Dad Dreamed It.

I Wrote It.

Special thanks to

Matthew Walters for graphic design

mattjwalters.com

<u>Chapter Index</u>

Chapter One   **3-39**
Big Fishes and Little Ponds
Chapter Two   **40-60**
Nightmares and Daydreams
Chapter Three   **61-73**
Anniversaries & Father Figures
Chapter Four   **74-109**
Peaceful Prayers & Broken Noses
Chapter Five   **110-136**
Pirates & Mexicans
Chapter Six   **137-158**
Provision & Perspiration
Chapter Seven   **159-181**
Coming to Light & Going to Church
Chapter Eight   **182-210**
Dying and Dreaming
Chapter Nine   **211-252**
Willing and Waiting
Chapter Ten   **253-280**
Holding Hearts & Cardboard Boxes
Chapter Eleven   **281-295**
Hide and Seek
Chapter Twelve   **296-325**
Words and Wasted Breath
Chapter Thirteen   **326-348**
Roses and Endings

Chapter One

Big Fishes and Little Ponds

Flying over the state of Indiana there is a view of corn
fields after hay fields, pastures, and flat plains that further
south descend into the rolling outskirts of the Appalachia
Mountains. In the winter every nook and cranny is white
with snow. In the spring it all burns vibrantly green and the
cow pastures are dark brown with sopping mud. In the
summer tractors dot the fields. Neat rows take shape, small
bales pop up, and wagons of tobacco haul into barns. In the
fall the grass starts to char brown and pumpkin patches start
to transpire. The hills churn with oranges, reds, yellows and
a few greens. A few metropolises stand out in the night,
creating their own kind of stars. South Bend screeches late
into the nights. Indianapolis, the capital, is encircled with
unceasing cars. And Fort Wayne stretches into the sky.

Outside the city limits small towns have to reach out a long
arm to greet their neighbors. One such town is Masonville.
In this town there is only one thing that is as popular as
Pastor Brown's Sunday morning church service; that is, the
Masonville High School boys basketball team.

"Well good morning, little town of Masonville! It is
7:30a.m *on the dot* on this fall day. We're going to continue
to have unusually high temperatures for November. We've
got the high today reaching the lower 60's around mid-
afternoon. There's not a cloud in this blue sky!" The voice
of Jeff Wallace comes booming through station 95.3. Static
accents the corners of his speech. "I think it'll be a good
day to get the rakes out, what do you think Will?"

William Bollinger joins his host. "I hope I don't have to Jeff!" The smile on Will's face is as audible as his words. Jeff Wallace laughs into his mike a deep manly kind of laugh. "That's right folks, we have Will Bollinger of *Bollinger's Hardware*, here in the studio with us today. I understand you have an announcement for us Will. Why don't you go ahead while everyone's listening in."

Jeff pushes his mike to Will. He clears his throat then the smile appears in his voice again. "Hey there everyone, I want to remind you all that this Saturday is the first game for our Mustangs here at Masonville High School. *Bollinger's Hardware* will be sponsoring our Mustangs this season. To open the season we're going to have a drawing at half-time for a *brand new* shop-vac. Raffle tickets are fifty cents each or three for a dollar. The more you enter the drawing the more likely *you'll* be taking home this *two point five gallon* Craftsman's shop-vac. It's a real nice one Jeff. I better see you there too."

Jeff and Will laugh together. Jeff slaps Will on the back and is now shaking him by the shoulder. He pulls the mike back. "There you have it folks, we have the season opening *this Saturday* at 7 o'clock. Bollinger's Hardware will have the half-time show after the Mustang cheerleaders. Now I know for a fact that Masonville has some good refreshments!"

"That they do!" Will laughs in the background.

Jeff laughs too. "They have hot-dogs, soft-pretzels, pop-corn, coke products and more. Here to tell us about what that "*more*" is, is Eleanor Brown. Eleanor, how you doing today?"

Jeff pushes the mike away once more. Eleanor Brown's soft voice comes through so quietly that listeners turn the radio dial up. This is to be expected from a Pastor's wife—a gentle, meek and as quiet as a mouse voice. By the sound of it one would picture her as a skinny skeleton of a woman but she's actually a hefty one. No one can blame her for her weight problem though once they've tasted her cooking. Pitch-ins at Masonville First Baptist Church is renown in this town. Anytime there's an occasion to eat, Mrs. Eleanor Brown has requests for all kinds of favorites from the community. Seems she's always fixing up a feast. "Hello Jeffery," she says. "I'm very well, thank you. A little tired today after all the baking we women at Masonville First Baptist Church have been doing all week." Eleanor giggles but it is so faint no one can hear it.

Jeff pulls the mike back toward himself, "Baking! Well now you've got us all listening Eleanor. Won't you tell us what you ladies have been cooking up now."

"This week we've been preparing baked goods for our annual fundraiser at the first basketball game of the season. Every year this bake sale raises enough money to supply Masonville's Children's Home with goody-bags for each child at Christmas time. This fundraiser is very near and dear to our hearts because the Children's Home is such a blessing in this community. This year they have 12 residents, ages 1 to 17. We really appreciate if you all stop by to support this good cause."

5

"Won't you tell us what kind of baked goods you ladies have cooked up for us," Jeff swings the mike around.

"We have all the pies you can think of Jeffery. We have cherry pie, apple pie, strawberry-rhubarb pie and our best seller, *the turtle-truffle pie*."

"O, say no more, Eleanor!" Jeff interjects with a deep laugh.

"We'll also have a wide collection of cookies, candy-barks, fudges and breads too."

"O land of the living!" Jeff bellows again. Eleanor's giggle can hardly be heard behind Jeff's bellowing. His fat round belly bounces like Santa's "bowl full of jelly."

"Thank you Eleanor, that sure does sound like a good bake sale. I know you convinced *me* to stop by."

Eleanor Brown shares a gentle giggle. "Well thank you Jeffery, and thanks for having me." She's probably the only woman to get away with calling two hundred and fifty pound Jeff Wallace, *Jeffery*.

He swings the mike back to his mouth again. The radio dial needs turned back down as he says, "If seeing the Mustangs play Saturday isn't enough for you to get to the Masonville gym this Saturday then I think you've just heard enough to convince you otherwise. Again, we'll have *Bollinger's Hardware* raffle at half-time and the ladies of Masonville First Baptist Church will have their baked goods stand right around the corner from Mustang P-Ride concessions. Well, that's enough chit-chat for now. Let's get back to the music. Here's *Rhinestone Cowboy* by Glen Campbell." The music of a guitar picks up the through the radio static.

Down the road from Myron Studios is the single four-way-stop in Masonville. At the corner is Masonville High School. Turning left at the four-way and then an immediate left is the parking lot. Straight ahead are the gymnasium doors. A large black mustang leaps over the doubled doors. Under its belly, inside and down the hallway to the right is the basketball Coach's office.

A large man with a balding head sits with his ball cap resting on his knee. He wipes the sweat from his forehead, not because it is hot weather but because he's a large man who always sweats. Talking seems to take the breath out of him these days. His gut hangs out of his shirt an inch above his pants. He rubs the top of his belly as he speaks to Coach Jackson. "I just can't do it anymore Coach," he says. "I've been wrapping ankles and wrists for 20 years now. I'm the one who's going to need wrapped these days."

Coach Jackson smiles and laughs a little. He nods his head in agreement even though he doesn't like the news.

"You need to find someone else," the large man finishes with a frown. "I'm sorry Coach."

Coach Jackson sits up straight in his chair and nods his head some more. He rests his arms on his wooden desk. The large man wrestles in his chair to get up. When he finally stands he says one more thing. "I'd check at that community college. They study physical therapy there now." Coach nods his head.

Outside the gymnasium, continuing down Elm Street, one single house lies beyond the fence separating its yard from the Masonville Elementary School playground. The house is rickety. One side balances on cinder blocks. The white stairs that lead to the front door are made of wet wood. The steps bow under the pressure of each footstep. At the top of the stairs the only entryway is a crooked hanging screen door. It flaps in the wind making a slapping noise. There, Philip Oliver swings his weed eater left to right, left to right. Phil Oliver is 17 years old. He stands as the tallest in his class at Masonville High School at six foot, seven inches. All of his classmates call him Ollie. He is well known in school. He is one of the best players on their basketball team. This year, his junior year, everyone knows he deserves the title of "team captain."

His golden flakey hair is mostly hidden under his red and white *Bollinger's Hardware* ball cap. The weed eater string slaps against the chain linked fence when Ollie gets too close to it. The two stroke purrs then roars, purrs then roars. Eventually he kills the weed eater and sets it down on the slowly browning grass. He wipes away the beads of sweat on his forehead. The sweat soaks into his tan leather gloves. He bends down and rips out one last vine that still clings through the diamonds of the chained fence. Then he picks up his weed eater and heads toward the home.

School starts in less than a half an hour. Ollie leaves the weed eater in the little shed out back then creaks up the white wooden steps of the porch. Ollie can hear the chaos inside before he opens the door. Once inside a handful of kids run across the living room giggling after each other.

Across the room Miss Stephen is brushing little Kirsten's hair. Her hair is always the rattiest of the girls. Her long dark hairs are so thin they spin together to form long tangles. Miss Stephen is always telling her to use more conditioner when she takes her baths. She jerks the brush through her hair in long quick strokes. Kirsten used to cry and complain the whole time Miss Stephen brushed it, but now she is used to it. She's not a "tender head" anymore, so Miss Stephen says.

Miss Stephen is in her upper forties. She has a small waste but very large hips and thighs. She puts her hair in 9 large pink rollers each night before bed. Every day her short brown hair is brushed up in the same bird nest kind of look. She doesn't wear any make up except for blue eye shadow that always looks slopped on. She always wears a thin summer dress, even in the winter. Her only variation is in the winter she wears thick black 'hose. And she always wears her yellow striped apron with two large front pockets that ties around the thinnest part of her body. All the children are told when they first arrive they are to call her *Miss* Stephen. After all, she has never married (probably never even dated). It's not that she isn't a nice woman . . . that is, Ollie finds her nice enough. Ollie thinks she's never married because she's never had time to meet anyone. For the last six years she's been here raising him along with countless others. And she was here even before Ollie was.

"Alright Kirsten, you're done." Miss Stephen pushes her away. She slowly gets up off the brown flower printed couch. She's been having trouble with her knees again. The spot where she gets up from is so worn the flower print isn't there anymore.

Kristen runs up to Ollie as he slides his leather gloves off. "Hey there Kirsten!" he says as he squeezer her into his stomach. The seven year old bounces up and down but doesn't speak. She's in first grade this year and still the teachers can't get a word out of her. Miss Stephen is all the time tempting her with different types of food or toys to get her to talk. It never works. The doctors think Kirsten must have had a traumatic life event before she came to the orphanage that has somehow equated talking with a bad thing.

But Kirsten has never seemed like a bothered child. She's been in this orphanage since she was three years old. From day one she has been nothing but smiles (except when Miss Stephen first started to brush her hair). She runs and plays with the other kids like nothing is abnormal about her at all. And the other kids don't bother her about not talking. They usually just make her the pet or baby in their games of house so she doesn't have to speak anyway.

Ollie tries not to have favorites in the orphanage but he can't help but really like Kirsten. She looks up at him now, her only being as tall as his belt. She says she's glad to see him with her big blue eyes. Ollie smiles back, pats her on the head and she takes off running again.

"You better hurry and clean yourself up Oliver before you're late to school." Miss Stephen has finally made it off the couch. She snatches a ribbon off the floor in one quick swipe. As the herd of kids makes their way running across the living room again Miss Stephen snatches one of the girls. Suzan whines in protest, frustrated that she is the one who got caught.

"Now you hold still," Miss Stephen says as she pulls Suzan's hair up into a pony tail. As she ties off the ribbon into a bow Ollie dodges his way down the hall to the bedroom at the end of the hall.

The room is lined wall to wall with four bunk beds. In between each one a rickety dresser stands. Some of the drawers are open with clothes hanging out of their lips. Ollie heads straight to them and begins shoving all the dangling clothes back inside. He makes his round to all four dressers, shutting each drawer. Then he heads back to the brown one with six drawers in the center of the room. His drawer is the top one because he is the only one tall enough to see into it. He quickly pulls out a fresh shirt as Ben and Ezra stumble into the room.

Ben and Ezra are both eleven years old in the fifth grade at Masonville Elementary School. They are inseparable but they also get along as well as dogs get along with cats.

"No you shut up Ezra!" Ben pushes Ezra into the bunk bed right inside the door. Ezra raises his hand to retaliate as Ollie turns around.

"Hey boys, let's get along now," he says. The boys hold their fists in midair then slowly their hands drop back to their sides. Ollie is always listened to. He is the oldest boy in the orphanage and he's been there the longest. Every kid knows he's the second boss, right after Miss Stephen.

Ollie smiles at them then swaps his sweaty white shirt out for a clean one. "You guys ready to go to school?"

Ezra and Ben slide their back packs out from under their bunk bed at the same time. They nod their heads then give Ollie a hug goodbye. Outside his window he can hear the school bus brakes squeal as it comes to a stop outside the orphanage. Ben and Ezra take off running already arguing with each other about shoving as they push through the front door.

Ollie watches Miss Stephen run out the front door from his window. She holds up a small pink back pack as she nearly falls down the white wooden front porch. She is yelling something but Ollie can't hear what over the hum of the bus. Little Kirsten turns to Miss Stephen before she climbs the bus steps. Miss Stephen hands her the back pack and waves her index finger at her. Kirsten never stops smiling though she is probably being reprimanded. Ollie shakes his head and smiles at her.

Behind the school bus a white Sedan is idling. It is Ollie's best friend Buddy Porter. Buddy started picking Ollie up for school at the start of this year. He spots Ollie through the window and a large white smile appears across his face. He waves his hand to motion for Ollie to come on. Ollie can't help but smile in return. Buddy has been his best friend since seventh grade. That's when Buddy moved here. Before then Ollie didn't have a best friend. He didn't have any enemies but he also didn't have anyone he really connected with.

He was put in the orphanage the summer before his sixth grade year. For the next year a half he felt like he didn't have the energy to talk all that much, much less make any friends. But then Buddy showed up one day before Ollie's science lab. After Mr. Bates announced Buddy as the new student he told the class to get their lab partners and begin their assignment. Buddy sat at his desk all alone looking like he was going to cry. None of the other kids seemed to notice. And since Ollie had always done his science labs partner-less, he decided he'd make friends with this Buddy fellow. From that day on they haven't left each other's side.

Buddy is the darkest kind of black you can find in a small Indiana town. He moved all the way across the state from Cincinnati, Ohio to this small corn-cropping town of Masonville. His father had been transferred with his company to the coal power plant here. It was a hard readjustment for Buddy to go from the city life to the town with one stop light. His ethnicity only made the move harder. With his family moving in that might have brought Masonville's African American population to ten.

Being six foot two inches, Buddy looks cramped in the front seat of the old white Sedan. His large white smile seems to take up half the windshield. "Come on man, we're going to be late," Buddy smacks the door of the car as Ollie walks around to the passenger side. The bus huffs off while he throws his nearly empty back pack into the back seat.

"Thanks for picking me up," Ollie slams his door shut.

"Man, I told you to stop saying that. You've thanked me every day this year." Buddy turns the radio dial up so Led Zeppelin spills out of the car windows.

Masonville High School is the largest building in the whole town. Originally, when it was founded in 1902, it was only a one room school house with a large bell tower on top. Now the original building stands to the front of the new school as a historical site. Ten years ago the school had another addition added to it—the Bagenski-Brown Gym. Largely funded by the Bagenski and Brown families of Masonville, a larger gymnasium was erected in honor of the first Masonville State Champions title. Though they haven't won another championship since, all of Masonville anticipates this is their year.

Directly inside the two double doors of the school a shrine of the first and only championship is encased in the middle of the hallway. Only a month into the school year and already Ollie feels he's been stopped at this shrine a hundred times by teachers and students who pat him on the back saying, "You're taking us all the way to another championship this year, Ollie!"

Ollie could care less if they win a championship title. He just loves the game of basketball. He figures God must have intended him to play or else he wouldn't have made him so tall. Nonetheless, Ollie has a good feeling about this year.

Each school day starts the same. For reasons unknown to Ollie, he's the most popular guy in school. He often wonders why it is everyone is always calling on him and following him around like he's a leader of a special club. He wonders because it is not like he's ever tried to be popular. He doesn't care about what clothes he wears, in fact, he only owns a week's worth of nice t-shirts and two nice pairs of pants. He's had the same sneakers for two years. He doesn't groom his hair or have his own car, and he's never had a girlfriend either. Why it is he's the most talked about fellow he feels he'll never know.

Unbeknownst to him, this is the quality that makes him most attractive—the fact that he doesn't try. All the girls fawn over him because of this modest attitude. While Ollie has plenty of reasons to brag, a prideful comment has never been heard from his lips. And that is what makes all the guys in school like him. They idolize his talent and respect that he isn't a threat to their girlfriends. What most often keeps people from being popular is the rest of the population hates them for it. Ollie doesn't have that problem. All of Masonville wants him to be better off. Most people fight to be on top of the one pedestal that resides in each high school. Masonville sat Ollie on top of theirs and from his feet they gladly cheer.

Ollie returns at least a dozen hellos as he walks through the parking lot. Buddy receives quite a few greetings as well. As the most popular kid's best friend, Buddy has quite the reputation as well. Some would argue however that the new guy, Corky Hammons, is creaking up the popularity ladder.

Corky moved here at the start of this new school year. He is originally from Chicago, Illinois. Once people heard where he was from they assumed he had to have a worldly knowledge no one in Masonville could offer them. He became a big fish in a little pond. He came with city slicker clothes, name brands that no one had ever heard of. He had a fancy rural hair-do, a nice slicked backed look with yellow highlights. So not only did he have the city life to his advantage to amuse the masses, he had his looks too. Take away the fancy clothes and the expensive hair coloring and Corky is still attractive. His tall six foot five inch figure is stout. Without asking him, one could look at him and know he is an athletic machine. Corky didn't have any trouble fitting into his new school. The girls were more than welcoming and Corky wouldn't know shy and modest any more than Masonville would know of malls and stadiums.

As soon as Corky entered the school that mid-August he made his purpose known. He was there to play basketball. Up in the Windy City he did all he could to make a name for himself, but in the masses he was lost. It was Corky's father's dream to play collegiante basketball. Over time it grew into Corky's as well. But his dad started to fear Corky's junior year when not a single college recruiter came near his son's school. He put it in his mind to find a smaller town then. He'd find a place where his son would be a lighthouse. And so for a family excursion, the Hammons started driving. They drove all through Illinois, Indiana, some of Ohio and some of Kentucky. The world may never know how it came to be that they passed through Masonville and noticed it was a town. It was a miracle Mr. Hammons remembered the name 'Masonville' from a local newspaper he had read while eating at a diner on that very trip. The headline had read, "Masonville Mustangs Trample Teams!" It revealed their progression toward the State Championship. And so fate sealed the deal. Corky and his family up and moved from suburbia to an abandoned farm house on the outskirt of Masonville, Indiana.

When his purpose was revealed that he would join the basketball team to take them to Championship level to in turn be recruited by a division one college, everyone pointed him toward Phil Oliver. Corky strutted himself right up to Ollie on the first day of school. He introduced himself and told Ollie he was either going to be "his new best friend or new worst enemy." Ollie smiled and shook the stranger's hand. "We should probably be friends," Ollie said. And so the duo became a tri—Ollie, Buddy and Corky.

Among the greetings, Corky runs up behind Ollie and Buddy. He jumps on Ollie's back with a hoot and a holler. "Howdy boys!" he yells. He thinks it is funny to "talk country" now. He disfigures his Chicago accent with a dramatic hill-billy draw. Ollie piggy-backs him a few steps as Corky swings his hand in the air like he is holding an invisible lasso, "Ye-haw!" The boys laugh at Corky's normal enthusiastic greeting.

Only one greeting is unique this morning. Angela Patterson waves at Buddy as they walk by her baby blue Pontiac Firebird. "Hello Buddy," she wiggles her fingers from behind her stack of books she has pressed to her chest. She stands with her four best friends—Sandy Mitchell, Patricia Combs, Mandy Wallace and Bekkah Brown. Each of them giggles when Angela speaks. Sandy nudges Angela as if to say *I can't believe you actually spoke to him!* Buddy falters for words. He merely wiggles his fingers back, which leaves the pack of girls in a frenzy of giggles.

Ollie shakes his head smiling while Buddy's face turns a bright pink through his dark brown skin. "Hi Buddy," Corky mocks in a girly voice. Buddy gives him a look that tells him he better not say a word. Ollie knows Buddy has the biggest crush on Angela Patterson but as any best friend should do, Ollie never rags Buddy about it. He thinks it is funny that Buddy, his hilarious, ever-so-talented, very popular best friend won't even speak to the girl he's liked since seventh grade.

The one time Buddy had a clear chance at making it with Angela he completely blew it. Angela had just gotten her baby blue Pontiac Firebird for her sixteenth birthday present last year. Everyone was gathered around her car in the school parking lot before the morning bell would ring for them to get to class. Ollie walked up through the crowd with Buddy on his heels to say, "Nice car Angela!"

Angela bounced on her tip toes, her long brown pigtails in their solid single curl bounced with her. "Thanks Ollie," she beamed then looked to Buddy. "Do you like it Buddy?" she asked with intense eye contact.

It seemed like the whole student body that had gathered there held their breath in anticipation for Buddy's answer. He was lucky Angela had asked him a yes or no question though. His large white smile appeared again and he nodded his head yes like an eager pup. That's when things took a turn for Buddy. Angela, with everyone watching, leaned on the hood of her brand new car, her hands one on top of the other, her cheeks cradled in her shoulders like an innocent little child, looked deeper into Buddy's eyes. "Well if you ever want to drive it sometime, you could come to my house. I'm sure if you asked my dad he'd let you take me out in it."

Every person there seemed frozen in time. All eyes turned from Angela and her beautiful new Firebird to Buddy. Some kind of noise choked out through his throat eventually but as soon as it did Buddy broke eye contact with Angela and started waving goodbye to her as if she was five hundred yards away. As he did so he tripped his way out of the crowd and ran into the school. While the rest of the crowd burst into murmurs and laughter, Ollie escaped to find his friend hiding in the boy's locker room. They never talked about it. Ollie just laughed and dragged Buddy out to class.

Since that day everyone in school is on pins and needles any time Buddy and Angela are in close proximity. They're all just waiting for the day when Buddy has the nerve to drive to her house to ask Angela's dad for permission to take her out in that hot Firebird.

Today Buddy actually says something about the situation. "One day," he says as they walk up the stairs toward the double doors, "I'm going to talk to her."

Ollie laughs and nods his head.

"Sure you are," Corky says. "The day you ask her out is the day a black man will be elected president." Buddy pushes him away as they laugh their way to class.

19

The bell sounds for the first class of the day to get started. Students file in from the hallway. Ollie and Buddy sit in their usual spots. Corky sits in the front row beside his girlfriend Roxanne.

Roxanne has to sit up front in all of her classes. It is no secret she will be the senior class President this year. She's brilliant. She's a member of nearly every club in the school. All of the girls are jealous of her for one reason or another. Most are because of her musical talent. Roxanne is the lead in every theater production, the best soprano in the choir and first chair violinist. She sings the National Anthem at most sporting events and she's the best baton twirler in the color guard. All of these things she participates in require dedication and steadfast discipline. There are only two things in her life she is loose with—her hair and Corky. As soon as he sits down she scoots her desk closer to him and kisses him like her tongue is an untamed python.

Buddy sits nearest the wall so no one can sit by him. He does this in every class just in case Angela ever tries to sit by him. He believes he can't afford the distraction, or the potential humiliation.

Two of Angela's girlfriends sit right in front of them. They giggle to each other as they glance at Buddy. Buddy never takes his eyes off his desk though Corky is all the time turning around making faces at them.

The last student comes in just as the final bell rings. As every day before it is Josh Acosta. He walks with slow heavy steps. His large black military boots make heavy thuds each time they contact the floor. Long silver chains hang from his bulky pockets going *clink* and *chink*. His long greasy black hair is brushed forward so it covers his eyes. His black hood is pulled up on his head. Mrs. Young pulls it off as he strides by her. She does this every day.

Josh sits in his chair with a chime from his chains clinging against the metal pieces of his desk. He sits right behind Ollie in the last chair of the row. He produces his yellow number two pencil from the pocket of his black jacket. He grinds it into his desk top adding more lines to the dragon with flames coming out of its mouth.

Mrs. Young gives a stack of papers to the front desk of each row. One by one the students take them and pass them over their heads to the next person in line. Ollie takes his sheet then holds the last one behind his head. He holds it there for a while. He shakes it back and forth hoping Josh will see it. When no response comes, Ollie turns his head over his shoulder. "Josh," he waves the paper again. Black fingernails wrap around the sheet of paper. His hand tightens around it so it crunches in his grip. Ollie shakes his head as he hears the paper form into a wad then fall to the ground.

The rest of the day goes as every school day does for Ollie. Each of his teachers smiles at him and hand back his "A" work papers. Every time he's in the hallway he gets half a million hellos. In home economics all the same girls want to be his partner. As always he chooses Emilee Stratton. The first day of home economics he noticed Emilee sitting all alone in the back corner. Emilee is a fat girl. She's so large her face is almost a perfect circle. She has thin blonde wavy hair that only goes to her shoulders, further accentuating her lack of a chin. She wears large square glasses that are brown and rounded around the edges. Her glasses do her a favor. They enlarge the bright green eyes beneath them. This is the first thing Ollie noticed about her—her wonderfully round, green eyes. To Ollie's surprise his kind act of asking her to be his partner has turned out splendidly. Emilee is a terrific cook!

Emilee wears her small smile that disappears at the edges into the creases of her fat pink cheeks. She watches Ollie as he kindly disappoints the swarm of females and gestures for Emilee to come join him as they move toward the lab part of the classroom where six different stoves line the far wall.

Today they are making all the fixings for the staff's pitch-in lunch tomorrow. Emilee and Ollie have been assigned the meatloaf recipe. When Emilee and Ollie first came together as partners Ollie assumed she was a very shy type of person. She hardly spoke and when she did it was with the volume of a barn mouse. For the first week Ollie had to carry conversations with himself. He finally figured he would only ask her yes or no questions to get to know her. Eventually Emilee found her comfort zone. Now, Ollie hardly gets a word in edge wise. She tells Ollie every detail of her previous day and morning. She often goes on rants about her older brother Patrick who is many years older than her and now has his first baby. Turns out, Emilee thinks Patrick is her parent's favorite and to make matters worse, Emilee doesn't even like babies. She equates her new nephew with an alien who has come to secretly ruin her life. She blabs about how she hopes this alien baby will eventually take Patrick back with it to Venus from whence it came. Ollie finds most of what she says to be comical but he tries not to let that on because Emilee seems very serious about it all.

After home economics Ollie meets up with Buddy outside the health room. Every day Buddy comes out of there in a cold sweat. It is the only class he has without Ollie that Angela happens to be in.

Today Buddy hustles out. As soon as he's out the door he's jerking Ollie's arm down the hallway. "I don't know why we have to talk about the most awkward stuff with *girls* in the room," he says as he looks over his shoulder (no doubt making sure he can't see Angela). Ollie had already taken health class last year. Tons of awkward topics run through his mind that he remembers from his time there—periods, STD's, intercourse, hemorrhoids and body parts. None telling what awkward thing Coach Jackson embarrassed Buddy with today. What makes the class discussion even more awkward is when Coach Jackson brings up his class topics at basketball practice.

Buddy, Corky and Ollie finish off their day with study hall where they do the five minutes of homework they have then spend the rest of the time talking. When the final bell rings they hurry to their lockers. Corky goes to his girlfriend's first, of course. Buddy always sprints to his locker, leaving Ollie behind. Buddy *"has to,"* he says, because the lockers are assigned in alphabetical order. Buddy Porter is only two lockers down from Angela Patterson. Ollie doesn't know why he even worries about it.

23

Buddy is always down in the gym with five minutes to spare by the time Angela gets to her locker.

Despite arriving way earlier than Ollie, Buddy always waits for his friend to arrive before they change in the locker room. Ollie only has one outfit he wears every day for practice. Each day he takes it home where Miss Stephen washes it, folds it and puts it back into Ollie's back pack for the next day. She's always amazed at how sweaty he gets it.

Today Buddy pulls out two pairs of gym shorts and an extra t-shirt. "Here you go. These shorts don't fit me anymore." Buddy throws the red Nike shorts down on the bench in front of him. Ollie looks at them carefully for a moment. He's never seen Buddy wear them before. True, Buddy is a little larger than Ollie around the waste, but it is nothing a little elastic won't fix. Anything that fits Buddy will fit Ollie. They look brand new.

Ollie picks them up and turns them in his hand. "These sure don't look like any old shorts I've ever seen you in."

Buddy shrugs his shoulders. "Here's a shirt too." He throws it at Ollie like it is nothing then digs deeper in his bag for his own clothes.

This time Ollie knows Buddy has went out of his way to get him these. "Buddy," he says, "this shirt still has the tag on it."

Buddy is caught. "What?" he stammers. The boys exchange a look for a moment. "O alright," Buddy slips his shirt off over his head. "My mom got em' for you."

Ollie simply nods his head. "Tell Mrs. Porter I said thank you."

Buddy sighs loudly. "I will, but I'm going to leave out the *Mrs. Porter* part. How many times has she told you to call her Colleen?"

Mrs. Colleen Porter has always bought things for Ollie since the day she met him in seventh grade. The first time Buddy had Ollie over to his house she was asking him a million questions about his parents and what they do and where they live and where they work. Finally Ollie was able to explain to her that his parents died in a car accident the summer before sixth grade. Having no other family to take him in, he moved into the children's home with Miss Stephen. Mrs. Colleen Porter stared at Ollie for the longest time when he said it all. Buddy didn't know the whole story then either. He just knew Ollie lived with a bunch of other kids and didn't have to ask his parents if he could go out, only a Miss Stephen. Buddy was deathly quiet like his mom. Ollie stood there like it was what it was. He was an orphan and that was okay with him. The first year before Buddy came, it was difficult, sure. But now, Ollie was alright. He was alright because of two reasons: the first being, he found Jesus at Pastor Brown's church and Jesus was mighty helpful to him; and the second reason he was alright was because this kind Jesus then gave him a best friend named Buddy. Ollie explained this and in return Mrs. Colleen Porter burst into tears. Ollie stood there wide eyed feeling sorry that he'd told her something that made her so sad. Buddy grabbed Ollie and took him up to his room to play with the avatar and it was never mentioned again.

Since then, Buddy's mom is always sending stuff to the children's home. She bakes cookies, buys groceries for their pantry, gives Miss Stephen gift cards to her hair salon, and though she gets all the kids in the children's home presents now, she is most kind to Ollie, always giving him extra little things throughout the year. She's even thrown him full out birthday parties three years running now. Each time Ollie sees her he makes sure to give her a large hug and thank you. Mrs. Colleen Porter does the same thing Buddy does, she wafts him away like what she does is nothing.

Ollie doesn't say any more about the new clothes. He suspects it makes Buddy feel awkward. So they head out of the locker room into the gymnasium where Coach Jackson is waiting in gray sweatpants, tennis shoes and a navy blue collar shirt with his keys and whistle dangling from around his neck. He is the only teacher allowed to wear jogging pants to work.

"Hustle up!" he yells as majority of the team emerges from the locker room. Corky is one of them. He always takes a long time to change, with his clothes being so nice and all. "Start warming up!" Coach blows his whistle then starts throwing orange basketballs from the little rack that stands beside him. Mr. Chris used to do this. He was the assistant coach for years. Coach Jackson told the boys he wouldn't be helping out this year. Ollie misses the fat man. He used to wrap his ankles and wrists before each game. He figures he'll do without this year.

Ollie runs onto the court in time to snatch a bouncing ball. He takes it in his large hand and instinctively dribbles it down the court to the opposite basketball goal. He runs all the way up for a right hand layup. It bounces perfectly off the upper right hand side of the square then into the white net, *swish.*

Buddy is right behind him jumping into his layup, then Corky with a show-boat twist. One after the other the rest of the team follows suit. A drill takes form as they all circle back around for more layups. Eventually Ollie leads the team into the next set. He purposely bounces the ball forcefully off the backboard so it jumps back to the next player in line where they have to catch it in the air and likewise bounce it off the backboard for the next person. It is a fast drill and before it has circled around again Ollie is already sweating, but so is the rest of the team.

Coach Jackson isn't seen but his voice is heard as he commands, "Sprints!" followed by two short blows on his whistle.

The team lines up on the blue line at the farthest end of the court. All the balls bounce to the sidelines. Ollie is the first off the line as they run to half court, touch the line then sprint back. Ollie slaps his partner's hand, Buddy, who takes off to do the same thing. They continue to run five more times to the halfway line before Coach Jackson sounds three short whistles. Then they run sprints the full length of the court five more times. One long whistle sounds telling the team they are finished. They all run to Coach Jackson who is standing with his legs wider than his shoulders, his arms crossed at his chest. He always stands like this, like he is some kind of Indian chief.

The team makes half a circle around the coach. All of them are panting and sweating. Corky is bobbing his head and mouthing words like he's singing a song in his head. It makes the guys around him smile. Ollie takes long breaths in through his nose and out his mouth to try to slow down his heart rate. Buddy has his hands on his knees like many of the other players.

"Alright," Coach Jackson begins. The team straightens up. "Listen up! We've got our first game this Saturday night. You all have been practicing really well so far this season. I think we've got a promising chance of going all the way to the championship this year." A few teammates clap their hands and nod their heads, "Yeah we do Coach!"

 "That isn't to say you guys still don't need a lot of work," Coach says. "Ya'll better not get cocky, just thinking this season is going to be handed to you. You've got to work for it like you're the underdogs. So today you'll practice like you're losers." A few groans escape some teammates. "You're going to run a mile then I'm going to make you shoot free throws until your arms fall off!" Coach Jackson smiles. He's a good coach but the team knows he's never as hard on them as he makes it sound. "A mile is 24 laps around the court. No cutting corners!" Coach stares at two players in particular. Percy Jackson, his own son, and Miles Clifton smile at each other the kind of smile that says *Coach Jackson just dared us to try to cut corners and boy, are we going to!*

"Well stop standing around here! Get started!" Coach blows his whistle long and hard. It stings their ears but it gets them going. "Yeah!" Corky yells. He pushes at Coach's shoulder which doesn't budge. Corky has been sucking up to Coach from day one. Coach doesn't even smile at him anymore.

Ollie leads the pack of them around the gym. Buddy strides along right at his side. Behind them they can hear Corky making some of the guys laugh. It isn't too far into the mile before Percy and Miles are passing them as they cut ahead through one of the corners. Percy and Miles are best friends. They're always the ones who get in trouble by the Coach for making ridiculous plays or lacking in their grades, or missing practice or staying out too late on school nights, or for getting in trouble at parties over the weekends. Percy and Miles are well known in school for how rowdy they can get at parties. They're notorious for having townsfolk call the police on them for underage drinking and noise violations. It can be assumed there aren't major consequences for Percy because he's the coach's son, and neither for Miles since he's Percy's best friend. Though Ollie is often embarrassed for the reputation Percy and Miles give the team, and for their profanities they throw at the umps during games, Ollie is still grateful they're on the team. There are only 11 team players. If they lost Percy and Miles, they'd lose two great guards and their team would suffer.

After three quarters of the mile is run Ollie spots Coach Jackson talking to a young girl near the exit of the gym. It is hard to focus in on who it is while he bounces up and

29

down but eventually Ollie concludes he's never seen this girl before. She looks older than him. He can only assume she's already graduated high school. Coach Jackson is nodding his head while she talks to him. Ollie rounds the corner of the gym so Coach and the girl disappear behind him. He hurries to the next corner so he can see more. When he finds them again Coach Jackson is pointing at papers on a clipboard. The girl is nodding her head like she understands then she takes it from Coach. He pats her on the back smiling. She returns a pretty smile while Ollie rounds the corner again so his back is toward them. When he turns to face them again the girl is gone and Coach is walking back in toward the team. A little disappointed, Ollie finishes his mile in another lap and sits on the bench beside Percy and Miles who have been done for a few laps now. Ollie gulps some water from the team bottles while Percy and Miles whisper about the party they crashed this past weekend.

"I'm telling you the truth," Miles nudges Percy. "Bekkah Brown really was there."

"Well I'm telling you I didn't see her there," Percy sets down his water bottle.

"Just 'cause you didn't see her there doesn't means she wasn't."

"Why in the world would the *pastor's daughter* be at a college party?" Percy enunciates as he glares at Miles.

Ollie rolls his eyes. Miles and Percy are always talking about girls. Sadly, they are always talking about them in a derogatory fashion. It is like Miles and Percy are in a competition with each other as to who will have the most girls. Since Percy's older brother Matthew went away to college three years ago, Miles and Percy have hit a party nearly every weekend, high school ones or college.

"I'm telling you," Miles continues, "it is the *pastor's daughters* that are the most fun."

"O stuff it," Percy throws his long shaggy hair out of his eyes as he tosses his head.

Miles brings his water bottle to his lips where he's trying to hide his childish smile. "Just you wait and see *Percy*. I'm going to be with her at the next one."

Buddy plops down at the bench as Percy concludes, "That'll be the day."

"What are you guys talking about?" Buddy squeezes in between Miles and Ollie. Ollie shakes his head, wishing Buddy hadn't asked.

"Miles here, thinks he's going to get with *Bekkah Brown* this weekend."

"Oh," Buddy whispers to Ollie, "Why'd I even ask?"

Corky jogs up to the bench next. "Hey guys, what ya'll talking about?" And Miles and Percy go at again.

The guys refresh with some water then they are back on the court shooting free throws. By the time practice is over at 5:30 Ollie's stomach is aching with hunger. The free plate lunch at school is never enough to hold him over until supper time, which is always served at 6 at the children's home. Miss Stephen is a good enough cook but when food is always served in bulk and on a budget, it tends to be repetitive. Today is Monday; that means it is meatloaf and boxed mashed potatoes. Ollie is just starting to dread this meal as he bounces the ball to Buddy to put it on the rack as Coach Jackson dismisses them with a final whistle. "See you all tomorrow!" He shouts as he snatches up his black zip-up sweater from the bench then resides to scold Miles and Percy for cheating the mile.

"You want to come over tonight?" Buddy asks him as they walk into the locker room. "I know it is meatloaf night and that's your favorite and all, but . . ." Buddy winks.

Ollie smiles back. "I'd love to but I have to get to Raymond Gibbs' place."

 "When are you going to be done working for that old man?" Buddy tosses his sweatbands into his locker.

"What old man? Who?" Corky asks as he walks by. He's always interjecting but never listening. The guys find it funny. They've learned to ignore him most of the time.

Ollie shakes his head. "He's all alone on that big farm, still trying to run it himself. I'm going to keep working for him until he says not to."

"Does he even pay you?" Buddy unties his shoes.

Ollie changes out of his shorts and wraps his towel around his waist. "Yeah he does," though Ollie has never felt right about taking the old man's money. He hadn't asked for money the first time they met. Ollie was just going for a walk down some back country roads one beautiful day early this past summer when he noticed Raymond Gibbs trying to hook a trailer to his pickup truck all by himself. Ollie took off running through the hay field toward the old man. Raymond Gibbs was hunkered down in his blue overalls. His forehead was so sweaty his blue floppy hat was hanging down over his eyes. The old man was startled with Ollie's sudden appearance and he slightly jumped. He didn't have time to protest. Ollie man-handled the wagon onto the hitch.

When he had it secured Ollie straightened up to face the old man. Raymond Gibbs looked taken aback for a moment before he finally spoke. "Well, thank you young man." Then he stuck his hand out. "I'm Raymond Gibbs and who might you be?"

Ollie shook the man's hand. "I'm Phil Oliver sir."

"Sir?" The old man looked stunned again. "How do you like that? A teenager who still has some manners. I thought I'd never see the day." Raymond smiled. Some of his teeth were missing and others were yellow and brown. But among all his wrinkles his blue eyes still held a lot of youth.

"I do appreciate the help," Raymond continued. "I thought I had the pin in well enough but I hit one little bump out here and the whole trailer came bouncing off."

Ollie continued to stand there, quietly.

33

"It seems like I'm always doing stuff like that nowadays."
Raymond swatted the side of his leg at some dried dirt.
Then he turned slightly and looked Ollie full in the face.
"Phil Oliver, you say?"

"Yes sir."

Raymond Gibbs nodded his head and kept looking at Ollie
like he was thinking really hard. "How old are you boy?"

"I'm 17, sir."

Raymond nodded his head again. Ollie began to wonder
what this old man was thinking. "You work around here?"
Raymond shifted his stance so his arms were crossed and
his back was straightened like a sudden serious man.

Ollie straightened a little too. "No sir, not for employment.
I help out plenty where I live and I'm going to be a junior
this year at school."

"Where do you live?" Raymond was quick to respond.

Ollie always hated to have to say it, knowing his next
comment changed how the rest of the conversations tended
to go. "I live at the children's home." Ollie relented.

The old man continued to look at him real hard but his head
nodding slowed down. "Well," Raymond finally broke eye
contact. He pulled a pipe from his front overall pocket and
a match from his leg pocket. "A sturdy young man like
yourself ought to be employed at your age." He put the
black pipe between his teeth. "When I was your age I was
working full time for the Amish building houses." He

struck the match to life off the side of his pant leg then puffed on his pipe till the match had done its work. Smoke started to drift out of the end. He waved the match in the air until the flame died then he threw it down at his feet where he stepped on it. "Built my own house by the time I was 25." He pulled the pipe out of his mouth and used it to point behind Ollie towards the old white farm house behind him. Ollie looked at it. "What say you start working here for me as my farm hand?" Raymond put the pipe back in his mouth and raised his chin to look Ollie full in the face again.

That was the last thing Ollie was expecting. He had just been thinking of getting a summer job on his walk. Ollie nodded his head. "I would like that very much sir."

A smile appeared at the edge of Raymond's pipe. "Can you get started right now?"

Ollie was so surprised he couldn't help but laugh at the old man. "Yes sir, I can spare an hour or so."

Raymond took his pipe out and jutted it into the air. "Now that's what I like to hear!" And with that he turned to his pickup truck. "Get in boy! We've got a lot to do if I've only got you an hour. What do you think this is I'm running here, a beauty salon? This is a farm son!" Raymond slammed his red pickup truck door. Ollie slid in on the passenger side. The truck smelled like dust and tobacco. Ollie went straight to work that day. He didn't ask any questions about pay. For some reason, he wasn't worried about it.

Ollie thinks about that first meeting again here in the locker room. He nods his head. "Yeah, he pays me real good."

Buddy huffs as Ollie disappears into a shower stall. "Well how do you like that? If he pays you so good why is my mom still buying your butt shorts?" The sound of the showerhead echoes through the locker room.

"I never asked Mrs. Colleen to buy me nothin'," he shouts.

"Yeah, yeah, I know. She's just a sucker," Buddy shouts back.

Corky bursts open Ollie's shower curtain, "Hey-O!" All the guys laugh. Ollie shakes his head and shuts it again. Buddy, per usual, yells at Corky with the fury of a hurricane. Then the guys leave while Ollie finishes up.

Ollie is always the last one left in the locker room. Most guys don't shower at school. But it is a lot easier for him to shower there than at the children's home. There's only one bathtub and Miss Stephen is always hauling one kid out of it after another. If Ollie were to shower at home, he'd be doing it in cold water in the middle of the night.

Outside the children's home little Kirsten is chasing two other girls—Julie and Suzan. She's barking like a dog. Ben and Ezra are hanging from the monkey bars kicking each other with their swinging legs. Three boys are in the sandbox—Matthew, T.K and Joshua. Matthew is no doubt looking after the other two. As the eight year old, he considers himself to be the best of the oldest boys since

Ben and Ezra are nightmares. T.K and Joshua are twins. They're the newest to the gang. They've only been here a shade over four months. They came just in time to start preschool. Ryan is standing with his arms crossed by the yellow slide watching the boys at the sandbox. His bottom lip is puckered out as far as it can go. He's undoubtedly upset with them for some reason. He's known as the pout box in the house. He's had eye problems all his life. Miss Stephen is always taking him to appointments. Because of it, the other boys like to pick on him, "Ryan's the sickly one!" The two oldest girls, Jennifer and Sarah are sitting on the front porch steps reading what looks like a love note on notebook paper.

Miss Stephen comes through the front door holding the last member of the gang as Ollie gets out of the car. "It looks like a zoo," Buddy says out his window. Ollie smiles back at him, "You should see em' at feeding time."

Buddy shakes his head and drives off. Meanwhile, Miss Stephen is shaking the finger of her free hand at everyone. "All of you GET IN this house! I don't know how many times I've got to tell you, supper is always at six o'clock. The longer you take to get in here, the colder your food is going to be. And don't come complaining to me when your meatloaf is cold." Little George sits on her hip, his thumb in his mouth. When Ben and Ezra run by he pulls it out and reaches his short arms toward them. Ben stops to make a face at him that sends little George into an adorable set of giggles. They continue inside while Jennifer and Sarah each stroke George's cheeks as they go by. Julie and Suzan dash by, nearly knocking Jennifer over as they squeeze in through the door. Kirsten runs after them still barking like a dog.

"Kirsten, stop that howling!" Miss Stephen waves her finger at her. "And Ryan!" Miss Stephen shouts as Ollie latches the fence shut. "Stop that pouting and get in here!"

Ryan continues to stand with his arms crossed refusing to move.

"Ryan Patrick Smith, if you don't move those legs right now you are NOT getting any dessert tonight."

Ryan stomps his foot once before he breaks off into a speed walk to the house. He cuts in front of Ollie as they head up the brick pathway to the steps. "That's what I thought mister," Miss Stephen concludes. Ryan gives a harrumph.

"The fence is looking good Ollie," Miss Stephen changes her tone to a gentler one as Ollie reaches the top step. Together they glance out over the yard. Ollie has been working on cleaning out the fence line for years now. So many vines had overgrown the fence Ollie couldn't see through it when he first moved here. He thought the house was surrounded by giant hedges.

Ollie nods his head in agreement then takes Little George from Miss Stephen's hip. He wraps his arms around Ollie's neck then gives him a kiss on the cheek which is really an open mouth of slobber.

"Raymond Gibbs called," Miss Stephen tells him before he goes inside. "He said he doesn't want you coming over through the weekdays now that it gets dark so early now.

He said he'll expect you Saturday morning. And he'll be picking you up from now on." Miss Stephen goes into the house in front of Ollie.

Ollie finishes off the day doing his part of the evening chores—dishes duty with Sarah and Jennifer. He washes, Sarah rinses, Jennifer dries and puts them away (all except for the large mixing bowls, Ollie has to do that since he's the only one tall enough to reach that shelf). When that is done the sun is already set. He reads Kirsten a bed time story about *The Giant Jam Sandwich* until she falls asleep on him. Then Ollie retreats for his time of privacy on his top bunk. The room is dark. Ezra and Ben are the only ones still fighting off sleep. Ben pushes with both his feet on the bunk bed above him. Ezra swats at him from above. Ollie touches Ben's feet and turns Ezra over in his bed when he comes in. Ben tucks his feet in his blanket and turns over. Soon the room is completely quiet.

Ollie changes in the dark then mounts his bed. He pulls his Bible out from under the corner of his mattress (that's the safest place for it). And like each night before for the last six years, Ollie reads some Scripture then says his prayers.

Chapter Two

Nightmares and Daydreams

Eleven year old Ollie bounces his red and white IU basketball off the pavement of his driveway. James Oliver shuffles his feet back and forth in front of his son. "Just try to get around me," he teases Ollie, swatting at the basketball. Ollie slightly turns his body so his dad can't reach it. Then he pushes his shoulder into his dad's chest, backing him up toward the hoop hanging on the garage. When he's close to the basket he pushes his dad one last time, hard enough to send him a foot away. With the extra room Ollie swoops his arm up for a hook shot, shooting the basketball into the air. It bounces off the backboard and swishes through the net.

Ollie breaks into cheers and runs circles around his dad.

Ollie's mother steps out of the side door of their house. "James, we need to go," she says. She has long wavy blonde hair that goes all the way to her hips. Half of it is pulled back with a barrette. Her green eyes are vibrant against the blue summer sky. Ollie thinks she is beautiful.

Ollie starts to fuss, "O dad, do you have to go?" James Oliver pats his son's blonde head. With his deep brown eyes he looks down at him. "I'm going to get this one, son," he smiles. This is the third interview he's had the past two weeks. Ollie had just moved here to this small town two weeks ago. It was *only* his third move this year. Altogether Ollie has probably moved fifteen times in his life. He wouldn't know it as an eleven year old, but his dad is a no-count at holding jobs. He's never held one longer than six months. Ollie would never suspect it but his father is known as a flake when it comes to money.

James Oliver spends his money as soon as he earns it. He says he spends it on sensible things. He says he is always investing in up-and-coming businesses (businesses that no one has ever heard of). But his wife, Jane Oliver, never says a thing about it all. She isn't supportive or argumentative; she is a quiet woman. She is also a sick woman. Ollie couldn't tell anyone the name of the sickness but when asked he would say, "It's her insides. She just doesn't have a good stomach and all that." And that is true. Jane Oliver is always puking in the bathroom anything she gets down, which is hardly anything at all. Still, Jane Oliver would never complain about her condition. She is too shy to. She is too shy to go to the doctor to get it fixed and she is too shy to cry about it to her son and husband. Ollie is just getting old enough to understand how sick his mom is. He is learning she can't work like so many other moms he knows. His mom is too frail.

Thus Ollie is dragged all over the state of Indiana. He's never been able to make any friends because he is never in one place long enough to do it. And he's never been able to play any sports though his dad tells him every time they play basketball, "Ollie, you are gonna' go pro one day! You're a natural!"

James Oliver tells Ollie stories of how he played basketball when he was a kid. That is until he got taken away from his parents in high school and put in foster care. James' parents were drug users. They were charged with child neglect and James was taken away when he was fifteen years old. He never saw them again. He tried to find them after he graduated high school a few years later but he heard his parents had ended up in prison and weren't worth finding anyway. With no one to hold him back, or steer him otherwise, James took the path of venture and never stopped.

Jane's family disowned her when she ran away with James at age fifteen, pregnant and out of school. She never reconnected with them.

"Come on Ollie. We'll drop you off at the park to play for a little bit," Jane smiles her weak but affectionate smile at her son. Ollie can't be mad at her for ending the fun when she smiles at him like that.

"The park is only a few blocks from where we'll be," James reassures Ollie even though Ollie isn't worried about being alone at all. He is used to being at the park without them, no matter what town they are living in at the time. And he doesn't expect his mom to stay with him while his dad is being interviewed. She never does that. She says the sun hurts her eyes and gives her terrible headaches. She is always inside though she apologizes to Ollie all the time: "I'm sorry I'm no fun." Ollie runs his fingers through her long thin hair. "You are a fun mom," he'd say. She'd smile at him and kiss his forehead.

The family gets in their little red Pontiac GTO, Ollie in the backseat with his basketball. Jane Oliver pulls a thin hard backed book from under her seat. Because she is so easily car-sick she keeps it there at all times. She says reading while driving keeps her mind off the moving car. Ollie recognizes the book right away. Bright yellow letters scribe the heading *Cinderella.*

As she cracks open the pages all sound is lost from memory. Ollie can see Jane Oliver moving her lips as her eyes scan the page. Her movements get slower and slower as if time is now in slow motion. Jane Oliver glances over her shoulder at Ollie as she points at a blurring picture then an ear-splitting crunch and squealing sounds.

Ollie jumps forward, sweat running down his forehead into his eyes. He feels the cold walls around him to his left and to the right is open space. He waves his hand in the air wondering where he is. Then he feels the sheets on his legs. Slowly his eyes adjust to the dark room. He's sitting upright on his bunk bed.

"It was just a dream," Ollie wipes the sweat from his forehead then his hands on his sheets. He's had this reoccurring dream more times than he can count. Every time he wakes up at that exact moment—with his mom looking into his eyes one last time. Ollie lays his head back down on his pillow and flops his arms out over the sheet because he's so hot. He takes a deep breath, reaccepting the haunting memory of his parent's death. For a while Ollie stares at the ceiling. He dreads falling asleep again, thinking the dream may replay.

He isn't able to drift off again before his alarm buzzes beneath his pillow. Feeling more tired than usual, Ollie slips out of bed at half past five.

With a flashlight, Ollie unlocks the small shed in the back yard with his key. He removes the padlock, opens the doors and swings the flashlight around until he finds his leather gloves and weed eater. He fills the small tank with fuel then makes his way to the fence in the back yard where he last left off. The chain link fence quickly disappears into the dense green vines. Ollie slips his head phones from around his neck up onto his ears. He pushes the play button on his cassette player. Loretta James *At Last* fills his ears. Ollie pulls the string of the weed eater until it comes to life. Ollie sways it back and forth, occasionally getting it too close to the fence, snapping off parts of the string. Grass and bits of vine fly into his face and leave a layer of green there. He works and sweats until he hears Miss Stephen yell above all the noise. He kills the weed eater and pulls his headphones down around his neck as he catches Miss Stephen pull the screen door open again. Her nine pink rollers are on top of her head. Ollie stops to take one good look at today's progress: three more feet.

After the same morning hustle of pulling Ben and Ezra off each other, Ollie slips into the car with Buddy and heads to school.

"I've made up my mind," Buddy says as soon as they've pulled away from the curb.

"What's that?" Ollie kicks his backpack away from his feet.

"I'm going to talk to Angela today," Buddy doesn't look at Ollie. He wipes his un-running nose so his shaking hand seems less noticeable.

 "You have a whole conversation planned out or you just gonna' say 'hi' and run?"

Buddy rolls his eyes. "I'm not just going to talk to her, see, I'm actually going to ask her out today."

Ollie is as taken aback but doesn't say anything. He nods his head at Buddy. Looking him up and down like he's looking at new man. Buddy starts to chuckle. Soon the best friends are full out laughing. Ollie turns the radio dial up and they bob their heads to the classic rock, unable to stop smiling.

When they enter the school parking lot Buddy stops laughing. He turns down the radio dial and squeezes the steering wheel as if he's driving on black ice. The car is quiet for a moment as they watch Angela's blue Firebird pull into the parking lot. Buddy swallows then he wipes his sweaty palms on his pant thighs. "Make sure of one thing, will you?"

Ollie grabs his backpack. "What?"

"Make sure Corky doesn't embarrass me."

Ollie nods his head then gets out of the vehicle. He walks slowly around it like all is normal but even from here he can see Angela staring at the driver's side of Buddy's car. Finally Buddy's door unlatches and simultaneously Angela's girl squad starts to whisper.

Ollie sits on the hood of the car. Buddy hesitates beside him for a second then takes a quick peek toward Angela. He thrusts his fists into his pants pockets, shuffles his feet then says, "Yep, let's go," as he starts to the school. Ollie jumps and blocks his way holding up his hands. Buddy pivots and spins around him. He's a good basketball player but Ollie is better on his defense. He's quickly in front of Buddy and pushes with both of his hands on his shoulders. "Now is your chance. Before Corky gets here," Ollie turns him completely around. To his surprise, Buddy doesn't stop. Once he's turned in the right direction, he heads straight toward Angela's car. Ollie stands in the middle of the parking lot in shock.

The girl's whisperings drift off until there's none left. All five of them stand there staring at Buddy. Angela holds a flirtatious smile. Buddy finally lifts his eyes off his shoes and takes them straight to Angela's. "Angela," Buddy says in a shockingly loud voice, "would you like to go out with me this Saturday night after the basketball game?"

It seems like everyone in the parking lot has frozen to hear each word. All eyes are focused toward Angela's Firebird.

A smile like Buddy has never seen before appears on Angela's face. He knows she's going to say yes before she even speaks. "Why I would love to Buddy Porter," Angela Patterson lets the words ooze off her tongue like honey.

The parking lot erupts with applause. Buddy turns away with a smile on his face so large Ollie thinks his friend's teeth might fall out. Ollie joins the applause with the rest of the school. He smacks Buddy's back a good five times. Buddy looks at his feet. "Let's go, let's go, move it," he says under his breath. They jog off into the building.

Buddy isn't in the locker room at the end of the day for practice when Ollie gets there. Ollie looks for him. He isn't in the gym. He isn't talking to Coach. Ollie heads back to the locker room to look again. But in the hallway leading to the gym Ollie spots Buddy. He's at the end of the hall wearing his huge smile. Both of his hands are stored in his front pants pockets. He sways like a little kid trying to persuade their parent to give them sugar too close to bedtime. In front of him Angela Patterson stands with her head cocked to the left looking up at Buddy like she's seeing a movie star. Ollie laughs at the interaction and decides to enjoy the show. He leans up against the wall, crossing his arms and his feet. Buddy's eyes catch the movement and upon spotting his best friend he stops swaying like a ballerina and jerks his hands out of his pockets. Ollie laughs as he waves at him. Buddy eventually waves in return. Angela sees the exchange. She waves too, "Hi Ollie!"

Ollie smiles, "Hey Angela, you joining the team?"

 Buddy shakes his head and Angela laughs. Buddy says something, talking partly with his hands then starts to walk away. Angela smiles at Ollie again. "Bye Ollie!" she waves. Ollie waves back then watches his best friend approach. He seems a foot taller to Ollie. The two turn together down the hallway toward the locker room. "Seems like someone is having a good day," Ollie says as they fall into pace with each other. Buddy nudges his friend against the wall.

Even if everyone on the team hadn't seen the Buddy-Angela interaction this morning, they knew something great happened to Buddy Porter. He plays the scrimmage game like it is the state championship.

Coach Jackson blows his whistle three quick times. The scrimmage comes to a halt and the team circles up by the bleachers. "Buddy Porter, where has that kind of playing been?" Coach nods his head at the rest of the team. "That is

47

the kind of playing I'm talking about boys! That's what I want to see!"

Corky nudges his elbow into Buddy's side. "Someone's got a pretty little *angel* on their mind."

"I want that kind of enthusiasm and *passion* Saturday night! Play like it's the last game of your life! Or in Buddy's case," Coach smiles, "Play like it's the first time you've talked to a pretty girl."

The team erupts with laughter. Percy and Miles slap Buddy on the back. Buddy shoves them away and shakes his head like he's embarrassed but he can't stop his smile from appearing. Coach blows his whistle one more time for dismissal.

Eleven year old Ollie stands looking at a burning mass before him. He doesn't know what he's looking at or how he got here. All he can hear is a terrible ringing sound. It becomes so loud he squeezes his eyes shut and covers his ears. Slowly more sounds creep into his ear holes. A high pitch screeching noise that sounds like tires skidding on a road comes through. He hears voices, most sound like they're screaming. Ollie slowly opens his eyes. He's looking down at his feet. One of his tennis shoe laces has come undone. He spots this through the golden pieces of dry grass he's standing in. The wind gently blows the grass across his ankles. He's standing in a field of dead grass. About thirty feet in front of him the burning mass still flares. He can hear it this time. The flames lick at each other. A steady hissing noise rises like a snake is being burned.

Ollie is about to turn away from it to see what else is around him when a woman runs by his side toward the burning mass. She circles it about ten feet away. When she's nearly on the other side she freezes then drops to her knees. She gets down on all fours like an animal. Ollie takes a closer look at the mass. To the far left he can make out a black protrusion facing the sky. A closer look reveals markings on the black thing. Finally it clicks with Ollie that he's looking at a tire. He's looking at a car; a car that is upside down; a car that is on fire.

Something in Ollie's system jolts forward telling him he was in a car and so were his parents. *Why isn't he in a car now? Where are his parents?* Frantic now, Ollie spins in a circle looking all around him for his parent's car or at least his parents. But even when he sees the road directly behind him, lined with tons of vehicles, he doesn't spot his parents. Among all the cars people are standing and watching. They're all looking his way. More so, they're looking over him at the burning car.

Behind him the peering woman yells, "They're in there! Someone help! They're still in there!"

Ollie turns back around to look at her. She's running around the burning car, stooping down on her knees occasionally and peering again into the car. She tries to get closer to it but flames reach out at her and the hissing snake warns her with a louder cry. She slowly backs away. Ollie can see she's crying huge sobs now. She finally looks at him full in the face and her sobbing chest stops. Then she walks up to him. Her face is blackened from being too close to the flames. Only peach streaks mark her cheeks from her tears. When she inhales her breath catches in her throat then she chokes out, "Were you in there?"

Ollie peers around her shoulder toward the burning car. Fear grips his body because as he looks at it he honestly doesn't know, but something in his gut tells him he was. A sudden gust of wind brings a strong smell of burning flesh to his nose.

Ollie springs forward in his bunk bed once more. Sweat is dripping off his nose but tonight Ollie cannot just wipe them away. His dream boils in his stomach. He jumps off the bed, having it jolt against the wall with a loud thud. He doesn't stop when the child beneath him whimpers from fright. Ollie runs to the bathroom where he lets the bubbling memory flow out into the toilet.

Uncontrollably the tears flow out of him next. He gags on more puke and spits it out into the toilet between sobs. He cries so heavily he fears he'll never be able to breathe again. At last air is sucked back into his lungs and he collapses his head against the toilet seat. Its coolness helps his feverish head but the smell is so bad Ollie cries some more.

The bathroom door starts to creak. Miss Stephen's pink-rolled head pops inside. Ollie tries to stop crying but even as he holds his breath willing himself not to make any sounds, the tears won't stop pouring out of his eyes. Miss Stephen slips inside and shuts the door behind her. The bathroom is so small her nightgown brushes against Ollie's face when she turns. She examines him after the door clicks. Ollie's bottom lip shakes like a dam about to burst. Her eyes stay on his and they hold the kind of fear that a mother has for her child when she knows her assistance is useless. Nonetheless, with her rickety knees, she sits on the floor with Ollie and with this act he moans with his tears. Miss Stephen runs her fingers through his sandy blonde hair until Ollie's moaning stops many minutes later. Miss Stephen simply asks, "The nightmares still?"

Ollie nods his head then he falls asleep leaning against the bathtub.

Though Ollie has had an awful morning he can't let it burden his friend because as soon as he's in the car ready to go to school he can see Buddy is living high in the clouds. There's a glow about him that only a girl can give a guy. Just seeing Buddy's happiness helps Ollie believe his day is going to get better.

But the most part of the school day isn't anything extraordinary. Amy Stratton is happy in Home Education but it isn't anything extreme enough to wipe away the visions of his dream. Hoping basketball practice will help him forget it Ollie jets out of his last class first and heads straight to the gym.

As he rounds the corner into the gymnasium he hears someone rolling the basketball cart onto the court. Assuming it is Coach Jackson he doesn't even look up as he passes into the locker room. He's ready before any other teammates enter. Figuring he can use his timeliness for some extra practice, Ollie heads out of the locker room.

The basketball cart is in the middle of the gym as it should be. Ollie props his foot on the bleacher to tighten his shoelace. As he straightens up he notices from the corner of his eye someone duck behind the cart. Ollie turns to face it. He studies it for a moment, wondering if he is seeing things or if someone is really there. He is about to yell after them when they appear.

The beautiful girl Ollie had seen earlier this week there in the gym talking to Coach Jackson stands on the other side of the cart. She doesn't look at him. She rotates the basketballs in front of her. Ollie looks around the gym for anyone else. As he scans the upper floor of the bleachers for Coach Jackson the sound of her voice startles him.

"What are you doing?" her voice rings in the empty gymnasium like a megaphone.

She is looking at Ollie with one light brown eye brow cocked. Even from here Ollie can see that her eyes are green. Apparently he takes too long to answer her because she eventually rolls her green eyes and takes back to rotating the basketballs.

Ollie shakes his head clear. "I'm here to play basketball." He walks toward the cart now having forgotten the images of his nightmare and how his day was doomed to be sad. "What are *you* doing here?" he asks her as he grabs a basketball off the opposite side of the cart.

She looks up at him. "I'm making it possible for you *to* practice," she says then looks back to her work. Her voice is monotone like she's bored. Ollie wonders if she's bored with him, rotating the basketballs, or life in general. He decides not to ask her.

"Well thanks," Ollie puts out his right hand to her.

She looks at it for a moment then cocks her eyebrow before she slowly pulls her hand off the basketball and places it hand in his.

Ollie smiles from ear to ear as she shakes it. "I'm Ollie. What's your name?"

The girl's eyebrow slowly goes back down and her face softens a little, replacing some boredom and curiosity with acceptance. "I'm Brandi," she says then she takes her hand away and puts it back to rotating a ball.

"Brandi," Ollie says out loud. He feels like he's back to his normal self. His joy has returned to his heart, having his head clear of all the baggage that filled it this morning. Brandi doesn't look back up at him. Ollie tosses the ball back and forth between his hands. "That's a nice name," he says.

Brandi doesn't acknowledge him. She rotates the last ball then turns her back on him as she walks toward the bleachers. Ollie is a little stunned with her lack of interest but not offended. Unwittingly he follows her. "So you play basketball Brandi?"

She doesn't turn around or even hesitate as she continues across the gym. "Not currently," she says.

"You want to?" Ollie bounces the ball off the floor. It echoes through the gym. Brandi reaches the cooler of water on the bleacher. She doesn't answer him. Ollie reaches the cooler and putting one hand on the bleacher he leans so he is facing her. Brandi takes a deep breath like she's trying to stay patient with a little kid. She doesn't look at him as she speaks, "Where are the rest of you guys? Why are you the only one here?" Brandi squeezes the cooler pump so water fills a team bottle.

Ollie smiles and slightly giggles, half-way content that he's annoying this girl so much. "I thought you were doing all of this for *me* Brandi," he jokes.

She smiles at the corner of her lip, "Not likely."

Ollie looks at her, wanting to see the smile appear again. In that moment of serene silence Miles and Percy round the corner into the gym talking obnoxiously loud about their inappropriate misgivings towards some girls in the hallway.

When alas they notice Ollie they quiet their voices, still having some pride among their team captain. They wave at him then disappear into the locker room. As soon as they're gone a flow of teammates begin entering the gym. Ollie knows his time alone with the new girl, Brandi, is over. Coach Jackson spots the two of them still at the bleachers.

"I see you've met our new assistant," he says to Ollie as he crosses the gym toward him.

At first it doesn't click with Ollie that he means Brandi. When it finally does Coach Jackson is patting Brandi on the shoulder with a 'well done'. "So glad we could finally get you here Brandi," he says then turns to Ollie. "This is Phil Oliver, he's the team captain." Coach squeezes Ollie's shoulder like a proud father. "If you ever need anything," Coach now has one hand on Ollie's shoulder and another on Brandi's, connecting the three of them like a chain, "Ollie here will help you. You can trust him. He's a gentleman if ever I knew one." Coach smiles between the two of them and nods his head like he's done them both a favor.

Coach squeezes their shoulders simultaneously one more time. Then, as if he has eyes in the back of his head, he sweeps his arm out just as Percy comes out of the locker room. "This fellow here is my son, Percy." Brandi and Coach walk away together toward the rest of the team. Ollie stays put watching her as they go. For a reason unknown to him, he feels intrigued by her. He's interested in her like he's never been for any other girl. He wants to know what makes her mind tick. Why she walks the way she does. Why she talks the way she does. Is she confident? Is she shy? Will she always be this unreadable? It is the appearance of his friend Buddy that wakes him from his thoughts of her and turns him back to basketball practice.

As each team member trickles in for practice the guys pass balls to each other. Like always, Buddy and Ollie pair off. After five minutes or so the team is finally collected. Coach sounds his whistle and together they all huddle at center court. Brandi stands by Coach. She's looking at each player but only glancing at them as if she's trying to catalogue them all in her memory merely by first appearance. She doesn't look at Ollie though. All the boys take their time looking her over. She looks tiny among them all. Even with her blonde ponytail at the top of her head she only comes to their shoulders. She's a mere five foot, two inches. The shortest on the team is Percy and he's five foot, six inches.

Coach slaps his hands against his clip board to quiet everyone. "Alright, listen up," he begins. "I've got someone I need you all to meet. This is Brandi Bollinger. She's going to be our assistant this season." Majority of the team shuffles their feet. Brandi puts her hands in her jacket pockets. Coach clears his throat. "That means she's your boss." He pauses and looks each teammate in the eye, hesitating over Miles and Percy a moment longer. "What she says goes. If she says you need to sit the bench, you sit. And I don't want to hear you ever try and argue with her. She's a college girl. She's got education to tell you knuckle heads if you done tore a meniscus or pulled a hamstring. She's studying to be a physical therapist. This here is her internship. She's going to wrap your knees, wrap your ankles, get your ice packs, get your water, get your towels . . ." Coach rolls his shoulders. "So that's Brandi." He looks to his clip board, sighs then starts barking orders in a totally different voice. Brandi looks a little shocked with the abrupt shift in character but none of the guys blink. This is how Coach Jackson talks. His voice flexes more than their arms do all practice. He goes from chit chatting to screaming faster than Angela's Firebird can go from zero to sixty.

Corky nudges his elbow into Ollie's side. "Check it out man," he clicks his tongue as he dances his eyebrows at Brandi. The team turns toward the court when Coach's whistle sounds. "I got a girl. Buddy's got a girl," Corky continues. He wraps his arm over Ollie's shoulders. "You catch my drift man?" Ollie pushes Corky away from him who bursts into laughter.

While they warm up with sprints and free throws and all through lay-ups, Ollie can't stop thinking of her. The more he thinks of her piercing green eyes, the larger a fire grows in his stomach. By the middle of their scrimmage game Ollie has resolved he must do something about this sickening sensation. Maybe Corky has a good point. But just as he is about to plan what he ought to do, Miles skids across the gym floor in front of him.

"Ouch! Oh, hold up!" he moans on the floor. He pulls his knee to his chest. The team comes to a halt and gathers around him. Miles stretches his leg back and forth from his chest to the floor, moaning all the while. In all his years playing basketball, Ollie has never had a teammate get hurt during practice. He now looks at Miles with suspicion as the rest of the team seems to as well. Coach breaks through the forming circle around him, "What is it now?" Brandi follows behind him.

"I think I tore something coach," Miles stretches his leg again.

Coach huffs as he crouches down on his knees beside him. "What do you mean you think? What happened Miles?"

"I mean I turned to guard Ollie here and I must have turned too quick." Ollie knows without a doubt now that he's fibbing. Miles wasn't guarding him in the least. "See I felt something tare in here or something Coach. It hurts real bad. I think it's starting to swell." Miles cradles his knee like it's a new born baby. Buddy and Ollie glance at each other and shake their heads with a common thought, *"He's got to be kidding."*

"What a weenie," Corky says.

Coach turns to Brandi. "Well come give this a look college girl."

Brandi, red in the face, takes a knee on the other side of him. Miles shifts toward her so his knee is over her thigh. From the corner of his eye Ollie catches Percy trying to hide a smile. Brandi pokes her finger at Miles' hands, "Can you move these so I can take a look?" she says. Ollie feels sorry for her and he knows Buddy probably feels the same way.

"Yeah, sure," Miles says as he relaxes back on his hands. It appears he's trying to flex simultaneously. It's simply revolting, just plain pathetic.

Brandi squeezes his knee in various places asking, "Does it hurt here? How about here? Well, then where does it hurt?" After a minute Brandi looks at Coach, "Nothing is wrong with him as far as I can tell."

Miles interjects before Coach can speak, "Well that doesn't mean it can't hurt. I'm telling you Coach I think I need Brandi to help me over to the bleachers and maybe get me an ice pack or something. I think it's swollen a little. See that Coach," Miles pokes his knee. "There's an indention there." Brandi crosses her eyebrows as she looks at the *"indention."*

Coach stands up and slaps his clip board against his knee. "In all my years coaching you Miles you ain't ever had a single injury and here you are only two days before the first game of the season saying you tore something DURING PRACTICE."

"Well what do you want me to do Coach?" Miles talks back, "keep lying here on the floor?"

Coach huffs a last time. "Brandi you two go over there and fix this. The rest of you all GET BACK TO THE GAME!" With a whistle, Brandi and Miles hobble over to the bleachers. Ollie stares at Miles whose arm is draped over Brandi's shoulder, his hand far too close to her chest. He feels the heat rise in his cheeks. He decides to let it all out the second half of the scrimmage.

The rest of practice Miles hogs Brandi. Each time she moves he asks her where she is going and then begs her not to leave him "in case his knee flares up again." Then when she sits back down by him he tells her stories of his weekend partying and hooking up with girls. Brandi keeps her eyes on the court, looking like she is the one in physical pain.

After a few minutes of uninterrupted discussion, Miles asks her if she is still listening to him. She nods her head so he continues on. "Blah, blah this and blah blah that. Insert random girl's name here and mention her bra size there." And while Miles is thinking he's the most clever ladies man, Brandi is lost watching Phil Oliver. She could easily reason she does so because Ollie is the best, but really she knows it is because Ollie is the best looking. Yet it isn't just his looks that catch her gaze. It is this, combined with lack of pride. She notices his encouragement to each team member. She notices that while he could keep the ball, shooting and scoring multiple times, he always passes the ball to give his teammates the opportunity instead. It is this that intrigues her. She wonders if he'll be like this all season or if he is just trying to put on a good guy persona for her first day here. She prays he isn't actually more like Miles: annoying, childish, fake, and just waiting for an opportunity to pounce on the only female on the team.

By the end of practice Ollie chooses not to ask Brandi what the fire in his gut had been telling him to. He figures she's had enough guy talk after having sat with Miles for nearly an hour. Instead he just smiles at her when Coach circles them all up for his last words. Then he goes home.

Chapter Three

Anniversaries & Father Figures

Friday Ollie wakes up feeling differently. He pulls the string of the weed eater so passionately it fires to life the first try. He swings the power tool like a dance partner. His cassette tape replays Loretta Lynn's *At Last* in his ears. Today it tells the story of his heart. *At last my love has come along. My lonely days are over. And life is like a song.*

Brandi's fiery green eyes burn a hole in his brain. As a straight A student Ollie has never struggled to enjoy class, but today he fights to be present. He feels slightly guilty for it when he realizes he's only half heard what Buddy has told him about the phone call from Angela the night before. And he feels even more guilt when he finds Emilee Stratton staring at him in home economics, apparently waiting for a response to the ten minute spill she had just given him. At this moment Ollie decides, *"I'm just going to have to ask this girl to go out with me, lest I never have a single thought to myself again."* With this conclusion, Ollie does the same as the day before: he is first out of his last class and first to the gym for practice.

Sure enough Brandi is there, pushing in another cart of basketballs. Her long blonde hair is pulled up with the same black scrunchy. It bobs against the hood of her black sweater as she walks. Her shoes slightly squeak against the waxed floor. She hears Ollie enter today. Her eyes meet his as soon as he rounds the corner. She notes his eyes are a ridiculously delicious shade of blue. They sparkle. They literally sparkle. She has to look away. As if he is some kind of trigger, sweat starts to form in her armpits. She coughs a little hoping her nerves will ease. *"It's his height,"* she thinks to herself. *"He's too tall. That's what is making me nervous,"* she tries to persuade herself.

Ollie feels absolutely no nerves on the other hand. "Miss Brandi," he announces as he walks into the gymnasium. Brandi's neck hair tingles so she tries to ignore him. Ollie tosses his back pack onto the first row of bleachers and continues to walk toward her. Brandi waits with the cart, rotating the balls face out.

Ollie stops just short of the other side. Smiling from ear to ear he puts one hand on the cart, slightly leaning, and crosses his feet. "Hi Brandi," Ollie feels his chest fill with a sweetness that comes from the sound of her name leaving his lips out loud.

Brandi's response is choppy as her eyes dart so quickly from his to the basketballs he isn't sure she even looks at him. "Hi."

Ollie is clueless to her lack of interest. He looks over the Mustang logo on her sweater down to her faded out blue jeans when the words on his mind flow freely out of his mouth, "You look beautiful today Brandi."

Her nerves block any signals from her brain to keep moving her hands. Brandi is frozen for a moment. Then her brain catches up with her. Thinking he must indeed be another version of a smooth talking Miles, Brandi hardens. She takes a step away from the cart so she can get a full view of Ollie. She noticeably looks him up and down then places her hand on her hip. "Is this what you're wearing to practice in today?"

Ollie stands up, taking his hand off the cart and uncrossing his feet. He looks down at himself then smiles as he puts his hands in his blue jean pockets. "No, I just wanted to ask you something before I went into the locker room."

The fire within Brandi flickers. Sweat starts to dampen her sweater in multiple places. She physically tries to shake it off. Rolling her shoulders she moves back behind her side of the cart, hoping to hide what she's feeling. Ollie follows her around to the other side.

"I was wondering if you'd like to go out on a date with me." Ollie's smile never falters and for some reason this is enough to rekindle Brandi's fire.

"Go out on a date with you?" She laughs at the idea of being seen in public with a junior in high school. "No. No way," Brandi rotates a final ball then starts to walk away. Ollie doesn't move from the cart. "Okay," he says, "Maybe tomorrow then."

Brandi stops, completely stunned. But when she turns around to correct him with a *"No way, not ever,"* Ollie is snatching his backpack from the bleacher and disappearing into the locker room. Brandi shakes her head wondering what in the world has just happened. *Why couldn't he take a hint? What did he mean 'maybe tomorrow'?* And among these wonderings Brandi notices she is actually excited about this prospect. If he really did ask her again tomorrow, she just might start liking this guy. And now with a heads up, she'd also wear an extra layer of deodorant.

To no one's surprise Miles is completely recovered. "Must have just pinched something Coach. I'm all better today. That college girl must have done something right." Miles winks at Brandi who rolls her eyes.

Coach, though a wonderful instructor in the game of basketball, is a rather dim man. So he nods his head, "Good to have you back Miles. We need everyone for our opening game Saturday. Like always, be expecting a big turn-out from both sides. AND LISTEN HERE," Coach moves his gum from one side of his mouth to a pocket in his cheek (he does this when he has something "serious" he wants to say). "I don't want *no one* conversing with the enemy." In Ollie's mind he wants to die laughing, and the look he exchanges with Buddy tells him his best friend is thinking the same thing. Corky claps his hands together. He loves it when Coach "talks rough." He says it gets the teams blood pumping. "We ain't playing Saturday to make new friends. WE'RE MAKING ENEMIES! You're going to play these wimpy Georgetown *Gofers*, or whatever rodent they are, AND YOU'RE GOING TO CRUSH THEM."

"Yeah!" Corky applauds louder.

"They ain't ever gonna' want anything else to do with Masonville Mustangs. YOU HEAR ME?" Coach yells over Corky.

Everyone applauds and nods their heads. Brandi still looks taken aback by Coach's abrupt screaming. It is going to take her a while not to jump every time he speaks.

Ollie knows Coach has said this for obvious reasons. Some of the team players, mostly Miles and Percy, have gathered a reputation for taking out the opposing team's cheerleaders after a win. They think it is a great way to "claim the win." Miles and Percy have used harsher terms, saying, "They're marking their territory." Words obviously gotten around in this little town and even though it's been going on for years, Coach seems to just be hearing about it, or at least to have just processed it. The culprits exchange looks around the circle, smirking to each other. Then it is back to warm-ups and a scrimmage. Ollie multitasks, playing the sport and watching Brandi on the side lines. Unfortunately, he has to bear watching Miles make embarrassing gestures to her all practice as well; winking, smiling, finger-shooting, trying to high five her as he runs down the sidelines. All of it gives the team something to laugh at.

Ollie asks Buddy to tell him about Angela's phone call one more time as they drive home after practice. Buddy isn't saddened in the least that Ollie didn't hear it the first time. He tells the story again in longer detail. After hearing it Ollie can't believe he missed it the first time.

"I can't believe Mr. Patterson answered the phone! What are the chances?" Ollie slaps his knee.

"I know!" Buddy laughs. "Here am I calling to talk to Angela and I end up talking to her dad more than her!"

"Hey, at least now he knows you're taking Angela out Saturday."

Buddy nods his head, "Yeah, but I wanted to ask him in person tomorrow before the game so he knows I mean business. But now with me calling, what if he thinks I was going to take her out behind his back? I mean, that was the first time I've even ever called a girl but he probably thinks I'm some kind of yanker."

Ollie laughs to ease Buddy's pain. "No man, once Angela tells him how nice you are, you don't have anything to worry about."

65

Ollie's comment puffs Buddy back up. He smiles again then gives Ollie a strange look. Ollie laughs at first but Buddy won't stop looking at him with his strange smile. Finally Ollie shove's his shoulder laughing, "What are you looking at me like that for?"

Buddy holds his awkward smile a moment longer then, as if they were back in seventh grade playing their secret detective game, he says in a very quiet voice, "I think you should ask a girl to come out Saturday night too."

Ollie knows instantly he's been caught. He laughs out a sigh and shakes his head. "Do you now? And who should she be?"

Buddy laughs full out, "Like you don't know! Brandi of course! I think she likes you."

Ollie finds this completely preposterous. "Like me? She won't even look at me."

"You've got to be pooping me a box of rocks," Buddy stops the car in front of the Children's Home. "Doesn't even look at you? You're all she looks at all practice. Er, you know, when Miles isn't in her face. She tries to make it look like she ain't but she is."

Ollie has no idea how Buddy would know this. Buddy has never lied to him before, so while Ollie severely doubts this to be true, he holds onto this little bit of hope. But he doesn't go forward with telling Buddy about having already asked Brandi. Instead, he tells his buddy goodbye.

Before he makes it to the steps Miss Stephen is holding open the front door, little George on her hip, his fist tight around a ring of her hair. "Ollie, old man Gibbs is on the phone for you in here, hurry up. Ouch! Now George I'm gonna' spank you if you don't quit trying to eat my hair!"

Ollie finds the receiver lying on the counter, the cord of the phone spinning in knots. "Hello Mr. Gibbs, what can I do you for sir?"

Raymond Gibbs clears his throat, "Yeah, uh, how you doin' son?"

"I'm just fine sir, how are you?"

"I'm good boy," Raymond sighs then clears his throat again. "You still up for workin' tomorrow?"

"Yes sir." In the living room Ben and Ezra are wrestling. Miss Stephen is yelling for them to get off each other. Ollie plugs his open ear.

"Well then I'll be there at seven a.m. sharp to pick you up. We've got some scrap to haul off. What time do you got to be back home? I know you have that negro-sport going on now."

Kirsten skids across the tile kitchen floor. She crosses her arms and legs around Ollie's leg. He tries to focus. "I need to be back no later than five, if that'll do you fine sir." Kirsten jerks his leg back and forth at the knee trying to communicate he should walk and take her on a ride. Ollie holds his finger up to her to tell her to give him a minute.

"That'll do just fine. See you bright and early."

"Thank you, sir. Goodnight sir."

Raymond Gibbs sighs, no doubt perplexed that Ollie still calls him sir after having told him numerous times to call him Raymond. "Goodnight Philip."

After a long night of pulling Kirsten around on his legs, Ben and Ezra on his arms, and Ryan on his back, Ollie sleeps without any interrupting replays of his past.

Despite only having one day of the week to truly sleep in Ollie is glad to wake up Saturday morning. Of course Ryan fusses when Ollie steps on his mattress to get down. But even faster than his school morning routine, he is dressed and out the door. Raymond Gibbs pulls up to the chained fence in his battered red pickup truck. Ollie waves at him from the sidewalk and the old man nods his head. His pipe is already smoking from his lips.

Ollie slips in through the passenger door, sitting on top of a pile of crumpled papers. Raymond waves his hand at him. Ollie leans forward and the old man snatches the papers out. "Gotta' take these to the BMV later today," he says as he smashes them into the glove box in front of Ollie.

"What are they for sir?"

The old man cocks his silver eyebrow at the boy, biting his pipe. "Getting nosey are we?"

Ollie smiles inside because he's grown to know the old man is actually a really big softy, he only talks gruff. "No sir," Ollie clips in his seatbelt and the two of them take off.

Once they're to the farm Raymond backs the truck up to a wagon with Ollie directing him through the back window. Once it's ready to go they drive through the dried hay field to what Raymond calls, "his back barn." Behind it old machinery and piles of junk line the fence. Ollie starts to take inventory as they drive by it. One by one they pass old tractors, a manure spreader, an old van, the skeleton of a car, the frame of a truck, a few truck beds, piles of tin, piles of copper, piles of steel, and piles of straight up trash.

Ollie is dying to ask why the old man has all this stuff but knows it will sound too rude. To his surprise Raymond answers as if he can read his mind. "I'm a bit of a collector, you'd say," he muffles through this pipe. Then he removes it. "My wife always used to yell at me 'I was a hoarder,' but that woman knew nothing. This ain't hoarding and I'm going to prove it to her today. We're starting at this end and we're pitching anything and everything that the scrapper will take. She'd have wanted it that way." He nods his head.

Ollie is surprised with the sudden mention of Raymond's wife. All these months working beside him, Raymond has never talked of the Mrs. "What was her name sir?"

The old man looks surprised for a moment. He takes his pipe out of his mouth and licks his lips a few good times. "Uh," he hesitates and clears his throat, "Margaret. Margaret Jane Gibbs."

Ollie smiles at the old man though he refuses to look at him. He imagines Mrs. Margaret Jane Gibbs. He imagines her as a tall, thin woman with dark hair, pulled back in a tight bun. She'd wear . . .

"She always wore a flower print dress," Raymond reads his mind again. "She and flowers, let me tell you. She was always wearing them flowers. Even her aprons had them flowers on 'em. And," the truck comes to a stop at the end of the scraps. Raymond puts the truck in park but doesn't stop talking. It is as if he's forgotten he's where he is. "She always wore my rubber boots." He laughs and coughs a little at the same time. "I kept em' by the back door so she'd always slip em' on when she'd come out to find me. She looked so goofy with that pretty flower dress of hers and my muddy black boots. They were so big on her, they'd come up past her knees." The old man wears a smile Ollie has never seen before. He gazes out the front window of the truck like he's looking at Margaret in the field. Ollie lets the silence fill the vehicle. After a while the old man looks like he's going to cry—his eyes misting over, his smile gone. Even his pipe is out of a light.

Ollie's heart aches for Raymond. "I've never heard you talk about Mrs. Gibbs before sir."

Ollie's words seem to awaken him. He snaps out of his trance and quickly strikes a match off his steering wheel. Puffing his pipe back to life he says, "Yes, well, today is our anniversary." And with that Raymond takes the keys out of the ignition and steps out of the truck. A deep sadness bites Ollie's heart but he knows not to press

Raymond. He will just try to make today great as a day it can be for the sad man.

If Ollie hadn't just been in the truck hearing what he did, he wouldn't have known Raymond had a sore heart at all though. The brisk fall wind seems to clean his slate. "Start here on this pile!" he barks through his pipe. And with that the rest of the morning is put into motion. Ollie tries not to take his eyes off his work, hoping to get as much done as he possibly can, but he can't help but glance at old Raymond every now and then. He just sits there on the edge of the wagon, looking out into the field where the invisible Mrs. Margaret Gibbs must be.

Alas, lunch time comes. Ollie has the whole first pile sorted through. Raymond calls after him, "Come on over here Philip. Eat yuh some lunch." From the bed of the truck Raymond pulls out a red and white plastic lunch box. From inside he tosses Ollie a brown sack. Inside is a bologna and cheese sandwich in plastic wrap. In another ball of plastic wrap are some bar-b-q potato chips and still another plastic wrapping of hard chocolate chip cookies. "Here's the canteen of water," Raymond sits the metal green canteen on the side of the wagon. Ollie sits beside him on the edge, the canteen between them. Raymond munches on his sandwich too.

After a few moments of silence Ollie feels he can't keep his words inside his chest any longer. "Sir, if you want to talk more about Mrs. Gibbs, I'd like to get to know her."

Ollie doesn't look up at Raymond and Raymond doesn't look at Ollie. The old man just stops chewing and gazes out at the field again. After a moment he chews his food again. "Well, what do you want to know about her Nosey?"

Ollie cracks into a smile. "Anything. Did you two have any children?"

Raymond answers robotically trying to act like this conversation isn't doing him the favor it really is, "No kids. Do I seem like the loving father type to you?"

Ollie laughs. Raymond even smiles a little. The old man hits his pipe on the edge of the wagon. Old tobacco falls out. He reaches into his pocket for his bag. "No, we tried but never could have none." He pinches out some black tobacco and stuffs it in the pipe. "Probably a good thing," he says mostly under his breath as he pushes his bag back into his coat pocket.

"Well I know lots of kids that would like to have you as a father." Ollie says it without really thinking. He wipes his sandwich crumbs off his fingers onto his pants. "Thanks for the sandwich," he finishes by crumbling his bag into a ball. He slips his chips and cookies into his coat pocket for later. Raymond looks at Ollie's face like he never has before but he doesn't say anything. Ollie gets back to work on the scrap pile.

Raymond doesn't move from that spot for the rest of the afternoon. Even when the wagon is overflowing, about to push into Raymond's back, the old man doesn't move. He is entranced again. Only he isn't looking at the field. He looks at the spot on the wagon beside the water canteen where Ollie had sat. Ollie doesn't bother him, only nods his head for Raymond to get in the truck when it is time for him to leave. They drive home in silence. Raymond doesn't touch his pipe. Finally at the chain fence of the Children's Home as Ollie is getting out of the old pickup truck, Raymond speaks, "Thanks for the help today Phil and," Raymond hesitates looking at his hands on the wheel. "And thanks for the talk." Then Raymond shoves his hand into his jean pocket and pulls out a few bills. Ollie takes them with a little pain but knowing to respect the old man he doesn't reject it. "You're welcome sir. Happy anniversary."

Chapter Four

Peaceful Prayers & Broken Noses

As Buddy and Ollie pull into the school parking lot they can't miss a blonde ponytail streaking across the pavement. If Ollie had thought Brandi was beautiful the first day he saw her in the gymnasium, he couldn't think of how to describe her now. Seeing her run through the parking lot Ollie feels his heart pounding with her feet. She is breathtaking. So before Ollie gets out of the car he notes to mention in his prayer his extra need for focus tonight.

As is custom, Buddy turns off the car engine but doesn't leave. He and Ollie bow their heads. "Lord God," Ollie starts, "thank you for this beautiful fall day. Thank you for the colorful leaves and for Mr. Gibbs. Thank you for all that you give to us and all that you take away." Ollie usually says that line every prayer. And since this is only their thousandth prayer together Buddy knows that line by heart. He mouths it in time with Ollie. Yet each time that line means more to him than Ollie knows. It is his favorite line. Each time he hears it he wonders what all that line entails for Ollie. It always chokes Buddy up. "And so tonight we hope this game of basketball will bring you joy Great Father." With Brandi in mind Ollie continues, "Please help us to focus so we can do our best. And keep my friend Buddy here safe so he can have a rocking date with his new girlfriend." Buddy cracks into a laugh as Ollie closes with an "Amen." Buddy shoves his friend's shoulder in their playful banter.

 Prayer time before the game always relieves them. Buddy gets a sense of serene presence when Ollie prays. It makes him feel like God will literally be hovering around him during the game. He's thanked Ollie tons of times for praying for him before each game but he still doesn't think Ollie really knows what it does for him. Not only have these prayers made Buddy feel closer to God, it has made him feel completely special. Ollie bringing him before his God so many times has shown him he doesn't need for any other friend. There is no greater sense of friendship than when your friend will petition for you before their God.

The first time Ollie stopped Buddy for a prayer was tryouts day for the eighth grade basketball team. Mrs. Colleen Porter was driving them back to the junior high after having taken the boys for ice cream after school. The dessert had calmed Buddy's nerves for a few minutes but again he was holding his chest trying to take deep breathes. He was sweating and Mrs. Porter was looking through the rearview mirror saying, "Just calm down Buddy Porter. You've tried out so many times. It's no big deal." Ollie stared at Buddy like his friend had been replaced by a hypochondriac. "My heart is going to implode! I'm dying mom. Say goodbye to your son. Goodbye ice cream," Buddy said to his half-eaten cone. Ollie watched wide-eyed. "Don't be so dramatic," Mrs. Porter called back. As she stopped the car by the curb Buddy began to rant. "Mom, take me home. I can't do it. I don't wanna' do it. Let's leave. Ollie, you go." Ollie hadn't known Buddy struggled with anxiety before this day.

"Buddy, you calm down. We are not leaving 'till you tryout." Mrs. Colleen was wrapped around the seat patting her son's knee.

"Mom, I can't. No, no, no. You don't understand."

Finally Ollie had enough. "Buddy Porter," Ollie's voice cut through the car louder than usual. Both Colleen and Buddy went silent. "Buddy," Ollie pat his hand on his friend's shoulder. "Let's just pray about this."

Mrs. Colleen and Buddy continued to stare at Ollie. Buddy knew his friend went to Masonville First Baptist Church and Ollie had even told him about when he became a Christian after his parent's died and he was moved to this small town. But the Porters were not Christians. It wasn't because they didn't believe in a God. It was because they never took time to believe in him. They weren't opposed but they certainly had no idea how to go about talking to a god. So when Ollie bowed his head and closed his eyes Mrs. Colleen looked to Buddy and Buddy looked to his mom before they nodded their heads and did the same. Afterward, Buddy felt a calmness he couldn't explain. The following Sunday the Porters found their way to the back pew of Pastor Brown's Church. They've been there ever since.

Coach is waiting for them in the locker room with a big cardboard box. As soon as the boys walk in he throws a white mass of material at each of them—brand-new jerseys. On the back of Ollie's "Captain" stretches across the shoulders in black letters. Corky sports his jersey overtop his clothes like a model. The feel of the new material in their grip fuels a hunger for the game that every first game of the season should have.

The locker room is louder today than it has been this season. Miles and Percy are laughing, snapping each other with their towels. Corky is still strutting like a turkey in his new jersey. Coach stands with one leg propped on the bleacher. His sweatpants are too tight on him so his crotch looks like a bulging V. He's studying his clip board like there's world breaking news there. He doesn't move until each player is sitting along the bleachers dressed in their new jerseys. They all stare up at him until finally he lifts his eyes from the manila clip board.

He slaps it once on his knee. "Well boys, here we are: the first game of the season."

Miles and Percy whistle. A few other boys cheer. Corky is looking past Coach at himself in the mirror. He runs more gel through his hair.

Coach moves his wad of gum to the other cheek pocket. "We're going to go out there and we're going TO SQUASH THEM CUPCAKES out there." Buddy and Ollie exchange their usual look of desired laughter as they can only assume he's referring to the Georgetown Gofers as "cupcakes." The rest of the team cheers.

"I DON'T WANT TO SEE a crumb of em' left behind. Enjoy the taste of this victory, boys."

"Oh, we will," Percy nudges Miles in the side with his elbow and together they share a mischievous smile that makes Ollie want to puke.

Coach slaps the clip board off his thigh again then stands up straight. "NOW we'll have the team captain say a few words and then we're ready to play."

Ollie hadn't thought of anything to say. He hadn't taken the time. He'd also chosen to not worry about it. He knew Coach's words would be inspiration enough. Nonetheless he stands now in the middle of the sweat-smelling locker room. "Nice looking new jersey's hu?" Ollie sports his while the boys laugh and some speak their agreement.

"I think it looks better on me," Corky winks.

Ollie smiles back while the boys laugh. Then the words come to Ollie about what he should say next. "Let's not dirty em' up with foul play or dirty words," he says. The boys get quiet. "Let's not stretch em' out with big egos on the first game of the season. Let's start and finish this season the way we want these jerseys to." Ollie looks around at each team mate. Everyone looks back at him with hesitation, or is it admiration? "Looking good, and smelling pretty good too." The team erupts in laughter and clapping. They all huddle together. Ollie says a quick prayer, as is custom. The boys put their hands together in a circle, throw them in the air on 'three' and run from the locker room.

The team is greeted by a storm of applause. Music tries to play through the gymnasium, cracking and moaning its way through the speakers. Their entrance doesn't need to be too dressed up though. The crowd is on their feet, roaring like the Masonville Mustangs are the heart and soul of the town.

Miles and Percy feed off the crowd's energy. They jump up and down pumping their fists in the air as they shout back at their crowd they are number one. Ollie knows they'll play really well tonight with an enthusiastic crowd like this. He can't remember ever having lost an opening game anyway. Corky stops mid court, his mouth open as he stares at the crowd. Ollie stops beside him. "I can't believe this," Corky says. In all his years playing in the big city he never felt such a welcoming. Ollie smacks him on the back.

Coach slaps them all on their behinds with his clipboard as the starters take the court—Miles, Percy, Ollie, Buddy and Corky. Corky takes center stage as their jumper. He meets the referee and the opposing team's jumper in the middle of the court. As the ref poises the ball on his palm between the two of them the crowd goes silent. Corky crouches down. Ollie bounces on his heels. Miles and Percy nudge their opponents unnecessarily. Then the ball is thrust upward. Corky springs into the air and connects with the ball first, tipping it to Ollie. Without hesitation Ollie is dribbling down the court. Only when he is feet from the goal does his opponent jump in front of him, his arms in the air. Ollie makes a quick spin, leaving number eleven behind him and he shoots a scoring layup. The crowd is up and chanting, "Oll-ie, Oll-ie!" Only ten seconds into the game and Ollie has the first two points.

He and the others run to the other side of the court, leaving the ball for the Gofer guards to take in. Ollie stops just beyond midcourt to guard his equal—the other point guard. Number eleven eyes angrily then shouts a play number. But as soon as he crosses the half court line Ollie makes a jab for the ball. He swats it away and it rolls across the court. All ten players move to get it but Ollie is first. He hits the ball off the ground into a dribble and he's off again. He scores another two-point layup. The rest of the half continues just like this. Ollie scores every point but four. The Mustangs break to their locker room at half time. The score is 48 to 14.

Over the crackling intercom Jeff Wallace tries to announce William Bollinger and the amazing new shop vacuum prize. The crowd erupts in cheers as Mr. Bollinger announces the names of the raffle ticket winner. Then the sound of the cheerleader's music quivers through the speakers.

Once in the locker room Ollie notices all of his stuff has been taken out of his locker. His clothes lie partly on the bench and part on the floor. He remembers putting it all in his locker. He opens it up to see if someone decided to reclaim it. Nothing is inside so he shoves all his clothes back in it. Many of the guys slap him on the back. "Ollie you're doing so good tonight!" Buddy says.

"You might break the school record this year," Miles says. Percy shoves him.

"Did you see me swish that three?" Corky squeezes Percy's shoulder.

"Keep your shorts on!" Coach yells as he enters the locker room. Brandi follows behind him.

Someone on the team shouts, "There's a girl in the boy's locker room!" Miles quickly removes his shirt.

"You better get used to it," Coach spits. "Ollie, great work out there son. You going to be able to play all the second half?" Ollie nods his head. "Buddy, Corky, you too?" They nod. "Good. Brandi you wrap up their ankles then." And with that Coach exits the locker room, no doubt to buy some cookies from the bake sale.

The locker room fills with talk again as Brandi kneels at Buddy's feet. He kicks off his shoes and pulls his socks off.

"Hope you don't pass out from the smell Brandi," Miles laughs.

Ollie can see Buddy's lips moving as he talks to Brandi but the locker room is so loud with laughter he can't make out what is being said between them. Brandi wraps Buddy's black leg with the bright white gauze-like material quickly. Then she circles his ankle with white tape to hold it all in place. She's done in only a minute. While Buddy puts his socks back on Brandi pushes her box of supplies the few feet over to Corky then slides across the floor so she's in front of him. Corky doesn't stand still for her. He stands, yelling over her head at the boys about his three point shot. He only notices her when she pulls a misplaced piece of tape off his leg. It rips his leg hair out. Corky sucks his lips together so not to yell. Brandi does too, but so she doesn't laugh. Corky pats her on the head like a child when she's done and the team laughs. Brandi moves to him. As she kneels in front of him she sees Ollie's socks have no elasticity. They are bunched down at the top of his horrible looking sneakers. He pulls them off and then his socks. They have holes in the big toe and on each heel. Brandi eyes them as he puts them into his shoes. Ollie doesn't seem to notice their ragged state. In her mind Brandi takes note of the most popular guy in the school having the worst socks and shoes she's ever seen. Then she starts to wrap his ankles.

"You're pretty good at this," Ollie says.

Brandi doesn't look up from her work. "Yeah well this stuff is so cheap there's really no point in taking my time with it. It's probably not going to do you much good anyway. Don't know why he's having me wrap you all in this." She cuts the gauze then holds the roll up to Ollie's face. She finally looks at him. "Is this seriously all that you guys have?"

Ollie looks at the white mass for a moment. "I don't see anything wrong with it."

Brandi rolls her eyes then goes back to work with the tape now. "Yeah, well you don't know what to look for." Brandi rips the tape free from the roll. "When you find this rolled down into the toe of your shoe you'll know its crap." She throws it all into her box then stands up. Ollie says thank you but he doubts she hears him as she maneuvers around Miles who is waving his jersey over his shirtless body like a lasso. Ollie wishes he could teach that boy a thing or two about respect and dignity. Instead he rolls his eyes and slips on his holey socks.

Shortly into the second half the Gofers call for a timeout. The guys rush over to Coach but he's busy telling a referee where he can put his whistle if he blows it that closely to his ear again. Brandi hands each boy a water bottle as they pass her. Ollie stops in front of her. "Brandi," he says, "would you like to go out tonight?"

Brandi's face turns a vibrant red. She looks around as all the guys have stopped to look at her. Ollie doesn't notice them. Brandi holds the water bottle in midair. "Man you're derailing!" Corky laughs.

 When Ollie looks back to Brandi she is squeezing the bottle until the sides touch together and water bursts out of the mouth piece. It squirts in a direct line at Ollie's chest. The guys burst into laughter.

"No," Brandi answers then hands Ollie the bottle. Ollie smiles and nods his head.

Corky slaps Ollie on the back, "Derailed!"

"She ain't got time to go out with you Ollie," Miles says. "She'll be too busy going out with me. Ain't that right Brandi?"

Brandi doesn't look at him as she continues to hand out bottles. "In your wildest dreams," she says.

The team erupts with laughter. Ollie can't help but laugh too. "In your dreams!" Percy yells into Miles' face. He pushes him away, his face redder than Brandi's.

Halfway through the third quarter Buddy flags down Coach with a time out sign. Coach eventually sends in a replacement when the opposing team gets foul shots. Ollie watches Buddy motion to his ankles. Coach motions to Brandi. Brandi kneels in front of Buddy's black legs. The bright white gauze is nowhere to be seen. Ollie looks at his feet. He realizes then that his wrap is gone too. Probably where Brandi said it would end up—down in the toe of his shoe by now. As he jumps to rebound the ball he can feel the wrap sliding down around his heels. He knows Buddy must have timed out to get this uncomfortable feeling out from under his arches. Ollie doesn't stop though. He scores 21 more points before the game dismisses. Score: 97,Mustangs; 31, Gofers.

In the locker room Brandi is hardly visible behind the cluster of rooting boys. Coach Jackson makes his presence known by slapping his clipboard against his palm a few

83

good times. "That's what I'm talking about boys!" He smacks his gum around. The boys root even louder. "Phil Oliver," coach points his clipboard, "you keep playing like that son AND YOU'RE GOING TO BREAK THE SCHOOL RECORD!" The team cheers again. Ollie nods his head. He notices all of his stuff is out of his locker again. He shakes his head and picks it all up again.

Buddy dances a nervous jig on his toes.

 "What's wrong with you?" Ollie laughs.

"I want to change and get out of here but Brandi is in here." Buddy sweats more now than he did the whole game.

 "Oh yeah," Ollie remembers. "You have a date tonight, don't you?"

Buddy jumps on his toes now. "Yeah and I don't want her waiting on me."

Ollie shakes his head laughing. "Man, Angela is a cheerleader. She knows how long it takes to get out of a game when it is over."

Corky appears with a loud slap that echoes off Buddy's butt. "Date night!" he yells then dances around.

Buddy's eyes widen like white glassy moons on his black face. "Man, tell me you're coming tonight even if Brandi turned you down. I can't be left alone with Corky. I may kill him."

Ollie laughs. "Yeah I'm coming. You're my ride remember?" Brandi leaves the room. Ollie pulls off his jersey.

"I've got an idea," Buddy slips into his blue jeans. "I'll tell Angela to invite her next time."

"Go ahead," Ollie wraps his towel around his waist. "But I'm going to ask her too."

Corky leaves first to save some tables for Buddy and Ollie at the Freezer Fresh. Buddy talks to Mr. Patterson in the gym about Angela's curfew while Ollie takes a shower. When Ollie is done washing up he sees his back pack is out of his locker again. It's on the floor of the locker room. He shakes his head. He's certain he'd put it all up before he showered. Nonetheless he shrugs it off, gets dressed then sweeps it off the floor. He turns off the lights as he leaves.

Sunday morning Ollie gets up earlier than everyone else like usual. The first hour of his morning he spends hacking at weeds choking through the fence around the children's home. He weed eats and pulls, weed eats and pulls. His routine is interrupted by Miss Stephen who he spots waving her arm at him from the front steps. He kills the weed eater, pulls off his head phones and walks up to her. She starts talking to him when he's still halfway across the yard. "Philip we ain't getting these children nowhere if that blasted van doesn't start." Miss Stephen uses his first name when she wants to express she's direly serious.

The children's home's van sits on the concrete slab of a driveway. It is rusted through its red casing around all four wheels. The hood is tinted pink from the sun. The back passenger side's wheel is the spare tire. It's been on there for about a year now. The home can't afford new tires, not even one. It is their only means of transportation. It only seats ten comfortably so all of the children can't go somewhere together all at once unless someone volunteers their services. Ollie's fixed at least a hundred different problems on the van since he was tall enough to see in the hood. He changes the oil, pumps the tires, charges the battery, changes the brake pads, etcetera. Still, there's only so much Ollie can do when all his repairs have to cost near to nothing.

He pats his leather gloves together then pulls them off his hands. "I'll see if it'll start."

Miss Stephen shakes her head, her pink rolls swishing from side to side. "These kids ain't ever gonna' know nothin' about Jesus and mother Mary if they can't ever get to church. And how am I supposed to expect them to behave if they ain't got no morals?" She stands on the front steps while Ollie turns the key over. The van huffs like an old geezer before it chokes out. Ollie turns the key three more times before the van sputters its last breath. The fourth time he turns the key the van only makes a clicking sound. Miss Stephen throws her hands in the air before she turns and goes inside. She knows it isn't going to start. Ollie knows he'll be going to church alone again. Miss Stephen says no one goes to church if they all can't go. It is just easier for her to keep an eye on everyone that way. Ollie can go because he's old enough to drive himself if he had the means. He wants to take the kids with him but there's no room in the Porter's car for anyone else and even if there was some, he'd have to choose who could go and he just couldn't do that.

When the Porters pull up to the fence many of the kids cling to Ollie's legs. "Don't go without us! Take us with you! We want to go!" Kirsten holds on to his leg for dear life. Miss Stephen has to yell at them all to get off before Ollie can make it down the steps. Guilt tears at his gut for not being able to take them. He says a little prayer hoping soon they'll all be able to.

Buddy talks the whole ride there and back, and even between hymns, about his date with Angela as if Ollie wasn't there last night. Buddy is going to see her again this afternoon. They are going to "study" together for the *one* class they have. Ollie spends the rest of the day trying to fix the van, all to no avail.

Monday through Thursday go by the same way. Ollie goes to school. Buddy hangs out with Angela after practice. Ollie tries to fix the van. Each day at practice Ollie gets there early to ask Brandi if she'll go out with him. Each day she says no but Ollie is not deterred. Thursday night the Mustangs play against the Manchester Muskrats. Ollie ends the game only five points short of breaking the school record for points made during a game. Brandi still turns him down.

By Friday, Buddy has his plan in motion.

"Angela is going to ask her tonight," he says.

"Brandi doesn't even know Angela, does she?"

Buddy looks a little uncertain. "Well, no." He finally says. "But girls have some kind of girl code. She'll say yes if a girl asks her."

Ollie hustles to the gym but Brandi isn't there. Technically they don't have practice right after school today. They have a half an hour before their pre-game warm-up. After a half an hour team members start to trickle in. As they change in the locker room, the cheerleaders arrive. When Angela walks in Buddy stops dribbling and travels across the court. Angela leads the pack of girls in the gym as the cheer captain. Among the chatty girls, Brandi's blonde ponytail bounces along. She looks more like a girl than ever surrounded by all the cheerleaders. Some of the girls hoot after Ollie. He waves. Buddy stops a foot from Angela twirling the ball around his waist. "Hey what have you been up to?"

Angela throws her long hair off her shoulder. "Oh, we just went to Freezer Fresh for a snack. I saw Brandi here and asked her to come along." Ollie tries to appear not to be listening. He slowly bounces the ball.

Buddy and Angela act like they don't know of any secret plan. "I asked her to come with us again after the game." Angela smiles first at Buddy then at Brandi. Ollie's heart stops with the ball in his palm. He holds his breath for Brandi's response.

"Oh yeah?" Buddy prods.

"Yeah, she probably will. Won't you Brandi?" A cricket somewhere in the bleachers chirps.

Brandi shrugs her shoulder. "Yeah, I might."

Buddy starts bouncing the ball, trying to hide his excitement. "Great, you can ride with Angela and me. And probably Ollie too." Buddy stops bouncing the ball and turns to his friend. "Ollie you coming tonight?" He yells as if the gym is loud with the single dribbling of Ollie's ball. Ollie shoots another three-pointer and tries to still his voice. "Yeah, I'll go." Brandi's cheeks turn red. Angela smiles like she's the craftiest person in the world. The girls disappear to practice and Brandi exits to the ice machine. When the gym is clear, Buddy and Ollie jump into each other's arms. Then they chase each other around the court in excitement.

This good bit of news drives Ollie the extra mile. He plays like he's an all star the first quarter. He's doing so well the Trojans captain has been yelling for Ollie to be double guarded. Despite the double defense, he's scored more this first quarter than he ever has. Coach Jackson eventually blows his whistle for a time out. "Ollie," he says, "you're going to break the record tonight! Heck, you'll break it before half time IS EVEN UP! Three weeks into the season and we're BREAKING RECORDS!" Coach smiles so big his wad of bubble gum threatens to fall out. "Miles, you've got to be picking for him. HE'S GOT TWO GUARDS ON HIM!" Coach points to Buddy and Percy. "And you two, YOU'VE GOT TO BE THERE for the rebound!" Spit dribbles down Coach's chin. "And Corky, FOR PETE'S

SAKE, stop flipping your hair out of your eyes and WATCH THE GAME PLEASE."

"I need more gel Coach," Corky runs his fingers through his hair.

Coach rolls his eyes. "Getbackonthatcourt!" Coach yells so loudly it comes out as one word. No one understands him when he gets worked up like that, but no one says anything either. Everyone nods their heads then the game is back on.

Across the court Coach Mannford for the Trojans looks like he's sucked on a lemon head and swallowed it down with hot sauce. His face is blistering red and he sucks in his cheeks until his lips looks like a fish's. He's known for getting thrown out of games for his temper. He doesn't like to lose though his team has never been known for their success. Ollie gets a sick feeling in his stomach when he makes eye contact with him. Ollie tries to forget about it as he takes in the ball. Two Trojan guards rush half court to guard him. Ollie has to use his fancy footwork to maneuver past them. After a number of spins, Buddy lands a solid pick resulting with one Trojan on the floor and Ollie's lay-up through the hoop. Coach Mannford is on the court yelling profanities at the ref. In the meantime, Percy smacks the ball loose from a Trojan. Ollie scoops it up and swishes a three pointer. Mannford's screaming accelerates. The Mustangs start to laugh. A clipboard flies across the gym floor. Ollie swishes another three. While Mannford paces the sidelines, Ollie slides by three defensive guards with a lay-up. The crowd is on their feet. The Trojans are trailing behind. Masonville pride rings with cow bells, blares with blow horns, and shakes with pom-poms. Even the old ladies from Masonville First Baptist Church, with their matching crocheted sweaters, stand on their crow-toed feet.

Ollie stops midway between half court and the three point line. He slightly bends his knees, extends his arms full length above his head, slightly jumping and thrusts the ball into the air. Trojans swat at it as it goes over their heads. The ball makes one crisp sound as it slides through the net. Then the gymnasium explodes.

The floor is rushed first by Coach Jackson, then the team, then majority of the high school from the bleachers. Ollie is met with full-speed-ahead enthusiast. Buddy wraps his arms around Ollie's thighs and lunges him into the air. Corky follows behind smacking what is visible of Ollie's buttocks. Coach Jackson jumps up and down smacking at everyone with his clipboard. "He did it! He did it!" Coach is yelling. Everything happens so fast Ollie doesn't comprehend what he's done until he's being passed around on everyone's shoulders. Through the crackling intercom he hears Jeff Wallace announcing, "Phil Oliver has just broken the Mustang record of shots made in one game *before half time*! BEFORE HALF TIME!"

It takes a good fifty blows on the whistle from the ref before anyone notices the clock has been running. Coach Mannford has cussed out every score board operator, every ref, even the school principal. But with less than a minute left of the first half he's mostly ignored. The buzzer sounds. Ollie is carried into the locker room where the explosion continues. Ollie notices Brandi is even smiling as he bounces up and down on the team's shoulders. Ollie thinks tonight couldn't go better even if he prayed for it.

The second half starts just as loud. But Ollie finds it near impossible to make any more shots. In fact it is hard for him to do anything. He can barely pass the ball as three, sometimes four, guards circle him. Multiple times the ref stops the game. Ollie's only shots are those he gets from being fouled. Two players are removed from the game for technicals. Coach asks Ollie after the third quarter if he is okay with continuing. Ollie feels beat up but he knows he can last the little bit left of the game.

"It's not fair what they're doing to him!" Percy yells.

"We can't even get close to him to make a pass!" Corky yells too.

Coach nods his head. "I know. I know. Just keep playing like you are. WE'RE STILL WINNING."

Brandi looks over Ollie like a wounded animal. "Maybe you should sit out the rest of the game."

Coach looks like she just asked to shoot his family dog. "He'll sit out if he needs to but he doesn't need to." Coach looks at Ollie. "Right, champ? You're fine, aren't you?" Truthfully Ollie thinks it will be easier for the rest of the team to finish out the game, but he knows Coach would feel that his victory might be threatened. He's never taken Ollie out of a game. He nods his head, "I'm okay."

The whistle sounds and the final quarter is underway. Immediately Ollie is rushed by the same three guards.

When the ref isn't looking they're bumping and pulling Ollie. Coach Mannford watches him like a hawk. After minutes of hardly being able to move, Ollie breaks free. He is passed the ball and goes in for a lay-up. But as he jumps an arm comes down on his nose with such force Ollie only sees a black gym roof. Sounds like whistles and yells are all around him but Ollie can't open his eyes for what feels like the longest time. When at last he does the first thing he sees is Brandi. She's behind his head, holding it up on her lap. "He's awake!" she yells.

Dr. Jameson is skids to his side. "Get me some tissues or something. We've got to pinch off the bleeding," he says.

 "I've called for an ambulance," Mrs. Jameson says over her husband's shoulder.

Ollie looks for Brandi again. She's looking at him but not into his eyes. It's like she's staring at his nose and she looks frightened.

"Ollie," fingers snap by his face. "Ollie, can you hear me okay?" Dr. Jameson is saying.

Ollie suddenly feels very confused as to why he's on the floor and all of these people are around him, but he remains calm. "Yeah," he says. But as the words leave him a pain like a heavy brick lands on his face. He winces.

"Alright, let's get this boy on the stretcher," Dr. Jameson says.

A stretcher? Ollie thinks. But before he can say anything his body is lifted. Brandi disappears from view.

"Wait, what?" Ollie finally gets out.

Dr. Jameson appears by his side. "You're alright Ollie. We're taking you to the emergency room to get you fixed up."

"Brandi," Ollie looks around.

Coach Jackson yells, "She's going with you. Brandi GET IN that ambulance with him. DON'T YOU leave his side! Makes sure he gets EVERYTHING he needs. I'll be there when the game is over."

Brandi's heart races. She nods her head then chases after the stretcher that's being pushed out of the gym. Hands reach out to Ollie as he goes by the bleachers. Everyone is still yelling, maybe still cheering him on. He feels a little nervous now that he doesn't know exactly why he's leaving the game this way.

He's thrust inside an ambulance. It's doors slam shut. Dr. Jameson is on one side of him. Brandi appears on the other. Ollie smiles with sudden joy in his heart. But as he does a sharp pain pricks him on the head and the edges of the ambulance go black. Ollie's eyes start to roll in his head. He tries to find Brandi again but more and more of the ambulance darkens. "He may pass out again from the pain," he hears Dr. Jameson say. And then he does.

———————————

In the blackness the siren of an ambulance blares. Eleven year old Ollie sees it skid its tires on the pavement of the highway beside this browning field. The woman in front of him, who is down on one knee, now gets up. She puts her arm over Ollie's shoulder. She starts to walk toward the ambulance, pulling him along with her. A fire truck siren catches Ollie's attention next. He watches as it bounces down off the highway into the field. It drives past him to the burning car. Men jump out in black and yellow suits. Some start to pull hoses from the truck. Ollie's attention is stolen again by the sirens of cop cars. At least six of them scream onto the scene. Some stop on the highway. Some pull into the field too. All of the officers run in their black suits and shiny medals. A few start to yell at the drivers who stare at him from the highway. Cars start to move out of the way.

The woman with her hand on Ollie's shoulder leads him to the back of the ambulance. There, two men with white and black uniforms, busts open the doors. "Is he okay?" one of them asks. The woman answers, "He's fine. It's a miracle!" Then the doors slam shut and the woman disappears.

Ollie jerks awake. All around him a white room glares with florescent light bulbs. He squints till his eyes adjust. Then he feels a warm touch on his right hand. As soon as he finds it Brandi slips her hand away. "You're awake," she says.

Ollie smiles. He doesn't feel any pain. He just feels a little lightheaded. "You were holding my hand," he realizes out loud.

Brandi's cheeks turn pink. She diverts her eyes. "No, I wasn't."

Ollie shakes his head because he isn't trying to embarrass her, but seeing her defensive kind of makes him happy. Ollie laughs. "Yes you were." His nose whistles as he breathes out. Ollie stops laughing at hearing the noise. Brandi turns to him like she can't believe what she's heard either.

Ollie breathes out again. His nose whistles with each exhale. Brandi puts her hand to her mouth. Ollie tests it out some more. He breathes out through his nose to the tune of *Old McDonald had a Farm*. His nose whistles along. Brandi starts to laugh behind her hand. Ollie starts to smile. "What is so funny?" he nudges her. His nose whistles even louder. Brandi's laugh races out.

"O my gosh!" she laughs so hard her arms wrap around her stomach. "Your nose!" she laughs some more. Ollie starts to giggle at Brandi. She laughs so hard tears start to come down her cheeks. "Your nose is squeaking!" Ollie laughs with her. The whistle in his nose gets louder. "Stop! Stop laughing!" Brandi looks at him now. "You're making it worse!" she says. Ollie can't stop laughing now though, not now that he knows how adorable Brandi is when she laughs. Brandi nearly falls from her chair beside Ollie's bed. Ollie moves his head closer to Brandi's ear. She tries to move away from him but she's laughing so hard she can't really move. Ollie leans forward in his bed putting his whistling nose right in Brandi's ear. She squeals in laughter and tries to push him away. This only makes Ollie whistle louder. Finally she flings her hand in the air by her ear. It smacks Ollie in the nose. He falls back on his bed in a groan.

Brandi stops laughing. "O my gosh! Ollie I'm so sorry! Are you okay?" She leans over him to see his face. Ollie holds his nose in one hand. Slowly he looks up at her. Then he starts to giggle. A subtle whistle comes from behind his hand.

Brandi plops back down in her chair. She smacks his shoulder. "I thought I really hurt you!"

Ollie moves his hand from his face. "You did!" he laughs.

Brandi shakes her head as her laugh starts to move up her throat again. Brandi laughs but for once Ollie feels she's actually looking into his eyes. "You look terrible," she says.

"Ouch, now that really hurts." Ollie laughs.

"Seriously," Brandi starts to say. She stops when the door to Ollie's room opens. A beautiful blonde nurse steps into the room. She's the bustiest woman Ollie has ever seen. Or maybe they just look bigger because they accompany a tiny waste. This nurse has the figure of an hour glass made by Hermione, the goddess of love. Her mounds of blonde hair are piled on her head into a Dolly Parton fashion. By the frame of her face her eyes are nearly as big as her knockers. Her dark eye lashes outline her big beautiful blue eyes and under her small feminine nose, rose-pedal lips burst with volume and moisture. It is as if the hospital knew she was gorgeous when they hired her, so they made her uniform special to order. Her top busts at the buttons. The bottom of her skirt doesn't come anywhere near her knees. She takes little steps across the room in her high heels. "Phil Oliver," she sighs as she grabs the clipboard from the file by the door. "O my precious thing," she says. Brandi's cheeks turn pink in jealousy. She looks the nurse up and down more than any guy in the emergency room probably had.

"I'm Sandra," the nurse says as she flips through the pages on the clipboard. She sits on the edge of his bed leaning down to his face. Brandi turns her head away, not wanting to see Ollie stare down Sandra's top.

Sandra runs her long red fingernails through Ollie's hair. "How are you doing baby?"

Ollie smiles, "I'm feeling good Sandra. How are you?"

Brandi huffs a little, rolling her eyes.

Sandra laughs, cute and little. "Well, I'm just fine." She puts her hand on her chest, "How sweet of you to ask."

At that moment the door of Ollie's room opens again. Dr. Jameson comes in. He's put on his white doctor's jacket but under his Friday evening game clothes are on. Sandra gets up from Ollie's bed and pulls at the bottom of her skirt so it makes its way back down her thighs. "He's wide awake and sweeter than ever Dr. Jameson," she says.

"Thank you Sandy," he says. "I'll take it from here."

Sandy turns to Ollie as she walks her baby steps toward the door. "Get well sweetheart," she waves. Ollie waves back while Dr. Jameson and Brandi both shake their heads.

The doc sits in the chair opposite Brandi. "Well Ollie, looks like that Trojan gave you a broken nose—a pretty bad one too. We reset it but it may not be perfect. There were at least five breaks in that short bridge of yours. Pretty much shattered it. I'd say you'll have to be wearing a face mask the rest of this season so it doesn't move out of place. Make sure Coach gives you one." Ollie nods his head. "Brandi, will you make sure that coach gets him one?" Doc looks at her with a sly smile. Brandi nods her head. Doctor Jameson's demeanor changes. He leans over the bed closer to Ollie. He nearly whispers, "Ollie, do you know if someone is coming to pick you up?"

Ollie looks at Brandi who quickly drops her eyes so he thinks she may not have heard. He sighs. "The home's van isn't working."

Doctor Jameson looks at the white bed sheets.

Brandi doesn't want Ollie to know she's heard but the quiet from the Doctor becomes too much for her. "I can take Ollie home," she says.

Doctor Jameson and Ollie look at her at the same time.

"Well," Doc smacks the edge of the bed and stands to go. "There are a lot of people out here to see you." He smiles at the both of them then opens the door.

Ollie calls after him, "Dr. Jameson, can I shower before I go?"

Doc knits his eyebrows a moment then nods his head. "You can use the one in my office."

Sandra sticks her blonde head through the door. "Sandy,

show Ollie up to my office. Let him use the shower there."
He nods to Ollie then leaves.

Sandy claps her hands as the door shuts. "O goodie! You
all ready to go big fella?"

Ollie sits up. "I guess so."

Brandi follows Sandra down the hallway. Ollie holds his
robe together behind his back.

"Alrighty," Sandra's heals stop clicking. She holds open a
door. Ollie and Brandi go in before her. "Here's your things
doll." Sandra places Ollie's clothes and shoes on Dr.
Jameson's desk. "You can leave your robe here on the bed.
You'll have to be extra careful pulling your shirt over your
face. You'll need someone to help you." Sandra poses for
the job by putting her hand on her hip and smiling extra
wide. She even adds a wink. Brandi's mouth hangs open.

"Brandi here can help me." Ollie says. "Thank you, Sandra.
You've been a real help." Brandi snaps her mouth shut.
Sandra's smile disappears. She bobs her hip once as an
"okay" then pats the clothes sitting on the table. "Don't put
your face directly in the water," she says. She and Brandi
exchange a look before she slips through the door. When
Brandi turns back around Ollie is peering inside the tiny
bathroom.

"I'll wait out here," Brandi says.

Ollie nods his head then disappears. Brandi sits while she
listens to the shower kick on. Before long she hears Ollie
singing. She can't make out exactly what it is but she can

tell he has an awful voice. She shakes her head, smiling at the thought of him. When the water turns off she feels her chest tighten. She straightens up in her chair, perking her ears.

After a moment Ollie's arm appears around the door. "Brandi, can you hand me my clothes?"

Brandi moves quickly, scooping the clothes off the desk. She puts them in his hand while standing feet from the door. She turns away when he opens the door to pull them in.

A moment later she hears Ollie muffle behind her, "Brandi."

"Yeah?" she asks without turning around.

"I think I need your help here."

Brandi's heart stops. She turns around. Ollie stands in the office, his arms straight up in the air. His jersey is halfway down his face, covering his eyes. One of the arm holes is stuck around his elbow. "Brandi?" he asks.

She smiles at the sight of him. How he looks like a helpless child stuck in his clothes. Then her eyes fall on his bare chest. He's chiseled like an Olympian god. She wants to touch it—the pale carving of David couldn't compare to this.

"She's right; it really does hurt my face." Ollie's muffled voice awakens her to reality.

Brandi curls her fingers around the bottom of his jersey. Ollie stops moving once he feels her. Brandi pulls the material as far away from his nose as she can before she pulls it down over his pecks, then his abs. Once his face appears through the hole she tries to look into his eyes instead of at his body. Time freezes in that moment. Brandi has no heartbeat. Ollie has no recognition of time or place or pain. Brandi knows she's in trouble. She's falling for this guy. Ollie knows he's in love. He's fallen for this girl.

Brandi moves away. She spots Ollie's tennis shoes still on the desk. His socks are stuffed inside. She pulls them out as Ollie comes nearer. One of his socks falls to the floor. Brandi quickly bends down to get it. On the way up her head connects between Ollie's legs. She feels his private parts squish above her neck. She jerks the rest of the way up pulling her hands to her mouth letting the sock drop to the floor. She gasps as Ollie winces his eyes shut. Then in one long whistle he puts his hands to his crotch and exhales.

As badly as she feels for having dismantled his manhood, Brandi can't help but laugh as the long whistle plays out. She tries to cover up her laughter. "I'm sorry. I'm so sorry."

Ollie leans against the desk and begins to laugh. "What are you trying to do to me Brandi?"

Through giggles she gets out, "Ollie, I. Am. So. Sorry."

Ollie nods his head up and down. "Uh-hu, sure you are." He smiles at her over his shoulder.

Brandi knows her cheeks must be the color of the blood that came out of Ollie's nose earlier. She shakes her head daring herself to keep the laughter in but this only shakes her body. She cracks again into a rolling laughter. She uses a hand to wipe away the tears of joy on her face. Ollie can't help but laugh as he watches her. He's never seen someone cry when they laugh. He thinks it's the best combination in the world.

"Alright, alright," he finally pulls himself up straight. "Without injuring me, can you hand me my sock?"

Brandi sighs one last long laugh out of her system. She steps a good foot away from Ollie before she bends over. Before she stands up she asks, "All clear?"

Ollie laughs a whistle out of his broken nose. "Yes, yes."

The door creaks back open. Sandra pokes her blonde head through. "Ready to go?"

Ollie smiles at her and holds up his sock. She disappears through the door again. He sits in the doc's chair and starts to pull on his sock. Brandi kicks into motion. She kneels at his feet and takes the sock from his hand. "I'll do it. You shouldn't bend over. Might make it bleed again."

Ollie sits up. He's reminded of the Bible story of Jesus washing his disciple's feet. Ollie is so humbled watching Brandi slip on his stinky shoes, he can't move. Brandi ties the final knot then stands up patting her knees.

The waiting room is so loud Ollie can hear it through the closed doubled doors. As they step through Corky is heard first, "There he is!"

Buddy reaches Ollie first. "Man, I was so worried! Are you okay?" Buddy notices his nose bandage and makes a grimacing face. "Ugh, what happened to your face?"

Ollie playfully shoves him away.

"Looks like I'll be the best looking one in this town now," Corky wraps his arms around Ollie's shoulders.

"You wish," Miles says.

"I'm so sorry this happened to you Ollie," Coach appears next. He is wringing his ball cap in his hands. He has a bald spot on top of his head. Percy looks embarrassed as he stands behind his dad. "Doc told me it is bad."

"I'm alright Coach," Ollie slaps him on the back.

The waiting room gets smaller around him as everyone is now standing trying to look at him, trying to talk to him, trying to see if Brandi is touching him. Ollie starts to feel sick. "I think I need to go home now," Ollie says. The crowd sighs in unison but then they all start to nod their heads.

"You want us to take you home?" Colleen Porter rubs her hand on Ollie's shoulder.

"Thank you Mrs. Porter, but Brandi already offered." From the corner of his eye Ollie sees Buddy's face light up.

"Okay, you let me know if you need anything Phil Oliver and I'll be there."

"See ya man." Buddy side hugs Ollie and winks when he's close to his face.

"O ho!" Corky starts to clap, "Bran . . ."

"No," Buddy tells him and takes Corky by the arm to lead him out. "What?" Corky says

Ollie and Brandi finally make it through the waiting room which feels like another gymnasium. Brandi opens the door of her car for him in the dimly lit parking lot. Ollie rests his head back against the seat. His nose is causing a throbbing through his whole brain.

Brandi slows as they come to the orphanage. "This one?" she asks.

Ollie smiles, "That's me."

Brandi stops the car and looks at her hands. Guilt is riding through her body. She knows this is the place. She's heard her friend's parents talk about the Children's Home; how it is all run-down; how the building is a hunk of junk—a sore spot to the otherwise visually appealing historical town of Masonville. She's drove past with her wealthy friends who shake their heads at the dozen of kids running around the ugly yard. They wrinkle their noses at the overgrown fence around the tiny house. They laugh at the old lady who runs around after the little kids, often with pink rollers still in her hair. They call the place a zoo, a mad house. Brandi hates herself inside for all the things she's said about the messy, dirty kids who climb around the play place in that grass forsaken yard. She shakes her head as she looks at the dimly lit shack.

"Don't think you have to say yes next time I ask you out because you feel sorry for me now." Ollie says. Brandi's heart starts to race. She didn't mean to be shaking her head in disgust. She turns her eyes from the home to her lap. "You know, for my smashed nose." Ollie clarifies. Brandi's heart relaxes.

She tries to smile cheerfully. "If I say yes it will be because I feel bad for hitting *your*," she nods her head down at his midsection.

Ollie starts to laugh. "You do owe me for that."

Brandi smiles, realizing she's lightened the mood. "Actually, I think driving your butt home makes us even."

Ollie laughs again as he pulls his door handle. "True. See you tomorrow Brandi."

"Wait, let me walk you in." Brandi says it without thinking of the repercussions. She merely notices Ollie's nose has swollen so large he squints through slatted eyes to see the door handle. There is no way he could get up those stairs by himself.

"Oh my dear lord!" Miss Stephen stands on the front porch. Her shrill voice scares Ollie and Brandi. She pats her thighs like she's trying to put a fire out there. Ollie drapes his arm over Brandi's shoulder. He tries to open his eyes wider.

The ground is fuzzy and the top half of Miss Stephen is blurry. Brandi guides him up the creaking steps.

"No one called me!" Miss Stephen sounds hysterical. Brandi reaches past the woman and opens the door. Miss Stephen follows behind them inside the house. "I had to hear about this on the radio! I have been worried sick! Why didn't anyone call me?"

Ben and Ezra appear around the corner into the living room. Their eyes are round as basketballs. "Woe, Ollie!" Ben points, "What happened to your face?"

"Philip you know I would have been there right away if I had the means," Miss Stephen runs around the couch to face Ollie.

He nods his head. "I know Miss Stephen. I know you would have. Sorry no one called."

"I hate to see what the other guy looks like," Ezra says.

"Ollie, we need to lay you down," Miss Stephen says.

"Which way?" Brandi asks.

Ollie waves his hand to the left, down the hallway.

Ben and Ezra run down the hall before them. They stop at their door as if to show Brandi which one. She leads Ollie down the narrow hall. Her shoulder rubs against some frames on the wall. She tucks her arm in so she doesn't scoot them off. When she reaches the door Ben and Ezra frantically wave their hands. "No girls allowed! Miss Stephen, this girl is trying to go in our room!"

Miss Stephen stands with her hand on the couch, holding her up. She's too tired to fight with them. And she's too shocked with how badly Ollie looks to follow him to his room. "Boys, get your butts back in bed!"

With that Ben and Ezra run through the door. Brandi moves Ollie in. A nightlight glows across the room. It illumines bunk bed frames and sleeping boys within. One has his arm draped over the edge. Another has most of his blanket on the floor. Ollie heads to the bunk across the room. Ben climbs to the top bunk next to an empty one. He sits Indian style as he watches. Ezra jumps into the bottom bunk. He lies on his belly with his head raised to watch.

Ollie unwraps his arm from Brandi's shoulders. He steps on the bottom bunk. Brandi puts her arms on his back to help him balance. "T.K," Ollie holds up a toy with the initials on it. "I told you to stop playing on my bed." Ollie hands a handful of matchbox cars to Brandi who sets it all on the floor. One handful after another Ollie hands down toys.

Finally, his bed looks clean. Ollie steps down from Ryan's bed. Miss Stephen stands in the doorway now. She has one hand over her mouth. She just can't believe her invincible Ollie has gotten hurt. Brandi sees her from the corner of her eye. She takes her hands off Ollie's back. He moves toward the ladder between the bunks. He is so groggy from his medication he can't think of anything else but how good his pillow looks. Once he's lying down he throws his arm over the rail. "Brandi," he twitches his fingers.

Brandi can no longer see his face. With the boys around her asleep she doesn't want to talk. She reaches her hand up and touches Ollie's fingertips. "Thank you," Ollie's voice is slurring. Brandi squeezes his fingers in reply then turns to leave. Miss Stephen steps out of the way for her but doesn't look at her. Brandi lets herself out.

Chapter Five

Pirates & Mexicans

Just before 7 a.m. the phone in Brandi's house rings off the hook. Brandi tosses in her bed hoping one of her parents will answer it soon. Eventually Brandi makes out her father's voice. She drifts back into sleep but only for a moment. She is shaken awake by her dad's yell from downstairs. "Brandi, get down here! The phone."

Brandi rolls around. Had she heard him correctly? She turns her head to the clock on her bedside table. 6:54. *6:54?*

Who would be calling at this hour on a Saturday morning? She stretches in her bed.

"Brandi!" Her dad's voice bellows again.

She kicks off her blankets and books it downstairs. Her dad stands tapping his foot. He's in his khakis and polo shirt. "I'm going to be late for work," he says as he hands her the phone.

Brandi holds the phone to her ear. "Hello?"

"Brandi!" Coach's voice sounds even louder in this morning hour. "You need to get a face mask for Ollie PRONTO! We have to be at the gym by TWO O'CLOCK to take the bus to Pendleton. You BETTER HAVE THAT BOY a mask before we leave!"

Brandi's head swirls. Coach Jackson continues, "I know he works for Raymond Gibbs on Saturdays so YOU BETTER PRAY YOU GET TO HIM BEFORE HE LEAVES. I've tried calling that old man and he AIN'T ANSWERING HIS PHONE. He's probably on his way to get Ollie RIGHT NOW! If you don't GET OVER THERE before he does Ollie will go and HURT HIMSELF even more! You tell old man Gibbs OLLIE HAS THE DAY OFF 'cause you need to get him a mask! Now get moving!" The other end of the receiver clicks. Coach Jackson has hung up on her.

Brandi stands puzzled. The phone line starts to buzz so she hangs it up. Still she stands in the kitchen dumbfounded. She wonders *who in the world is Raymond Gibbs?*

"What did the Coach want?" William Bollinger asks as he zips up his coat.

"I have to get Ollie a face mask. Apparently it's life or death." Brandi squeezes the top of her nose. She has a slight headache from the abrupt rush to her early morning.

"Well basketball is all that kids got." Her father's words surprise her, hurts her a little. "It's the only shot he's got to be something." William picks up his lunch box and smiles at his daughter as he heads out the door.

Brandi hopes that isn't true. She looks around the kitchen. The time on the stove catches her attention. 7 a.m. She jumps into action. She runs into her room. She stops in front of the mirror to see her hair standing on end. She grabs her brush and tries to smooth it down. She grabs the same pair of socks she wore yesterday. Hopping on one foot she tries to slide one on. Her mother appears in the door as she tries to hop into the other sock.

"What in blue blazes are you doing up this early?" she says.

Brandi sits on the edge of her bed and tries to slide her foot into her tied shoe. She has to give up and untie it. "Coach called. I have to make it to Phil Oliver's before he leaves for work this morning. I'm supposed to find a face mask for him before the game today."

At last both shoes are on. Brandi's mom shakes her head and goes down the hallway. Brandi meets her mom on the steps. She nearly pushes her over as she scurries by. But once she's at the bottom she stops then turns around. "What is it?" her mom asks.

Brandi runs back up the stairs. "I probably should wear a bra!"

The bra makes an uneasy exit from her drawer. It gets caught. Brandi pulls it multiple times before it snaps out at her. Brandi's mother is laughing at her as she runs through the front door.

When Brandi pulls up to the home there are a line of cars down the street. She looks in her rearview mirror one more time. She tries to smooth down her hair. When she gets out of the car Miss Stephen is standing on the front porch with a baby on her hip. Brandi hesitates. Miss Stephen does not look like she's in the mood for more company. She still has large pink rollers in her hair. Brandi zips her coat further up toward her chin. The early December breeze cuts right through her sweatpants.

"Hi," Brandi tries to sound chipper.

Miss Stephen shifts the infant to her other hip. "Hiya," she says.

Brandi stops at the bottom of the porch steps. The large woman looks down at her, one eyebrow cocked.

"I'm here to see Ollie," Brandi says.

Miss Stephen purses her lips. "Who isn't?"

Brandi realizes all the cars lining the street must be people here to see Ollie. "Coach Jackson called me. He asked me to take Ollie to get a face mask today before the game." Brandi shuffles.

"My Ollie shouldn't be going *nowhere* with his face looking like a red balloon. I done told off that Raymond Gibbs this morning and I ain't afraid to do some more telling off."

Brandi starts to get an uneasy feeling in her gut.

"But that Coach Jackson scares the daylights out of me." Miss Stephen's words surprise her. "So if he says you *gotta* take Ollie, then you're gonna have to take him." Brandi breathes a sigh of relief. "Now get in here before you freeze clear through. You ain't nothin but skin and bones." She holds the screen door open long enough for Brandi to lunge up the steps and catch it before it smacks shut.

Once inside it is as if the world here doesn't know that an early morning exists. More children than Brandi can count run across the living room and down the hallway then back again through the kitchen and down the opposite hall. Two boys wrestle between a coffee table and the television. Miss Stephen starts to yell at them as a little girl runs into Brandi's legs. The little brunette wraps her arms around Brandi's leg and looks up at her with big round eyes. She doesn't speak, just smiles. Brandi feels extremely awkward but she pats the little girls head, "Hi." Two other young girls spot the first and go to wrapping their arms around the rest of Brandi's legs. She wobbles to keep her balance.

"O they'll get you alright," Miss Stephen smiles at Brandi from across the room.

Ben and Ezra stop wrestling. "The girl," Ezra whispers to the other.

Brandi smiles back and braces herself against the door while the two new girls shout up at her, "Walk with us! Try to walk with us!"

"All of them boys is in his bedroom." Miss Stephen points down the hallway.

Brandi smiles and nods but looks down at the three girls on her legs. She knows she can't move. Miss Stephen saves her. "Girls! Get yourselves up off that floor and off that nice girl! What do you think you are? Velcro? Get in here to this table and get yuh some breakfast."

The girls immediately let go of Brandi and run with the rest of the kids to the large table in the kitchen. Brandi makes a move for it down the hallway. Toys are against every inch of the wall. School pictures of all the kids are in frames down both sides of the hallway. Brandi moves slowly by them. Just before the door in the hall she spots a picture of a young boy who looks like a young version of Ollie. He has freckles on his cheeks and his ears are sunburned. He has the same smile as Ollie. His eyes look through the glass of the frame right into her soul. She wonders how it could be that no one ever adopted this beautiful boy.

Brandi can hear a bunch of voices coming from the boy's bedroom. She recognizes Corky's voice first. Brandi runs her fingers through her hair one more time. She wishes she had taken her time this morning now that she knows everyone is here.

"Miss Stephen, that girl is going in our room again!" Brandi hears a boy yell. She steps through the door before she draws more attention to herself.

Corky is standing in the middle of the room when she peeks her head around the door frame. "I got right up in that Trojan's face and . . ." Corky stops with his fist in midair. He spots Brandi first. Then the rest of the team sees her.

"Brandi?" Many of them say at the same time.

Brandi feels heat rush to her cheeks. She looks around the room for Ollie. Boys are sitting on every bottom bunk. Miles and Percy whisper to each other though their eyes are on her. Buddy sits beside Ollie below his bunk. They smile at her.

Corky puts his fist down as Ollie gets up off the bed. "Hey Brandi," he says. "What are you doing here?"

All eyes are on the two of them. Brandi tries to ignore the rest of the guys. She looks at Ollie. His face is puffy and red. "Coach called me.," she says loudly enough for everyone to hear. "He told me to get here as soon as I could in case you made a run for it with . . ." She tries to remember that old guys name. "Raymond Gibbs."

"That's why all of us are here," Corky walks up to Ollie throwing his arm around his shoulders. His hand comes dangerously close to Ollie's face. Brandi flinches. "We all had to make sure he wasn't going to work on that *stupid* fence today either." Corky smiles at Ollie. Brandi has no idea what he's talking about.

Ollie laughs. A hardly audible whistle comes from his nose. He bends over a bottom bunk to fix its blankets. "Everyone seems worried about that today. Miss Stephen already told him off this morning. Poor guy."

"Poor guy?" Percy says. Corky removes his arm from Ollie. Everyone looks to Percy. "That guy ain't poor. He's got one of the biggest farms in this county."

A murmur of agreement rises. Guys break off into their own conversations around the room. Corky still stands there. He looks Brandi up and down. "So what are you doing here?" he says. The room goes quiet again. All the boys look to her.

Brandi looks at Corky puzzled.

"You see that he didn't go to work today so what are you still doing here?" Corky clarifies. Ollie shakes his head in embarrassment.

"Oh," Brandi fidgets with her coat zipper. Then she swallows the biggest gulp of saliva she's ever had in her mouth before. "I was wondering if you wanted to go with me today. To get the face mask," she finishes.

Corky nods his head for the whole world to see. He spins in a circle to make a face of awe at everyone in the room. All the guys respond by smiling or clapping their hands or making "Ooooh" sounds.

Ollie doesn't acknowledge any of them. He can't take his eyes off Brandi. When she finally is able to look him in the eyes, he nods his head.

"Looks like the big guy is leaving us!" Corky announces to the room.

Buddy finally stands and makes his way to the three of them in the middle of the room. "After all of us guys got up at the butt crack of dawn to see you," he slaps his best friend on the back. "As soon as Brandi gets here you're ready to go."

All the guys laugh. Ollie can't help but smile. "Hey guys," he says. "I really appreciate all of you coming over here."

"Don't go getting a big head," Miles says as he stands.

"Dad would have killed me if I didn't come," Percy stands too.

One by one the guys start to leave the room. Some grab Ollie's hand and smack his back with the other. Some high five him, some just nod their heads. Corky picks Ollie up in a bear hug. Brandi winces at the sight. Ollie moans as Corky squeezes his arms tight around his torso. He finally puts him down. "See you later homo." He says to Ollie. To Brandi he smiles coyly, "Behave Brandi."

Brandi blushes and rolls her eyes. Corky pushes her shoulder as he spins his way out of the room. She can hear him yelling after the guys as he goes down the hallway and all the way through the living room until he's out the door.

Buddy and Ollie exchange a handshake. "See you later man. Brandi take care of him." He pats her on the shoulder as he leaves.

17

Ollie and Brandi stand alone for a moment. The air in the room feels lighter to both of them. The way Ollie is smiling at her makes Brandi turn her eyes to her shoes. "This is the first time I've seen you with your hair down," he says. Brandi freezes, becoming too keenly aware of her bed head. "You look beautiful," he says.

Brandi knows he's got to be loving this. He's tried so hard this season to get time with her and she's successfully turned him down every day. Now she's the one coming to him. She lets him take it in for a moment longer. "Well, come on then. You ready or what?"

Ollie turns to his bunk bed and pulls off a coat that is hanging on the post. "Ready," he says.

Brandi knows right where to look. The local pharmacy has to have something.

After a few minutes of searching for the mask they find one. Ollie studies it. "I'm going to look really hot in this. Aren't I?"

Brandi scoffs. "Covering your face definitely won't set you back."

At the counter Brandi pulls out her wallet to pay for the mask. She figures it is her responsibility since Coach asked her to take care of it.

"Phil Oliver?" The cashier says. Brandi looks up at her. The woman smiles at Ollie like he's a superstar. "It is you, isn't it?" she says.

Ollie nods his head. He sticks his hand out across the counter. "Ollie."

The pharmacist and other cashier turn at the sound of his name. All of the employers are now watching them.

The woman's smile broadens even more. She shakes his hand like it might disappear in seconds. "I heard what happened to you on the radio last night." The woman stops smiling but doesn't stop shaking Ollie's hand. She curls her lips down in a frown. "That is just so sad." She looks at his nose.

Ollie finally frees his hand. "I'll be fine," he says as he slips his hand into his jean pocket.

The pharmacist approaches along with a male cashier. The three employers stand behind the counter looking at Ollie with a mixture of amazement and sadness. The pharmacist says, "It is a real shame what happened to you." The three of them nod their heads. "That was an unfortunate way to end your record-breaking night." Ollie and the three of them laugh together. Brandi watches, still perplexed at what is happening.

"So you must be the intern," the female cashier finally acknowledges Brandi's presence.

Brandi nods her head but Ollie answers, "This is Brandi Bollinger. She's the team's physical therapist this season. She's really good for what she has to work with."

The female cashier laughs.

"What do you mean "with what she has to work with"?" the male cashier steps closer. Brandi notices his nametag says *Manager.*

"Well, the gauze the team has is really terrible. No matter how well Brandi tapes it up it always falls down our ankles."

The employees look shocked. They exchange a look with one another before turning back to Ollie. "Can the team not afford anything else?" the pharmacist asks.

Ollie and Brandi both shake their heads. "Well then," the male cashier with the manager tag says, "this is on the house." He pushes the face mask across the counter to them.

Brandi is stunned. She looks at Ollie thinking, *Who is this guy?* Ollie shakes the man's hand.

As they leave the store Ollie asks, "Can we go the dollar store real quick?"

Brandi is still trying to get her bearings on what happened inside. She shrugs while Ollie waves for her to follow him.

"What do we need here?" Brandi asks when they enter.

"One of the kids at home had surgery on his eye. He's got some nasty looking stitches now. I don't think he's too happy about it. I've got an idea for something that will cheer him up." Ollie leads the way through the store. He makes his way to the toy isle. Slowly he looks over each toy as he walks by.

"What's this kid's name?" Brandi asks.

Ollie looks closer at some coloring books before walking again. "Ryan. He's kind of the loner in the boys anyway. He's got a patch over his eye now, kind of like I do over my nose." Ollie laughs. "Anyway, he's pretty down now." Ollie stops at a rack of styrofoam swords. "Perfect," he says.

Brandi looks down at them. She thinks it's a weird present for a kid. Ollie draws a sword out of the rack. He admires it in the air as if it is a real one. "What do you think?" Ollie swats the sword at Brandi's stomach.

Brandi tries not to smile. "You can't be serious."

"What?" Ollie swats at her hair. It brushes back off her shoulder.

Brandi drops her mouth as if she's aghast at him. "What are you? Five year old?"

Ollie seems not to hear her. He steps back in a fencing position, one arm behind his back, the other pointing the sword at Brandi. He smiles and moves the tip of the sword in circles. "Choose your weapon."

Brandi shakes her head. "This isn't really for a kid, is it?"

Ollie swats the sword at her leg. Brandi steps back just in time to miss it. Ollie comes at her again, then again and again. She grabs the nearest toy to be her defense—a hula hoop. She blocks the sword a few more times while her laughter comes again. Ollie moves in fast and steels the hula hoop onto his sword. Soon he has it over his head and around his waist. He moves his hips but the hoop drops in only a few seconds. "Give that here," Brandi says. "You suck at that."

Ollie laughs but hands it over. He has her right where he wants her again. Brandi pulls the hoop over her head and starts to swivel it around her body without any problems. She holds her hands up while it goes. "That's how it's done."

Ollie sticks his sword out so her hula hoop is knocked to the ground. Brandi raises her eyebrow at him. Ollie shrugs his shoulders. "You're so dead," Brandi says.

"Let me see what you got *Brandi*," he toys with his sword.

Brandi can't believe what she's about to do but she does it. She jets after Ollie who mockingly squeals like a girl and runs away. The two of them chase each other about the store until they successfully knock over a bin of rubber balls. "What are you? Five years old?" Ollie teases her. She pushes him away as they walk to the checkout lane.

At the register Ollie pulls out his wallet. Inside is a one dollar bill. He reaches into his jean pocket and retrieves seven pennies. Brandi wonders if that's the only money he had. Ollie knows it is.

On the drive back to the home Ollie massages his forehead.

"Time for more pain killers, huh?" Brandi notices.

Ollie nods his head. "I think so."

When they reach the house Brandi turns off her car. "Let me walk you in," she says. "You don't look so good."

"Would it help if I put the face mask on?" Ollie smiles at her.

Brandi shakes her head. "Nothing is going to help that face."

Ollie laughs as he steps out of the car. Brandi doesn't put her arms around his waist like the night before but she stays close enough to be in reach.

Inside, the same little brunette girl runs to Ollie and wraps her arms and legs around his waist. He pats her head, "Hi Kirsten." She smiles at him then lets go. Ollie goes to the couch where a little boy sits. His arms are crossed around his chest. The television isn't on but he stares at it. His bottom lip puckers out. The wrinkles on his forehead show he's angry. Over his right eye he wears a white patch.

"Got you something," Ollie says to the boy. The kid doesn't move. Ollie slips the sword out of his belt loop. The little boy turns his head toward it. The wrinkles on his forehead disappear.

Ollie presents the sword by holding it in both of his hands, his palms up as if it is for a royal knight. "For Ryan the pirate," Ollie says.

A hungry smile breaks across the boy's face. He reaches his hands out for the sword. Ollie wraps his fingers around it first. "But," Ollie says before Ryan can take it away. "You have to be a good pirate. You can only do good things with this." Ryan nods his head slowly, his left eye looking deep into Ollie's. Ollie unclasps his fingers. Brandi feels a warm blade is entering her heart. She smiles at Ollie then says her goodbye.

———————

It is the first game in Ollie's basketball career he has to sit the bench. He doesn't mind. He cheers on his team. It is the first time he's really gotten to watch his best friend play. It is also the first time he gets to watch what Brandi does during the games. She is constantly going. She is refilling water bottles, wrapping ankles, wrapping wrists, fetching pain killers from parents in the stands, and trying her best not to look at Ollie the whole time. Ollie asked her before the game how his facemask looked. He made a girly pose when he did it. Brandi tried really hard not to smile. She just shook her head and waited for him to ask her out again. "If I promised to wear this mask, will you go out with me?" She said no.

Sunday at church everyone coddles his face. He gets put on the prayer list which he finds extremely funny but also kind. Buddy can't stop talking about Angela again. But Ollie doesn't mind. He knows if he had a reason to he'd talk about Brandi just as much. Afterward he asks Miss Stephen if he can please call Raymond Gibbs to come get him. She shakes her head at him nice and slow, staring at his big broken nose. But because Ollie has the eyes he does, she caves in just like she always does.

Raymond pretends to sound annoyed with the sudden work shift. Ollie says he'd like to not get paid for it anyway.

Raymond objects to that right away and says he'll be there in three minutes flat. He is.

Ollie is surprised when Raymond pulls in the drive. In the passenger seat is a young man. He looks to be in his thirties. He is a shorter man than Raymond who sits on a stack of papers to see through the windshield. They aren't speaking to each other.

The young man gets out of the truck when Ollie steps through the fence. Ollie waves to him. "Hi there. I'm Ollie." Ollie sticks his hand out to the new guy. His handshake is returned. "Hi," the man says. "I'm Carl…" He's cut off by Raymond who yells from inside the truck, "I'm not paying you two to chit chat. Is this going to take all day? What are you? Girlfriends?"

Carl looks frightened. Ollie laughs as he climbs in to the middle seat.

"Long time, no see," Raymond says. He puts the truck in gear and starts to pull away as Carl tries to shut the door. He shakes his head like he can't believe this old man.

"This here is Carlos. He'll be working on the farm with yuh now." Raymond says with his pipe bouncing in his mouth.

Ollie looks from Raymond to Carl. The new guy shakes his head. "I've told you, my name is *Carl*. Not *Carlos*."

Raymond makes a grunting sound. Ollie reiterates. "His name is Carl."

"Enough chit chat," is all Raymond says.

As they pull into the farm's driveway Raymond takes his pipe out of his mouth and jabs the power button on the radio. "First things first," he says into the silence. "You go feed the hogs. Take some bales of hay out of the loft and line their stalls."

Ollie and Carl nod their heads as the truck comes to a stop outside the red barn. As the boys walk toward the barn Raymond yells out of his window, "Ollie, make sure Pedro knows what I said."

Ollie looks back at Carl who flaps his arms against his legs. "Mr. Gibbs my name is Carl. I know what you said. I don't even speak Spanish!"

"I don't understand a word that boy says," Raymond rolls his window back up.

Carl stands in the barn loft. He throws square bales down to Ollie one at a time. "When did you start working?" Ollie asks.

"Just started Wednesday," Carl says. He tosses down the final bale then swings from the rafters so he lands on the barn floor with a jump.

"You from around here?" Ollie pushes the bales off the edge of the barn floor to the lower level the pigs squeal in.

"I am. I moved away for about fifteen years. Just got back into town a couple months ago. Been looking for a job." Carl grunts as he shimmies between two boards until he's down into the pig pen. "I was standing by the hardware store when Raymond pulled up." He stops to catch his breath. "He yelled at me from the side of the road he had work to be done on his farm and he'd pay cash." He wipes the sweat from his forehead and looks to Ollie. "I'm pretty sure he thinks I'm a Mexican."

Ollie can't help but break into laughter. Carl somewhat laughs at the idea too. Ollie climbs down in with the pigs too. The two of them start cutting free the bales from their strings.

 "If you don't mind me sayin'," Carl says, "what did you do to your nose?"

Ollie laughs, "Broke it playing basketball."

"O you're that kid?"

Ollie looks at Carl for a second. Then he grabs the pitch fork resting against the stall.

"I heard about yuh in town the other day. You broke some school record that game too I hear?"

Ollie forks some hay and spreads it over the mud. Carl grabs his own pitch fork and starts too. The pigs squeal with delight. "Yeah, something like that," Ollie finally answers.

"Everybody is talking about you, you know? You're like the town celebrity." Ollie begins to sweat in his armpits. The conversation is making him feel awkward.

"Are you two done lolly-gagging in there?" Raymond's hoarse voice echoes through the barn.

Ollie and Carl exchange a knowing grin. They hurry up to find Raymond waiting in the truck.

The old man doesn't stop driving when his driveway comes to an end. He veers off into the field. Ollie knows they're heading to the white barn with all the scrap behind it. He notices Carl must have been working while he hadn't. More scrap piles are gone and the old van is gone too.

"Looks like you've been working hard." Ollie nods to Carl.

Carl wears a look of exhaustion, "Raymond doesn't go easy on you, that's for sure."

"Mr. Gibbs," Raymond corrects him.

Monday morning Ollie starts his normal routine on the fence as a light snow starts to fall. Miss Stephen doesn't let him get too far. "Get your stupid head back in that bed boy! You is staying indoors for sure."

"God love her for caring," Ollie thinks.

He gets to practice early to ask Brandi out again. It has become such a routine she is waiting with one arm propped on the basketball rack. She faces the entry and watches him run in.

"Brandi—a vision today as always . . ."

"No," she says.

"Let me finish," Ollie laughs.

Brandi cocks one eyebrow. Now-a-days she is able to look him in the eyes without blushing.

"Brandi, would you like to go out with me …"

"No," she turns to her cart of basketballs.

Ollie laughs. As he runs off, Brandi mouths the words he always says as he says them again, "Maybe tomorrow."

When Buddy drops Ollie off after practice a large white van is in the driveway. On the side "Myron Studios" is in big black letters. Ollie finds the legs of a man sticking out from under the home's van. When he approaches the man is scooting his way out. He turns over on his belly and half his butt crack greets Ollie.

"Hey, can I help you?" Ollie says.

The light snow that had fallen this morning melted. The mechanics knees of his jeans are soaked through. He wipes his black greasy hands on his uniform jacket. "Hi there," he says. He has two brown front teeth. "Myron Studios, here to fix your van." He turns to face his work and pats his belly with pleasure. "Think I got her all fixed up."

Ollie can't believe it. "Who asked you to do this?"

The round-bellied man smiles at him. "Doc Jameson came by the studio. Boss tells me to fix the van. I fix the van." He hawks up a loogie but smiles as though he doesn't know it is disgusting.

Ollie stares at the van while the mechanic drives away.

On Tuesday Ollie hurries to practice for his daily routine of asking Brandi out. But as he enters the gym Coach Jackson is there talking to her at the basketball cart. He turns to spot Ollie as he runs around the corner. "Ollie, son, get yourself over here," he waves at him. "Myron Studios wants you over there today to do a little interview." Coach says. "Brandi's got a car. She's going to take you." Coach moves his clipboard between the two. "That'll also give you time to ask her out another dozen times." Coach smiles so most of his gum wad sticks out between his teeth. Brandi's mouth gapes at the Coach while her cheeks turn pink.

Ollie slaps him on the back, "Thanks Coach."

He nods his head, "Hurry up now."

Brandi doesn't even look at Ollie. She watches Coach walk away with her mouth still hanging open. At last she shakes her head then turns away from Ollie toward the gym doors.

Brandi doesn't know how her internship has come to this. She started this whole thing trying to avoid Ollie, now she is his personal chauffer. It is as if the whole town is on Ollie's side, trying to get the girl to say yes to him. Truth is, Brandi doesn't know how much longer she'll want to say no. Talking with him is becoming as natural as the rest of her day.

"How's your day Brandi? What have you been up to? You look beautiful today by the way." Ollie says it all as soon as he slips into the passenger seat.

She shakes her head at him, letting Ollie know she thinks he talks too much. "My day is fine. Just went to school and came here. Same as always."

"Do you like the community college?" Ollie asks. Brandi hoped he wouldn't ask that. She wants to be honest with him, to tell him she is severely disappointed with her current education situation, but she also wants to be pleasant and not such a downer all the time. So she shrugs her shoulders. "It's okay." Ollie looks at her like she's supposed to say more. Brandi glances both ways at the four-way stop then continues. "It's just a two year degree so it's not like I'll be there forever." Ollie is quiet so Brandi clears her throat, "Have *you* thought about college?"

Ollie nods his head, "Yeah, I mean, I want to go to college."

"What do you want to study?"

"The Bible. I want to be a pastor."

Brandi suspected Ollie might be religious. His kindness is too unwavering to be a show.

The car pulls to a stop at Myron Studios. Jeff Wallace waves at them from a large bay window. Inside you can see all the music equipment. Brandi hopes she isn't asked anything. She hesitates in the car wondering if she can wait here. Ollie turns to her as he walks through the parking lot and waves for her to come after him. She sighs but follows.

Jeff Wallace laughs so loudly into his microphone his gut bounces. He slaps his knee once then clicks a few buttons on his panel. As a new song comes through the speakers he opens the door for Ollie. "Heya' son!" he says. "You come on in here and take a seat right there. And you brought your girl with you?" Jeff sticks his hand out to shake Brandi's. She looks to Ollie for correction but Ollie says, "This is Brandi, Mr. Wallace."

"Brandi Bollinger," she finishes.

Jeff thrusts his hand into Brandi's and pumps it up and down. "Bollinger? Will Bollinger's girl of *Bollinger's Hardware*?" Brandi nods. "Well I'll be," Jeff laughs. "Your pop is a good man Brandi, good man. Worked with him at the shop for a good minute before this gig. Good man. Take a seat, take a seat," Jeff shuts the studio door. He doesn't stop for a breath as he continues. "When this song is done I'm going to introduce you and we'll get on with the questions. Just a few questions for you Ollie, nothing hard and then you're ready to go."

Ollie nods his head and before Brandi can think the song is over and Jeff is swinging his mike around like a monkey with a vine. "And welcome back folks, it is Jeff Wallace here with special guest Phil Oliver, the Captain of our Masonville Mustangs!" Jeff pushes a button and some fake applause sounds. "For those of you who weren't there Friday, a new basketball record was broken by this young fellow here. Ollie you want to tell us what that was?"

The mike swings across the table to Ollie. "The record was points made in one game."

Jeff doesn't move the mike, he just talks even louder. "What was the score to beat Ollie?"

"Samuel Tweety had set the record with 52 points made in one game."

Jeff bellows a laugh. "And you blew that out of the water! What is the new record Phil Oliver?"

"I scored 79 points." Brandi watches Ollie with amazement. At a moment where he could suck up all the glory, Ollie merely answers factually.

Jeff is whooping and hollering Ollie's praises. "And then the stadium went wild." Buttons are pushed, more applauses and shouts, bells and horns. "Every person in that gymnasium was on their feet! And you Ollie, you were on your teammate's shoulders. Tell us, how did that moment feel?"

Ollie smiles, "Felt pretty good sir."

Brandi smiles too and shakes her head. Jeff says just what she's thinking. "We've got a modest star on our hands Masonville," he laughs. "Now that was the first half of the game. The second half did not go so good. You got elbowed right in the nose and escorted to the hospital, am I right Ollie?"

Ollie only has time to say "Yes," before Jeff is shifting gears again. "To my understanding your beautiful lady friend who is here with you today is the one who stayed with you through the whole event." Brandi's worst fears are coming to life. She feels her stomach curdle, not just from the thought of being called Ollie's girlfriend on the radio, but Jeff is looking right at her and she knows what is coming. "We have Brandi Bollinger here. Brandi, tell us about that hospital visit."

Complete silence fills the studio. Jeff's smile starts to waver. He pushes the mike closer to her face and whispers "Don't be shy now. We're live on the air."

Brandi clears her throat and blinks extra hard. "Well," she starts, "Ollie suffered an almost completely shattered nose. Dr. Jameson said there is at least five breaks." Jeff makes a grunting noise. Brandi looks at Ollie for reassurance. He is smiling at her. "Ollie is tough though and he was out of the hospital that night and at the game on Saturday."

Jeff laughs and nods his head at Brandi like he's so proud of her for speaking up. She couldn't have done a better job for him. "You must be doing well Ollie. How's that nose treating you?"

"My nose is fine sir, but I was actually wondering if I could add something to that doctor's visit?"

Jeff nods his head like a mad man. "Well of course! Go ahead!"

"I'd like to thank Brandi here for riding with me in the ambulance and staying by my side the whole time." Ollie looks into Brandi's eyes as he says it. Shockingly, Brandi doesn't feel her face light up with fire. She feels her heart warm instead. Jeff makes an "awe" sound from the board. "I'd also like to thank Dr. Jameson and my nurse Sandra for how well they attended to me. Dr. Jameson actually left the game to take me to the hospital. He wasn't supposed to work that night at all but he did. He also did me and the children at the home a great blessing. He spoke with employers here at the Myron Studio to fix the Orphanage's broken van."

Jeff Wallace sits like a stuffed animal frozen in a pose of disbelief. His eyes are of admiration and shock. "So I'd like to thank Myron Studios as well." Ollie finishes but Jeff still sits staring at him. "Thank you Mr. Wallace," Ollie says. Jeff finally blinks and licks his lips. He pulls the mike into his mouth again. "You are most certainly welcome. That is Phil Oliver and Brandi Bollinger folks. Be sure to see them at their next home game this Friday at seven o'clock. Now back to the music." Jeff flicks off some switches and on some others. Music fills the studio again. Jeff gets up to open the door for Ollie and Brandi. He sticks his hand out, "Ollie, thank you so much for your words." It is the most quiet and gentle Brandi has ever heard the husky man. He clears his throat. "Good to see you young folks. You come visit anytime." Brandi and Ollie nod as they make their way out the studio. "And why don't you two get a t-shirt on your way out? Trisha!" Jeff yells. "Trisha, get these two a t-shirt." Jeff shuts his door to his studio as the secretary appears with two 95.3 radio t-shirts.

Chapter Six

Provision & Perspiration

As soon as the Mustangs exit the locker room and grace the gymnasium floor the crowd erupts. Every single fan is on their feet. The team is so stunned they all stop only a few feet onto the court. It is their first home game since Ollie had his nose demolished. It will also be the first game he plays since the accident. A chant starts to take form. At first it isn't audible but it grows. "Oll-ie! Oll-ie!" The crowd claps the syllables of his name. Buddy rubs his hand on Ollie's back. Corky starts to jump up and down chanting along. The paralyzing feeling runs its course through the guys and soon Percy and Miles are running around the court with their hands stretched out to those on the front bleachers. They all slap their hands as they go by. Coach stops beside Ollie. He turns and smiles at him. "Everyone is glad you're back, Ollie." He slaps him on the shoulder with his clip board.

Absolutely nothing could make Ollie frown the rest of the evening. He is a wide-eyed young peacock. He flutters all over the court and no one can bring him down. The crowd of Masonville gets the show of their lives. They feed off his energy. They jump from the bleachers. They can't sit down. They whoop and holler and carry on with cow bells. Ollie slips and slides between players with such stamina and grace Coach Jackson almost mistakes him dancing with the ball. And unbeknownst to Ollie, this is the perfect night for such a performance. God is undoubtedly looking over him. College scouts are visiting.

A sleek, professional jock stands off the court leaning against the gym wall near the entrance doors. His hair is an organized mess. The lanyard from his neck holds at least 12 keys. He doesn't come with a clipboard or even a pen. His philosophy is if he can't remember the player's name or jersey number they aren't good enough for Butler University anyway.

Another college scout sits at the opposite end of the gym. He wears dark large rimmed glasses and his hair is perfectly jelled to a plastic looking comb over. Sitting down makes his khaki pants raise enough to see his long white socks with two red stripes at the top. He isn't the basketball coach, but Liberty University doesn't send their coaches, they send him—the sports recruiter. Based on looks alone, no one guesses he's a sports recruiter. But there is no mistaking Ollie tonight. Everyone is looking at him in awe . . . even Brandi.

At the sound of the second half buzzer she watches Ollie bound onto the court like a gazelle. His leg muscles pulse with each step. She takes him in slow motion like a lion to its prey. His ankles bend and his calf muscle extrudes like a cliff. His shorts are tight around his thighs. She can make out the different muscles around them. She sees flashbacks of his jersey stuck around his elbow over his head in the hospital. His abs so perfectly outlined they could be a coloring page. His arms bend as a ball is thrust between his hands. His bicep flexes. Brandi sees a nun running over the hills of his arm muscles singing they are *'alive with the sound of music'*. The longer she looks at him the hotter she gets. When her forehead is covered in perspiration she wills herself to stop. Her body wants to lose control. She forces herself to look at the crowd as a reminder she's in a public place. She never would have guessed a high school boy would arouse her.

Ollie and Buddy smack each other on the behind as they run down the court. They laugh out loud. At one point Corky leap frogs over Ollie's head. The ref yells at him but everyone else cheers. The final buzzer sounds as Ollie swishes his last shot. The score board adds another three points. The Batesville Bandits have lost by 30 points. The gymnasium explodes with cheer. "Oll-ie! Oll-ie! Oll-ie!" He tries to find Brandi but one by one his teammates surround him. Together they all jump up and down.

"Ollie! Ollie!" Coach appears through their circle. "Ollie," he gets him to meet his eye. Coach draws him in toward his face so he can hear over the all the chanting. "There's scouts here," he says. Ollie gets a tingle in his stomach. "One of em' already told me he wants to talk to you." Ollie smiles at Coach. Mr. Jackson looks like a proud father. He slaps Ollie on the shoulder. "Well come on son. I'll introduce you. But take off that RIDICULOUS mask first."

Ollie slides the mask off his head. "Hold on Coach," he holds up his index finger. He turns around the circle looking for his best friend. "Buddy!" he spots him. "Buddy, come on!" he waves at him.

"What is it?" Buddy asks.

"There's scouts here that want to talk to us." Ollie pats him on the shoulder like Coach had done for him. Buddy's white smile breaks out across his dark sweaty face. "No way!" He jumps up and down and pats both of Ollie's shoulders.

Coach is a little confused. He wonders why Ollie is talking to Buddy. But when he hears Buddy shouting "No way!" he knows Ollie has told him about the scouts. He leads both of the boys to the sleek looking one still leaning against the gym wall.

He doesn't lean away as the boys stretch out their hands to him. He's too cool to move. He doesn't want to look like he's desperate as he is to have Ollie for his team. He has to remain looking like he's only slightly interested. He doesn't really know why the black boy is there too. He told the coach he only wanted the tall blonde looking one but what the heck, he might be interested in this one too.

"I'm Coach Reynolds," he says. All 12 keys jingle.

Ollie doesn't get a good vibe from the guy. His posture against the wall says sloth-fullness to him. Buddy looks like a young puppy ready to fetch anything the guy throws. Coach Jackson stands slightly to the side and behind them with his hands crossed feeling like a body guard.

"What's your names boys?"

Ollie sticks his hand out first. "I'm Phil Oliver, sir. This here is my best friend and the greatest center you'll find on this side of the Mississippi, Buddy Porter." Ollie holds his hand out to motion toward him.

Buddy jerks into gear. He thrusts his hand into the Coach's. "I'm Buddy Porter, yes sir." He pumps the man's hand up and down until Ollie thinks he might draw oil. Coach Jackson clears his throat at him from behind. Buddy stops.

Coach Reynolds looks back and forth between the two of them, a little quizzical. He finally bobbles his head and relaxes further into the wall. "Well, I'm the Coach at Butler University. . ."

"I LOVE Butler University!" Buddy interrupts.

Ollie slightly shakes his head. Mr. Reynolds raises an eyebrow then continues.

"I was mostly interested in you here," he looks Ollie in the eye. Buddy's shoulders droop. "You've got skill kid. Now, don't get me wrong you still need some major work but I think we have just the program to whip you into Butler material."

Ollie and Buddy look at each other. They're both thinking of how much they don't like this Mr. Reynolds already. Ollie sticks his hand out again toward the man. Coach Reynolds looks questioningly at it for a moment before taking it in his own. Ollie shakes it. "Thank you Mr. Reynolds but I'll decline. Sure do appreciate you coming all the way out here to watch us play though."

While Buddy breaks into a big smile Coach Reynolds finally leans off the wall to stand on his own two feet. He looks at Ollie with stunned disbelief.

"Have a safe drive home," Coach Jackson says from behind. Buddy and Ollie turn away. Coach Jackson couldn't look more pleased.

"Hey Corky!" Buddy yells. "That there college coach wants to talk to you about Butler University."

Corky jerks his head in the direction of Mr. Reynolds. He is still standing there staring. He looks over at Corky when Buddy shouts. Corky runs to the man and jabs his hand into the even more puzzled coach. Buddy and Ollie laugh some more.

A man in khaki pants and dark rimmed glasses stands before them now with a clip board and a thick manila folder in hand. He shoves it all under one armpit, pushes his glasses up on his nose then puts his hand out before them. "I'm Patrick Wackalliton from Trinity College," he says with his hand still wavering in the air.

Ollie puts his hand into it, "Phil Oliver."

The man moves his hand over to Buddy who shakes it, "Buddy Porter."

And lastly the man sticks his hand out toward Coach. "Coach Jackson," he says through smacks of his gum.

The skinny man pushes his glasses up his nose again. "So nice to meet all of you," he says. "I'm here on behalf of Trinity College as I said before. This is a private Christian school in Connecticut." He keeps his eye contact moving between the three of them. He nods his head as he talks. "I work in the recruiting department. I've been traveling on behalf of Fred Veal, our basketball coach, for the last month or so now. And I must say, this is the best sort of sportsmanship I have seen all season."

Coach Jackson tries not to smile. Mr. Wackalliton smiles enough for all of them. His head keeps moving like a bobble head on a dash board. Ollie has a good vibe about this guy. Each time he says Trinity College something kicks him in the gut. It's a good feeling despite the description.

"I know Coach Veal would enjoy meeting you boys for a possible tryout. If you're interested. . ." He looks between Buddy and Ollie now. The boys look at each other then back to Patrick. They nod their heads at the same time. "I know I would," Buddy smiles. "I'd be very interested," Ollie says.

"Wonderful," the recruiter says. He pulls the folder out from under his armpit. His fingers quickly play through the pages. He pulls out two sheets of white paper with typing all over them. "Here you are," he hands one to Buddy then another to Ollie. "This explains what you'd need to do for tryouts, what to bring, what to wear, etcetera. It also has our school address so you can find us and down below that are the dates scheduled for open tryouts. Tours of the school are also available. My phone number I've wrote at the top here." He points to the top of Buddy's paper. "And that's my name there. You guys can contact me any time. If you have questions about possibly staying overnight on campus or things of that nature I can answer your questions." He nods like he's coming to an end. "Be sure to discuss this with your parents of course and we look forward to hearing from you."

"Thank you," Coach Jackson steps forward and shakes the man's hand first. His chest is puffed out like an arrogant rooster. Buddy and Ollie take their turn shaking his hand too before Mr. Wackalliton departs. He has a funny last name for his funny looking character. No one would have ever guessed he was a basketball scout. Maybe he did that on purpose.

Ollie is mesmerized by the white paper in his hands. He studies the blue crest of the school logo at the top of the paper. Something in him knows he wants to be part of this school. He can hear God telling him this is his future. He just knows it.

Ollie looks up to see Brandi putting water bottles in the cases. He moves in her direction hoping tonight may be the night she actually says yes to his question. When he's only feet away from her, three of Angela Patterson's cheerleading girlfriends step in front of him.

"Phil Oliver!" they cry simultaneously.

"Are you going with anyone to the Freeze tonight?" Sandy asks.

"Do you want to go with me?" Patricia lays her pom-pom on Ollie's shoulder.

"Do you want to go with *us*?" Mandy hits Patricia in the stomach with her pom-pom.

Brandi hears the whole thing. She wills herself not to turn her head or let her mouth fall open like a dead fish. Instead she jams the water bottles in their cases with unnecessary force.

"Oh," Ollie feels dumbfounded. "No thanks girls." He manages to say it but there is a quiver in his voice.

The girls moan before they mope off. When Ollie is free he sees Brandi walking away from him carrying the cases of water bottles. As Ollie follows after her Corky jumps off the bleachers where he's been kissing Roxanne with such ferocity his lips are hot pink like she tried to suck them off. "Thanks for telling me about the recruiter man!" Corky wraps his arm around Ollie's neck so their heads touch.

Brandi comes to a stop outside the boy's locker room. She sets the water bottle cases down outside the entrance. "Brandi," Ollie catches up to her. Corky loosens his arm around Ollie's neck but leaves it draped over his shoulders.

"I was wondering if you wanted to go out to the Freezer Fresh with me tonight."

Corky nods his head at Brandi who rolls her eyes at him. "No thanks," Brandi says. She takes a roll of gauze from her jacket pocket and puts it on top of the water bottles.

"Oh well that's alright," Corky announces. Brandi straightens up. She looks at him curiously. Ollie looks at his friend like he's a mad man. Corky glances at Ollie but he looks at Brandi as he says, "Ollie has plenty of girls that want to go with him tonight." Ollie's face flushes. He shakes his head at his friend. Corky never says the right things at the right time. Brandi throws the roll of tape from her pocket onto the water bottles before she walks off. Corky and Ollie turn to watch her leave. "She'll come now for sure," Corky says as he moves into the locker room. Ollie shakes his head at his friend's backward thinking.

The rest of the team makes a quick exit from the locker room. They don't care about going to the Freezer Fresh still smelling like a sweaty gymnasium. Ollie is the last one inside. When he comes out of the shower he finds all of his stuff out of his locker again. He doesn't care anymore though. He dresses quickly then flicks off the lights as he leaves.

In the parking lot most of the basketball team waits by or in their cars for Ollie. All of them have a girl or two with them. Miles proudly holds Bekkah Brown on his elbow. Percy has one arm on Patricia's back and the other on Mandy's. Everyone hollers as Ollie appears out the gym doors.

45

Two young girls Ollie recognizes as underclassmen run up to him before he's down the stairs into the parking lot. "Ollie, we want to go with you to the Freeze," the red head says. A girl at the bottom of the stairs yells up, "I was going to ask you Ollie!"

Ollie stands with his mouth open. He tries to look around the two girls into the parking lot for Buddy. They stand on their tip toes trying to get in his vision. Ollie starts to feel a panic when something tugs on the tail of his shirt that hangs out of his coat. He turns to see Brandi pulling on it. "I'm taking him," she says to the girls. Then she pulls at Ollie's shirt until he's following her down the stairs. The ball team goes wild as the girls go silent.

"Hey we're going to Freezer Fresh, right?" Someone yells from another car.

Buddy stands one foot in the car and one foot out. "Yes we're going to Freeze. Where else would we go Mandy? Get with it." Angela laughs.

Ollie follows Brandi to her car. When they reach it she finally lets go of his shirt. "Get in," she says. Even in the dark Ollie can tell her face is red. She still hasn't looked him in the eyes. Ollie has never felt so confused and happy at the same time in all his life. He doesn't argue with her. He doesn't even speak to her. Ollie just gets in the car.

The ride to Freezer Fresh is less than two minutes if you don't get the single red light in town. Tonight it feels like infinity to Ollie. When at last they pull in the parking lot it is packed. It always is after a game. All the team players usually come here. And most of the time there are the same sets of parents who crash their teenagers night out. Take for instance poor Griffin Lytle who sits dreamily watching the rest of his classmates from the corner booth his parents always get.

Freezer Fresh is notorious for its ice cream. You can get soft served, hand dipped, a milkshake or choose from 100 different Frozen Twister options. Everyone stares down the menu for a solid three minutes. Each person tries to get all 100 options so they can get their picture on the wall of Twister Champs.

Ollie has never ordered anything for himself. For as long as he can remember Buddy has always ordered two of everything and given Ollie his seconds. He's asked him a 100 times not to. Buddy always says, "Man stop saying that. You know my mom would kill me if I ate in front you and you didn't have anything. Shut up and eat." Ollie knew Mrs. Porter probably gave Buddy extra money for this very purpose. Buddy truly is a good friend. Any other teen would have told their mom they did spend it on their friend but would really keep the extra cash for themselves.

But tonight Ollie would be ordering for him and Brandi. He remembered to pull a five dollar bill out of his sock money just in case tonight was the magic night. He doesn't have loads of money to spare. That's why he never spends it on ice cream on a regular day with Buddy. Tonight is a special occasion.

The Freeze is so full it's nearly 85 degrees with everyone's body heat. Christmas decorations hang from the ceilings.

47

Tinsel is over the table tops. Corky and Roxanne sit at a table in the center of the shop. When Brandi and Ollie walk in, Buddy and Angela right behind them, Corky waves his arms then sticks two of his fingers in his mouth and whistles. Roxanne, who sits on his lap, covers her ears and giggles.

Ollie sits across from them. Buddy takes the other empty seat. Angela doesn't hesitate. She plops down on Buddy's lap in the same stance as Roxanne who now has Corky's earlobe in her mouth. Brandi looks around the shop. The place is so packed there isn't a single empty chair. She takes a deep breath then sits on Ollie's lap too.

One of Buddy's long legs stretches across the aisle. Everyone has to step across him as they go to and from. The waitress gives him an annoyed look at first. Brandi recognizes her. It is a girl from her graduating class. Brandi hadn't known she'd stayed around Masonville.

"Can I take yall's order now?" she says.

"Raven?" Brandi asks. The waitress looks taken aback.

"Brandi? What are you doing here? I haven't seen you in forever." Brandi is a blushing mess. She's so hot she's certain she'll faint from heat. Raven taps her pencil on her pad.

"I'm at the community college right now." Raven eyes her and Ollie. Before she has time to ask, Brandi says, "I thought you were going away for college?"

Raven moves her gum from one side of her mouth to the other. "Yeah I am. I'm just working over my Christmas break." Brandi wishes she hadn't asked. "So you're into younger guys huh?" Raven smiles as she waves her pencil between Brandi and Ollie. Corky laughs so loud Roxanne has to let lose his earlobe. Ollie and Brandi stay completely silent. "Oh, I'm only joking Brandi," she laughs. "So what'll it be?"

Thankfully Corky jumps right in on ordering. Brandi looks around the crowded restaurant. No other college kids are here. This makes her both glad and concerned. *Am I acting immature hanging out with these high school kids?* She thinks. *Why am I even here with Ollie? What could possibly come of this?*

"What would you like?" Ollie's sweet voice shakes her back to reality. He smiles at her with a deep understanding in his eyes. Looking at him makes Brandi realize he knows she was embarrassed by Raven just now. Something in his eyes tells her he's hoping she'll see he's more than just a high school boy.

Brandi sighs, "Peanut Butter Twister." Raven scribbles then disappears, nearly tripping over Buddy's leg on the way.

Ollie's hands rest on the top of Brandi's thighs. He looks up at her from around her shoulder. Buddy is talking his head off about the game but he's only partly listening. He's taking in every angle of Brandi. He listens to her talk about her high school days with Roxanne and Angela; how she played softball and would never have considered being a cheerleader. "No offense," she says to Angela.

Eventually it is just Angela talking. Brandi bobs her head up and down. The girl can talk so fast she should do it for the Olympics. Ollie drifts from their conversation back into Buddy's. He must not notice then what he starts to do to Brandi. She, on the other hand, notices nothing but it. Ollie's hands start to move up and down her thighs. He rubs her legs slowly at first. His fingertips touch the end of her knees then slide to the bend in her hips. They go back and forth like this. He raises his hand every now and then to talk. It slaps back down on her thigh and goes back to work. Brandi's heart rate increases. His hands stop only for a moment to slide a twister in front of Brandi and the other in front of him. With one hand he holds the Twister. The other hand continues its track on her jeans.

Ollie finishes his Twister in only a few minutes. He sets it down on the table and both of his hands take back to Brandi's legs. She's happy he's done so fast. One thigh was getting extremely warmer than the other.

The chilling Twister doesn't seem to help Brandi's body temperature. Ollie's hands moving up and down her thighs are making her blue jeans stick to her. Even though she holds ice cream in her glass cup, her palms are sweating. Her heart beats faster the closer he pulls his hands toward her hips. Brandi looks down at him wondering if he's noticing what he's doing to her. Ollie is deep in conversation with Corky and Buddy. He feels her eyes on him so he turns to smile at her but then he returns to his conversation without ever slowing his hands.

Brandi looks down at Angela's thighs to see if Buddy is doing the same to her. Buddy has one arm wrapped completely around Angela's waste. His other hand is on the table tapping his fingers. Roxanne has sucked two hickies on Corky's neck and is working on a third. Brandi looks around at the other girls sitting on their boyfriend's laps. Some of them stare into each other's faces. One couple moves in for a kiss. That's all it takes for Brandi's thoughts to start running wild. She pictures herself grabbing Ollie's hands, unable to take it anymore. She pulls him from the bench and tugs him through the Freeze after her until they are in the parking lot. As soon as they're out the door she'd turn to kiss him and it would be slow at first but then raging with passion. Brandi stops herself. She is starting to breathe like she's run a marathon.

"Ollie," Brandi interrupts. All three boys stop talking to look at her. She didn't realize her voice would come out so loudly. She whispers to Ollie now, "I'm going to the restroom, be right back." Ollie nods his head and goes back to his conversation.

Brandi maneuvers through the crowd until she's in the restroom. Four girls stand in front of the mirrors above the pink sinks. One reapplies lipstick; another is running her fingers through her hair. Brandi waits for a curly red head to finish washing her hands. As soon as she moves Brandi steps toward the pink sink. She turns the faucet back on. She lets her hands bathe under the cold water while she looks at her damp forehead in the mirror. Her long blonde hair is pulled back in a tight ponytail. Brandi turns off the faucet, flicks her fingers then pulls the ponytail out. Her

51

hair falls down over her shoulders. She shakes her head so her hair parts. She wipes her hands on her jeans and tries to smooth down her hair without it getting too wet. A couple girls watch her from a mirror over. Brandi leans against the sink for a second. She takes a deep breath in. She feels the warmth between her legs slightly diminish. She hopes it is enough to get through the rest of the evening. She straightens up and walks back out of the bathroom.

When she rounds the corner from the hall to the bathroom she sees everyone at her table is standing up. Ollie spots her across the room. Her long blonde hair glistens from the lights of the Freezer Fresh. Ollie remembers the morning Brandi stopped at the orphanage to get his face mask. Her hair was down that day too. She looks even more beautiful to him with her hair down.

"There she is!" Corky yells as Brandi approaches.

"We're heading out Brandi," Angela says. "I'm so glad you came out with us tonight."

Buddy and Ollie exchange a routine handshake. Corky smacks them each on the butt as he pulls Roxanne behind him with his other arm. "See you queers!" And with that he and Roxanne run out of the Freeze.

"Bye Angela," Brandi says as Buddy takes his girlfriend's hand and leads her out of the restaurant as well. They watch them go then turn to each other. Ollie smiles down at his date. He knows he'll never forget this day. Brandi smiles up at him. A tiny hint of purple lies under one of his eyes but the swelling is gone. Ollie's nose is perfect again.

Brandi sees now how perfectly his face goes together. His eyes are just the right size and set apart correctly. His eyebrows are fair like his blonde eyelashes. The tops of his cheekbones are slightly darker than the rest of his face. A brown freckle by his left eye draws her attention to his glistening baby blue eyes. Brandi has to physically sigh to relieve some of the emotion she's experiencing inside.

"Ready to go?" Ollie says.

The word 'go' gives her a curious idea. From the corner of her eye she sees Raven wave at her. Brandi turns to wave back. Their waitress wears a mischievous smile. Her eyes look from Ollie back to Brandi. Brandi knows what she's thinking. She blushes again. *If only you knew what I was thinking,* she says to herself.

Cars squeal out of the parking lot driven by anxious teenagers, ready to be alone with their partner. Part of Ollie feels their anxiety. Brandi feels all of it. She pushes Ollie's head down into the car like she's a police officer. "I've got something I want to show you," she says.

Brandi drives away from town toward the country. "Where are we going?" Ollie asks.

"Somewhere special," Brandi says. She turns and looks at him. Ollie sees the green in her eyes glinting off the moon light. Her eyes look wild. They sort of scare him. He wonders what in the world is going through her mind. She licks her lips and says to him, "Somewhere we can be alone."

Ollie feels his heart racing when she finally stops the car. They've drove up a long gravel driveway. She tells him to get out of the car when she stops. He feels it's a little aggressive but he obeys. She grabs his hand when he's at the front of the car. She pulls him along behind her in the dark. "Where are we?" he nervously asks.

Brandi doesn't slow down. "We're at my Grandpa's. Well, technically I live here too but this is my Grandpa's side of the farm."

Ollie tries to slow her down. Unlike her, he doesn't know where he's walking. He prays he doesn't trip over something in the dark and bust his already busted nose. "You live with your grandpa?" Ollie tries to keep conversation going.

"No," Brandi quickly replies. She side-steps between two bushes. Ollie does the same thing. "Are these roses?" he asks.

Brandi pulls Ollie along. "Yeah, this is the rose garden," she says. "They're obviously not in season though." The plants are bare and short. Ollie's footing changes. The ground beneath him changes from a rock path to hollow sounding wood. "What are we on?" He tries to pull at Brandi's hand to slow her down. She finally stops. "This is the dock on the pond."

"We're on a dock?" Ollie looks around. The night is so black he can't see the water all around him.

Brandi pulls his hand again. "Come to the end with me," she says. "I like to lay here and look at the stars." He follows her, even more cautiously now, to the end of the deck. She lets go of his hand and sits down. Her legs dangle off the deck above the water. Ollie feels his way down onto the dock, not wanting to fall into the freezing water. Brandi lies down on her back. She pats the deck beside her. Ollie feels tightness in his chest but he lies back too.

Brandi feels for his hand until she finds it. She pulls it off his chest and holds it against her side. Ollie never imagined Brandi would be so forward with him. She's been playing hard to get this whole time. Now, on their first night out, she drug him to the middle of nowhere with no one in sight and won't let go of this hand. He takes a deep breath and tries not to think.

The stars above are beautiful. It is so dark Ollie can see the Milky Way. He points to the sky, "That there is the Little Dipper." Brandi doesn't respond. She moves closer to him so their sides are touching. She wraps her other arm around his so he feels locked in her grip. He clears his throat and points again. "So if you follow the end of it, you'll find the Big Dipper." Brandi's breathing is the only thing he hears. Her hand moves up and down his arm. "So you share a farm with your grandparents?" Ollie tries again.

Brandi turns her head to him. Her nose nearly touches his cheek so he doesn't face her. "My parents built a house on my grandparents land. My grandpa's house is on the other side of the lake."

Ollie is relieved she's talking to him in full sentences. "I see," he says.

"My grandparents retired and my family does the farming for them," she says.

"Oh," Ollie nods. "That's a good thing." Brandi's hand goes back to rubbing his arm. He's thankful he has on his coat to provide some distance between them. He doesn't see how Brandi is standing the cold. The deck wood under him is freezing and hard. Brandi doesn't notice though. She's still burning up from the Freezer Fresh. She rubs his arm like he was rubbing her legs. She moves her hand from his arm and onto his belly. She reaches around him until her hand is around his other side. She pulls herself closer to him so she's on her side. Ollie's spit gets caught in his throat when she turns her body over on his side. He coughs trying to hack it up. Brandi's leg drapes over his so her shoe is between his knees. He tries to squirm but Brandi holds him tighter. She puts her head on his chest. He's about to say, *I thought you wanted to look at the stars*, when Brandi's hand moves down his gut toward his pants. Ollie's heart starts to race. He hopes he's mistaken in what he's thinking Brandi is about to do. He exhales so his breath makes a cloud above him.

Brandi breathes slowly through her nose. Her heart races too. The warmth between her legs is the only sensation she can concentrate on. She wants it so badly she can't stop. She moves to the zipper on Ollie's blue jeans. As her index finger and thumb move around his button his hand closes on hers. Her eyes dart up to Ollie's. His grip is firm so she can't move her fingers. He pulls her hand away from his crotch and places it on his chest. Brandi lifts her head off Ollie's chest so she can see his face. He unfolds her hand so it is flat under his. She can feel his heart thumping under his coat. Ollie says to her, "I wanna' make sure you hold my heart the way I hold your heart."

Brandi is flooded with shame and affection at the same time. Cold chills run down her spine and the heat between her legs vanishes. She takes a deep breath as she removes her leg that she isn't entangled in Ollie's. She sighs as she leans back against the dock. Her hands rest on her stomach. She searches the sky. Ollie slips his finger under her palm. He slides his fingers through hers and brings her hand back to his side. Brandi turns her head to Ollie. He turns to face her as well. They look at each other for a moment. "You're holding it," Brandi says. Ollie isn't sure if it is a question or comment. He squeezes her hand in his. "No," she turns her head to face the stars, "My heart."

Chapter Seven

Coming to Light & Going to Church

Brandi's mother pulls on her daughter's foot. Brandi hides under the blankets. She tugs her leg this time. Brandi moans. "Will I ever have a Saturday to sleep in again?"

Mrs. Bollinger leans over the foot of the bed and swats what she assumes is her daughter's buttocks. "Get up!" she says as she walks out the door. "They'll be here shortly," Brandi hears her mother say as she walks down the stairs.

Under the covers Brandi sighs. Her family Christmas is today. Mrs. Bollinger has been overly excited for this for weeks now. Her cousin's new baby is the main reason for it. She has a love for babies that makes Brandi fear for her virginity. This makes Brandi think of last night. She covers her face with one of her hands still partly ashamed for how she behaved. She got called out by a junior in high school. *Was he really more mature and self-controlled than her?* Then again, a sweet thought comes to mind. He wants to hold her heart. *Hold my heart? What does that even mean?* She wonders if that is some kind of Christian scripture— *"To hold the heart of your lover is to hold the hand of God."* Brandi laughs out loud.

Phil Oliver, on the other hand, has been out of bed for a couple hours. He swings the weed eater at the base of the fence at his home. Mr. Gibbs will be there soon to pick him up. He kills the weed eater and leans it against the fence. With this leather gloves he pulls at the poison ivy growing up through the chain links. He's lost count of how many times he's gotten the gooey bumps from the awful stuff. Still, he has a mission. He pulls until vines break away. The bitter wind cuts through his thin coat. It is a hand-me-down from a young man at church. It doesn't have a hood. Ollie's ears burn from the cold.

Brandi's feet jerk up toward her—a reaction they have to the cold hard wood floor they meet. Brandi uses her big toe to feel for her house slippers that have disappeared under her bed. When she finds them she slides her feet into the warm pink fuzz. She sees herself from the mirror that hangs above her dresser as she goes to her door. Her blonde hair flies in the air from the static her sheets caused to her head. Brandi wipes her eyes as she feels her way down the stairs.

Ollie hears Mr. Gibbs arriving before he sees him. His old red truck makes a coughing sound like a heavy cigarette smoker. As he puts the weed eater in the shed the truck's breaks sing a high note as Mr. Gibbs stops. "C'mon boy!"

The old man yells out his window. A cloud forms in the air from his breath. Ollie surveys his work as he approaches the truck. Half the fence line has been cleared. Part of the Elementary School building is starting to show in the distance. Carl nods his head at him as he lets Ollie slide into the truck by the old man. Carl never sits in the middle.

Mrs. Bollinger puts a bowl of cereal on the island in front of Brandi. Milk sloshes over the side onto the counter. Brandi rubs her eyes one more time, "Cereal?"

"I don't have time to slave over a breakfast for you two," Mrs. Bollinger says to her daughter and her husband. Will looks at his daughter who looks back at him in bewilderment. They sit on the bar stools at the island. They each sigh as they pick up the spoon next to their bowls.

"I've got a ham in the oven, yams on the stove, bread rising, don't think for one minute I want to create more dirty dishes for myself." Brandi's mom holds a spatula in one hand. She swings it as she talks. She has more utensils in the pockets of her apron. "Brandi, you're going to feed the animals this morning. William, if you don't have that toilet fixed by the time they get here, you're fired."

"Fired?" Brandi's dad says as milk dribbles down his chin.

"*Yes fired,*" his wife doesn't turn around from the pot she stirs on the stove.

"Fired from what?"

Carol looks over her shoulder with one eyebrow raised, "Fired from being my husband."

"You can't fire me," Will and Brandi both laugh.

"Oh, yes I can." Mrs. Bollinger turns back to her yams.

Ollie is taken aback when he sees the fence line behind the white barn. The scrap piles have been cleared out. All the junk is gone. All the vehicles and farm machinery are gone. Carl nods his head and wears a proud smile. Ollie claps him on the knee a couple times as in "good job."

"We don't got much time today thanks to city boy's ball playin'." Raymond takes his pipe out of his mouth. "So fix the fence quick today. No fartin' around." Carl opens the truck door. It makes the sound like a tin can popping. "*Vamanos Jose*," Raymond yells. Carl rolls his eyes and Ollie laughs.

Brandi pours a scoop of the dry red and brown balls into the cat bowl. "Bon appetite," she strokes the white fur of her favorite kitten. It is the odd ball of the bunch. She doesn't know how it happened but this kitten has the hair of a wooly mammoth. The rest of its siblings have short silky fur. This kitten's hair stands on end. It is so long the cat looks like a walking fur ball. Brandi calls it Edison because it looks like it got fried with electricity. She laughs every time she sees it. The mommy cat circles Brandi's feet. She has made a home for her five kittens in the warm hay loft. Brandi hasn't told her dad about them. There is a chance this old mommy cat would get the boot if he found she had another litter.

Brandi makes her way around the porch to the dog house in the back yard. Sampson is so old he looks like an overused mop head flopped on the ground. He hasn't moved in so long leaves are starting to blanket his back. "Sampson, are you still alive you old hound?" Brandi jokes with the dog but inside she knows his days are ticking down. It makes her sad to think of it.

Sampson lifts his head a few inches. His ears are so long half of them stay on the ground. The skin under his eyes droops. The red there makes the dog look like he hasn't slept in years but truly that is all he does. Brandi opens the metal lid on the large trash can behind his dog house. At the sound of it Sampson wobbles his way onto his paws and over to his bowl. Brandi knows she isn't supposed to but she gives the old dog an extra half a scoop. She pats his head that used to be deep brown but now is graying. He'll eat on that all day as slow he chews.

Ollie pulls on the hammer that is anchored to the fence and lodged against the post. The barbed wire tightens. Carl hammers the fence in place. Raymond sits on a stump ten feet away. "When you gonna quit this basketball life and become a farmer?" Mr. Gibbs grumbles this. The smoke from his pipe bubbles with his words.

Ollie laughs and shakes his head. "I ain't no farmer Mr. Gibbs." With that he grabs the whole digger and jams it in the ground. He works the two arms to move the mouth of it open and closed. "Carl here should be the farmer."

Mr. Gibbs laughs one hardy time. "Ha! *A Mexican cowboy.* That'll be the day."

Brandi slips off her boots in the mud room. Her mother appears in the doorway. "Tell me those aren't covered in manure," she eyes the boots like they might be diseased.

Brandi plops them in the corner. "I didn't go in the pasture mom, calm down." Carol looks appeased then disappears. Through the wall she can hear her dad grunting and pipes tinking off tools. "Why you . . ." she hears him say under his breath.

"Seriously kid," Raymond removes his pipe. "What are you going to do after you graduate? You gonna stay here, marry a pretty girl, help me keep this place runnin?" Ollie feels a quick, sharp pain of sadness for the old man. Raymond doesn't look at him. Ollie can't imagine leaving the old guy with this huge farm all by himself. If he did go away to college and Raymond died, would he be alone? The thought of it makes Ollie's heart stop. For a second he thinks he should throw away basketball and college and just stay here. But as soon as those thoughts enter he knows they aren't his calling.

Ollie clears his throat in order to practice the tough love he's feeling. "I hope to get a free ride for basketball sir. I'd like to go to college so I can learn about the Bible. I want to be a pastor." Carl moves ahead like he isn't hearing anything.

Raymond repositions on the stump. The hard wood is hurting his old boney butt. "Well you'll meet lots of pretty girls at them fancy colleges." He says with a little defeat in his voice.

Ollie laughs. "I don't need to go to college to do that."

"What, you already found you a pretty girl in Masonville?"

Carl stops working to hear Ollie's reply. "Yes sir. I found the prettiest girl in the world right here in Masonville."

"That's unlikely," Carl says.

"Back to work *muchacho*," Raymond points his pipe at the man. Carl harrumphs. Raymond continues, "I doubt she's the prettiest in the world Philip, but I'll give you pretty cute."

Ollie laughs. "Why is that sir?"

Raymond sits up pointedly. "Because *I* got the prettiest one."

At half past eleven Brandi's cousins pull in the driveway. Carol runs from the living room to the bathroom waving her hands above her head. "Cheryl is here! William, Cheryl and Tom are here!"

Brandi watches from the bay of windows in the living room.

"I got it. I got it." Her dad says from the restroom. He exits wearing his tool belt around his waist.

Brandi's mom follows behind him. "Go change your shirt!" Carol comes back to the window beside Brandi. She only stays a second to watch the Stratton's car door open. She moves to the front door. Brandi watches her Uncle Tom and Aunt Cheryl lift out of the front seats. Her cousin

Emilee gets out of the back left. Behind them another car parks. Her cousin Patrick, his wife, Patricia, and their new baby get out. Emilee slinks around the car like she's in the pits of hell. Brandi feels sorry for her. She hopes kids at school still don't call her "pig-ily Emilee." By the looks of her cousin though, Brandi knows they must. She raises her big eyes up from behind her large rimmed glasses to the house. She makes eye contact with Brandi who smiles at her. Relief seems to wash over her cousin.

"Cheryl!" Mrs. Bollinger cries like a little girl who hasn't seen her sister in years even though they talk every day on the phone.

"Sis!" Cheryl cries back. She throws her purse over Carol's shoulder as they embrace. They teeter back and forth in each other's arms giggling. Tom catches sight of Mr. Bollinger as he comes down the stairs in a fresh shirt. They exchange a wide-eyed look.

Cheryl and Carol are twins. They both have fair skin, light eyes, and thin mouths. Their muscle tone and build are identical. While Carol's hair has darkened over the years from blonde to brown, Cheryl's hair has always had a red tint. They thank God for this minor detail; otherwise, distinguishing themselves would have been much more challenging.

Emilee tries to remain sane as she shivers in the cold on the front porch waiting for her mother to get inside. By the time Emilee crosses the threshold Patrick is at her back trying to walk over her. He holds the baby now. He showcases the bundle above Emilee's head.

Patrick and Emilee are similar in their faces. Both have round, fat cheeks and a tiny pointy chin like their father. Patrick also wears large rimmed glasses that magnify his eyes. However, he stands a foot taller than his sister. He is husky, but he isn't fat. None of the Stratton's are but Emilee. She resists the urge to elbow her brother in the stomach and makes her way toward Brandi.

Mrs. Bollinger takes the baby as soon as she's let go of her sister. Tom Stratton wiggles around them to shake Jeff's hand. He lifts a pie carrying case in the other and Brandi's dad motions for them to go in the kitchen.

Last in the door is Patrick's wife Patricia. She's not an attractive lady. She's skinny but in a way that makes her have pointy features—her elbows, her knotty knees, her cheek bones, her spiky spine. She's shorter than them all. Her frail wrists look like they'll snap as she lifts her coat onto the rack.

Patrick beams from ear to ear. He unwraps his scarf and hangs it over Patricia's head. She ducks in under his arm like a chick and holds onto his waste. Emilee looks at Brandi. Her eyes say, *"This is what I have to deal with on a daily basis."* Brandi laughs at her cousin. She wraps her arm around Emilee's shoulders. "Let's get out of here, what do you say?" They sneak up the stairs.

Mr. Gibbs puts his fingers between his lips and blows a whistle. Ollie and Carl have moved ahead of his stump fifty feet or more. As they approach Raymond makes his way to his old red truck. He pulls two sack lunches off the dashboard. He throws them at the boys as they come by.

"Why can't we eat in the house where it's warm?" Carl says. Ollie thinks about that statement. He realizes he's never been in the old man's house.

"Be grateful for what I get you *Ricardo*." Carl rubs his arms to warm them. "We ain't living in no tropics up here," Raymond continues. "I don't see no Mayan ruins 'round here. Do you Ollie?"

Ollie looks to Carl who is gritting his teeth. "Aren't you cold Mr. Gibbs?" Ollie asks.

"I'm always cold," he says. "I put the old in cold."

"Ain't that the truth," Carl sniffs.

"We speak *ingles* around here amigo," Raymond shuts his truck door.

"I'm speaking *English,*" Carl pulls his sandwich from his brown baggy.

"This here is Em-Erica." Raymond taps the old tobacco out of his pipe. Ollie smiles as he bites into his cold ham sandwich. He shakes his head as Carl and Raymond go at it.

"So, been applying to colleges?" Brandi asks as she jumps onto her bed. Her unmade blankets jump after her. Emilee takes her time sitting on the bed. Her weight makes the mattress sink. Brandi rolls onto her elbow so she doesn't fall down the hill Emilee has created in the mattress.

"Yeah, and scholarships like crazy," she says as she pushes her glasses up her nose.

67

"What do you think you want to study?"

Emilee leans back against the head post. "Food," she smiles as a flame flashes in her eyes.

Brandi laughs. "Oh yeah?"

"Yep," Emilee folds her hands in her lap like she's getting comfortable yet formal. "I've fallen in love with Home Education class this year." Brandi laughs some more then repositions so she's sitting Indian style facing her cousin. "Not to mention the hottest, nicest guy in school has been my partner all year," Emilee's fat cheeks turn slightly pink but she looks Brandi in the eye without any shame.

Brandi pulls one shoulder to her cheek. "You don't say."

Emilee laughs and pulls her legs onto the bed to sit like Brandi. She's always admired her older cousin. Brandi has always been beautiful, graceful, energetic and fun to be with. Emilee has stayed over with her cousin for more sleepovers than she can count. All of Emilee's birthday parties included Brandi, sometimes only Brandi. They've had pillow talk on this very bed about every subject Emilee think of. "Yeah, his name is Phil Oliver and . . ."

"Phil Oliver?" Brandi slouches, her hands landing hard on the bed in front of her, making the bed springs vibrate.

 "You know him?"

Brandi can't believe it. "Know him? I'm with him like every day."

Emilee's mouth drops open a little. "Why?"

"I've been working with the basketball team. Duh Emilee. You knew that, didn't you?"

She inhales like she's remembering. "Yes, now I remember that. Isn't he the nicest human being ever?"

Brandi laughs a little. She sits back. "I don't know," she shrugs.

"What do you mean *'you don't know'*?" Emilee looks at Brandi with some fun in her eyes but also seriousness. "He is Brandi," she says. "Trust me. He's the nicest person ever."

Brandi feels a heart string tug. "Why do you say that?" she probes.

Emilee shakes her head madly and slaps her hands on her thighs. The smacking noise is loud off her fat. "*Because,*" she looks at Brandi. "Look at me Brandi." She holds her hands out away from her body so her cousin can get the full picture of her blubber. Brandi wrinkles her forehead. Emilee pulls her hands back in to her lap. "No one wants to be my partner. No one even wants to be my friend. And have you seen Phil Oliver?" Emilee looks at Brandi like she's crazy. "He's like the most gorgeous creature on the planet. All the girls in Home Ed want to be his partner. He literally has to *push through* swarms of girls every day in that class. And he wants to be *my* partner." Something swells inside Brandi's chest. It takes her breath away. Emilee continues to shake her head. "And he listens to me. He asks me how I am every day. He never talks about himself. I mean," Emilee takes a deep breath. "He could whine and complain every day about the life he's been handed but instead he's so," her eyes search the ceiling for a moment. "Optimistic. Haven't you noticed that about him?"

Brandi is quiet for a moment while her cousin studies her face. Brandi breathes deeply so the swollen mass of pride in her chest makes a little room for her words to come out. She nods, "I have."

After her family leaves, Brandi and her parents sit on the couch staring at the wall. They soak in the silence. Mr. Bollinger starts to drift off to sleep. When Carol slaps her hands on her knees he jumps forward in fright. Brandi and her mom giggle. He wipes the salvia from his bottom lip, "What now?"

"Well now that we have Brandi alone for a few minutes finally, I think we should ask her about that thing." Carol gives William a look Brandi can't read. She suddenly fears she's in trouble.

"What thing?" Will looks back at his wife like she's gone mad.

"You know . . . the radio thing." Brandi sits next to her mom on the love seat. Mr. Bollinger sits in his recliner. They face each other. Brandi feels she's in a trap. Her dad continues to sit there having no idea what Carol is talking about. Finally she slaps her knees again. "Brandi," she turns to her daughter. "We heard you on the radio last week."

Brandi doesn't know where they're going with this. She slowly nods her head.

"Oh!" Will finally catches on.

Carol rolls her eyes. "So we heard the news."

"And we're not too happy we had to hear it from *Jeff Wallace* instead of our own daughter." Will finally puts in his two cents. Brandi is really scared now but she still has no idea what they're talking about. Her parents wait in silence.

"Do you have something you want to tell us?" Brandi's mom puts her hands in her lap and sits up straight.

Brandi hates it when her mother does this. It is the perfect stance for a guilt trip. Brandi shrugs her shoulders. "What are you talking about? I didn't know Jeff would put me on the air. I was just there with Phil Oliver."

"Yeah, we know," Will sounds like a child.

"With your boyfriend," Carol crosses her arms in front of her chest.

"What? Boyfriend? Phil Oliver is *not* my boyfriend." Brandi looks back and forth at her parents who now look at each other in bewilderment.

"He's not?" Mrs. Bollinger looks to Brandi who shakes her head no.

"I told you Caroline. Brandi wouldn't hide something like that from us." Will looks at Brandi with pride and nods his head.

Carol uncrosses her arms. "Well Jeff Wallace said you were his girl."

Brandi recalls the conversation now. She plays back that day at Myron Studios. She shakes her head at her mom. "Jeff was just assuming. Trust me. I'm not dating Ollie."

"Then who did you go to the Freezer Fresh with? Don't think we didn't notice you got home later than usual. You know we listen to the games on the radio when we're not there. You got home *way* after it was over." Carol crosses her legs. One foot bounces. It is a sign she's upset.

Brandi sighs. She knows now she has to confess. She looks at her dad who is biting his upper lip. He gets nervous when the Mrs. is upset. "Well, I did go out with him *that* night but that doesn't mean we're dating."

"I knew it!" Mrs. Bollinger claps her hands together and uncrosses her legs at the same time. She has a broad smile on her face. Brandi is immediately confused.

"Brandi, you know the rules." Her dad looks at her, trying to be stern but inside he's still writhing with worry.

"What rule?"

"We have to meet the boy. You know that. I don't care if you're calling him your boyfriend or not. If he's taking you out and I'm not invited, I need to meet him."

Carol holds her hands together in front of her face. They can't hide her huge smile.

"Well, I wasn't expecting to go out with him. It just happened."

Carol puts her hand on Brandi's knee. She leans in, "Do you think you'll go out again?"

Brandi can't help but smile. Her mom looks like a little kid. Brandi's smile says yes. Carol claps her hands again. She bounces on the couch until she's scooted so close to her daughter she can't move any further. "Do you like him? Did he ask you? Did he pay?"

"Hey, hey, hey," Brandi's dad interrupts. "We're not turning this into girl talk. I'm serious Brandi," he widens his eyes. "The next time you two go anywhere, is here."

Brandi smiles and nods her head. Carol holds her daughter's hands now. She's squeezing them and pumping them up and down. "Okay," Mrs. Bollinger uses her serious voice. "Now go away William so we can talk."

Mr. Bollinger moans and rolls his head. Carol and Brandi smile at each other like little girls.

Coach Jackson paces the locker room floor. Brandi sits with her extra wrapping material in her hands. Everyone sits, in uniform, looking at their sweating coach. He finally stops, wipes his forehead then looks around the room. His eyes stop to hold Ollie's. He claps his hands together.

"Boys, I've got some news. There is another record in the making here boys."

The boys sit up straighter. "What is it dad?" Percy asks. "I mean, Coach."

Coach purses his lips then smacks them before he speaks again. "Someone in this room is going to score THEIR THOUSANDTH POINT this season."

Corky claps his hands, "That's what I'm talking about!"

"NOT YOU Hammons," Coach snaps. Corky drops his hands. Coach Jackson looks into Ollie's eyes. "Phil Oliver, I'm not telling you this not to psych you out son, but to INSPIRE you," he points at the rest of the team, "ALL OF YOU." The team bursts into clapping. Buddy slaps his friend on the back. Corky says something about being a close second. "It may be too soon for me to be saying this but I have a feeling we're going ALL THE WAY THIS YEAR." The glass case of the last basketball state championship comes to Ollie's mind. "Ollie, you're going to reach another record, AND WE'RE," Coach waves his clipboard around the room. "WE'RE GOING TO WIN THE CHAMPIONSHIP!"

The clapping escalates with cheers and shouts. The team moves to their feet and bounce their way toward the middle of the room. When they're huddled together as tight as they can they jump up and down as one organism. In the center of it all Coach Jackson and Phil Oliver clasp hands and hold them high above their heads. The rest of the team attaches to them. None of them ever want this moment to end but with one last hoorah they break up and scatter onto the gym floor.

The best team of the district, the Hanover Hornets, can't keep up. The Mustangs fly circles around them. The gymnasium is packed from floor to ceiling. People stand in every corner, in every knick and cranny. They hardly sit down. They shout praises like they're in Pastor Brown's church. When Corky swishes his infamous three point shot, from his sweet spot, someone sings "Hallelujah!" When Buddy smacks down a ball in midair only inches from going in the rim, another person shouts, "Thank you Lord!" When the team is down by two points and Miles fouls number seven who gets to take two foul shots but misses, the gym screams "Praise God!" And when Ollie jumps like he's never jumped before, putting the basketball through the hoop then hangs from it, the choir moves to their feet proclaiming, "Sweet Jesus!"

Ollie didn't know he had it in him to dunk a ball. He'd never done it before. He doubts he can ever do it again. But in the moment of hanging on the rim by his two hands, he pulls his knees to his chest and swings about. When he lands he's surrounded by Corky, Buddy, Miles and Percy who squeeze him in all the places they can. They throw him in the air. The ref blows his whistle but no one hears him. The Hornets look like they've had their wings ripped off.

Brandi smiles so much she can't feel her cheeks anymore. Behind her a man in the stands yells at anyone who will hear him: "Who is that boy? I'm with Purdue University and I must have him! I've never seen a high school boy dunk. Someone! Tell me his name!" The recruiter moves

75

around the bleachers trying to get in people's faces. Everyone looks around him. They can't take their eyes off the boy he yells for.

The Hornets pretty much give up after Ollie's dunk. They don't press him when they guard. They keep their distance like he's a celebrity. When the final buzzer sounds the Mustangs have won by twenty seven points.

It is becoming a Masonville tradition for the fans to swarm the court as soon as the winners are declared. "Masonville Mustangs have trampled the competition AGAIN!" And the gymnasium nearly loses its roof with the cry that comes after. Everyone tries to get to Phil Oliver. They want to touch him. They want to say, "Good job. Remember me when you're famous." College recruiters try to talk to him. He gently declines or yells for Corky who amuses them. Brandi longs to be at the center of the gym with him, but she stands on the bleacher instead, trying to peer over the crowd at him. She finds a blindingly blonde head approaching him. She recognizes it from across the gym.

"Phil Oliver!" The blonde waves her arms madly.

Ollie peers through a gap in the crowd toward the voice. He recognizes her in an instant. "Sandra, how are you?"

She reaches for his hand through the crowd. Ollie holds it as she pulls him toward her. Her other hand is pulling another man after her. "Phil Oliver, why I never! You were incredible!"

The men around Sandra stare. The teammates stare. The cheerleaders push at them, their mouths open in shock at the woman.

Sandra's button-up blouse is so tight upon her chest the gaps between the clasps are spread open. The buttons look like they are holding onto the material for dear life. The top three buttons are taking it easy. They aren't buttoned at all. Her blouse opens around her throat and shoulders. The bottom of her shirt is tucked into her blue jeans which are also so tight one can make out the imprint of a coin in her front pocket.

Ollie manages to free his hand from hers. "Thank you," he says.

"Oh Ollie! This is my boy toy Mr. Ramirez." She pulls the man behind her until he's at her side. He's a few inches shorter than the tall thin model he's with. But his body is fit. His button up shirt is tight as well but not busting at the seams. He wears a matching tie, business pants and on his arm his blazer hangs. Sunglasses rest in shirt pocket, along with an ink pen. His black shoes are polished. They shine off the gymnasium floor. His black hair is slicked over on the side and glares off the lights. He wears a smile on his face that says, *"Yes I know I'm here with the sexiest woman in town."*

Ollie shakes the man's hand, "Nice to meet you Mr. Ramirez."

"How do you do?" He has an accent Ollie has never heard in these parts before. It sounds sophisticated.

"Fine, thanks."

"This is the boy who talked about me on the radio Ronnie!" Sandra says to him.

Mr. Ramirez nods his head but doesn't look at her. He keeps eye contact with Ollie who feels a little intimidated. "You speak sweet thanks to my love on the radio Phil Oliver," he says. "I appreciate your kind gesture." He finally breaks his eyes from Ollie to look at Sandra who tucks her shoulder to her chin and smiles at him. She blinks with her flirtatiously long eyelashes. Sandra turns to Ollie again. "He's the owner of Speaker City. He's a very well-to-do man. You know of him, don't you Ollie?"

Ollie hasn't heard of him but he nods his head yes. The way Ronnie is looking at Sandra seems he's undressing her right there in the crowd. He longs to be alone with the woman but obviously this little kid means something to her. He turns to Ollie. "I offer my assistance if ever there is anything I can do for you young man. As a thank you," he looks to Sandra, "for acknowledging my sweet's greatness."

"Awe!" Sandra pinches the man's nose then turns to Ollie. "Isn't he great?"

Ollie nods his head again but then an idea hits him. "Mr. Ramirez," he says. The man takes a deep breath to pull his eyes off his prize. He looks at Ollie. "I don't know if you heard tonight, but our speaker system is terrible." The man's face changes as if he wasn't expecting the twerp to really take up a favor from him, a stranger. "I'm sure, by the sound of it, you could do something really amazing." Ollie says.

Sandra wraps her arms around Ronnie's arm. The touch of her large breast against his arm makes him more urgent. "I'll see what I can do," he smiles.

"Oh!" Sandra kisses him on the cheek. "You're such a rich man!" She smiles at Mr. Ramirez who now feels his privates are going to squeeze off and fall onto the gym floor if he doesn't get this woman alone with him.

Sandra turns back to Ollie. "I'll make sure he gets it done real soon," she says. Then she wiggles her fingers on her hand that sticks out between Ronnie's arm and his side. "Goodbye Phil Oliver."

"Toodle-lou," Corky says over Ollie's shoulder as Sandra walks away.

"Man, look at that package," Miles says as he watches Sandra's hips sway.

"Hasta la pasta," Percy says.

Ollie shakes his head at Buddy who is shaking his head back. The two of them make their way through the crowd. Brandi steps down from the bleachers when he starts to approach. She starts to pick up the water bottles. He reaches for the bottle Brandi has. He grabs her hand instead. Brandi straightens up at his touch, leaving the water bottle on the floor of the stands. She looks into his eyes. Ollie goes breathless at the touch. He shakes his shoulders then reluctantly lets go of her hand. "Did you have a good time at the Freeze?" he says.

Brandi looks him in the eyes a moment longer before she nods her head. Ollie smiles but as he speaks Brandi does too. Together they say, "Would you?"

"Oh," Brandi laughs, "You first."

Ollie laughs then clears his throat. "I was wondering if you would want to go to church with me tomorrow."

Ollie never ceases to surprise her. *Church? Of course Phil Oliver's next idea of a date would be to the house of God.* Brandi laughs again. Then she thinks of her parents. *Church would be a perfect place for them to meet Ollie.* Then she's obeyed the rules without asking Ollie to awkwardly meet her parents when they weren't even an item. She nods her head. "Yeah, that's actually a good idea."

Ollie laughs at her word choice and knits his eyebrows. Brandi shakes her head and laughs. "I just mean, yes. That'll work."

"Alright," Ollie laughs. Then he braces himself for the awkward part. "I usually ride with Buddy, if you . . ."

Brandi stops him right there. "No, I'll go with my parents and meet you there."

Ollie feels relieved he doesn't have to go further. He thinks of the Bollinger's being at church. He's seen them there for Christmas and Easter, but that is about it. He wonders for a moment if Brandi will be able to get them there. He decides not to worry though. He'd understand why if she didn't show up tomorrow. Together, Brandi and Ollie go back to picking up water bottles. They smile at each other through the corner of their eyes.

Chapter Eight

Dying and Dreaming

Brandi sets her alarm clock for an early rise. She'll need time to curl her hair. She lies in bed smiling at her ceiling. Her nerves for tomorrow make her fingers trace the lines in her quilt. If all goes according to her plan, she'll hurry her parents so much in the morning they won't have time to argue with her about going to church. If she's lucky they won't even have time to ask her why and she won't need to mention Ollie asking her or Ollie at all. They'd just arrive at Pastor's Brown's Church, see Ollie, who would undoubtedly introduce himself and then they'd be satisfied with their little rule. That's all that would become of it and her mission would be accomplished. She could continue going out with Ollie without making a spectacle of it.

When her alarm clock rings Brandi jerks forward. How she managed to fall asleep she'd never know. She kicks off her blankets and runs to her mirror. She pulls open her vanity drawer. Ribbons and bows overflow out the sides. She digs under the mess of material until she feels her iron. It cracks off the bottom of the vanity as she pulls it out. This causes her hairbrush and container of ear rings to fall to the floor with a clash.

"Brandi, are you up already?" Her mother's voice travels from her bedroom to Brandi's. She freezes. After a moment of silence she tugs at the end of the cord of her iron that is stuck between the drawer and vanity. It finally releases and sends Brandi stumbling backward into her bedpost.

"You're in a hurry," her mother stands in the doorway.

Brandi drops her shoulders in a predicted defeat. "What are you already doing up?"

Carol looks at her daughter with an eyebrow raised. "I was going to ask you the same question. You're never up this early on a Sunday morning." Brandi fumbles with her cord until she finds the end. She jams it into the plug in beside her dresser mirror. "And do I remember correctly, you saying you wish for *one day* to sleep in?"

Brandi scoops her hair brush off the floor and drags it through her hair. "We're going to church today," Brandi says. "Go get ready."

Carol straightens up. "What? Church. Why?"

Brandi starts to curl her hair. "Because mom. Please, let's just go."

"You've never wanted to go to church before. It is hard enough to get you to go on Jesus' birthday."

"Mom, please." Brandi squirts the hair spray.

Her mother waves the fumes away from her face. "I'm not going unless I get an explanation young lady."

Brandi drops her shoulders again. Her hair starts to smoke where the iron is. She removes it then looks at her mom who has her lips sucked together like she's got a lemon in her mouth.

"Phil Oliver asked me to go, okay?"

Carol's face relaxes. She leans against the doorframe again. "So, you have a car. Drive yourself."

"Ugh," Brandi's head falls.

"Well, honestly Brandi. What does this have to do with me?" Her mother raises her hands in question. Her pink bathrobe opens to show her puppy pajamas underneath.

"You guys said you had to meet him, so I thought this would be the perfect way to get dad's stupid rule out of the way." Brandi turns back to her mirror.

She doesn't see it but her mother smiles. "Oh, I see." Brandi hears her trying not to giggle. She rolls her eyes.

"O!" Carol suddenly throws her arms in the air and turns. She runs down the hall to her bedroom with her arms flapping like a chicken. She says, "O! O! O!" the whole way.

"What? What is it?" Brandi yells after her.

Her mother sticks her head out from her bedroom door. "I wish I had a little warning Brandi Marie Bollinger!" Her head disappears again.

"What is going on up there?" Brandi hears her dad yell from downstairs.

"William, get up here and get ready!"

"Get ready for what?" William yells.

Carol sticks her head back out of the doorway, "For church!"

When Brandi is ready she hurries down the stairs. She spots the bottom half of her mother. The top half is hid by the freezer door of the refrigerator. On the counter beside her is every frozen item.

"Mom, what are you doing?" Brandi moves around the island to see.

"I'm trying to find something to make for lunch!" Her mother's voice muffles out of the freezer.

"Can't we worry about that when get back. We need to go." Brandi leans around the table to see if her father is in the living room and ready.

"No we can't worry about it later. I need it to slow cook during church so it'll be ready when we get home." She starts to put the frozen items back in the freezer. "I can't very well have a guest over and have *nothing* for them to eat. I can't believe you did this to me Brandi."

Brandi stops looking for her dad. Her head moves back to her mother. She puts her finger in her ear and twists it around. "I'm sorry what did you say about a *visitor*?"

Carol looks over a package of fish in her hands. She throws it into the sink then shuts the freezer door. "O no you don't," she shakes her finger at Brandi. "I am not going to church last minute just to shake this boy's hand and never see him again." She retrieves a pan from the cabinet. "He's coming over here for lunch, bet your biscuits!"

Brandi puts her hands to her head, "But *why*?"

"Oh shush," is all her mother says. She sweeps seasonings from a cabinet.

"Well," Brandi looks at the time on the stove. "Can't we just go out for lunch?"

Carol turns quickly on her toe. She puts one hand on her hip. This is a sign of trouble in the Bollinger house. "So he thinks I *can't* cook?"

Brandi puts her hands over her eyes. She knows she can't argue with her mother, especially when the hand goes on the hip. She shakes her head at how stupid she was for believing her plan would go as she hoped. Now her goal is just to get to the church on time.

Buddy can tell something has happened to his friend. Ollie walks out of the Children's Home with a wider stride. He waves at Mr. and Mrs. Porter in the front seats so much they giggle at him. Ollie puts his Bible down in the middle of the seat when he gets in the car. Like always, Buddy shakes his head at it. The seam of the book is cracked down the middle. The side with the pages is brown like a million cups of coffee have been spilled on them. Buddy imagines Ollie trying to keep the book sacred in that home. He envisions Ben and Ezra pulling it apart, Kristen carrying it in her mouth when she pretends to be a dog, and Miss Stephen pushing it with her vacuum under a couch. Buddy is surprised his mom hasn't bought him a new one of those yet.

Ollie pats the cover of his Bible like it is a baby's bottom. With his other hand he strums his fingers on the car door. He bobs his head, lost in his song. *"I found a dream that I could speak to; a dream that I can call my own."* Buddy finally hits him. "Hey man, what's gotten into you?"

Colleen turns her head around her seat to look at Ollie. She notices the extra sparkle in his eye and how his knee can't stop jumping up and down. Ollie smiles at Buddy. But before he can tell them the good news Mr. Porter speaks up from the driver's seat. "Been talking to them college recruiters at the games Ollie?" Colleen shakes her head at her husband. She finds he is always clueless to his surroundings. The rest of the drive to church Mr. Porter talks about different colleges and which ones he wants Buddy to go to. They talk of college visits, try-outs, scholarships, and through it all Ollie tries to still his nervous knee from thumping a whole in the Porter's car.

Ollie scouts the parking lot for Brandi's car. He doesn't see it. He cranes his neck as he comes to the sanctuary doors. The greeters stand with a bulletin in their hands. They look at each other when Ollie isn't paying attention to them.

Their bulletin waits in the air. Buddy grabs his friend's arm. He gives Ollie a *"what in the world is up with you?"* glare. Ollie takes the bulletin without his usual eye contact and 'thanks'.

The Porters sit in the middle row on the left side of the sanctuary. All around people grab each other in hugs and handshakes. The church is active, like a beehive. Voices echo off the high ceiling to make a buzzing noise. At the front of the church to the left of the altar the organ blares through pipes that climb the wall. To the right side the pianist tries to play along but she's so old her eyesight is failing her. Nearly every note she plays is off key. No one has the guts to tell her she needs to retire. Pastor Brown is up front behind his pulpit trying to fasten his tie clip to his shirt. Mrs. Brown eventually comes to his rescue. Ollie watches them. Mrs. Brown pats her husband's cheek a few times as she looks up into his eyes. They smile at each other. Then she moves to her seat in the front pew.

"Welcome everyone! Find a seat and we'll get started here shortly." Pastor Brown says then ducks behind the pulpit to fetch a bottle of water.

Ollie turns his body to make sure his seat is clear before he sits down. It is a habit he's had to pick up from the orphanage. No telling how many times he's sat on a sharp toy, a tool, Miss Stephen's sewing needle, or a kid. When he does, his eye catches a yellow ball of blonde hair gleaming off a sunbeam coming through the sanctuary doors. As the glare disperses Brandi's face comes into view. Her long blonde hair is in curls around her shoulders. Buddy looks up at Ollie who is smiling at the doors. Buddy

87

turns in his seat. He sees Brandi Bollinger slipping her arms out of her coat. "Oh," Buddy says. He smiles and shakes his head.

A greeter takes Brandi's coat and scarf from her. Behind her, Mr. and Mrs. Bollinger cling to their coats. The usher puts his hands up in surrender. Mrs. Bollinger pushes at her daughter's back to move her down the aisle. They look stressed, rushed, and a tad uncomfortable. Carol and William search the pews for an open section. They don't look at anyone. Brandi searches every face however. She looks for Ollie. When she sees him, he's looking directly at her. She can't help but smile at him because he's the only one standing and he's in the middle of the congregation. Meanwhile, her mother clutches her shoulders like a hawk to it's a prey. She moves Brandi about like a stick shift. Brandi and Ollie don't look away from each other even as Mrs. Bollinger pushes her down into a pew. Their eye contact breaks when Pastor Brown welcomes everyone again. The sanctuary doors shut with a clonk. The noise makes Mrs. Bollinger jump. Ollie turns away from Brandi who now sits in the back row.

Pastor Brown preaches on forgiveness. He pounds his fists off the pulpit. He parades his Bible around. Mrs. Brown nods her head the whole time. An old man gives his "amen" a hundred times. The choir sings. The pianist squints at her sheet music and hits every wrong note. A baby cries through ten minutes of the sermon. Colored pencils roll down the aisles. Mr. Porter falls asleep twenty minutes in. Mr. Bollinger is too nervous to, though his head bobs. And Ollie and Brandi smile the whole time.

When the closing prayer finishes Ollie turns his head to the back pew. Brandi catches his eye and smiles back. Carol and Will stand. They still have their coats on. Ollie exits his pew, leaving the Porters looking after him in curiosity.

Ollie slides into the second from last pew. He excuses himself as he wiggles past the people trying to get out of it. He stops in front of William with his hand held out. "Mr. Bollinger, sir, I'm Phil Oliver. It's a pleasure to meet you."

Will looks at him for a moment in a great confusion before he sticks his hand out too. Ollie smiles at him as Will slowly shakes his hand. Brandi watches the encounter in horror. Finally, understanding crosses William's eyes. His handshake tightens. "So you must be the reason we're here."

Ollie laughs. His hand is still trapped in Mr. Bollinger's. "I'm so glad you came with Brandi today. I've been wanting to meet you."

"I'm Carol Bollinger, Brandi's mom." She pulls William's hand out of Ollie's to replace it with her own. She only holds onto it for a second.

"Pleased to meet you Mrs. Bollinger. Phil Oliver."

"Oh, I know who you are," Carol smiles at him then at Brandi. "I didn't know you went to this church."

"I could have guessed as much," Will says it more to himself but everyone hears. Carol slaps him in the gut.

"Will you be joining us for lunch then Phil?" Carol puts her hand on Ollie's. Brandi widens her eyes. Ollie looks to her to see if this is what she wants. He can't read Brandi's expression. So he stumbles for words.

"Brandi this *is* why you drug us here today, is it not?" Carol looks at her daughter. "You want him over for lunch, don't you?" Carol turns to Ollie with a smile on her face. "You don't have plans, do you?" Ollie starts to shake his head but he still doesn't know if that's what Brandi wants him to do. She stands there, not saying a word or even nodding her head. At last, she looks at Ollie and smiles shyly. Ollie smiles in return. The jitters in his gut start dancing for joy.

"Ollie, who are these nice folks?" Mrs. Porter appears at the end of the pew. She starts to side step between the pews towards them. Mr. Porter and Buddy follow behind her.

Ollie shakes his head. He can't believe he'd almost forgotten them. "Mrs. Porter, this is Mr. and Mrs. Bollinger and this is Brandi."

"Oh, I know Brandi," Colleen smiles at the girl. Then she shakes Mr. Bollinger's hand. "William," he says. "And this is my wife, Caroline."

Mrs. Porter shakes her hand. "I'm Colleen. I'm Buddy's mother." Mr. Porter shakes hands next. Buddy follows. "Brandi is just a lovely girl," Colleen winks at Ollie.

"She's doing a real fine job with the boys." Mr. Porter nods his head.

"Thank you," William says.

"That's so nice of you to say," Carol says with her hand over her heart.

"Well," Colleen turns to Ollie. "What's your game plan, son?"

"I don't think he's riding back with us," Buddy says it loudly enough that only Ollie appears to hear him. The boys smile at each other.

"Well we just invited him to lunch with us if that is okay," Carol says to Colleen.

"That's perfectly fine with us. We're just the drivers," Colleen laughs. Carol giggles with her. The two of them look like they could be good friends in just a matter of minutes.

"If you don't mind, I think I'll join the Bollinger's for lunch today." Ollie doesn't want to hurt the Porter's feelings. He feels guilty he's had them drive him here only so he can abandon them for another family. He usually spends a good portion of Sunday afternoons with them.

"We don't mind one bit Phil Oliver." Colleen puts her arms around his waist and hugs him. As she pulls away she kisses him on the cheek. "We'll see you later." The three of them start to side step back out of the pew. Buddy waves at Ollie as he walks out.

Ollie calls after them. "Thank you. See you tomorrow!"

Mr. Bollinger claps his hands together. "Shall we then?" He makes his way out the aisle. Ollie follows behind Brandi. He watches her curls bob as she walks.

Mr. Bollinger opens the car door for Ollie. He stands, holding it until Ollie sits inside. "So Phil," Carol plops down in her seat.

"He likes to be called Ollie mom." Brandi says from the back seat.

"Oh, my apologizes." Carol clips her seat belt as William starts the car. "I hope you like fish."

The driveway to the Bollinger home is long. The house can't be seen from the road. The woods open up to the house eventually and a clearing lies behind it. Beyond the house is a gazebo then a lake. Further back is a small house on the other side. Ollie assumes that is her grandparents. He recognizes the small rose bushes he walked through the night Brandi brought him here. He had no idea he'd been this close to her house. It is one of the prettiest Ollie has ever seen. It is an old, two-story, white farm house. Smoke drifts from the brick chimney at the roof. A porch swing hangs on the front porch. Large oak trees in the front yard have lost their leaves. To the right of the house is a large white barn. A fence starts at its corner and heads over the hill. Beside it a red tractor sits.

"Welcome to Bollinger farms," Carol says. She lays a hand on Ollie's knee. Her smile is so inviting to him he already feels he's part of the family.

Ollie follows them up the brick sidewalk to the front porch steps. Christmas lights are stapled around the posts. William holds the front door open for them all. He nods his head at Ollie as he walks in. Inside, it smells like Brandi—a combination of fresh linen and gingerbread. In front of Ollie is a narrow staircase. To his right is a living room where a fireplace crackles. It continues on to an unseen mudroom and bathroom. To the left a dining room table has six chairs around it. Beyond that is a kitchen, separated by an island with bar stools. The smell of fish wafts from there.

"You can hang your coat here," Carol touches a set of hooks by the front door. "Brandi, why don't you show Ollie around? Dinner will be ready in a few minutes." Mrs. Bollinger disappears into the kitchen. Mr. Bollinger walks up the stairs.

Brandi still stands with her coat on. "Well," she shrugs her shoulders. "Do you want to see the farm first?"

Ollie follows her back out the front door. She looks funny to him still being in her Sunday best, walking toward a barn. She wears black stockings, black shoes, and a button up red velvet coat. The bottom of her blue dress sticks out underneath it. She turns around when she's close to the barn doors. She sees Ollie watching her. She waves her hand for him to catch up. Ollie smiles and jogs to her. Brandi climbs a ladder to the hayloft. She sits on a hay bale in the corner. Ollie sits beside her on another bale. In front of him kittens lay one on top of the other. Their mother curls around them, asleep. Brandi picks up the furriest one and puts it in her lap. Then she scoots closer to Ollie. "This

one is Edison," she whispers. "Don't tell my dad."
Together they laugh quietly so not to wake the babies.

Brandi shares with him a few stories about cats in her past. They laugh together when she tells him of her father's hated for felines and how she always snuck them into the house anyway. Once, she even had a cat birth a litter of kittens under her bed. They stroke the kittens for a minute more. "You have to meet Sampson," Brandi says.

Ollie smiles, "I agree. I have to. Who is he?"

Brandi pushes against him with her shoulder. She leads him out the barn to the back yard. "Sampson is probably the oldest dog you'll ever see."

"The Methuselah of dogs," Ollie jokes. Brandi doesn't get his Bible reference.

"Sampson, come on boy," she says to a pile of leaves. Ollie looks harder to see a hound dogs head sticking out from underneath. They brush the leaves off Sampson until Ollie can see the whole hound. He wags his tail in greeting but doesn't move anything else. Brandi pets his head, "I've had him since I was in fifth grade."

"That's amazing!" Ollie pets Sampson's side. Slowly the dog rolls over on Brandi so Ollie can rub his belly.

Brandi's mouth forms an O. "He must like you," she says. "He doesn't move for just anyone." Ollie laughs and scratches the hound's fur. Sampson's leg starts to kick, his mouth curls into a smile. Brandi shakes her head in amazement.

Mr. Bollinger yells from the back porch, "Time to eat!"

Mrs. Bollinger has the table set for four. There are two plates, two forks, a knife, a napkin, and a glass of ice at each place. In the center of the table a bowl of rice steams. Next to it is a plate full of fish filets. There's another bowl of broccoli, a basket of rolls and a pitcher of sweet tea. A small vase of flowers stands in the midst. The placemats have Santa and his reindeer riding across them.

Carol is still in her Sunday dress. She wears a yellow apron over top it. It is smudged and spotted with flour. She's tucked her hair back in a large clip out of her face. Ollie thinks the table setting is beautiful but Mrs. Bollinger looks amazing. He can see what Brandi will grow into. "Ollie, what would you like to drink?" she says to him. "Tea, water, milk, coca cola . . ." She holds the tea pitcher in her hands.

"Tea is fine, Mrs. Bollinger. Thank you."

"Carol, please." Ollie nods his head.

Mr. Bollinger walks in from behind Ollie. He takes his seat at the head of the table. He looks up at Ollie and pats a corner of the placemat to his right. Ollie takes his seat. Brandi sits next to him. Mrs. Bollinger pours tea into all the glasses. "What is this Caroline?" William pokes a filet with his fork in disgust. "Fish?" Mrs. Bollinger gives him a look that could kill. William meets her eye only for a second. He pulls his fork back to his plate. "Looks delicious!"

It sounds like Carol mumbles, '*That's right. You better say it looks delicious.*' But no one asks her to speak any clearer.

When she is seated William reaches for the basket of rolls. She slaps his hand. "Not before we say grace," Carol raises her eyebrows at him. Once again, Mr. Bollinger looks baffled.

He clears his throat. "*Right*. And you want *me* to say it I'm assuming?"

Mrs. Bollinger rolls her eyes at him but she turns to smile at Ollie in a way that says, *'Silly, forgetful husband.'*

William sighs then bows his head. He folds his hands in front of his chest. To Ollie he looks significantly smaller in this position. Brandi bows her head but she looks up at Ollie from the corner of her eye. "God, um, thank you for this food. It looks delicious," Mr. Bollinger looks at Carol from the corner of his eye. She looks like she's trying not to laugh. "And thanks for church this morning. Amen." He claps his hands when he's finished then reaches for the basket of rolls again. Carol doesn't stop him this time. The food begins to pass around.

"So Ollie, tells us about yourself. You're a senior this year, right?" Carol smiles up at him while she scoops broccoli onto her plate.

"Junior," Brandi answers for him.

"Any plans after you graduate?" Mr. Bollinger says as he hands him the plate of fish.

Brandi feels her chest tighten. She worries the next half an hour will be an interrogation.

"I want to go to college sir."

"College huh?" Mr. Bollinger only takes two heads of broccoli.

"Where to?" Carol says.

"Brandi stabs her broccoli extra hard to try to get her parents attention. Neither of them notice.

"I'd like to go to Trinity College."

"Trinity, I've heard of that," William says. Brandi doesn't know why her father is talking so loudly. Everything he says comes out in a booming voice.

"It's a Christian school, isn't it?" Carol asks.

"Yes ma'am." Ollie uses his fork and knife to cut apart his fish filet. Mr. Bollinger pokes his.

"What would you like to study?" Carol's voice is softer than usual, like she thinks Ollie is extra fragile. Or maybe she's trying to give her husband a hint.

"I'd like to study the Bible, ma'am. To be a pastor," Ollie takes his first bite of food. The fish tastes delicious to him. Mr. Bollinger coughs like he's choking when he takes his bite.

"*A pastor*," Carol says it like it is the sweetest thing she's ever heard. She smiles at Brandi who tries to shake her head at her mother without Ollie noticing. "That is a virtuous trade, Ollie." Carol blatantly ignores her daughter.

"Thank you," Ollie says. He crunches on his broccoli. He isn't a huge fan of the stuff but he can't recall the last time he had a green vegetable.

Mr. Bollinger cuts his broccoli into tiny pieces. "Talked to any college recruiters from there?" He mixes it in with his rice.

Ollie nods his head. "Yes sir. A Mr. Wackalliton said he thinks the school would like to have me. I just need to make it up there for try-outs."

"You have a car, don't you?" Mr. Bollinger doesn't look up from his plate as he cuts away at his fish. Brandi tries to stare a hole into her father's face to get his attention.

"No sir. I don't. But I'll find a way there."

William looks up from his plate, his fork has stopped. Carol looks at him with her eyes wide. She grits her teeth and waves her head toward Ollie.

"Well, Brandi has a car. I have a car. I'm sure we could get you there if it comes to that." William looks at his daughter for the first time. She's biting the inside of her cheeks.

"I appreciate that sir."

"But uh," William waves his fork in the air. Brandi can tell by the look on her father's face he's going to say something embarrassing again. She tries to stop him by waving her fork across her throat. "Are you working, saving up for a car?"

Brandi drops her head. Mrs. Bollinger kicks her husband under the table. He grunts and looks around the table in shock.

Ollie doesn't react at all. He takes a sip of his tea then says, "Yes sir. I've been working with Mr. Gibbs on his farm."

"Mr. Gibbs?" Carol says in a high pitch voice.

"I thought that old man was dead," William says. Brandi rests her forehead on her palm in shame.

Ollie laughs, "No sir. He's very much alive and temperamental as ever."

"Is that so?" Mr. Bollinger gut laughs. "The old man's a slave driver huh?"

Ollie laughs along with the rest of the table. "He certainly doesn't go easy on me that is for sure."

The table laughs some more. Brandi feels all her anxiety leaving her as she watches the smiles on her parent's faces. "You must stay pretty busy then with basketball and working," Carol says.

"Yes ma'am." Ollie swallows his food. "If I'm not playing ball or on the farm, I'm fixing something in the home. There's always something wrong there."

The table goes quiet. Brandi feels her heart drop to her stomach. The Bollinger's all look at each other while Ollie puts another fork full of rice in his mouth. Carol looks at her husband in desperation.

"Like what?" William wipes his mouth with his napkin.

"Oh, you know. The usual." Ollie looks around the table as if he's noticing the quiet for the first time. "The bathtub is always leaking. The sink gets stopped up. I'm trying to fix the kitchen chandelier." Ollie puts a piece of broccoli in his mouth.

Mrs. Bollinger looks at her husband with her eyes as slits. She grits her teeth. With her fork she points at her husband. Her eyes dart from Ollie back to Will. Mr. Bollinger gets the picture. "How about I come down and take a look at that tub," he says.

Ollie looks up in surprise. "Oh," he says. "That would be awful nice of you sir. Thank you."

Carol still looks at her husband with her bottom jaw tightened. "*And* the sink, and chandelier of course." Mr. Bollinger says it looking at his wife. When he's mentioned everything she smiles at him. William relaxes his tensed arms. He goes back to his rice.

"I'll make sure he gets to it real soon." Carol smiles. "How long have you lived there Ollie?"

Mr. Bollinger's fork clinks on his plate. Everyone looks at him. "Caroline," he says with pink cheeks. "Maybe Ollie doesn't want to talk about . . ."

Ollie interrupts. "No, it's alright. I've lived there since I was in the sixth grade."

Carol and Ollie smile at each other. "Before then, did you live nearby?" Mr. Bollinger eyes his wife while he bites into his roll. Brandi can't feel her heart beating.

"No," Ollie searches his memories. He can't place any names of the towns he used to live in. "I don't think so. I don't really remember."

Mrs. Bollinger knits her eyebrows. "Do you remember much about your life before . . . Masonville?" she decides upon the word. Mr. Bollinger puts the rest of the roll in his mouth so he can hardly breathe.

"Yeah, I mean I remember my parents and moving around and," Ollie's eyes glaze over.

"What happened to your parents?" Carol is too intrigued to stop asking questions.

"Mom," Brandi's face flushes. Mr. Bollinger starts to choke on the bread. He beats his fist off his sternum.

"I'm sorry," Carol takes her napkin from her lap and wipes her lips. "I didn't mean to ask you that."

"It's okay," Ollie says. He looks to Brandi for a second then back to Carol. "My parents died in a car crash."

"We're sorry to hear that Ollie." Mr. Bollinger is quick to say. His mutilated roll is in his napkin on his lap. He looks to his wife. "We didn't mean to bring this up at dinner."

"I'm so sorry," Carol waves her hands in the air. "I didn't mean to get into that. So now, what other stuff do you like to do Ollie?"

Ollie waves his head around trying to roll a thought into his mind. "I play a little piano every now and then."

Brandi leans back in shock, "Really? I didn't know that."

"That is really something Ollie," Candi wears a proud smile. "Where did you learn to play?"

"Oh, the home gets a state stipend for kids to take music lessons."

Mrs. Bollinger leans back in her chair. "That is so neat. So all of the kids get an opportunity to play an instrument?"

"No, no," Ollie shakes his head, "only the ones who are there a long time. It makes them more sell-able." He shrugs, "And gives us something to do." Ollie looks around the table. The Bollinger's hold their forks in midair. They don't move or speak. None of them know what to say. Ollie begins to feel slightly uncomfortable. He regrets mentioning the piano lessons. Mr. Bollinger finally leans forward over his plate. He clears his throat then reaches for another roll. "Did you learn how to play ball from your dad?"

The pressure in Ollie's chest breaks apart. He takes a sigh of relief. He's suddenly very grateful for the man. "Yes sir," Ollie smiles. The table fills with light conversation again. Ollie and William lose themselves in the topic of basketball. They discuss every game of this season. They go over plays and Coach Jackson's style. After thirty minutes of ball talk Brandi and her mom slip away unnoticed. While they wash the dishes Ollie and William don't move from their spots at the table.

Brandi looks over her shoulder at the two of them. She watches her father push at Ollie's shoulder then bend his neck backward in laughter. "He is really something," Brandi hears her mother say. Carol looks over her shoulder at the two of them as well. She shakes her head, grinning. "You got a good one Brandi." Brandi holds a plate in her hand, a drying towel in the other. She nods her head.

At a quarter after three Brandi and Carol walk back into the dining room. Mrs. Bollinger puts her hands on her husband's shoulders. "William," she shakes her husband. "I think Ollie's ears are about to fall off." Ollie laughs. Mr. Bollinger shakes his head. "Ollie, you are welcome here anytime," Carol says.

Brandi's heart feels like it is a hot air balloon that has just been ignited and is starting to float around her chest. She beams at her father. Ollie nods his head. "Thank you."

They all stand. Carol moves around the table to Ollie. She wraps her arms around his neck so he has to bend down to embrace her. "It has been so nice meeting you Phil Oliver." She pats his back a few times before letting go.

"Nice to meet you," Ollie laughs a little.

"We need to take him home, don't we?" William looks down at his wife.

Carol pulls him to the stairwell. "We're letting Brandi take him home." She hopes Ollie doesn't hear. But Ollie can hear Mr. Bollinger still questioning as they walk up the stairs. "Why can't we go with her?"

Brandi and Ollie stand in the same spots around the table. They smile at each other until they hear no more from her parents. She drums her fingers on the back of a chair and sighs, "Ready to go?" Ollie knows he could stay in this warm house for a lifetime. But he retrieves his coat and follows Brandi outside to her car.

———————

Ollie stands in the middle of a dying field. The brown grass tickles his ankles. One shoe lace is untied. He bends down to tie it. When his hands reach for the string he sees they are bleeding. He stops. He turns his hands over then back again. There are tiny pieces of glass stuck in his skin. He forgets about his shoe and slowly stands. His heart starts to sound in his ears, a loud, audible thump. He looks down at his long legs in his blue jeans. They are ripped. Dark spots outline the rips, telling him he must be bleeding there. His eyes move up to his shirt. His white t-shirt has gashes in it as well. It turns pink in multiple places before his eyes. But he notices he's well-built. He's not small. He's 17 years old. He looks at the burning car in front of him. He wonders why he's seventeen when he should be eleven. His heart beats faster.

A woman runs by him to the car. This time the woman looks different. It is Mrs. Bollinger. She stoops by the car, just the same as the other woman had. She looks up inside. She screams toward the high way behind Ollie, "Help! They're still in there! Someone help!" She sees Ollie then. He wants to puke. She looks right into his eyes. Ollie looks back at her in wonder. Something in her eyes tells Ollie she knows who he is. Then the engine on the car bursts. The loud noise knocks Carol back onto her butt. The look on her face is replaced with horror. She scoots away from the burning mass.

Ollie wants to move. He wants to run to her, to rescue her, to save her. But he can't move. He's never been able to move in his dream. He tries to yell but when he opens his mouth nothing comes out. He's never talked in his dream before. Ollie is so confused his heart beats faster.

Mrs. Bollinger gets up. She looks into Ollie's eyes again. This time she looks at him like she's afraid. Behind him, Ollie can hear cars squealing their tires as they brake by the road. He fears one will veer off the road and hit him without seeing it. But he knows he can't move. He just watches Carol.

She moves in slow motion toward him even though she's sprinting. Her beautiful face is covered in black. It is moist with sweat from the heat of the fire. When she's only feet from him, she moves in real time. She was sprinting so fast she skids as she tries to stop by Ollie's side.

"Ollie," she says breathlessly. "Ollie, were you in that car?"

Ollie blinks then he stands facing an ambulance. He's about ten feet away. Mrs. Bollinger stands beside him. Red and blue lights flash in her eyes like they are pools.

Brandi appears. She holds open the ambulance door. She looks right into his eyes but Ollie doesn't think she knows who he is. He crosses his eyebrows wondering why she doesn't recognize him. He wonders if his face is mutilated. His urge to puke grows. He moves his bleeding hand toward his face. Everything moves in slow motion. There is no noise. Mrs. Bollinger grabs his fingers before they reach his cheek. She steps toward the ambulance. Ollie follows her.

Brandi doesn't change her face. She looks at everything as if it is ordinary. There is no life in her eyes. She is calm. Ollie doesn't look at anything else but her face. He doesn't hear his heart beat anymore. He looks down at his chest. The pink spots in his shirt have turned to red. The largest area of blood is on his gut by his hip. He touches it. It feels like a hole is in his skin. Ollie begins to panic. He looks up as an emergency responder appears at his other side. He doesn't look at Ollie. He looks beyond him at Mrs. Bollinger. His eyes are asking her a question. Ollie looks to her. Carol slowly nods her head yes. Her face is blank too. Ollie looks back to the responder. It is the same man who has always been in Ollie's dream. But this time he is robotic. He doesn't sweat, or look at Ollie like he is a miracle child. He doesn't run or mess with any equipment.

Ollie kicks in his bed. He doesn't understand why everyone is acting like zombies. He wants it to move in real time. He slams his fists off his mattress in anger. He wants them all to move. He wants Brandi to know who he is. He tosses to and fro. He grits his teeth and moans. He wants to yell but he knows his dream won't let him be heard.

The medic holds his arm out. He is motioning for Ollie to get in the ambulance. Ollie turns to Mrs. Bollinger for help. He doesn't want to go inside the ambulance. She looks at him with a blank face. She then moves her arm in the same fashion. Ollie looks to Brandi who still stands with the door in her hand. She looks him in the eyes as her arm lifts then her finger points toward the inside of the ambulance.

"No," Ollie says to her. But she doesn't move. He looks in the ambulance. The stretcher turns into a coffin—a black, silky looking coffin. Inside another medic starts to open it, his eyes on Ollie, his face emotionless.

"No! NO! NO!" Ollie's voice breaks through. He can hear himself in his dream. He sounds so loud. The medics, Mrs. Bollinger and Brandi all start to back away from him in fear.

Then weights appear on his wrists. He tries to move his arms but he can't. He continues to scream, "NO!" He jerks his body but it isn't moving. His face feels cold and wet.

"Ollie! Ollie!" someone yells.

He stops yelling. He stops trying to move so he can hear who it is. No one in his dream appears to have spoken.

"Ollie, wake up," someone says.

Ollie freezes. Brandi and the ambulance start to fade away. He blinks again. It is white. He looks closely at it all. Everything is white.

"I think he's okay now boys." Ollie turns to the voice by his ear. Miss Stephen holds a damp wash cloth on his forehead. She looks at him with pity. Ollie looks down at Ben and Ezra. Each boy is holding onto his wrist. They're pushing his arms down with all their weight. Their eyes are wide. They look at Ollie like they're afraid. Slowly, they ease up on his wrists. They sit back on their haunches. Behind them all the kids in the home stand. They all have their mouths hanging open. Little Kirsten is crying. Jessica holds onto her from behind. Ryan is sucking his thumb. A tear runs down his cheek. Suzan holds baby George.

Ollie looks up. He sees the white ceiling. The lights are on. He bends forward until he's sitting up. Ben and Ezra scoot away from him. "Are you alright Philip?" Miss Stephen removes her wash cloth. Ollie doesn't know what to say. He looks around the room at all the children. Their faces start to change from fear to sadness. "You were having a bad dream," Miss Stephen says. She pats his hand. "You all go back to bed now. Ollie is fine. He was just having a bad dream." Miss Stephen waves her wash cloth in the air at the kids. The girls peel their eyes off Ollie and start to disappear through the door. Ollie sits in the middle of the boy's bedroom. He doesn't know how he managed to get on the floor from his bunk bed. The boys still stand looking at him. "Go on now," Miss Stephen says to them. Ben and Ezra slowly get to their feet. One by one they all slide into their beds. Ollie looks at the floor. Miss Stephen pats him on the back. "You too," she says. Ollie looks at her weary face. Her eyes have compassion. "Go on to bed. I'll make sure nothin' happens to ya." Together, Ollie and Miss Stephen stand. She watches him climb the ladder then lay on his sheets. She flicks off the bedroom light and is gone.

Ollie lies on his back looking at the ceiling. He feels it welling up inside him. He tries to close his eyes tight enough that it can't come out. He tries to hold his breath. But eventually he sobs. He holds his hands over his eyes but the tears run out so quickly they fill his ears before they soak his pillow. He feels the mattress around his feet move. Then little hands hold his arms. A head lays on his chest then another. When he opens his eyes Ben and Ezra are on his chest. Ryan and Matthew hold his stomach. Jason and T.K wrap their arms around his legs. They all pat him with their little hands. Then they all fall asleep.

Chapter Nine

Willing and Waiting

Miss Stephen stands in the doorway looking at the bunch of boys piled on the top bunk across the room. She debates if she should wake them. Perhaps she'll let them stay home from school today. She's certain none of them got the rest they should. Still, she can't imagine what the schools would say if none of her children showed up. They'd probably accuse her house of having bed bugs or lice. She flicks on the light switch. "Time for school," she says. "Up and at em'."

Ollie is the first to open his eyes. He lifts his head as far as he can. He sees a puddle of drool on his chest coming from Ezra's mouth. He can't get upset though. One by one the boys start to move. They yawn and stretch and finally climb down the ladder. Ollie's arms and legs are asleep so he leans forward and shakes his torso until the needle-feeling passes through his body.

None of the boys say anything to Ollie about the nightmare. Some of them question if it wasn't a dream of their own. It is the girls who bring it to Ollie's attention. "What were you dreaming about?" Suzan asks.

"You know we all had to wrestle you down to the ground last night so you wouldn't fall out of the bunk?" Jessica says.

Little Kirsten's eyes are swollen from how she couldn't stop crying through the night. Miss Stephen says it was because she was so worried. Ollie can't help but think it is because he scared her to death.

Buddy's car horn sounds louder than normal this morning. As Ollie moves to the door Miss Stephen steps in front of him. She puts her hand under his chin, her thumb under his bottom lip. She pulls his face down until his eyes meet hers. She doesn't have a lick of make-up on today. She looks much older than normal. Guilt grips Ollie's stomach for putting the woman through all he has. Her eyes tell him she's not sorry though. She shakes her head at him. Clicks her tongue twice then hugs his body. Ollie has never felt Miss Stephen was like a mother figure. But in this moment he rests his head on her stiff hair and is in no more need for love.

"You look like crap," Buddy says as Ollie shuts the car door. He doesn't have the energy to rebuttal. He just smiles and nods his head. Buddy asks him about Sunday with Brandi. Ollie tries to be as energetic as possible.

When they arrive at school Corky is too much for Ollie. He can't muster the energy to react when his friend slaps his rear or tries to jump on his back. It takes all he can offer to just get through classes without slumping into his chair.

After the final bell, Ollie walks into the gymnasium. Brandi waves at him, standing on her tip toes, grinning from ear to ear. Ollie feels his heart lighten at the sight of her. To his left he catches a glimpse of a dark object high in the stands. It is the black suit of Mr. Ramirez. He holds a clip board and pen. He looks from the ceiling to his paper over and over again. Ollie climbs the bleacher stairs to him. "Mr. Ramirez, what are you doing here?"

The man looks at Ollie over top his spectacles that at the bottom of his nose. He pulls them off his face, "Ah, Phil Oliver," he says. "How are you?"

Ollie reaches the man and shakes his hand. "I'm fine sir. How are you?"

"Ah," Mr. Ramirez puts his glasses back on the end of his nose. He looks over his paper. "I'm well, I'm well." Ollie looks toward the spot in the ceiling Mr. Ramirez keeps turning to. It is the main set of lights in the center of the gym. They are simple florescent bulbs. "I'm getting started on my project Sandra promised you," he smiles at Ollie.

Coach Jackson walks to the bottom of the bleachers and yells up, "Ollie, what are you doing? Leave the man to his work. Come on now." He waves his hand for him to come down.

Ollie nods at Mr. Ramirez. "Good to see you." He starts to walk away. "And thank you."

"Don't thank me yet," Mr. Ramirez calls after him. "Not until you see what I do with this *disaster* of a gymnasium." Ollie smiles one more time at him while Coach Jackson makes his way up the bleachers in his turn.

For the first time all season, Ollie doesn't ask Brandi if she wants to go out with him. He doesn't have to reach out to her at all. When he rests on the bleacher, she sits beside him. When practice is over, she offers to take him home.

There's a glow in her eyes Ollie has never seen before. Her smile and her stride are wider. As he takes her presence in, he filters out the bad—the vision of her blank face from his dream, the bloody t-shirt, the nausea; he lets it drain from his body to make room for Brandi's joy.

When Ollie gets home it is time for supper. Miss Stephen has the food ready on the stove. Ollie scoops peas and noodles onto the smaller children's plates as they pass through the kitchen toward the table. Jessica pours the drinks. Suzan hands out the silverware. Miss Stephen places a piece of fried chicken on each plate while she bobs baby George on her hip.

"Baby George and I had some visitors today while you was at school," she says to Ollie.

He looks up at her in surprise. "Oh yeah?"

"Yes we did—*Bollinger's Hardware* store. The owner himself, William Bollinger was here."

Ryan nudges Ollie to serve him more noodles. Ollie unfreezes. "He was? Did he say why?"

"He was measuring stuff. He wrote down a bunch of things. It was all jibber to me. But he says he's coming back tomorrow with the stuff he needs to fix some things." Miss Stephen nods her head, her lips pursed out.

"Well, that's really nice." Ollie says.

"Yes it is. Curious how he knew the sink and tub needed fixin'." She doesn't look at Ollie but she knows it had to have been him who had made it possible. Ollie doesn't answer. He smiles at the thought of Mr. Bollinger getting to the home so quickly. Carol must not have let him forget it.

On Tuesday the gymnasium looks like a construction site. Mr. Ramirez walks around with his clip board and pen. He points and things either appear or vanish. Men follow him around like minions.

Practice becomes a game of trying to keep the ball out of taped-off areas. Large boxes sit in corners of the gym. Coach tells the boys they aren't allowed to disturb the workers, especially the one in the suit. So Ollie only waves at Mr. Ramirez.

When Brandi pulls up to the orphanage after practice, two of her father's company trucks are parked on the street. She follows Ollie up the porch steps. When they open the door they hear noises unfamiliar to the home. Drills screw. Saws cut. Men yell from one room to the next. All the kids are out of sight. They're forced to stay in their bedrooms until the workers leave.

A man in a *Bollinger's Hardware* baseball cap stands on a dining table chair. He uses a drill around the base of the chandelier hanging above the table. Wires and light bulbs sit on the table. In the bathroom a man puts the finishing touch of caulk around the tub. Another man finishes sawing through his last piece of plywood. His partner takes it from him, fixes it into the floor and begins to hammer it down.

Miss Stephen stands at the stove, cooking. She looks over her shoulder at Ollie and Brandi when they walk in. She tries to yell at them over all the noise but they can't hear her.

Brandi moves to the sound of her father's voice. Mr. Bollinger lies on his back, his head and shoulders are in the cabinet under the kitchen sink. Miss Stephen stands a few feet away shaking her head at the man. He yells for a screwdriver, his hand groping the floor around him. Ollie squats by him, putting the tool in his hand. "Thank you!" he yells. Ollie and Brandi smile at each other. After a minute William shimmies out of the cabinet. When he sits up a quick look of shock crosses his face. "When did you two get here?"

Brandi laughs at her father's hair, all disheveled and covered in dust. "Just now," she says.

William looks at his watch. "I didn't realize it was that time already." He grunts as he stands to his feet.

"Mr. Bollinger," Ollie says. "Thank you so much."

"Oh, don't mention it," William slaps his hands across his pants. He looks to Miss Stephen behind him. "Should have done this a long time ago."

"There's always more to be done." Miss Stephen stirs something in a large pot. "But you boys have done enough today." She points her spoon at William. "You got to eat now. Get your crew to the table. It's supper time."

William holds his hands up in protest. "Oh now we couldn't possibly," he shakes his pink face.

"Mr. Bollinger," Miss Stephen leaves her spoon in the pot. "You know I can't pay you. So you're not going to argue with me concerning dinner." Mr. Bollinger looks at the woman with a combination of fright and pity.

"What ya cooking?" the man standing on the kitchen chair yells.

Miss Stephen smiles, "I got some chicken noodle soup. And plenty of it."

"I'm in," the young man says.

Mr. Bollinger takes a deep breath. He sighs as he shoves his gloves into his back pocket. "Ollie, go get the kids and other men," Miss Stephen says.

The New Year brings a new kind of slothfulness to the team. Still caught in winter break, most of the team jogs heavy with Christmas feasts. Coach makes them run extra laps. He blows his whistle three short times. "YOU ALL ARE DISGRACEFUL!" Coach slaps his clipboard off his thigh. "You expect to entertain an audience tonight WITH THIS KIND OF MOVEMENT?" He looks everyone in the face. His gut sticks out further over his pants. If anyone gained any weight, it was the coach. "Now I don't know what all this *Speaker City* has done to our gymnasium," he holds his clipboard above his head. Everyone looks around the ceiling. No one sees anything. "But I *guarantee* it isn't going to distract the crowd FROM YOUR AWFUL PLAYING. You've got to LIVEN UP! Put on a show! The people come to see you. OLLIE," Coach points at him with his clipboard, "more dunking. CORKY! Get to your sweet spot no matter what you got to do. I don't care if you skip, flip flop, and bee bop there." The team giggles. People start to trickle into the gym. Coach looks around. "Alright, head to the locker room. Get ready." He looks at his watch, "GAME TIME in thirty minutes." The boys start to walk away. Coach hollers after Brandi. "Wrap the starter's ankles!"

As the boys sit in the locker room, Brandi wrapping Ollie's ankles first, they start to hear music. Slowly, heads come up. They look around curiously.

"Where is that coming from?" Buddy asks.

"You hear it too?" Percy replies.

Miles stands on the bench, his ear to a vent. "I think it's coming from the gym."

 As the boys quiet down the music grows louder. The bass makes their hearts thump. The words aren't yet audible, the tune hardly noticeable, but the boys start to move. They shuffle their feet and ring their hips. Corky hoots and hollers. He runs around the lockers snapping his jersey shirt at the boy's butts. The room fills with noise again.

When Coach Jackson enters he has to whistle to quiet them back down. "Brandi did you get them boy's ankles wrapped?"She nods her head. Coach looks about the room. "There's a lot going on out there tonight, SO KEEP FOCUSED. No distractions."

"What's going on out there Coach?" Miles asks.

Coach ignores him. He waves his hand at Ollie who knows what to do. He takes a knee. Buddy follows suit. He leads the team in prayer: "Dear God, thank you for this day. Thank you for this team. Thank you for basketball. Thank you for all that you give and all that you take away. Please help us get this victory tonight and to make you smile. Amen.

"Huddle up!" Coach yells.

The boys lay their hands together in one pile. Ollie counts off, "One, two, three . . ."

The team yells together, "MUSTANGS!"

As soon as the boys exit the locker room the music takes new volume. It thumps in their ears so they can no longer hear their heartbeat or their shoes squeaking off the waxed floor. The crowd cheers. Their mouths are open screaming as loud as they can. Still, their volume cannot compete with the music. Every word, every note, of the song is heard.

The only voice to top it is that of Jeff Wallace. "Here they are: the Masonville Mustangs!" The boys run in, clapping at hands as they go by. "This has been the hottest basketball season in Masonville history. I'll even venture to say we have division one players in the making here." Jeff Wallace sits in a concrete box on the second floor of the bleachers. His fiberglass window looks out over the court.

A hush falls over the crowd as Roxanne makes her way to the center of the court where a microphone waits for her. Corky nudges everyone around him to look at his thespian beauty. Then, a spotlight shines down from over her head.

Everyone looks up in amazement at the ceiling. The cluster that used to be florescent lights is now a jumble of large, moving lights. The center one is the largest. It beams down, making a halo around Roxanne. The crowd goes completely silent. Music starts to play. Jeff Wallace asks everyone to stand, for the gentlemen to remove their hats. Roxanne begins to sing the National Anthem. *"O say can you see?"* Corky wears the proudest smile of his life. When Roxanne bows her head the gymnasium erupts with applause, cat calls, and whistles.

Mr. Ramirez appears behind Buddy. He taps on his shoulder then points his finger at the other four boys. Buddy waves his hand at them to come over. The five of them circle around the man in his black suit. "When your name is called, do something." He looks at the boys in their eyes. None of them seem to understand. "Like a signature." He looks around the gymnasium. He nods his head once and winks before turning away. The five of them stand looking at each other.

Lights, the colors of red, blue, green and yellow, start to swirl from their mount above. The colors dance on the gym floor in round balls. Music starts to play. Jeff Wallace bellows through it, "And now, for your Mustang starting lineup!"

The players look back and forth to each other. All of them have their eyes wide open, asking each other without saying a word, *"Can you believe this?"*

The center spotlight stops on Percy. He turns back around to face the court. Jeff Wallace announces, "For your power forward, the Coach's very own son, and the Mustang's speed, we have number 31, Percy Jackson—*the Stallion*!" Upon hearing his name, Percy knows exactly what to do. He puts his arms in front of him like he's holding reins, and he gallops forward. He makes a full circle in the court before stopping.

The team busts into laughter. "The *stallion*?" one says.

"Who thought of that dumb name?" says another.

"He looks ridiculous," Miles says.

The spotlight moves from Percy to Miles. He quickly shuts his mouth. "For your other starting forward," Jeff says, "notorious for his intense guarding, number four, Miles Jackson—*the Aggrivator*!" Miles jogs to center court. When he gets there he treads in place, pumping his arms like he's boxing. The crowd applauds. The team laughs.

Jeff Wallace is so meticulous with each word it can only be assumed he's reading from a script. Ollie spots Mr. Ramirez in the stands. He wears Sandra on his arm like a handbag. He nods his head as he looks at the box in the stands. Ollie figures Mr. Ramirez must be the author of the script tonight. Coach Jackson would have agreed to anything he asked for having done all these lights and sound system.

The spotlight hovers over Buddy. "For you center: the unmoving, unshakable, number 12, Buddy Porter—BUH . . . BUH . . . BUDDY THE BOULDER!"

Buddy runs onto the court. He stops at Percy and whispers something into his ear. The crowd watches in anticipation and wonder. Percy nods his head and says something to Miles beside him. Buddy moves a few yards back from them. Then he runs forward toward Percy. Both boys cross their hands in front of their chest. Buddy bumps Percy's chest so he stumbles backward into Miles. Both boys fall to the floor. Buddy raises his arms and flexes. The crowd roars with laughter.

The boys get to their feet as the spotlight settles on Corky. The bright light makes his highlights look florescent. He points his fingers at the crowd like he's shooting guns. Ollie shakes his head at his friend. He's always thought Corky should perform in the high school theater group with his girlfriend. He'd love being center stage and the crowd always eats him up.

"For your shooting guard, all the way from the Windy City, we give you number eight. Put Corky Hammons in his sweet spot and he's sure to swish a three every time. So it's no wonder why we call him *CASH MONEY*!"

Corky runs to left side of the court. He stops at his sweet spot on the three point line and fakes throwing a ball up. "Swish!" Jeff Wallace shouts. The crowd jumps up and down in the bleachers. Ollie feels the gym floor vibrating under his feet.

The spotlight makes his face feel it is in direct view of the burning sun. He puts his hand up across his forehead to shield his eyes. Jeff Wallace pushes some buttons so a thumping beat starts to play. The crowd starts to clap with it. Ollie's heart thumps to the rhythm. "And now, for your captain, and point guard. You've seen him break the Masonville record for shots made in one game," the crowd claps even harder. "You've seen him fly through the air to *slam dunk* the ball." The stadium screams. "You know him as Phil Oliver, number thirteen, but we know him as our FLIGHT COMMANDER!"

Ollie looks around the gymnasium. Everyone is on their feet. Brandi claps and smiles at him. Coach Jackson waves his clipboard at him to get moving. Ollie doesn't know what to do, but when he turns to see the other four starters on the court he is shown what to do. All four boys have their arms spread open, straight from their shoulders to their fingertips. They move in circles like they are planes. Ollie looks around the gym once more. The crowd starts to join in. They hold their arms up, moving as much as they can, like they are aircraft.

Ollie follows suit. He stretches his long arms out, opening up his chest. He runs around the court in this position. He runs so fast he feels he may actually take flight. The crowd reaches out their hands to him. He runs closer to the bleachers, letting their hands slap against his.

Brandi has to hold her breath she's so overcome with excitement. She feels her eyes begin to water with a gust of pride. She moves her hands in front of her face to clap so no one can see her emotion. She turns to find her parents in the stands. She has to know if they are as proud of him as she is in this moment. She finds them in the highest bleacher of the first stand. They are clapping and screaming so intensely Brandi can see the veins bulging in her mother's forehead and in her father's neck.

The screaming doesn't stop the whole game. The gym floor doesn't quit vibrating. The music never ceases it's thumping. Jeff Wallace gives a play by play that can actually be heard without static or breaking voices. No one misses a shot. The only points made by the opposing team are their free throws. They get plenty of those given Miles is determined to live up to his name—the Aggrivator. He fouls out before the first half is done. It seems everyone is trying to fit their new nick name. Percy runs extra fast. He also sweats so much the team jokes saying his name should be changed to "the slippery stallion." Buddy doesn't worry with running to the other side of the court most of the time. He focuses on hardening his chest so his picks and blocks are brick solid. Corky dances his way down the court when he swishes his three point shots. Ollie feels longer, like his arms are really wings and his legs are weightless. They feel famous. They feel timeless. And the scoreboard reassures them they are. 100 points: Mustangs; 12 points: the losers.

The school newspaper and Masonville Township Tribune interview Ollie on the same day. A tall, thin boy called "Muskrat" Wilson stops Ollie in the hallway. His high-waters look like they're squeezing the life out of any testacies that he may have. Following suit, his voice is high pitched. He walks toward Ollie like he's incredibly uncomfortable, with his legs wide apart yet still on the tip of his toes. He pushes his thin rimmed, square glasses up his nose. He holds his pencil in front of him like it is his

23

compass. He walks straight up to Ollie at his locker so the tip of his pencil almost guts him. Ollie is taken aback by his close proximity.

Muskrat Wilson looks around for any bullies, then without looking Ollie in the eye, asks, "Can I get an interview with you for the Mustang Time?"

Corky slaps Ollie in the butt as he walks by. He stops when he notices the Muskrat. He raises one blonde eyebrow. Muskrat hides his head between his shoulders like a turtle sinking into its shell. Corky looks to Ollie who nods his head. He grabs Roxanne's hand and continues down the hall, everyone parting for him as he goes.

"Sure Wilson," Ollie says. "I'd love to."

Muskrat doesn't look up. His eyes look around for any threats. He nods his head once. "I'll find you during your study block." He turns with his pencil and darts down the hall, bumping shoulders with everyone as he scurries.

In his last class the principal comes on the intercom. "Phil Oliver, Corky Hammons and Buddy Porter, please report to the main office. Ollie, Buddy and Corky to the main office," he repeats. A loud clink sounds after.

Ten minutes before school is out Ollie shakes hands with Michael Deaton, the sports-columnist for the newspaper. They sit in the principal's office. Mr. Deaton brags on all their accomplishments. Before he asks a single question the final bell rings.

"It's alright. We're going straight to practice anyway," Corky says. And so the raving continues until he finally says, "And to top it all off you're an orphan." He points his pencil at Ollie. "Tell me about your journey, Ollie." The tip of the pencil is poised at the paper.

The next day the school newspaper has Ollie's school picture in the corner. Beside it a headline reads: *Ollie leads the Pack*. A larger picture of the whole team takes up the bottom half of the page. Wilson describes Ollie's successful season as captain and record-breaker. Ollie recognizes all the basketball lingo is worded exactly as Ollie described. He'd spent most of the interview explaining the game to the Muskrat. His pencil swirled about the paper like a tornado.

Everyone that has the courage to slaps Ollie on the back as they hold up a newspaper in the other hand. Some simply hold it up and nod at him smiling. Each of his teachers mention it. Josh Acosta crumples it in his large hand. He drops it on the hall floor and kicks it out of his way.

The next day is the same. The *Masonville Tribune* publishes Michael Deaton's article. Ollie takes the time to read it in his study block. His teacher placed it on the corner of his desk. "You should read this," she said.

A Mustang Miracle is the heading. A tiny picture of Michael Deaton is beside it. Down the length of the newspaper a picture of Ollie's long body flies in the air. The tips of his fingers touch the basketball rim. The basketball is falling through the hoop. Underneath, Buddy stands like an Indian chief, his arms crossed and his face stern. A Georgetown Gofer is bouncing off him.

The article talks about the Mustang's successful year. It mentions the renovations and how it has brought in a larger audience. It proposes an addition will need to be made to occupy the growing fan base. Corky and Buddy's lives are abbreviated. Their dreams for the sport and hopes for the season are packed in a few paragraphs. All three boys are termed "division one worthy athletes."

The article continues on 7B. Ollie flips to it. A picture of Ollie sitting on the shoulders of Corky and Buddy is blown up. The rest of the team is in the background. Michael writes about the picture: *Saddled upon the backs of his teammates, Philip Oliver leads the way to victory.* The article goes on. Ollie's journey is there in three long columns. Mr. Deaton makes it sound like a rags to riches story—*the orphan gone super star. "The Flight Commander has taken off!"*

Ollie folds the paper up and puts it in his teacher's hands as he heads out the door. He feels her sympathetic stare. He's never read about his parent's death before, or saw in numbers his long years in the orphanage. He's never read about himself as a child who has never been claimed. It didn't make him feel any better to read, *"If only potential parents would have known what Phil Oliver would become today."* He wishes he hadn't told Mr. Deaton the whole "sob story" of his life. He doesn't want others to look at him as though he's publicizing for pity.

"Shake it off man," Buddy pats Ollie on the back.

"Yeah," Corky says. "No one reads the paper anyway."

Coach Jackson waves the *Masonville Tribute* above his head. Ollie sees him as he walks down the hall to the gymnasium. "That's my boy," Coach squeezes Ollie's neck between his elbow. "You're making us famous!"

Brandi walks through the front of her house. Pans bang together in the kitchen. Her mother is putting away dishes. The smell of fried chicken comes from the stove. William Bollinger sits in his arm chair. The newspaper is spread wide to 7B. It covers his upper torso. He lowers a corner when the bottom step of the stair squeaks.

"Brandi," he catches her. He waves his corner of the paper so she comes to him. "Have you read this?" he asks. Brandi glances at the cover of the *Tribute* as she goes to the couch. "It's about your boyfriend," her dad says.

Brandi sits on the couch with a huff. "He's not my boyfriend dad."

"Shame," she hears him say under his breath. His eyes have gone back to the paper. "I'm almost done here then you can have it." He glances over a bended corner of his paper again. "You can scrapbook it." He grins. Brandi huffs again and pushes herself up from the couch. "No, no, no," Mr. Bollinger says. "I'm done," he hands her the paper.

Mrs. Bollinger calls for the two of them to come eat dinner when she's a column from being done. She hollers back,

"Just a minute!" When she walks into the kitchen her heart is still wrestling with the article.

"Brandi, did you see the *Tribute*? There's a long article about your beau." Mrs. Bollinger says as she sets the last dish on the table.

"He's not *hers*," William says to her. "Supposedly," he smiles at Brandi.

"That boy," Carol says as she sits down, "he's going places. He is a big deal."

"He *might* be going places," William says partly under his breath.

"Excuse me?" Carol unfolds her napkin in her lap.

William looks up in surprise. He was so distracted by the food he hadn't realized he'd said anything out loud.

"You read the paper," Carol continues. "He said he wants to go Trinity College. Wouldn't you call that going places?"

"How do you suppose he gets there Caroline? I did read the article. Didn't you? That boy don't have two nickels to rub together." William holds a fork in one hand, a knife in the other.

Carol drops her little bottom jaw. "Well I seem to know someone who has plenty of nickels."

William looks at his wife with his eyes slowly widening at the idea of what she's suggesting. She puts one hand on her hip. The two of them look at each other for a long moment. Brandi watches, amused at how her large father can look so frightened by her tiny mother. Finally William lays down his silverware. "Well, what do you want me to do about it?"

Carol removes her hand from her hip. She relaxes back into her chair. "You're going to take him, of course."

Brandi is as curious as her father is now. "Take him where?" she says before William can.

"To Trinity. For his college visit and try-out." Brandi and William look at each other with their hungry bellies swirling with questions. "We'll go too, of course." Carol scoops a pile of beans onto her plate. William and Brandi sit looking at her. "Well, go call him," she waves her fork at her husband.

William slumps in his chair. "What? Caroline . . ." he starts to protest.

"No buts," Mrs. Bollinger looks up at last to her husband's face. "William," she says. "You've said it yourself—basketball is that boy's only chance." Brandi feels her throat tighten. "If we don't give him this opportunity, he'll never get it. You're going to call him and we're all going to visit Trinity College."

William and Brandi look at each other once more. Carol nods her head, pleased with herself. She grabs herself a biscuit. William nods his head. "Alright," he says. He reaches for a biscuit.

His wife slaps at his hand. "Call first."

Mr. Bollinger groans like a little kid who has been reminded to wash their hands before they eat. "Caroline, right now? Can't I eat first?"

"No," Carol sucks her lips together. "You'll forget. Now hurry before your food gets cold."

Brandi laughs at her father who slaps his thick hands on his thighs as he pushes away from the table. Carol and her daughter smile at each other as if Brandi was in on this plan.

———————————

Ollie is surprised to get a phone call from someone other than Mr. Gibbs. Miss Stephen waves the phone at him as she bobs baby George on her hip. "It's the handy man," she says.

Ollie is shocked to hear Mr. Bollinger's voice. He talks quickly, "Hey Ollie. Read about you in the paper today. Me and the Mrs. have been talking and we want to take you to Trinity for your college visit. How's that sound?" Ollie is too stunned to speak. "Ollie, I'm kind of in a hurry son. Caroline is withholding my dinner until I get an answer." William partly chuckles.

Ollie's heart lightens at the image of Carol slapping away her husband's hands at the table. "I would appreciate that sir. I just . . . You don't have to do that."

"Nonsense," William is quick to reply. "We want to. You still have that paper with the open try-out days you got from the recruiter?"

Excitement beyond belief floods Ollie's body. "Yes sir, I do."

"Good," William says. "You give me dates and we'll get up there."

"Thank you sir."

"Sure, Ollie. Talk to you later."

"Bye Mr. Bollinger."

The next day Ollie gives Brandi his sheet from Mr. Wackalliton with the dates for open try-outs on it. Brandi smiles when she looks down at it. "Did you have anything to do with this?" Ollie asks her.

Brandi looks up at him and scoffs. "Are you kidding? You think I want to ride in a car with you all the way to Connecticut?" They smile at each other. Her eyes tell him she can't wait.

Miss Stephen nearly faints when Ollie explains to her the Bollinger's are driving him to Connecticut for a college visit. She squeezes him and tells him, "Ollie this is your chance. You're going to make it son."

————————————————

The Bollingers pull up to the orphanage Thursday before noon. Miss Stephen explained to the school in advance that he'd be missing today and tomorrow for a college visit. With Brandi still being on her winter break from the community college, it is no problem for her.

William takes Ollie's backpack. He puts it in the trunk. "Is that all you're bringing?" he asks.

"Yes sir," Ollie says. He has butterflies in his stomach. His palms are all sweaty. He's never felt this feeling before. It takes everything in him not to squeal with delight when he slides in the backseat. Brandi smiles at him from ear to ear. "Ready for a 13 hour drive?" she says.

They play games Ollie had never heard of: games involving other vehicles, their license plates, waving, broken headlights, and games involving billboards and the alphabet, and games with the radio too. Not one second of the drive is boring for him. When there is silence he admires the beauty out his window, but even more so, he admire the beauty in the seat beside him.

Around hour 11 Brandi drifts off to sleep. Carol's head bobs up and down. She asks William for a bathroom break. When they all return to the car she gets in the backseat by her sleeping daughter. "You sit up front with William, Ollie. I'm falling asleep."

William throws back some *Mountain Dew*. He adds another empty bottle to his collection in the plastic bag by his seat. "Ahhh," he says. "I'm good for another three hours."

It is after two a.m. when they pull into the hotel parking lot. The girls go straight up to the room while Ollie and William wrestle the luggage onto a rolling cart. By the time they get upstairs Brandi is under the blankets on the twin bed. Carol is brushing her teeth. William throws the cushions off the sofa and pulls until a bed appears. He unfolds it and throws the cushions back on it for pillows. He taps it twice, "This is yours."

Ollie puts his backpack on one side of it. He lays there until William and Carol have finished using the restroom. When they're in bed he slips in to take his shower.

Brandi sleeps through the morning ruckus. William and Carol chatter as they go about the room, from the bathroom to the bed, to the mini fridge, to the duffle bags. When Carol turns the hair dryer on full blast Brandi finally stirs. She rolls over in her sheets to face Ollie's sofa. He has his bed shoved back inside. He leans against the arm rest, his legs stretched across the couch, reading a book. Brandi rubs her eyes. When they refocus she notices the book is Ollie's bible. He turns a page, not noticing her. She begins to drift off.

Her mother slaps her thigh a moment later. "Get up, sleepy head. Breakfast closes in a half an hour."

By the time Brandi is out of bed, her family and Ollie have gone downstairs for the continental breakfast. Brandi spots the microwave clock. She jolts out of bed when she realizes she only has ten minutes until the free breakfast is over. She shyly slips in the lobby still in her pajamas. She tugs at the long sleeves of her top. Her fully dressed parents and Ollie grin at her when she appears with her bed head still intact.

A short mile down the road from their hotel a sign welcomes them to Harford. They see the campus before they're on it. A large brick clock tower stands atop a cathedral looking building. Large stained glass windows play in the sun. Surrounding the building is more of the same brick, making a sidewalk as wide as a street. It leads to other buildings of the same mold, some with more modern additions. Two brick columns form an entrance to the campus. A plaque on one says: *Trinity College Est. 1592.* On the other column a statue of a rooster stands.

"We're here!" Carol exclaims.

As they drive through, William says, "Brandi, *you* should go here. Check this place out!"

Brandi and Ollie smile at each other. Brandi hadn't thought of such a thing before. As she peers out her window, she tries to imagine her and Ollie sitting on the bench they just drove by. The beauty of this historical campus is luring her in.

William spots the gymnasium first. He jerks the wheel into the parking lot so quickly Brandi puts her hand down on the seat to balance, placing it on top of Ollie's. He squeezes it and smiles at her before letting it go. He can't believe what a beautiful life he has right now.

Ollie flings his backpack over his shoulder as he gazes upon the large building. "Ferris Athletic Center" is carved in the concrete above the sets of double doors. Inside feels even bigger to him. He stands in the open area before the next set of double doors that lead onto the court. He looks through the glass of the doors. He's never seen a court so large before in all his life. The Bollinger's, on the other hand, are not overwhelmed. "What division is this school, anyway?" William asks.

"It's only a three," Brandi says to him. Ollie isn't listening.

The Trinity team is in uniform. Slowly the balls stop dribbling and they all congregate in the center of the court. Ollie has to strain to see the other half of them. Mr. Bollinger stands behind him trying to peer over his shoulder in the same direction. "Do you see the coach?" he asks.

At that moment, a man taps him on the shoulder.

"Hi, there. I'm Patrick Wackalliton." Ollie recognizes the scout. He reaches for Mr. Wackalliton's hand before William can process it. "Ahhh," recognition crosses Patrick's face. "Phil Oliver, right?" Ollie nods his head. The women stand in awe, unbelieving he could remember that. "Good to see you again. And you must be Mr. Bollinger?" Patrick moves his hand to William's.

"I am," he says in reply.

"You're the one I spoke with on the phone?" Patrick still pumps William's hand.

"Yes, yes," Mr. Bollinger says.

"We're so glad you could bring Phil up here." Mr. Wackalliton removes his hand and grabs the folder of papers he's had tucked under his armpit. "You're right on time," he shakes his head. "Did you have any trouble finding us?"

"No, no, not at all," William speaks in his deep manly voice now.

"Well Coach Veal is ready for you when you are. I'll show you to the locker room where you can change and you all can go ahead in there and sit anywhere you like." He motions to the Bollinger's who nod their heads. They give Ollie one last look. They pat him on the back and push through the double doors.

"This way," Patrick says to Ollie.

He leads him around the corner to a hallway. Each side has banners and plaques from various sports. They pass door after door—*Boy's Tennis; Girl's Tennis; Girl's Swimming; Boy's Swimming*—until they come to a short hall to the left. They pass a few offices and the Girls Basketball room until they reach the boy's. Before going in the door with "Boys Basketball," Patrick points to the door at the end of the hall. "That leads you into the gym," he points at it. Ollie nods his head, then they go in. "Over here are the shower stalls, the toilets, urinals, and over here," he rounds another corner, "are the lockers." Shiny metallic blue lockers line the walls and stand in rows. "So get dressed and go through that door I showed you, okay?"

"Okay," Ollie nods his head.

"See you in there," Patrick says.

Ollie takes the bright yellow Dollar General bag from his backpack. It is rolled up tightly. He lets it spin down so it flaps open. He pulls out his old Mustang uniform. The numbers and "Oliver" on the back of it are cracked from the folding. The head of the mustang on the front looks like it is missing a tooth from the plastic like material it is made of chipping off. Ollie removes his blue jeans and folds down his long white socks. He slips on his jersey, then his shorts. He re-ties his shoes so they're tighter on his feet. He looks at himself once in the mirror, only a glance. He takes a knee, prays, then heads out.

The Batman Roosters are sitting on the front row bleacher. They all turn their heads toward him when the door slams behind him. Ollie stops there, outside the court line, looking back. The Bollinger's sit directly across the way looking at him too. Slowly, a fit man, with broad shoulders and a small waste, in a ball cap and sweat suit, turns as well. The Coach looks at the new boy standing across the gymnasium in an old, ratty uniform. But his frame is slender, strong even. He notes that the young man's face doesn't look frightened, nor cocky, just uncomfortably aware that he's the center of attention.

The coach turns full face now to look at the boy. Ollie doesn't move. Loud noise from the stands breaks the silence. Mr. Wackalliton nearly falls down the steps as he pushes his glasses up his face. He rushes to Ollie's side. He smiles at him and pats him on the back. He looks to the coach then back to Ollie.

"You Phil Oliver?" a voice echoes across the gym. Ollie and Patrick turn toward the coach. Ollie nods his head at the man.

"Yes, this . . . this . . . this is the one," Mr. Wackalliton nervously rubs his hand on Ollie's back.

The coach turns back toward his team, his face looking at his clipboard. "We're ready for you," he says.

"They're . . . they're . . . ready for you," Patrick pats Ollie's back. Ollie nods his head at the small man. He walks across the gym to the rest of the team. It is completely silent but for a light slapping noise. Mrs. Bollinger is the first to find the source for the pesky noise. The soul of Ollie's shoe flaps off the gym floor as he walks. Carol goes red in the face, her lips sucked together like she's just been given a lemon head. She squeezes her husband's knee so hard William pushes it away. "Ouch!"

Carol turns to him with eyes like fire. "Go get that boy new shoes right now. And clothes," she looks back at Ollie who is still walking across the court. "Look at him. For his tryout . . . an old uniform? Go, go get him shorts, a shirt, and new shoes for Christ's sake."

William blushes but doesn't dare protest. He's embarrassed by Ollie's appearance too. All three of the Bollinger's look at him, not feeling contempt for how they must appear in their good clothing, while the orphan they drove here is in shambles, but they are embarrassed they hadn't thought of the clothing and shoes beforehand. William stands, "I saw a gift shop right outside. I bet they have something."

"Do whatever it takes," Carol whispers loudly.

The coach holds out his hand to Ollie while he's still a few steps away. "Coach Veal," he says. "Heard a lot about you Phil Oliver." Ollie doesn't know what to say. He partly smiles. "This here is the team. Most of them anyway," Coach holds out his clipboard to display the boys. They look Ollie up and down with wonder in their eyes. "What I plan on doing today is having the boys play a game. Only difference is, we're throwing you in the mix." He talks clear and crisp and at an even volume. Ollie can't help but notice how different he is from Coach Jackson. His teeth are white and in a straight line. He is clean shaven, not even any stubble. His hair under his ball cap is thick and brown. His eyes still hold youth, his skin still vibrant with color. "We want to see what you got," he says.

Ollie smiles in return, "What position sir?"

"You play point, don't you?"

"Yes sir."

Coach nods his head. He says the names of nine other boys and throws his thumb over his shoulder to motion them onto the court.

"Do you want me to run drills with the team sir?" Ollie stands.

The coach looks at him with an eyebrow raised.

"Do you want me to show sportsmanship and how I can lead?" Ollie clarifies.

Coach Veal drops his eyebrow but raises his head. "Sure," he says. "Involve the whole team. No need for show-boating."

Ollie nods his head once with a smile on his face. He jogs to his end of the court where the ball is thrown into him. He dribbles down the court looking for open players. He passes the ball off and sets picks. He cheers the others on. He slaps them on the back as they make their shots. He extends a hand to one who falls down after going up for a rebound.

Coach Veal watches him. Ollie, the junior in high school, is taller than all the others. Coach notices he's faster too and his dribbling makes the other boys look like they've just learned to walk. His passes are fast and right to the chest. Some of them are so fast the college boys fumble with the ball as it smacks into their hands. They look at Ollie wide eyed. They listen to him like he is their own team captain.

"Seven, watch number two," Ollie yells. "Bring your arms in tighter," he tells another. "Throw it up, take your shot," he encourages one. "Get open nine!" The gymnasium is full of Ollie's voice. The college boys start to clap and smack him on the buttocks. Brandi and Carol sit on the bleachers. They smile at each other and lean into one another when Ollie runs by. They see it as the coach is seeing it—Ollie is better than the very team he's trying out for.

"Philip!" Coach Veal yells. Ollie stops midcourt, still bouncing the ball. "Run the court," Coach says.

Ollie nods his head at the man, understanding completely what he's asking of him. Coach Jackson uses the same vocabulary—"run the court." It means "enough team building; show me what you got."

Ollie feels a gush of renewed energy come in through his nose, down his throat and fill his arms and legs. Mr. Bollinger climbs the bleacher steps to his wife and daughter, a gift bag in hand. "I had to run across the street to get the shoes," he says breathlessly. He quickly throws the box and bag down and sits. The three of them don't speak as they are now mesmerized by their Phil Oliver.

Ollie charges the court with unfounded speed. He twirls around picks as they if they are ballerina poles. He places the ball in the hoop effortlessly. The Roosters don't understand what has happened. Ollie is so quick. Over and over again he throws the basketball through the hoop. It arches like a rainbow and swishes through the net. He's so quick he leaves the team on the other end of the court as he steals away a ball and runs it to the basket.

Coach Veal starts to laugh at the sight. He thinks it can't be true. He can't believe this boy would want to come to this small Christian school when he could be playing division one. His joy starts to bubble out of him. He laughs on the sidelines as Ollie bounces the ball between a player's legs and retrieves it behind him, leaving the boy looking between his knees for the ball. Ollie stretches his long legs so they pulse as they move him down the floor. He pushes off the floor and flies through the air. His left arm stretches for the rim but it doesn't need to. Ollie has jumped so high his chest aligns with the square on the backboard. He pushes the basketball through the hoop then grabs it with both hands as his body comes down. He swings from the rim like an ape, with his knees tucked to his stomach, his arms bent at the elbows.

The Bollinger's mouths drop as they watch him sway. The team stops, frozen in awe underneath him. Coach Veal drops his arms to his side, his pencil slides to the floor. Then Ollie drops. He stands back up to greet the silence with a dropped jawed audience.

"You can dunk?" number seven asks.

"He can dunk," number twelve says.

"He can dunk," Mr. Wackalliton whispers.

"He can dunk," Coach Veal smiles.

For supper, the Bollinger's decide to have a mini party for Ollie's successful day. They order pizza and buy sodas from the vending machines. They can't stop talking about Ollie's performance. Mr. Wackalliton tried to give them a campus tour but instead of talking about each building and available degrees, he went on and on about Ollie's future with the basketball team. The Coach had shook Ollie's hand after the dunk. He blew his whistle, went up to the Ollie and just shook his hand. He only said one thing, "You're on the team."

Mr. Wackalliton said the Coach told him to give Ollie anything he wanted. He told him to use any means necessary to be certain Trinity was Ollie's first choice. A full-ride athletic scholarship was on the table. But Ollie didn't need convincing. He can feel it in his bones. Trinity is his future. William and Patrick got lost in conversation about Ollie's season with the Mustangs thus far at one point. So Brandi, Ollie and Carol wandered into the Campus Chapel. While Mrs. Bollinger "ooo-ed and awe-ed" over the carved manger pieces, Brandi slipped her hand into Ollie's. He looked down at her and smiled, his breath caught in his throat. She held it until her mother turned around. Then they slipped out of the Chapel and back onto the leader-less tour.

"We'll celebrate at the pool!" William exclaims as he throws Ollie's new bag of clothes onto the hotel couch.

Ollie takes out his new navy "Trinity College" t-shirt and gold knee-length shorts. "Why'd you do this?" He asks as he opens the shoe box to find black sneakers with a white swish mark on the sides.

Mrs. Bollinger is quick on her feet. "You have to own something sporting your College at practice, now don't you?" The Bollinger's smile at one another. Carol gives a wink while Ollie turns his sneaker in his hand.

"Let's head down to the pool," William has slipped out of his pants and into swimming trunks. "We can meet the pizza guy in the lobby. He should be here any minute. Caroline, Brandi, don't forget the drinks." With that, he disappears through their room door.

"I don't know if he's excited about Ollie still, or the food." Carol jokes. Ollie and Brandi laugh because they know it's true.

Ollie takes the cans of soda. He heads down to the pool so the girls can have the room to change. He waits in the pool room while William talks to the delivery boy in the lobby. Ollie sees Brandi before she enters the room. The wall facing the lobby is all windows. When he spots her stepping out of the elevator, chills run up his arms leaving goose bumps. She wears a white towel wrapped around her chest. The rest of her flesh is bare. Her hair is piled high in a bun on the top of her head. When her eyes meet Ollie's he starts to rub his arms to warm them. He suddenly is frozen to the bone in this 80 degree pool room.

William catches up to the two of them holding a box of pizza and a smaller box of breadsticks. Ollie pulls four chairs closer together and scoots a small stand in the middle. William sits it down and plops onto his chair before anyone else. He flips open the lid, rubs his hands together, his tongue sticking out the side of his mouth.

"William, really?" Carol eyes him.

"Sit down. Hurry up," he replies.

When they all sit, Ollie is prepared to watch Mrs. Bollinger slap at her husband's hands. But Mr. Bollinger doesn't move. "Ollie, want to say prayer?" he says. Brandi and Carol look at him with all the bewilderment in their body. William doesn't notice. He's bowed his head. Ollie doesn't waste time. He knows this large man is near starving. So Ollie thanks God for the family in front of him, for Trinity College, for the successful try-out and campus tour, and even for Mr. Wackalliton. William claps his hands together when Ollie is finished. "Amen!" he yells. He digs into the pizza but Carol doesn't stop him to remind him guests go first. She's too proud of her hulking man for stopping to pray before filling his gullet for the first time in a long time—maybe in all their marriage.

"So what did you think of the campus Brandi?" Mrs. Bollinger asks halfway through their eating.

"I loved it!" Brandi replies quickly. She doesn't question why her mother is asking her instead of Ollie, whom which the tour was intended for.

"I wonder what a school like that costs a semester," William says through a mouthful of breadstick.

"Oh the money doesn't matter," Carol says.

"Money does *too* matter," William's eyes widen.

"I could apply for scholarships," Brandi says. "And grants," she adds.

Ollie looks at her beautiful face. He can't believe she's actually considering this place; that she wants to come here; that she could be with him. William looks like he's taking it in too. He has a hard time swallowing but picks up another slice of pizza.

"I think we could do it Brandi. It's a reach-able goal." Carol reassures.

"God will provide," Ollie says to Brandi. She doesn't much believe it because of the God part, but because Ollie's eyes show her truth and hope. His eyes would never lie to her. She nods her head which is flooded with confidence.

"Alright, William folds the last half of his slice into his mouth. "Fime, fo fim," he says. Carol slaps him in the gut as he gets up from his chair.

"Aren't we supposed to wait thirty minutes after eating?" Brandi jokes as she watches her dad's gut appear when he pulls his shirt over his head. With a wad of pizza still in his cheek he kicks off his sandals, runs then as he jumps tucking his body so he forms a cannon ball. The water splashes all over the three of them. William emerges trying to swallow his pizza and laugh at the same time.

"William Todd Bollinger," Carol clicks her tongue and wipes at her hair.

Brandi stands, her towel still tucked under her armpits. She moves away from Ollie and kicks off her sandals. Ollie tries not to stare but when her towel drops he forgets time and space. Brandi, too shy to linger in her bikini, quickly jumps in the pool.

"Ollie, where are your swimming trunks?" Mrs. Bollinger's voice turns his head. "Didn't William tell you to pack any?"

A ball of saliva sticks in the middle of Ollie's throat. After all the Bollinger's have done for him today he really doesn't want to say what is next. "Yeah, he did. But I don't have any."

Carol sighs like she is aghast with this news. She slaps her hands on her thighs. "William!" She quickly turns to the pool. Ollie's face blushes. He wishes this wouldn't happen.

"What?" William asks, part of him knowing he's about to be sent on another errand.

"Ollie doesn't have any shorts. Did you bring an extra?" Ollie tries not to look at Brandi who he knows is looking at him.

"No," William says quietly.

"Well go get him some," Carol says.

Ollie shakes his head. "No, it's okay, really . . ."

Carol holds her hand up to him. He shuts his mouth. "Hurry up," Carol says to her husband.

Mr. Bollinger doesn't protest. He looks down at his feet as he wades through the water to the ladder. Ollie feels bad. "It's no problem," Carol smiles at him as she gets up. She goes to William's shirt and hands it to him. Ollie sees William hold his arms away from his body to display his dripping shorts.

"Don't be a baby," Carol says. He pulls his shirt over his head and his arms through their holes. She kisses him on the cheek then smacks his butt. Ollie doesn't feel as bad when Mr. Bollinger winks at his wife in return before heading out the door.

Ollie isn't sure if William just had to find another gift shop in the hotel or if he had to go into the freezing January night to a store across town, but he's back in a short time. Ollie changes in the lobby bathroom then rejoins the family in the pool.

Carol and William take Brandi and Ollie on in a few rounds of "chicken." The four of them laugh and splash each other so much their guts start to hurt.

William sighs, "I think I'm done for the night."

"I'm out for the count too, hunny." Carol wraps her arms around her husband's waste as they wade out of the pool. "You two come up when you're done." She waves her hand over her head at Ollie and Brandi.

"Pool closes at ten," William looks Ollie in the eye. "We've got an early start tomorrow," he finishes. Ollie nods his head so William can look away.

When they leave Brandi and Ollie aren't sure what to do. Ollie finally hits the water so it splashes into Brandi's face. She giggles before retaliating. Soon they are swimming after each other in a game of tag. When Ollie catches her, he feels his hands slide across her slick, soft skin. "Gotcha," he laughs. She squeals in return. His hands find her waste under the water. They slip around her back so he can pull her into him. Ollie stands on the slope of the pool floor. His head and top half of his chest is out of the water. Brandi's toes barley touch the floor. She jumps off it to keep her head above water. But as Ollie pulls her into his chest, he keeps her lifted. The closer he pulls her to him the quieter they get. They stop giggling and squealing. When their stomachs touch, skin to skin, even their breathing gets quieter. Brandi's arms have nowhere to go but around Ollie's shoulders. She nervously lets them take their place. Ollie's hand slips up her spine until he feels her bikini strings. His other hand feels the top of her bottoms. Her legs rub against his. To him they feel smooth, like the water itself. She feels his hair and it sort of tickles her. Ollie's arms wrap completely around Brandi's small waste so his fingers feel the ends of her ribs. The cloth of her bikini top is the only unnatural texture he feels against his skin. The water calms until the pool room is completely still but for their beating hearts.

Brandi looks at Ollie's lips. They are partly open. The bottom lip has a single drop of water hanging on. They look pinker tonight under his rosy cheeks. While she looks at them she lets her arms glide on Ollie's wet shoulders until they are around his neck.

Ollie studies Brandi's face, her neck, the tops of her shoulders and part of her chest. Her skin glistens with its wetness. The blue and green pieces of her eyes sparkle off the water. Beads of water slowly drag down her temples and off her blonde hair around her ears. He wonders if she can feel his heartbeat as her chest touches his.

Brandi's fingertips feel the hair on Ollie's neck. The texture draws her eyes from his lips back to his eyes. He's looking down at her collarbones and how there is two small pools of water there. She runs her hand up his neck and her fingers hide in his hair. The movement pulls Ollie's eyes to hers. While her fingers curl into his hair he slides his hand up her spine until he can draw her neck to him. Both of their worlds go black. Nothing else can be thought; no other feeling can be felt. Their wet lips sink to each other. Their bodies fall into one another. Brandi pulls Ollie's head into hers. Ollie's arms tighten so Brandi wonders if her body will ever be her own again. They kiss until they can't breathe. They suck in air and kiss again. Both of Brandi's hands crawl into Ollie's blonde hair. When Ollie's left hand starts to push at the top of Brandi's bottoms he pulls his head away and blinks. He loosens his grip so water floods between their chests.

Brandi wants to kiss him more. Her hands slide down from his head and back onto his shoulders. "Brandi," Ollie says. "Be my girl."

Brandi feels suddenly cold. She removes her arms from Ollie so her neck disappears into the warm water. "I will be," she says. "One day."

Ollie lets his hands slide away from her sides. His chest swells with a deep breath. He smiles on exhale, "Okay."

The drive home seems longer. Brandi keeps pinching the skin between her thumb and index finger. She plays the pool scene over and over again in her mind. The mere thought of it makes her armpits sweat. She can't quite hear anything anyone is saying. A sentence her father flings out manages to connect with her. "Yeah, well that girlfriend of yours back there will give you a run for your money," he says over his shoulder. Mrs. Bollinger is asleep. Ollie is leaning forward from the back seat, his head close to Mr. Bollinger's shoulder. They must have been talking to one another while she was lost in thought. Brandi watches Ollie for a response.

"Oh, she's not my girlfriend," he says.

"What?" William asks. "You kids call it something else now-a-days?"

Ollie laughs a little and shakes his head. "No. I've asked her but she keeps saying no."

Mr. Bollinger rolls his head to the side and sighs. "She's a nut head," he says.

Ollie laughs a little more and nods his head. He turns to look at her. Brandi quickly shuts her eyes and pretends to be asleep.

Chapter Ten

Holding Hearts & Cardboard Boxes

Monday there is no school. It is martin Luther King Jr. Day. Ollie works at old man Gibbs'. The team doesn't have a game or practice so Ollie is able to work from sunup to sunset. Carl and Raymond squabble all day. Mr. Gibbs says, "Carlos doesn't know how to do anything."

Carl says, "You're blind old man." Ollie says nothing.

By five o'clock Carl has had enough. He says goodbye to the two of them. Ollie makes one last round feeding all the livestock—the pigs, the chickens, goats and cows—by himself. When he comes out of the barn Raymond Gibbs is leaning against his old red truck smoking his pipe. He pulls it out of his mouth. "Philip, you're looking as thin as a fence post." Ollie reaches the truck and rests his back against it like the old man. Raymond twists his pipe in his palm a few times. Finally he grunts. "Get in the truck. The sight of you is making me sick. We're going to get something warm to eat." Ollie looks confused. "Go on, get in the truck." Raymond doesn't look at Ollie. He moves his knotty knees around the hood of the truck to his door. Ollie sits in the passenger side.

Mr. Gibbs drives the truck up to the old white farm house. It looks similar to Brandi's home, but smaller and lacking a woman's touch. The gravel drive thins to worn grass. The sidewalk leading up to the house is cracked and uneven. One blue shutter hangs from a single nail. It swings with the wind. Raymond leans down on his cane to get up the steps of his porch. He slips inside letting the screen door slap behind him in Ollie's face. Ollie pulls it open and follows inside.

The old man doesn't remove his coat. Ollie doesn't either. The house has a draft. The fire in the fireplace whips like a breeze is hitting it. A pile of wood is on the floor beside it.

Mr. Gibbs heads toward it. Ollie beats him to the stack before Raymond can bend over. He throws a few logs into the fire. It crackles and pops.

"The kitchen is this way," Mr. Gibbs points with his cane. Ollie follows him to the small room. An old green refrigerator has pictures magnetized to its front. A small round table with four rickety chairs is in the corner. In the center is a vase with dried flowers. Raymond sits in a chair that looks the most worn. On the placemat beside him is a picture of a woman in a flowery dress and rubber boots. Her graying brown hair is pulled back in a bun above her neck. In one hand she holds the corners of her apron up. Something is in it making it appear she's using it as a bowl. She is dropping something from her hand. Chickens surround her feet. Her head is down but her eyes look up at the camera as if she's been caught off guard.

Raymond moves his head toward the refrigerator. "Get what you can find out of there. We'll warm it up on the stove here."

Ollie does as he's told. He notices small pictures of the same woman on the door, along with other people he's never seen. He pulls a bowl of sliced turkey, a pot of corn, and a dish of carrots from the shelf. "Anything else?" he asks.

Raymond eyes the goods and shakes his head no. Ollie puts the pot of corn on, slides the dish of carrots onto the table and transfers the turkey to a skillet. Raymond moves from the table. He pours Ollie a glass of tea and himself a cup of coffee then sits with them at the table.

Ollie puts half the food on a plate for Mr. Gibbs and the other half on one for himself. He sits across from the old man at the table, the picture of Mrs. Gibbs between them.

"She wasn't much into fancy things," Mr. Gibbs says.

Ollie looks around the small kitchen. He could have guessed that without being told. "Is that her?"

Raymond looks at the picture between them. "Sure is."

"She's very pretty," Ollie says.

"Skinny old thing," Raymond partly laughs. Ollie takes a closer look at the picture. The woman is frail looking. "Of course that was taken when the sickness took hold." The old man doesn't look at Ollie, as if it may be too intimate.

"What was wrong with her?" Ollie asks.

Raymond's hand shakes as he lifts his mug to his mouth. When he's swallowed he answers, "Her muscles stopped working, just started shrinking like until she was curled into a ball. The doctors used some fancy words but I couldn't tell you." He looks at the picture briefly. "Couldn't eat. Couldn't drink. Couldn't lift her head no more." He sighs, "She never had no babies, but it was like I had one. There at the end."

Ollie finds it difficult to swallow his food. The old man leans back in his chair. He finally looks at Ollie. "Had to quit my job," he says. "She became my full time. The hardest thing I ever had to do." He slaps his hands on his thighs. "Almost lost the farm. Doc said she couldn't understand me when it got to the worst of it. Said her brain was mush. But when I told her I was going to lose the farm her eyes went crazy. I know she understood me. Couldn't lose this farm," he shakes his head. "No sir. She didn't care much for worldly things, but this farm," he nods his head, "this was her heart." The old man leans forward and starts to eat in fork-full's then. He doesn't lift his head again until all his food is gone.

"Well then I'm glad I get to work for you sir," Ollie finally says.

Raymond nods his head. "Yeah, you're a good kid."

Nothing more but goodbye is said. Raymond drops Ollie off at the home and drives away. Ollie goes to sleep and dreams of the old man and of that beautiful lady in the picture. In his dream, the Gibbs are young and in love. In fact, Ollie and Brandi are their same age. The four of them are good friends. They all live in Raymond's house. Brandi and Mrs. Gibbs walk the yard together, throwing feed to the chickens at their feet.

The Tuesday game begins with the new Mustang tradition. The five starters are announced with their new nick names. Ollie is the last to be called. Holding his arms out like wings, he flies around like a celebrity. Small children actually take him aside for an autograph on a local newspaper or scrap piece of paper. They ask for Buddy and Corky's too. Policemen are stationed at every corner of the gym. One stands at the hall entrance that leads to the boy's locker room. They watch the three celebrities of their town closely. Coach Jackson says they are here for crowd control, but Corky says they are his body guards.

The Georgetown Gofers are back. The poor things look at the Mustangs with wide eyes. They stare at Ollie in all his glory. None of them want to play. Their coach basically kicks them onto the court.

The Mustangs show no mercy. Because the lack of defense, Ollie throws up shots like he's never done before. It seems he's shooting the ball every second. In the background noise he picks out Jeff Wallace's voice. He announces over the music, "Phil Oliver is just points away from scoring his thousandth point in his varsity career."

Coach Jackson calls a time out after the third quarter. He puts both his hands on Ollie's shoulders. He leans in so his face is inches from Ollie's. "Son," he says. "Tonight is the night. You have worked for this for three years now. You're going to make it." Ollie can't believe how seriously he is taking this. He hadn't been working for this. He'd just been playing ball. Now with the look in Coach Jackson's eyes, Ollie feels it may be a bigger deal than he had thought.
Coach slaps him on the back. "That Mr. Ramirez has a surprise for you when you do it."

The ref blows his whistle. The boys scurry back onto the court. But for some reason Ollie doesn't make contact with the ball as much. Corky seems to have taken over. He swishes threes from his sweet spot over and over again. The clock ticks down on the fourth quarter. Ollie concludes he isn't going to get another shot this game. But just as the last minute of the clock starts to count down, Buddy rebounds a ball and throws it down the court to Ollie. He squares up, bounces on his heels and takes his shot. As the final buzzer sounds the ball swishes through the net. At the exact moment the ball bounces off the floor Jeff Wallace booms through the speakers, "He's done it! Ollie has scored 1000 points! Another record met and stampeded!"

A loud boom echoes through the gym. Some kids and women scream at the noise. Some men dunk their heads, searching the gym for danger. But they discover confetti falling from the sky. A large cannon sits in the balcony of the gym. Shreds of paper in various colors pour down.

Once again Ollie is hoisted up on his teammate's shoulders. Ollie is lost in the world of color falling from the ceiling. Jeff Wallace continues to bellow praises and people slap at Ollie from below. To him, it feels like déjà vu.

On the third Monday of every month Jeff Wallace hosts what he calls "The Coach's Corner." The sports writer for the local newspaper comes. Jeff invites whichever coach or coaches he wants into his studio for a debriefing on their team and season. It is no surprise to Coach Jackson when he receives the call from Myron Studios.

On Monday morning he shows up in Ollie's fifth period. He whispers to the teacher then waves his hand at him. "Ollie, get your stuff. We're leaving for the day."

At the studio, Jeff Wallace has cups of hot coffee and powdered donuts on the desk for them. He dunks one of his in his cup before seeing Ollie and Coach. He quickly puts it in his mouth then waves for them to come in. He motions for them to sit while he wipes his face with a napkin. "We're going to get started in just a minute. You all help yourself. I got you each a coffee."

The sports writer sticks his hand out as they sit down. "I'm Michael Deaton. Nice to meet you," he says to Coach. "Hey Ollie. Good to see you again," he shakes Ollie's hand.

Coach Jackson sits like he's on a throne. He's been interviewed for Coach's corner multiple times, but never alone as the priority coach. He's always been paired up with the girls coach. This time he knows everyone will be listening in for his secrets to a successful season. For once in his life, he feels bigger than what he is. He's more than a high school basketball coach. He is a dream-maker for a young orphan. He pats Ollie's knee beside him.

Jeff clears his throat before he flips a switch to light up a sign saying, "LIVE ON AIR."

"Hey there Masonville! It is the third Monday of the month so you know what that means. Welcome to Coach's Corner." Fake applause fills the room. Coach Jackson joins in, clapping his hands.

"Today it will come as no surprise who we have in the chairs. He's been head coach of this particular team for six consecutive years. He's coached two of his own sons. To summarize, this coach is on fire!" Drum roll sounds. "It is Coach Jackson of the Masonville High School Mustang's boys basketball team." More applause and whistles are sounded. "Of course Michael Deaton of the sports section in your *Masonville Tribune* is here. And we have the star of many of his columns here with us as well. Michael, you want to say who it is?

A drum roll starts again. Mr. Deaton speaks after it clangs in conclusion. "Have you read a newspaper lately?" He laughs, "Then you know who we're talking about—Mr. Philip Oliver!" Ollie wishes Brandi was there. All the attention is making him feel out of place, and misunderstood.

"Coach Jackson, we'll start with you." Jeff says. "It is no secret you're having a killer season. The secret we want to know is: how are you doing it?"

Coach laughs into his mike. "Well if I told you it wouldn't be a secret no more, would it?"

Jeff and Michael laugh. Mr. Deaton reads off his notes. "Have you tried something new this year?"

Coach leans back in his chair. He rubs his belly. "Well I haven't been any nicer to them this year I can say that."

They laugh some more. "Ollie is that true?" Michael asks.

"Coach Jackson has been whipping us into shape that is true," Ollie smiles.

59

The questions come one after the other. Short breaks are taken with music and commercials. Even some phone calls are fielded. Someone asks Coach Jackson why he became a coach and if it is his dream job. Another asks how it is to coach his son. One phone call leaves the men cracking up. A woman's voice came through the speakers. She asked how old Ollie was and if he wanted to play some games with her. Jeff had to cut to commercials because he couldn't hold himself together. The phone rings again. "We've got Samuel Ray on the line. You're live on the air," Jeff says. What is your question?"

A man's voice comes through the mike. "Yeah, I have a question for Ollie."

"Go ahead," Jeff says.

The man clears his throat. "Well, I read in the paper that Ollie wanted to go to Trinity College. I want to know why when he easily could go to a division one school."

"That is a very good question," Jeff says.

"Great question," Michael repeats.

The men look at Ollie for an answer. He leans forward to speak into his mike. "Hi Samuel," Ollie starts. "I want to go to Trinity College so I can study the Bible. I visited the campus and tried out for the team. I felt I was in the right place there."

The men nod their heads. "So you don't want to pursue basketball as a career?" the man on the phone asks.

"No sir. I want to be a pastor," Ollie answers. "But if I need to play basketball through college for a scholarship I will."

"We all know you could get a scholarship anywhere," Michael says.

"So true," Jeff agrees.

Another caller comes on the line. "I just want to say I read your article in the newspaper." The men aren't sure who the woman is talking to, Ollie or Michael. She continues, "I was sorry to learn about your parent's car accident. My question is, do you think you're making your parents proud Ollie?"

The room is quiet but for a soft buzzing noise coming from the woman's end of the phone. Ollie leans into his mike. "My dad loved basketball," he starts. He sees his dad playing ball with him in one of their unfamiliar driveways. "He always told me I would be good at it. I think he'd be at every game if he were here. Him and my mom would probably be my biggest fans." Ollie partly laughs. "But I'm not sure if they were Christians. I don't really remember them ever talking about God and we never went to church. So I don't know how they'd feel about me wanting to be a pastor." Ollie licks his lips and breathes into the mike. "But pleasing my Father God is what matters now I guess."

The woman on the other end of the line whispers what sounds like, "Wow." Jeff breaks the silence. "We've got to take a quick commercial break folks. We'll be right back," he pushes buttons until the voices of commercials fill the air.

"Sorry about that Ollie," Michael says. Ollie shrugs his shoulders.

"Here have a donut," Jeff says throwing a cinnamon sphere at him. Finally, they are asked for their closing statements. After Coach proclaims they will win the state championship this year it is Ollie's turn.

"Well I'd like to take this opportunity to thank some people again," Ollie says. Mr. Deaton picks up his pencil and pad. "I'd like to thank Speaker City for giving us a new sound system and light board, specifically to Mr. Ramirez, the owner." Jeff pushes an applause button. "And I want to thank William Bollinger and his coworkers from the hardware store for fixing up the Children's Home." Jeff pushes the button again. "That's all," Ollie says.

Jeff nods his head at the kid. Michael still scribbles on his notepad. The two of them are dismissed while Jeff and Mr. Deaton finish the show by predicting the Mustang's future in the tournament. They examine each player, his pros and his weaknesses. They can't find the right words to say about Phil Oliver. His thanks still play in their heads. On the streets, people turn down their radio dials and they turn into *Bollinger Hardware*.

William Bollinger hears the radio broadcast. He always tunes in for coaches corner. Never before has he heard his name come up though. For years he's ran this business. For years he's had a commercial on the radio. His store has sponsored so many things for Masonville High School halftime shows he can't estimate a number. He's put up billboards. He's put ads in the newspaper. He's made business cards. He's done it all. Come to find out, the best advertising ever done for him is an orphan's thanks.

Immediately following the Coach's corner edition for January, his parking lot starts to fill. Local townspeople keep complementing him. "I had no idea you guys did so much volunteer work." "I'm moving my business here," contractors say. "We want to invest in those who invest in our community," carpenters say. And the comments don't stop there. The shopping bags have to be restocked more often. Part time employees start working full time. Mr. Bollinger's store changes. Mr. Bollinger's *life* is changing because of *one* boy his daughter brought home *one* day.

William can't stand it. He can't stand to hear all these comments about his "servant heart" when he feels he hasn't done anything, at least, not nearly enough. Then he has a thought—a thought so provoking he can't finish his shift at work. He leaves right at that moment. He goes to Myron Studios.

Jeff Wallace sees Mr. Bollinger pull in rather speedily. He gets up from his chair to watch William jog into the building. When he sees William pointing toward the recording room, talking to Trisha, the secretary, he sticks his head out his door, "William, everything alright?"

Trisha looks back and forth between the two men before she nods her head. "Go ahead over there," she motions to Jeff then turns away.

William slides his hands out of his gloves and shakes Jeff hand. Jeff now stands with his right foot propping open the door, "What can I do you for?"

William puts his gloves in his coat pocket, "I've had an idea Jeff." William smiles from ear to ear.

Jeff straightens up. "What is that?"

Music plays through the studio. "Well, ever since Ollie said what he did during your Coach's Corner, my store has been full every single day. Business is crazy, I'm telling you."

Jeff laughs and slaps his gut with one of his hands. "I hear you William," he smiles. "Same thing happened here when he mentioned the studio fixing up that home van. More people buy their cars here now than I've seen in decades. Radio listeners went up too."

William nods his head madly. "That's what I'm talking about Jeff. He's done so much for our businesses. Can't we do something for him?"

Jeff goes silent and the smile disappears from his face. He rubs his belly with his fingers. "Well I understand you asking *me* that Will. But *you* do something for him? Sounds like you've done a lot for that kid."

"No," Will is quick to respond.

Jeff holds up a finger to him. He disappears into his room. The song overhead is ending. Jeff pushes some buttons until another song comes on. He comes back to the door. "What do you mean 'no'?" he says.

"I haven't done enough." Mr. Bollinger shakes his head. "This town thinks I'm a saint now or something just 'cause I fixed a leaky sink. Now," William looks Jeff in the eyes. "I didn't ask that kid to say anything about my store on that radio. And you didn't ask him either. Jeff, I want to do something for him."

Jeff pulls his lips together like he's thinking. He slowly nods his head once then pulls it back over his shoulder. William follows him inside his room.

Saturday morning Mr. Gibbs honks his truck horn so the sleeping boys murmur. Ollie throws his coat on as he walks down the path to the old red pickup. He slips into the passenger seat on top of a stack of papers. He pulls them out from under his butt and scoots them to the middle of the seat. "No Carl today?" Ollie asks.
"Who?" Raymond says through gritted teeth, his pipe clinched there.

Ollie laughs, "The guy who works with us."

"Oh," Raymond nods. "Carlos you mean. The Mexican. He ain't working today."

Ollie shakes his head at the old man. As the truck turns left at the four way stop, instead of right, Ollie turns back to Raymond. "Where we goin'?"

Raymond pulls his pipe from his lips. He taps it on the papers between them then puts both hands on the wheel.

Ollie picks them up. They are papers from Myron Studios. There is a list of materials with prices by them. "Gotta pay a bill?" Ollie asks. Raymond nods his head. Ollie doesn't snoop through the papers any more.

They pull into the shop side of Myron Studios and park. Raymond takes his pipe from his mouth and taps the tobacco out into his ash tray. "Come on," he says. Ollie follows him into the shop. He stands a few feet away while Raymond talks to a man at a desk in an oily blue uniform with small black stripes down the length of it. He nods his head, "Follow me. It is out back here. Got her done yesterday around noon."

The three of them go out a back door to the back parking lot. Ollie recognizes the vehicle right away. The old van from Raymond's scrap pile is sitting on four new tires. It has a new windshield so Ollie can see the new interior. The seats that once had cigarette holes burned throughout have new gray material. The plastic that was cracked down the front of the van, no longer holding the radio in place, is replaced. Raymond looks at the outside of the van, circling it. He opens each van door and scans the inside. When he seems to be satisfied he slams the driver's door shut and nods his head. "I'll take it," he says.

The mechanic laughs. "It's already yours."

"It ain't mine," Mr. Gibbs says. "It's going home with him." Raymond points at Ollie. Ollie stands dumbfounded. He looks around. There's no one else in this parking lot but the three of them. Raymond had to be pointing at him.

"Oh," the mechanic says. "Got if fixed up for Phil Oliver, did ya'?" Ollie looks at the man with the grease smeared on his cheek. He doesn't know the guy but somehow he knows him.

"No, no," Raymond grunts. "It's for the orphanage."

Ollie feels his heart swelling in his chest. His whole world seems mixed up. He can't be witnessing the hard old man he works for do such a generous thing. To Ollie, it isn't making sense. The mechanic says something about "good deeds going unpunished," but Ollie is overcome by gratitude. He runs to the old man and throws his arms around his boney shoulders. He squeezes him until Raymond makes a suffocating sound. He eases up but still holds Mr. Gibbs. "Thank you sir," Ollie says again and again.

Raymond pushes the boy away. "Enough," he says. "You're welcome. Now maybe I won't have to pick your scrawny butt up for work no more."

Ollie sees him smile as he walks away. The mechanic leads him into the building, back to his desk. Ollie turns back to the van. He runs his hand over the cold metal as he walks around it.

"Phil Oliver?" a man says behind him.

Ollie turns to see a clean shaven man at the back door of the shop. He wears a navy blue suit and yellow shirt, a white tie and white shoes. He waves his hand at Ollie. "Come on in here son," he says.

Ollie finds the man approaching a desk inside. When Ollie reaches him he is pushing papers sideways on his desk. The man looks quickly through them until he spots a paper with red ink at the top of it. He pulls it out and reads it over before nodding his head and sitting it back down. He looks up, "Ollie, right?" Ollie shakes the man's hand and nods. "I'm Gordon Myron, owner."

Ollie feels a little nervous but says, "Nice to meet you sir."

The man moves around Ollie so he can sit on the front edge of his desk. "I've had a pretty interesting week here Ollie," he says.

Confused, Ollie says, "Oh yeah?"

"Yeah," Gordon wipes his nose. "It is my understanding you're going to be a senior this Fall." Ollie nods his head. "Then you're off to college?"

"Yes sir."

"To . . . where was it? Connecticut?"

Ollie has no idea how this man knows him, beside he's probably read all this in the newspaper. "Yes sir," Ollie answers.

Gordon Myron nods his head, "Follow me." He stands from his desk and leads Ollie through the studio to the far door of the building. It leads them out to the far side parking lot. The used vehicles are parked in rows. One salesman is leading a family around the cars.

Gordon walks until there are only three rows of parked cars. "You'll be needing a car to get back and forth from school," Mr. Myron says. He stops and holds his hand out to display them. "Pick one."

Ollie looks at the man like he's crazy. He doesn't even know this man. It must be a trick. Ollie shakes his head, "What are you . . .?"

"I've got it worked out with a couple guys," Gordon says. "Besides, Ollie, you've brought more people into this parking lot than my Granddad Dietrich Myron ever thought possible. He started this dealership 56 years ago. And 56 years later, this is has been the best two quarters this place has ever seen. We can afford to give you one of these." Ollie looks into the man's face for any sign of a lie.

"There you are," Raymond's voice turns Ollie's head. "Did you pick one yet?" Ollie's breathing catches in his throat.

"I don't think he believes this is real," Gordon laughs behind him.

Mr. Gibbs laughs in return. He walks past Ollie to the man. The two of them shake hands. "I'm glad it worked out this way," Mr. Myron says to him.

"Dang convenient is what this is," Raymond answers him.

"What's going on?" Ollie finally says.

"You're getting a car aren't ya'?" Raymond answers.

"But how?" Ollie holds his hands up.

Raymond starts to answer but Gordon puts his hands on the old man's shoulders. "Some of your friends have arranged this all with me, Ollie. And they contacted Raymond about it also. I don't think you need to worry about all the details son. They just wanted you to have a vehicle for school and when they told me the idea, I was all for it. Now, please. You've got these three rows to choose from. Any car. It is yours. You're driving it out of here today. No payments. Nothing."

Ollie tries to take a deep breath in but he can only manage short ones. He shakes his head and looks at his hands. "I don't know how to . . . what to . . ."

"Stop blubbering," Raymond walks to him. He slaps him on the shoulder a few times. "Go get ya' a ride kid."

Ollie looks at the old man who smiles at him. He winks then moves away. Jeff Wallace watches from the window of the back door. He smiles at the sight of Ollie then heads back to his recording room. Mr. Myron kicks into salesman's mode. He moves down the rows showing Ollie the ones he thinks have the best potential. At the end of the second row a small two door Toyota pickup truck is parked. It has a small tool box in the bed. The back windshield has two small doors that open up. Ollie cups his hands so he can see inside. Gordon says he's found a good one. One with good gas mileage and the space to haul his dorm stuff in the bed.

"It's good for a farmer to have a truck," Raymond adds.

Ollie shakes hands with Gordon Myron. He drives his new silver pickup truck to the orphanage. The mechanic who did Raymond's paperwork follows behind him in the van. Gordon Myron follows behind him. When they stop Miss Stephen comes out to the front steps. She stands on the porch, George on her hip, looking at the two cars. "What in the world?" she says.

Ollie doesn't say a word. He walks straight up to her and puts his arms around her neck and over baby George's head. "Ollie," she tries to say. But Ollie is too happy to try to explain. He's grateful Mr. Myron has volunteered to drive the mechanic back and while he is here, to do the explaining to Miss Stephen. He comes up the steps and shakes her hand. He presents the van to her as a gift to the Children's home. Miss Stephen cries, "Now all my babies will be able to go to church."

Gordon explains Ollie's new truck. He can't say much though before Miss Stephen has tossed George at Ollie and thrown her arms around Gordon's neck. She sobs and sobs until Mr. Myron feels uncomfortable with a snotty wet spot on his shirt. "God bless you," she says. "God has blessed us!"

On the last day of practice before state tournament games begin, Ollie finds a man standing in the gym with Coach Jackson. Before he rounds the corner into the locker room he gets a look at the guy's face. He recognizes him from somewhere but he can't place it.

When Ollie comes back out he doesn't see the man. Instead he spots Coach Jackson lugging a large cardboard box to the bleachers. Ollie jogs to him to help out. Coach's fingers barley wrap around its edges. He's smashing the box into his gut, his head leaning back so he can see his feet. Ollie takes it from him. It is light. He puts it up on one of his shoulders and walks it to the bleachers. "What do we got here?" Ollie asks.

"Just had a donation," Coach says, partly winded.

"Donation?"

"Yeah, the Pharmacy gave it to us. I just talked to the manager. He said they've been wanting to do this for a long time but something about it taking a long time to be approved and what have you." Coach pulls a box cutter from his sweatpants pocket. He slices open the box while Ollie says, "That was really nice of them. I wonder why . . ."

"He said we had pretty crappy material to be using on division one athletes," Coach answers. "It's true. Boys like you need the best. This dang school just can't afford it." He pulls out clear zip lock bags full of gauze. He hands things one by one to Ollie—a roll of tape, a box of metal pins, some creams and lotions, gloves and scissors. Ollie's arms are too full to hold anymore. "There's more in here," Coach exclaims. "Good grief. There is at least three hundred dollars worth of supplies in here." He pushes things around in the box. He looks like a child at Christmas. "I just can't believe this," he says. Coach looks up at Ollie, what he can see of his face behind all the materials he holds, "Looks like you've got some more thanking to do," he laughs.

The next day the school has a pep rally planned for the boys basketball team. The cheerleaders and pep club have decorated the hallways with orange construction paper basketballs. Each of the teammate's lockers has his jersey number taped to it with streamers. Red, white and black balloons cover the floors. Angela stands on a plastic red chair at one side of the hallway. Patricia stands on another at the opposite side. They hold a long white banner between them. "A little higher *Patricia*," Angela scolds. Patricia stands on her tip toes. "There," Angela yells. "Tie it!"

The girls fasten the banner between the ceiling tiles above them. They let go at the same time. When the banner dangles in the air they cheer. Josh Acosta reads it as he walks down the hall. In bright red letters "TOURNAMENT TIME" stretches across it. Underneath in smaller black letters the cheer leaders have signed their names and wrote, "Go boys' basketball!" he reaches his hand up as he walks under it. His fingers crunch the paper as he pulls it down. Angela, still on her chair, watches her banner fall to the floor. "No!" she screams. "Are you serious?" she yells after the guy in the black trench coat.

The last hour of school is set aside for the pep rally. The cheerleaders get the high school worked up. They lead the school body in chants and cheers and even the school theme song until the school principal takes a microphone and shushes everyone. "I am so proud of our boys' basketball team this year. This is the best season I have ever seen!" The school can't be quieted. They applaud and cheer. "I could go on and on but that isn't my job today," the principal laughs at himself. The gym is silent. The principal waits a moment then shrugs. He holds his arm out to his side, "Here to introduce the boys' basketball team—Coach Jackson!" The school applauds as Coach walks to the center of the gym. He shakes hands with the principal then takes the mike. He nods his head at the crowd to encourage their enthusiasm. One by one he calls each player's name as they jog to their place on the court. The cheer leaders continue to rally the crowd, chanting the player's jersey number or name as they come out. The volume noticeably rises when Buddy Porter is called. Angela throws in some extra cartwheels. The noise gets even louder when Corky Hammons dances his way onto the court. He swivels between the cheerleaders, shaking his butt and shimmying up on them. He smacks each of the player's butts as he runs by. Coach Jackson audibly sighs into the mike. Then he announces "Number 13, Phil Oliver!" The whole gymnasium rises to their feet in outrageous chaos. The teachers worry Ollie will be trampled by fans or smothered by the girls. "And we can't forget our physical therapist this year," Coach Jackson says. "Welcome everyone, Brandi Bollinger."

Brandi walks across the court the same as some of the guys did. Ollie didn't know she was there. She looks slightly embarrassed like she didn't know Coach would announce her either. The gym applauds for her like she's one of the players. The cheerleaders lead a chant, "Bran-Di, Bran-Di!"

Ollie smiles at her reddening face. She lifts her hand to her shoulder and waves at the crowd. When she reaches Ollie's side she puts her arm between his and around his waist. She tries to hide her blushing face in his armpit. Ollie laughs, as well the rest of the team does. He puts his arm over her shoulder and squeezes him into her so her face comes out from hiding again. Then they let go of each other and stand apart.

Media coverage the high school has never seen before turns up at the first game of the state tournament. The local channel news is there. They stop Corky and Buddy on their way to the locker room before the game starts. Ollie manages to slip away.

Ollie never dreamed the materials the Pharmacy donated would make such a difference. Brandi wraps his ankles in what feels like pillows. The tape she binds it with is stiff in place. Ollie stomps his foot on the locker room floor. The material doesn't budge. "You're not losing this stuff," Brandi smiles up at him. Miles pretends his wrist is hurting him so Brandi has to use the new material on him as well. Coach Jackson slaps him in the back of the head when he sees it.

"Alright listen up," Coach moves to the center of the locker room. "This is the first game of the tournament. Now it is double elimination so there isn't as much pressure but," he shakes his head and stares holes through everyone's eyes. "Let's play like this could be our last game of the season."

"Or second to last," Miles says.

Coach gives him a glare. He shakes his head again. "Alright Ollie," Coach bows his head.

Ollie takes a knee. Buddy is the only other player who follows suit. The others respectfully bow their heads, but getting on their knee in the dirty locker room, they've never agreed to.

"Dear God," Ollie starts. "Thank you for this day, for this season, for this team that I can call my friends. Thank you for all that you give and all that you take away. Keep us safe Father. Help us bring you glory. May all the praise be to your name. Amen." A murmur of 'Amen' follows.

The news reporter tries to stop Ollie during half time multiple times. Ollie manages to slip away. But at the end of the game, as Ollie scores the last point, they invade the court.

"Ollie, great game," a skinny woman with curly black hair says. She holds a large microphone in front of her face. She pushes it on Ollie when she asks questions. "How do you feel about the state tournament this year, Ollie?"

Ollie wipes the sweat from his forehead, wishing they weren't recording him when he is such a stinky mess. He sighs, "I feel really good about it. The team is awesome. We've been fighting all season. Haven't lost a game yet and I don't think we're going to start soon."

The reporter laughs. She wears a huge smile on her face. "Think you'll win the championship?"

Ollie nods his head. "I think we can."

She pulls the mike back to her lips. "You've been getting a lot of buzz here lately. Do you think any of it is getting to your head?"

Ollie laughs, "You tell me."

The woman laughs along. Ollie starts to walk away. The reporter hops along behind him. "Ollie, do you have any more thanks you want to hand out?"

The question makes Ollie remember. He turns around. The reporter looks a little shocked but she jabs the mike in front of him. "Yes, I want to thank the Pharmacy just down the road here for donating supplies to the team. They provided us with new materials to wrap our ankles and wrists. It's the best stuff we've ever had. Coach Jackson was blown away with the generosity and I can say on the team's behalf, we only played as good as we did today because of what the Pharmacy gave to us. So, thanks again," Ollie nods his head at the camera. He smiles at the reporter as he turns away. He can hear her speaking into her mike as he escapes. "There you have it, another gulp of gratitude from Masonville's Orphan Ollie."

Saturday morning a similar cardboard box is sitting on the little front porch of the Masonville Children's Home. Ollie doesn't see it when he goes out in the dark of the early morning. He swings his weed eater until a numbing sensation comes into his forearms. He pulls weeds from the fence line until his hand muscles cramp. The frost makes the vines give a crisp snapping noise when he pulls them.

The chain fence sounds like a bell when he bangs against it. When the tips of his eyelashes start to freeze together he calls it quits. On his way into the home is when he spots the box. He squats down and picks it up. He maneuvers until he's in the front door.

Miss Stephen is frying sausage patties on the stove. She looks at him over her shoulder. "What do you got there boy?"

"I don't know," Ollie answer. "It looks like the box the Pharmacy sent the team though."

Miss Stephen leaves the patties sizzling in the frying pan. She looks over Ollie's shoulder as he sits down on the couch, putting the box on the coffee table in front of him. "Open it," she says.

Ollie uses the shed's key to slice open the tape on the box. The first thing he sees inside is a white sheet of printer paper folded in half on top a line of bubble wrap. He doesn't open it. He hands the letter to Miss Stephen. She reads it out loud. "We should have thought of this a long time ago. From now on, contact us for any medical supplies or toiletries. Courtesy of the Pharmacy." Miss Stephen looks up from the letter with her eyes wide.

When Ollie removes the layer of bubble wrap Miss Stephen gasps and sits on the cushion beside him as if the wind has just been taken out of her. Ollie pulls things out one by one, placing some in Miss Stephen's hands and some on the coffee table. It is packages of band aids, gauze and tapes, ointments for everything imaginable like burns, itches and bee stings. There are boxes of medicines for allergies, sinuses, colds and ear aches. There are bottles of eye drops and alcohol. There are sterilizing wipes, cotton balls, deodorant, shampoo, conditioner, and there's more. Miss Stephen starts to cry. She pats at her cheeks with the tip of her apron. When the smoke alarm sounds she jumps. "Oh I forgot about the food!"

Ollie puts everything back in the box. He stares at it for as long as he can before the kids are awake and crawling onto his lap. He tries to process the gift as he drives his new truck to Mr. Gibbs, but he can't. He simply can't grasp the outpouring of God's love he's been experiencing this year. For the first time in a long time, Ollie can't even pray he's so overwhelmed. He laughs at this complication. "God," he says out loud. "You're the only person I don't seem able to thank."

Chapter Eleven

Hide and Seek

February seventh the team is scheduled for their next tournament game. Coach doesn't know how it's happened but the game will be played on their home court. The team practices with more fervor. The court floor is waxed, the goals shined, the balls pumped. The principal inspires the school body to attend the last home game of the season. Sure enough, it seems everyone in grades nine through twelve shows up, early even. The boys can't practice much with the gym already being crowded. Coach Jackson tells them to forget about it and to head into the locker room.

"It's my last game at this tiny little school," Corky says as they walk in.

"This tiny little school made you famous," Coach Jackson snaps his fingers at him.

"Dang skippy it did," Corky laughs. "I'm actually gonna miss this place."

"It ain't gonna miss you," Buddy chuckles. Corky puts him in a chokehold while the rest of the team nags them on.

Brandi wraps Ollie's ankles first. She smiles up at him periodically as she works.

As she finishes wrapping Corky's, which is difficult with his anxious knees bouncing, Coach gets everyone's attention. "Let's give em' a show tonight," he says.

"Like always," Corky adds.

Coach nods his head. "Let's give this hometown something to talk about!" The team claps their hands. "Lord knows this town doesn't have anything else."

"So true," Corky smirks.

"You all are the biggest thing Masonville has." The boys nod their heads in agreement but quiet down with this realization. Of course Coach Jackson doesn't realize the seriousness of these comments nor the pressure they may imply. He claps his hands together one loud time. "Don't let em' down," he finishes. The boys don't move or say anything. Coach Jackson smiles at them. He starts to chuckle. "And have fun," he adds. The boys relax again. They shake their heads at one another at their ridiculous coach. But they smile too because though they wouldn't admit it, they love the results feeling pressured brings.

Coach nods at Ollie who takes a knee once more. He repeats his usual prayer then has the team gather with their hands all together in a pile. "Mustangs on three," he says. "One, two, three, MUSTANGS!" Their hands fly in the air. Cheering follows. Corky smacks at any butt he can reach as they run out the short hall into the gymnasium.

For the first time in Ollie's career, the cheerleaders have made a run-through. It is only a solid sheet of white paper on his side. The side facing the audience has a large 'M' in red marker. Ollie leads the team. He puts his head down and runs straight through. A ripping noise follows. He lifts his head when he feels it rip through. The gymnasium is bursting with applause. Music is playing so loudly Ollie's heart thumps to the beat that radiates up through the concrete floor. The team makes a big circle around the court, slapping hands that reach out to them. Ollie comes to a stop at the bleachers where Coach Jackson stands, his arms folded on top of his belly with a smirk on his face that says, *"Yes I am their leader."* Brandi stands beside him looking small but shiny like a diamond in the ruff.

Each player is announced from the other team. The Mustangs clap along with the guests to show their sportsmanship, that is, everyone but Miles and Percy. Then the home team is announced with booming music and Jeff Wallace's thundering voice. Each of the starters do their infamous signs—Percy galloping, Miles boxing, Buddy tumbling them over, Corky shooting his invisible three pointer and Ollie flying around the court like an airplane.

The Trojans are the opposing team. They watch the Mustangs with a new appreciation. Something in their eyes says they know they aren't going to win today. When Ollie runs by them, his arms straight out like wings, they partly fear him. Number nineteen wonders if Ollie will pummel him. Flashback of Ollie's broken nose plays through him. He hears the crunch under his elbow and a cold chill shoots down his spine. He feels sorry for what he did now that he's read so many articles and heard the broadcasts and seen the news. He didn't intend to be the bully who crushed a poor orphan's nose.

Ollie, having been free from his face mask for a week now, winks at number nineteen as he spots him across the court. The Trojan's face blushes, his eyes dart away and he grips his hands together.

Corky jumps and tips the ball to Ollie as soon as the whistle blows. Number nineteen sits on the bench, suddenly too queasy to play. A short stalky body guards Ollie now. The boy's arms look too long for his body but in this sport it is a good thing. His reach is amazing. He swats at the ball but Ollie bounces it between his knees in a circling motion until he is able to lunge it at Buddy who is right under the goal. The first points are made as quickly as the game began.

Taking what Coach said to heart, Corky has fun as he moonwalks down the court. Coach raises his finger to stop him at first, but when the crowd starts to laugh, he shakes his head. "That kid sure can dance," he says under his breath. Brandi hears him and smiles.

Jeff Wallace can be heard over the mob. "There goes Phil Oliver with another lay-up, and it's good!" He follows each player, each play, and he drags out certain words which gets the crowd's attention. "Ollie is charging the court, and here it comes. It's goooooooooooooood!"

Ollie puts up the ball more times than he can count. He stretches his arm, his veins pumping with adrenaline, and slides the ball in with a tender tap like it is all made of glass. "The captain is in control!" Jeff blows.

The Trojan coach never says one word. Typical for being a loud mouth, the spectators watch him for an outburst. Multiple times he bites at the insides of his lips. He wants to yell and scream but, like number nineteen, he doesn't want to be known as the coach who made a conniption fit playing against the future all-stars. When he does call timeouts, he speaks with his teeth gritted together to hold in the volume and curse words he wants to use.

Coach Jackson pulls out his little white board he's only used once this season while the Trojans huddle up. "Buddy, Ollie, this is what I want," he curls his finger so the five starters come closer to him. He quickly puts some circles and arrows in black dry-erase marker. The boys look at Coach like he's lost his nuggets when he's done explaining.

"Are you serious?" Buddy laughs.

"Just for kicks and giggles," Coach smiles. He shrugs his shoulders, "We're thirty points ahead."

When the opportunity is right, just a minute before the half time buzzer sounds, Ollie holds up the new play number. Buddy smiles at the one finger his best friend holds up. The team moves into place. Defense presses against them as best they can but the play unfolds perfectly. Ollie passes to Corky who passes to Buddy under the basket. He bumps his guard away until he's where he needs to be. He chucks the ball at the backboard with great force. It ricochets through the air, unintended to go through the hoop. Flying through the air, Ollie catches the ball. In one long jump he reaches the goal. To spice up the Coach's play, Ollie rolls the ball around his waist before he sinks it through the net. He slings from the rim like a slinky before he lands on the ground. The half time buzzer sounds but it isn't heard over the multitude.

The news reporter turns to her camera only a foot from its lens. "Did you see that?! Phil Oliver just dunked!"

The cheerleaders get the crowd chanting, "Oll-ie! Oll-ie!"

The team doesn't stop moving. They hustle from the court into the locker room. They know if they don't the townspeople might delay the game by pulling them into the stands and making them surf the crowd. They choose to make the audience hungry for more. They hide away down their hall. They rejoice in the locker room like they've already won the championship.

"We're awesome!" Miles yells.

"You were freaking unbelievable!" Percy screams into Ollie's ear as he goes by. All of his stuff is out of his locker again on the bench, some of it on the floor. He bends over and picks up his shirt. Corky smacks him on the butt when he's in position.

"Did you see me steal that ball for you?" he shouts at the back of Ollie's head. "I've got you son!" Corky yells. "I've got you!" He starts to jab at Ollie's ribs like he's a punching bag. The boys start to laugh. Ollie raises his knee to block shots then starts to tag Corky back. Buddy grabs the both of them and squeezes them together until he lifts them into the air. "I'm the master!" He shrieks into their ears. The team rolls with laughter. Coach Jackson doesn't even try to stop it. He smiles at Brandi who stands shaking her head at the madness. "Boys," she says to him.

A buzzer sounds over their heads. "Time already?" Percy yells.

"Go on, get out there." Coach Jackson smacks at them with his clipboard. Ollie hadn't realized how quickly half time would pass. He throws his shirt on the bench and runs out with the team.

The boys squirt water into their mouth before they take the floor. While Ollie is replenishing, Brandi pinches his arm. He gulps then smiles down at her. She smiles back at him. Ollie quickly puts his arm around her shoulders and squeezes her into his side. She laughs while she pushes away from him, "You stink!"

"Ollie, let's go!" Coach Jackson pushes him along until he breaks eye contact with Brandi. She shakes her head at him as he goes. To her, he's acting like a kid tonight. But this boyish behavior makes him look even cuter to her. His innocence is so inviting she wishes she was alone with him, wrapped in his strong but gentle embrace.

The boys play, not like it is a serious tournament game, but like the game doesn't matter at all. They're having a ball. They laugh with each other so much they don't even blink when a Trojan makes a point. Coach Jackson finally sits on the bench, like the Trojan coach. The Trojan coach sits with his arms crossed knowing nothing he'd say would make a difference. Coach Jackson thinks the same thing, only he leans back on his hands so his fat gut sticks out, like he's tanning on the beach.

Corky makes the last shot of the game. He sinks it from his sweet spot. The short, stalk-y boy who had been guarding Ollie tries to chuck the ball from half court into their basket before the buzzer sounds. It misses and nearly knocks out some of their cheerleaders. The crowd goes wild for the Mustangs. Buddy and Ollie lift Corky onto their shoulders.

"Who's the master now?" Corky rubs Buddy's black afro. Cannon of confetti fires from the second floor, the same as when Ollie reached his 1,000 point shot. Some women and girls scream but this time more people are prepared for it. It cascades down like rainbow snowflakes. Mr. Ramirez admires it with Sandra on his arm. She squeals in delight and jumps up and down. Her boobs nearly bonk her in the face when she does.

The guys drop Corky off on the bleacher. He runs up them to his girlfriend Roxanne. He dips her and kisses her, leaving her mother alongside her looking really uncomfortable. Buddy turns to find Angela springing into his arms. Brandi walks up to Ollie. He watches her come, his chest pounding from excitement. She holds up her hand for a high five. Ollie smacks his against it but then ties his fingers into her own. Her eyes widen in surprise but a smile appears on her face. They stand with their hands intertwined for a moment before their arms fall to their sides, their hands releasing. Brandi brushes a strand of hair from her face. Ollie reaches for the same strand and tucks it behind her ear. "If I shower can I get a hug?" He smiles at her.

She's enthralled with the way he can speak with his eyes. How his baby blues can twinkle at her. Brandi figures Ollie probably doesn't know it, but he's always giving himself away with what his eyes tell her. "Use soap," she smiles in return.

Ollie laughs at her as he walks away. Corky catches up with him as they round the corner to the locker room. His mouth has a pink stain around it like Roxanne's lips were suction cups. "Ollie, you want to go to the Freeze tonight? We've got to celebrate man!"

Ollie nudges his sweaty friend away. "I don't know Corky," he laughs, "probably."

Buddy is already in the locker room slipping into his clean t-shirt. "Ollie, you riding with me?" he asks as soon as Ollie walks in.

"Yeah, yeah," Ollie feels the hurry his best friend is in. Half of the team is in the same position as Buddy—already stuffing their jerseys into their bags.

"You gonna shower?" Buddy asks.

"Of course he is," Corky answers for him. "He's not like us Buddy. He's got a *college girl* to impress."

"Yeah them college girls like a man in cologne," Miles says while tying his shoe.

"How would you know?" Percy flicks him in the ear.

The team laughs. "From personal experience," Miles kicks Percy in the shin.

"Judging by how often I've seen you shower after a game you must have *a lot* of experience," Corky looks around the room. Everyone looks at him to finish. ". . . In getting turned down!" Corky slaps his shirt off his knee. Everyone busts into more laughter, but Miles.

Buddy grabs Ollie's plastic *Dollar General* bag full of shower supplies from the bench and his towel from under it. "Here," he hands it to Ollie. "We'll wait for you in the gym."

"Hurry up man," Corky slaps Ollie's butt on his way out.

Ollie undresses in front of the shower before stepping behind the curtain. While he turns on the water and unrolls his bag the locker room grows quiet. As he puts shampoo in his hair he hears one last locker slam shut and a boy scuffle out.

However, there is still someone among the lockers. Phil Oliver's metal locker door quietly swings open. A black military boot steps onto the bench. The only noise is a distant changeling from chains brushing along the inside of the locker walls. Ollie doesn't hear anything but the echoing sound the water creates in his ears and the hissing noise from the shower head.

A black trench coat slides off the wooden bench as the other black boot steps down. The coat pulls apart when a step is taken. The barrel of a twelve gauge shot gun runs the length of the black pants. The tip of it is unhidden at the hem of the coat. The steps are slow so no sound is made. Ollie rinses the soap from his hair. He doesn't know anyone is around until his shower curtain starts to slide on the railing.

Ollie wipes his hands over his eyes as he turns to see who is there. His first thought is that Corky has lost his patience and has come to flash Ollie's naked butt to whoever Corky would bring in with him—probably Roxanne—but when he turns that isn't who he finds. He blinks some water out of his eyes to be sure of who he is seeing. "Josh?" He wipes his eyes again. When he opens them a barrel of a shotgun is rising from the black coat. "Josh?" Ollie says again.

Josh pulls the bottom part of the barrel toward his gut until it makes a clicking sound. Ollie's heart starts to race. Josh's hand slides the part forward. *Chick-chick.* Ollie puts his hand on the water facet then a *boom* fills his ears. The gunfire is so loud it vibrates through the concrete shower and rings through Ollie's ears. He puts his hands to his head to stop it, but finds he's falling at the same time.

Everyone in the gymnasium hears the sound. They search the ceiling for more falling confetti. When none appears they all start to mutter: "What was that?" "Did you hear that?" "I heard it too." "It sounded like a gun." Then it seems to hit everyone at the same time. Buddy and Corky make eye contact first. Both of them think the same thing. Buddy's heart flutters, "Sounded like it came from the . . ."

"Locker room," Corky finishes.

Coach Jackson is the first to run. He sprints so that his belly jiggles and it hurts him but he ignores the pain. When the cop sees him approaching he turns in the same direction. They move down the hall, past the Coach's office, toward the locker room. The deputy puts his hand on his gun as they round the corner to face the lockers. The only sound he hears is the running water. He pivots toward the shower area.

Josh Acosta stands tugging at the underside of his shotgun. The part pulls back but it isn't clicking.

"Stop! Stop what you're doing!" the deputy yells. He unsnaps his holster and puts both of his hands on the gun.

Josh looks up briefly at the man but his focus stays on the gun. Coach Jackson stands stunned behind the cop. The deputy removes one hand to wave the coach back. "Kid, I said drop the gun!"

Coach Jackson puts his hand up when he sees Buddy running into the room. He yells, "Stop Buddy! Don't let anyone in here!" Corky slides to a stop behind him. Brandi follows on his heels. When Corky hears the coach he turns around and grabs her. Brandi is too confused to know what is going on. She can't catch her breath.

"I'm warning you!" the deputy's voice echoes through the room and down the hall. The police officers left in the gym are ordering everyone out of the building.

Josh doesn't listen. He raises the barrel to get a better tug on his jammed gun. The officer fires. Brandi screams. Coach Jackson's heart leaps so his breath is taken out of him. The officer's hands shake so his gun quivers in the air. Josh stumbles backward, his shotgun still pointed in the air, the butt of the gun poised on his hip. He pulls and pulls at the trigger. The deputy fires again. Brandi drops to her knees, unable to breath. Corky moves to his knees, still holding her. She fears he's holding her too tightly because she can't inhale.

Josh falls back against the wall. The barrel of his gun hits the floor first, then the rest of Josh's body slumps to the floor, his hand still wrapped around the trigger.

Coach Jackson looks toward the shower. Blood and water sweep out of it all over the floor and under Josh's legs. Ollie's jersey is an island in the river of his blood. The cop moves toward Josh, his gun still rose. Those the cops couldn't order out of the building have gathered at the mouth of the hall. They scream things like: "What's going on?" "Get out of there!" "Is anyone hurt?" "Let us in there!"

The deputy uses his foot to prod the boot of Josh. He puts his cheek to his walky-talky on his shoulder. "Shots fired. Suspect hit. Keep everyone out."

Coach Jackson pushes the curtain until it is fully open. Phil Oliver lays, his knees tucked to his stomach, like an infant in the womb. His side is over the drain so the water and blood are building up around him. Coach fumbles with the wet knob until his shaking hands turn the water off. He kneels beside his boy while the deputy talks into his receiver. "Emergency responders needed. Two males are down; shotgun wounds. Repeat: emergency responders needed immediately."

Coach Jackson doesn't know what to do. The pale face of Ollie frightens him so much he can't bear the thought of touching it. He starts to shiver uncontrollably. Tears run down his face. Blood and water flow until Buddy can see it moving toward him around the wall. His guts churn inside him until he's sure he'll throw up. He falls to his knees certain he's seeing the blood of his best friend. Corky notices Buddy fall first then looks around him at the blood and water. He quickly jerks his head away and forces Brandi's head into his chest. He covers her eyes. Brandi starts to cry. She isn't certain of anything but she's frightened feeling Corky's body tremble against hers.

Doctor Jameson is the only one allowed down the hallway. William and Carol Bollinger hold on to each other. In the parking lot the news reporter holds her mike with one hand and points with the other at the school behind her. "We're not sure what has happened inside yet. All we know is three shots have been fired in the gymnasium area. Police officers, here for crowd control, started to order everyone out of the building." Sirens fill the air. More police cars peel into the parking lot. The camera follows them. An ambulance follows behind them.

Two medics jump out of the back before it has completely stopped. One has a red bag in his hands. The other unfolds a stretcher in one quick motion. The two of them grab a side and run with it into the building. Police officers run in as well with their guns up at eye level.

Everything happens quickly for all involved. A second ambulance arrives with another stretcher carted in. Parents who huddle in the parking lot start to cry and hold their children to their bodies. Vehicles, once driving by the school, pull into the parking lot to find out the matter.

When Ollie's body is lifted onto the stretcher, the hole in his stomach widens so Coach Jackson leans into the shower and vomits. Everyone follows Ollie out into the parking lot. Brandi stands by the ambulance door as they lift his stretcher in. She feels nothing. She isn't sure if she's really there, if any of this is actually happening. She doesn't notice Corky is still holding her. Corky is unaware he's got her. He only knows if he isn't holding something he will have to try to hold himself together. For Buddy, the world is so utterly mad with noise and speed he thinks his eyes are going to fall out of his head. But for everyone, all goes deathly quiet when the ambulance pulls away.

Chapter Twelve

Words and Wasted Breath

Eleven year old Ollie tries to count the light poles as they pass by his car window. Jane Oliver feels for the skinny hardback book under her car seat. She pulls out *Cinderella* (one of her favorite stories). James Oliver turns down the radio dial for her. Ollie unfastens his seat belt and scoots to the middle of the back seat. He loves to hear his mother read.

Seventeen year old Ollie sits against the window in the back seat of the car too. He watches his younger self lick his lips in anticipation. His eyes seem dreamy as he looks at his mother. Ollie watches Jane, her lips parting, her frail fingers flipping pages. Seventeen year old Ollie looks into the rearview mirror to see his father. His eyes fill with tears. He can't believe he's here, in this old familiar Buick, with his parents.

"Just then Cinderella came into the ballroom." Ollie turns to his mother. He hears her voice. For the first time in six years, Ollie hears his mother's voice. She reads her book. "When the Prince saw her, he bowed. 'May I have this dance?' he asked. 'Yes,' said Cinderella."

Jane smiles and points her finger at the picture of the blue ball gown and prince in his red trousers and white shirt. Ollie lets the tears fall from his eyes as his mother smiles back at the eleven year old him. Her long blonde hair glistens in the sun that comes through her window. Her voice is gentle and sweet.

She turns the page. "All night the Prince danced only with Cinderella. They danced around the floor as if in a dream. Everyone said: 'How lovely is she! Who can she be?'" Jane

Oliver turns the book so little Ollie can see the pictures more clearly. Then Jane's eyes find seventeen year old Ollie's. "Someday," she says to him. "You'll find your princess."

———————————

Brandi sits on the edge of her bed looking out her bedroom window. It has been two days since the shooting. News reporters have stopped at her house twice already this morning. Her dad asks them to leave. He tells them his daughter isn't ready to talk about it. They don't dare turn on the television. They let the newspapers lie on the kitchen table, untouched.

The boys aren't sure how to pass the time. The team sits together in the locker room of their next tournament game. It is about to begin but they aren't talking about the game. "It's been two days," Corky says. He looks around at the rest of the team. His eyes rest on Buddy's, "What do you think Ollie would want us to do?"

Buddy shakes his head slowly. He isn't sure what his best friend would want now. Ollie never wanted anything. He didn't have anything but this team and that rickety old Children's Home with that blasted fence around it. *The fence,* Buddy suddenly thinks. "The fence," he says out loud. The boys look at him inquiring. Buddy stands up, suddenly full of energy and purpose. "Ollie was always working on that stupid fence at the home," he clarifies.

"The chain link one around the yard?" Miles asks.

Buddy nods his head. "Yeah, always weed eating and pulling weeds. He was clearing it out. I don't know why, but . . ." His eyes search the teams. They know what he's thinking before he says it.

"Let's finish it," Corky stands.

Buddy nods his head at his friend. "But first, there's something else Ollie would do." Many of the team members are drying their eyes. They look to Buddy for an answer. He moves until he's kneeling. One by one they get the idea. The team moves until every one of them is on their knee. They bow their heads. "Dear God, thank you for this team. Thank you for this sport. Thank you for all that you give and all that you take away." Buddy chokes. He sucks in a sob. Coach Jackson pats him on the back. More sniffling fills the locker room. Buddy clears his throat. "Thank you for Phil Oliver." Corky finishes the prayer for him. "Amen," he says. The rest of the team repeats, "Amen."

Brandi watches a school of birds fly from the roof of the barn to the power lines. She starts to cry again. "You're so stupid," she says out loud. "You said no. How could you say no to him so many times?"

Mrs. Bollinger stops in the hallway before she goes down the stairs. She hears her daughter in her bedroom, scolding herself. Her heart brakes for her daughter but there is nothing she can do for her. Carol goes to William for some comfort.

Brandi curls up in her bed. She tucks her knees as close to her chin as possible. She imagines a world without Phil Oliver. When she closes her eyes she sees him smiling down at her the day they were in the chapel at Trinity College. She feels her hand slide into his, that warm, soft hand.

Today is Josh Acosta's visitation. Everyone will dress the way he did—in all black. They all will act as he did—with their faces down and forlorn, possibly even angry at the world. But Brandi isn't going to go. She can't. She won't look that murderer in the face even if it is looking up from a casket. Brandi just doesn't understand how anyone can go. She tries to imagine what they will say at the funeral tomorrow. Will they say he was tormented and misunderstood? Will they admit no one knows why he did this horrible thing? Brandi can't imagine. How will people shake his parent's hands today? What condoling words can they have for them? Brandi thinks of what she'd say to them. *"Did you know your son was a killer? Did you know he had a shotgun? Did you even know where he was the night he decided to hide in a locker during a basketball game? Did you know Phil Oliver? Did you know he was the kindest, sweetest . . ."* Brandi can't continue. She grabs her quilt and pulls it onto her face.

It takes a long time, but because she hasn't slept for two days, she starts to drift to sleep. In the distance she hears a telephone ringing, then a thudding noise that grows closer. Finally, a crashing noise jolts her awake. Her father has pushed her bedroom door open so quickly her backpack that was hanging on her knob falls to the floor, spilling her books.

William Bollinger doesn't pay it any mind. His wife Carol follows right behind him. They come to the edge of Brandi's bed. William leans down, "Brandi, he's awake."

The Bollingers rush to the hospital. They find Coach Jackson and Percy sitting outside Ollie's room. "The cops are in there," Coach says as they approach.

"When did he wake up?" Carol asks.

"A couple hours ago," Percy says.

"Did someone call Miss Stephen?" William asks.

"She's here," Coach says.

They stand in silence for a minute. "Are they letting anyone in?" Carol asks.

Coach takes a deep breath. "They finally let Miss Stephen in there. The cops showed up about a half an hour ago."

"No one was here when he woke up?" Carol asks with tears in her eyes.

Coach looks partly ashamed as he shakes his head. "Nurse went in to check his fluids. Found him with his eyes open."

Carol finds a chair opposite the hall and sits down.

William strokes her back. "What are the cops doing?"

"Probably explaining to him why he's in a hospital bed with a hole in his stomach." Percy looks at Brandi for a moment then puts his head down. He looks like he's been crying. He doesn't want her to see his face.

Coach nods his head and adds, "They probably found the motive."

Eventually they all find seats. Brandi picks up the newspaper from her chair before she sits. She reads the headline: *A Masonville Massacre* by Michael Deaton. She throws it under her chair. A nurse tells them they'll be able to see him when the cops give her an okay. She disappears down the hallway and minutes go by.

Everyone's head turns up when Ollie's door opens. Two officers in black uniforms step out. They both look the same age, in their early forties or thirties. They see the family and stop. "Bollinger's?" one of them asks.

William stands up. "Yes, that's us."

The officer nods his head then looks around the room like he's searching for someone. His eyes stop on Brandi. "Brandi?" he asks. Brandi nods her head.

The officers shuffle their feet. "Can we talk with you all?" One of them waves his hand for the family to follow. William looks at Coach with a little bit of worry as they pass.

They follow the officers down the hall until they reach an empty waiting room. "Would you all like to sit?" one of them asks.

"We're fine," Carol quickly replies.

The officer nods his head. They exchange a look then one nods his head. "First of all, we're really sorry for all that's happened." The Bollingers nod their heads. Brandi wishes she was sitting. "Second off, we found out the motive." Again the officer looks at Brandi.

"Well, what is it?" Carol asks.

The officer doesn't look at Mrs. Bollinger. "Brandi," he says. "You were in Josh's grade at one point weren't you?"

Carol and William look to their daughter. Brandi searches her tired mind. She tries to visualize Josh without all the blood and being slumped against the wall, or laid out on a stretcher. "Maybe," she says. "Yes, I think so."

The officer nods his head. "Do you remember ever having any contact with him?"

"What is this about?" William butts in.

The officers don't move their focus from Brandi. She shakes her head, thinking it would be absurd for her to have been on speaking terms with that *Goth* at one point. Brandi continues to shake her head. "I haven't slept," she says. "It's hard to think."

The officers nod their heads in understanding. "It's alright," one says. They turn their attention to William and Carol. "We're still fairly certain of what happened."

The other officer explains. "We found pictures of your daughter in Josh's locker."

"Notes, drawings," the other adds in. The two of them continue to go back and forth, filing in each other's sentences.

"Come to find out, Josh used to be in Brandi's grade. He ended up failing his junior and senior year."

"Putting him in Phil Oliver's grade."

"He apparently had a pretty big crush on Brandi."

"His notes were addressed to her, but obviously never given to her."

"Some of them were dated from the beginning of this year. We have reason to believe he would have more letters from previous years."

An officer pulls out a sheet of notebook paper from his chest pocket. It is folded up multiple times into a square. He unfolds it while William and Carol look to their daughter with concern.

"If you read this middle section here," the officer holds the paper out to William. With his finger he shows him where to read. William reads it quickly, Carol peering over his elbow to read it as well. She puts her hand to her lips. William hands it to Brandi.

She reads the chicken scratch: *"Brandi, why can't you see? I'm the one who loves you. I've loved you since ninth grade. I try to talk to you and you don't hear me. I walk behind you to class and you don't see me. I follow you everywhere. You are my angel."*

William and Carol read another note the officer has produced. They pass it down to Brandi as well. *"I'm sick and tired of that orphan. I'm going to kill him. I saw how he grabbed you at the pep rally. I know you didn't like it. I can tell what you like and don't like. He's forcing himself on you. He thinks because he's so good at basketball he can get whatever he wants. I'll help you Brandi. I'll get rid of him. I'm going to kill that orphan."*

The paper drops from Brandi's hand to the floor. She puts her hands over her face and starts to sob. Carol and William wrap their arms around her. "It's okay," her father whispers over her head. They move Brandi to a sofa and sit her down. She sucks in deep breaths and wipes at her face until she's able to sit up.

An officer clears his throat as he picks up the notes from the floor. "We asked Ollie if he had any idea or if he noticed anything weird." The Bollingers look up at him.

"He said he'd noticed all of his stuff would be out of his locker in the locker room pretty much every time he went in there. He said he doesn't remember ever opening it back up to the stuff back inside. We think Josh had been taking Ollie's stuff out so he could fit in the locker."

The Bollingers all wear a curious face. William shakes his head. "Why? Why would he do that?"

"We think Josh had been watching Ollie from the locker."

"Waiting for an opportune time, perhaps."

"Or maybe just learning Ollie's routine so he could plan out how to . . . how to do it all."

"He'd been watching him all season?" Brandi asks.

The officers nod their heads. "We talked to Josh's parents. They said he never came home after school. And they could point to some nights that he wasn't home either that just so happen to line up with basketball games."

"Josh was able to pick up something on Ollie's routine." Brandi strains her brain trying to follow along.

"Ollie confirmed with us he takes a shower in the locker room after *every* practice, *every* game."

"He was always the last one in the locker room," an officer pulls his lips into a frown. "He was a sitting duck."

Carol shakes as she holds her daughter's hand. William rubs his forehead.

"Brandi," the officer says. She looks up at him with dark rings under her eyes. "Were you and Ollie seeing each other publically?"

The pool scene floods her mind. She feels Ollie's hands, smooth as butter, slide around her hips to pull her into his hard chest; his sweet lips sucking her bottom lip into his mouth; the tip of his tongue touching hers. Then how he pulled away and asked her to be his girl. The room was quiet. They were utterly alone. The chapel scene: Brandi pulls her hand out of his when her mother turns around. She sees him pulling her into his side at the last basketball game. She had pushed him away, *"You stink!"* And lastly, walking through the Freezer Fresh parking lot; pulling him along like a rag doll; driving him to a remote, secluded location. It hits her then. All Ollie wanted was for her to be his girl *in public*. He wanted to hold her hand and call her 'his'. He wanted to drive her from place to place and kiss her on the lips and sway with her in his arms in front of anyone.

Brandi swallows. "That's what he wanted."

Everyone stays still. The officer cocks his head. "Did *you* want that, Brandi?"

Brandi thinks of Josh's note. He thought she didn't want Ollie to hold her at the pep rally. She sees days and days of Ollie running into the gymnasium, her arm on the basketball cart waiting for him. *"Brandi, will you go out with me?"*

"No," she would say.

"Maybe tomorrow," Ollie would answer.

Brandi starts to cry again. Carol rubs her back. "Yes," Brandi chokes. "Yes I wanted to be with him . . . all the time."

———————

Miss Stephen comes from the room and says Ollie has fallen asleep. It is late into the night. Coach Jackson and Percy, the Bollingers, the Brown's, Porters and Hammons families all drop their heads in disappointment. They long to see Ollie. One by one they nod they stand to leave. They shake Miss Stephen's hand, or hug her neck as they go. She tells them to come back tomorrow. Brandi lingers at Ollie's door. The little glass window at the top of it only shows her a large white curtain that is drawn across the middle of the room. Miss Stephen pats her on the back. "He really wants to see you," she says. "But he doesn't realize his own pain. He needs rest." Brandi nods her head then leaves the hospital.

Ollie doesn't remember anything after the gun fired. His dream was the only real thing to him. Now, as he looks around his glowing hospital room in the dead of night, he realizes all of this is real. He wiggles his toes. The ones on the left move, but the right foot won't move. He can't feel much of his right leg. He tosses his sheet off his waist. He pulls his gown until it reveals white bandages. A large square of gauze and tape covers the lower half of his torso. His leg is in a contraption that keeps it straight. He can't move the bottom half of his body on that side. He lies back in the bed trying to piece together the past two days. The nurse told him he had been in a severe state of shock that made him unconscious over 36 hours. She said it was his body's way of tolerating the pain. She also said Miss Stephen had left him a gift.

On the table beside his bed is a *Golden Treasures* book. He picks it up and holds in the light of his heart monitor. *Cinderella.* Miss Stephen had plowed through Ollie's nurse yesterday when she yelled out the door "He's awake!" She said she had been there the whole time he was asleep, that Pastor Brown and his wife were watching the kids for her.

She stroked his face and told him, "I thought I was losing you. You kept saying *'Mom, read me* Cinderella *again.'* I thought you was in heaven." So she handed him the book and wiped her tears away.

Ollie holds it now. Part of him wishes he really had gone to heaven. He misses his mother more now than ever before. But as he flips open the book, there is a picture of Cinderella on her knees. She is supposed to be scrubbing the floor but she's looking up at bubbles. Ollie sees his beautiful blonde Brandi kneeling, her hands wrapping material around his ankles. He can't imagine heaven without her. He closes the book and falls asleep.

Ollie wakes up to the sound of a familiar voice. *"It can't be,"* he thinks to himself. When he opens his eyes he is happily surprised. "Mr. Gibbs?"

Miss Stephen and Raymond sit opposite each other, Ollie's bed between them. They both jump when Ollie speaks. "Philip!" Raymond's hoarse voice comes. "It's about time you woke up!"

Ollie and Miss Stephen laugh. "What are you doing here?" Ollie smiles at the man.

Raymond snorts, "What am I doing? I came to drag your butt to work. Don't think this hospital bed is going to get you out of anything boy." He grabs Ollie's knee and shakes it. Ollie is thankful he's on his good side.

"Well, thanks for thinking of me," Ollie jokes.

Raymond laughs a little while looking at Miss Stephen. She taps Ollie's arm and stands. "I'll leave you two alone." She smiles over at Ollie on her way out.

Raymond coughs a little like he's uncomfortable. Ollie feels something is coming. "Ollie, I wanted to talk to you about something," the old man says but doesn't look at him.

Ollie notices Raymond is sitting low to the ground. He tries to sit up higher. Mr. Gibbs sees what he's doing. He puts his hands down at his sides and pushes. He rolls back from Ollie's bed, seated in a wheelchair.

"Mr. Gibbs," Ollie says.

"Now, now let me say what I want to." He rolls back to Ollie's bedside. "Something's happened to both of us. When that something happened to you I thought of me. When that something that happened to me I thought of you." Raymond wears a small childlike smile suddenly. He shakes his head as he says, "You remember that day at the farm when you said you knew plenty of kids who would want a father like me?" Ollie watches the man, unsure if this is the same Raymond Gibbs he's worked on the farm with. He looks unfamiliar without his pipe dangling from his mouth and how he's using so many words unhindered by it today. He does remember that day though. He nods his head.

Raymond smiles broader then. "You've been like a son to me. You have. So I was thinking of things fathers do and how I took care of my Maggie when she got like a child.

You remember what I told you about her?" Raymond looks up at Ollie, half his eyes hidden by his white bushy eyebrows.

 Ollie nods his head again. "You said the farm was her heart."

Raymond nods his head. "That's all my baby girl wanted. So," he pauses, "I want to give you my farm Phil." Raymond doesn't look up still. He smacks his lips together to swallow the taste of salty tears in his throat. Ollie doesn't speak or move so Raymond continues. "Of course not right this minute or nothing." He looks up at the boy. "You've still got school and then college after that. But Miss Stephen said it first son. You're almost 18. You can't be staying with her after that. And after college, what then?" Ollie barely shakes his head. He doesn't know what will happen to him. He hadn't thought of leaving the orphanage this summer. He hadn't ever dreamed any of this would happen to him. "Exactly," Raymond nods. "I'm thinking of both of our futures."

Ollie feels hot tears are the on the brink of overflowing. He lowers his head and shakes it. "Mr. Gibbs, I . . ."

"You like working on my farm boy?" Raymond cuts in.

Ollie lifts his head back up. "Yes sir, but I'm no . . ."

"You *are* a farmer." Raymond tells him. "If I've taught you anything, it is how to farm."

Ollie and Raymond look at each other for a while before the old man drops his eyes again. "Nothin' more needs to be said." Raymond pushes away from the bed. "You take care of yourself." He uses his hands to roll the wheels toward the door. "You've got a home when you get out." He stops at the door. "And an old man to take care of too," he winks.

Ollie smiles while tears fall down his cheeks. "Thank you," he calls after the old man as the door of his room shuts.

Minutes later the door is opening again. Ollie, who had been crying, quickly wipes the tears away. Percy Jackson sticks his head through the door. He starts to pull back when he first sees Ollie but he is called after, "Percy! Hey!" Percy comes in with a smile on his face. His dad follows. "Hey Coach," Ollie says.

"Well don't you look pretty as ever," Coach walks to the bed. He is smiling but his bottom lip quivers. He tries not to cry.

"What's going on?" Ollie asks.

"The rest of the team is on their way." Percy looks up and down Ollie's body though he can't see anything because of the blanket. "If you're up for it.

"Of course. Sure," Ollie says.

The three of them talk. A nurse comes in to change Ollie's bandage so they leave briefly. When they come back , Corky, the Porters and Miles are with them. Corky pushes through the guys straight to Ollie. He leans over his body and hugs him. Ollie groans in pain but Corky squeezes harder. He slightly shakes his friend. "Don't you ever do that to me again," he says.

"Corky, get off him," Buddy pushes. Corky relinquishes so Buddy can grab his best friend's hand. The two of them do their own handshake. They smile at each other the whole time. Best friends don't often need to use words. Mrs. Porter pushes her son out of the way when they're finished. She too hugs Ollie, only gentler. She cries so tears run down Ollie's neck. She pulls away wiping her nose. "Pull yourself together Colleen," Mr. Porter tells her.

"Look what you're doing to everybody," Miles says. A smile creeps across his face as Ollie looks at him. "Always the center of attention," he shakes his head. A little giggle runs through the room. Corky puts Miles in a headlock and pretends to punch him in the gut.

The rest of the team trickles in through the door. When it appears everyone is there Buddy stands up from the chair beside Ollie's bed. "We've got good news for you," Buddy says. The boys stop wrestling and start nodding their heads enthusiastically.

"What is it?" Ollie can hardly contain his excitement. Buddy smiles at the boys in the room. They all look back at him with a knowing glow in their eyes. Ollie laughs, "Come on, what is it?"

Buddy turns to him. "We finished the fence for you."

Ollie goes still. His smile fades and his heart machine shows a slow in rhythm. The boys are anxious for his response. Ollie blinks once. "Did you really?"

The boys slowly start to smile. "We sure did," Corky slaps at the foot of the bed.

"It was a pain in the neck too," Miles says.

"It took us hours," Buddy smiles.

"Why in the world did you start that project?" Miles asks.

Ollie rubs his head. He can't believe his friends have done this for him. "I did it so the kids could start walking to the elementary school."

The boys stand with quizzical faces. "Don't they ride the school bus?" Percy finally asks.

Ollie laughs a little. "Yeah, but I mean, now they can walk over to the playground whenever they want. Miss Stephen wouldn't let them out of the yard because she couldn't see past the fence. I figured if I cleaned it up, she could see through it. Now she can watch them walk to school or play at the playground."

The guys start to nod their heads in understanding. "Thanks guys," Ollie says. "I can't believe you did that for me."

"Well, apparently we didn't do it for you," Miles says. "We did it for the old lady and the fifty kids that live in that place." The boys start to laugh. Corky puts Miles in another headlock. The room fills with small talk. The boys lift Ollie's spirit. He practically forgets he's in a hospital bed.

Brandi can hear the laughter as she approaches the door. William looks through the little glass window. He sees all the people and pulls at Carol's arm. "We'll stay out here."

Carol gives her husband a shocking glare. "We'll go in when there's not so many people in there," he tells her.

They nod their heads for Brandi to go on in. She's nervous to do so. She isn't sure how she'll react. She might burst into tears as soon as she sees his wrangled body. What if everything between them has changed? She takes a deep breath and pushes through the door.

As soon as Brandi sticks her blonde head through the door the boys brake into cheer: "Brandi's here!"

"There's our girl!" Coach says.

Corky reaches her before the door has shut. He grabs her around the waste and hoists her into the air. He jumps with her so her blonde ponytail thrashes. When he sits her feet on the ground Buddy pushes him away. He slaps his hand into hers and pulls her into him so he can slap her back with his other hand in a brotherly hug.

The rest of the team nods their heads at her. Brandi waves at them. She looks to Ollie, reclining in his hospital bed. His face is still radiant, his smile still sincere, his eyes are serene. His blonde hair is sticking up in the back from lying flat on his bed but Brandi thinks it's cute. She goes to his side, sits in the chair by his bed and grabs his hand. Ollie's heart machine starts to beep faster. *Beep . . . . . beep . . .beep . . beep .beep, beep, beep.* The boys start to laugh and Ollie's face turns pink. Brandi has no shame anymore. Now that she knows she could have lost him she never wants to waste another moment. She'll hold onto him as long as she can. If all these guys weren't in here she'd be kissing his face off.

Brandi looks to Ollie. They smile at each other. Her eyes start to water so she turns away. The guys continue to make jokes and fill the room with laughter. Eventually the door opens again. A white cloak is seen first. Ollie's doctor looks down at his clip board as he enters. The boys erupt again: "Doctor Jay!"

Doctor Jameson looks up with a startle. "Boys! My goodness Ollie, you've got the whole team here." The room laughs. Doctor Jameson moves around Ollie's bed. "Just need to check a few things here." He looks at the machines scribbling things on his clipboard. "How you feeling today Ollie?"

Ollie nods his head. "I feel good."

Doctor Jameson notices the two of them holding hands. "I'm sure you can't feel any worse holding a pretty girl's hand." The boys laugh at them. Brandi blushes but doesn't dare move. Doc winks at her. "How you doing Brandi?" She smiles at him. "Seems like you were just here yesterday." Ollie and Brandi both think of when he broke his nose. They grin at each other. Doctor Jameson takes Ollie's blood pressure.

"He looks okay to me," Miles says. "He's just faking it Doc so Brandi will hold his hand."

The boys laugh. "Yeah, when is Ollie going to be out of here?" Corky says. "We've got a tournament game tomorrow."

The boys laugh again while Doc removes the sleeve from Ollie's arm. He smiles but sighs at the same time. "Unfortunately boys, Ollie won't be out of here for a couple more days. Then he'll have weeks of extensive therapy." The room grows quiet. The boys slowly nod their heads.

"So what exactly is wrong with him?" Buddy asks.

Doctor Jameson turns to face the room. He folds his arms in front of his chest, his clipboard pressed against him. "He's had severe hip trauma. The bullet penetrated the tip of his pelvic bone. I'm not sure how familiar you are with the weapon that was used, but," he pauses briefly. "It was a twelve gauge shotgun. The bullets used in this type of gun burst out in tiny shards. The closer the target is the more solitary the entry wound. Ollie was shot at very close range." Doc waves his clipboard out toward Ollie. "So there was one main bullet hole, but it is very large." Some of the boys feel faint. "Ollie is very lucky to be here with us. But . . ." The boy's search Doctor Jameson's growingly pale face. He sighs, "Ollie won't ever play ball again."

Ollie already knew the news so it doesn't affect him like it does the others. He slowly nods his head while the others all drop theirs. Buddy's burst into tears catches everyone off guard. He buries his face in his hands, shaking his head. Corky moves to him first. Brandi starts to but tightens her hand around Ollie's instead. Other boys wipe the tears running down their faces. Buddy's shoulders bounce up and down. Hiccup noises come from behind his hand. Corky rubs his back and whispers to him. With one long inhale, Buddy sucks the snot and tears up and removes his hands.

 While Ollie wipes the tears from his face Doc clears his throat. "Everything is looking good, Ollie. Are you hungry for lunch yet?" Ollie nods his head. "We'll get you something up here real soon." He moves to the door. "And maybe up out of the bed today, yes?" Ollie and Doctor Jameson exchange a smile. Doc pats Buddy's shoulder as he passes through the door.

The boys take a bit longer to return to chatter and laughter but they eventually do. After a while Miles approaches Ollie's bed. He sticks out his hand to him. "I'm going to head out of here Ollie."

Ollie shakes it, "You going to the funeral?"

Miles stops immediately. The room goes silent. Everyone looks to each other to be sure they really heard what Ollie said. Miles stitches his eyebrows together. "What?"

Ollie releases his hand, "The funeral. It's today isn't it?"

Miles looks around the room at the other boys. He turns back to Ollie shaking his head, "Josh's funeral?" Ollie doesn't understand the confusion and shock. He nods his head. "You want me to go to *Josh*'s funeral?" Miles almost laughs the words.

"Check his pain killer drip," Corky jokes.

Ollie shakes his head. "I'm serious guys. You all should be going."

"You want us to go to the funeral of the guy who *shot* you?" one asks.

"The one that tried to *kill* you," says another.

Buddy looks at his best friend with deep concern. "Why would we do that?" he asks.

Brandi still holds Ollie's hand but she too fears he must not realize what has happened to him.

"He was still our classmate," Ollie says.

"He was a jerk," a teammate says.

"Guys," Ollie sighs. "You've been asking me if there's anything you can do for me." The boys know then what he's going to ask. "This is it," Ollie says. "If I could go, I would."

"You'd go to your *shooters* funeral?" Miles still layers his words with cynicism.

Ollie sighs more deeply this time. Coach Jackson speaks up from the back of the room. "Think of his parent's boys." The team looks to him. "If we can't go for Josh, think of how his parents must feel."

The boys don't know what to think. Some of them mutter under their breath. Miles finally turns to Ollie again. "You seriously want us to go?" he asks one more time.

Ollie nods his head, "Please." Miles nods. He squeezes Ollie's hand then heads to the door. One by one the boys say goodbye to Ollie. When Coach Jackson approaches, Ollie clings to his hand. "Coach, can you do me a favor?"

He nods his head, "Of course. Anything."

"Give my condolences to the family." Coach finds it hard to nod his head. He can't understand how this young mind before him is so wise and forgiving.

At last, Brandi is alone with Ollie. When the door last clicks shut she jumps up from her seat. She leans over Ollie's bedside and pushes her lips against his. She kisses him until she fears his oxygen levels may suffer. When she moves away Ollie wears the biggest smile she's ever seen. Brandi sits down and laughs at herself.

No one really understands why they are here. They sit in padded metal chairs. Brandi sits between her mom and dad. She turns around to see who else has come. Buddy is right behind her with his parents and Angela. Coach Jackson, Percy and Miles are to her left. She turns to her other side. Corky and his parents are there. Behind him the rest of the team is spread out. Brandi doesn't know many others. The boys recognize some classmates but not many. As far as anyone can tell, Josh didn't have any friends. The table displaying pictures of him only has a couple. In each one he's looking at the camera as if he is about to attack it. The table is mostly bare. There are no certificates, no major accomplishments, trophies or awards. There are only a few of his drawings. One is of a warrior on a black horse. It tramples over soldiers in metal helmets. Another is of a dragon flying through some clouds. This is the only one in color. Brandi actually finds it beautiful. Josh was a good artist.

His parents sit in the front row feet from the casket. No one has gone by it yet. They wait, listening to a preacher talk about how life is a precious gift. The team and Brandi mostly block everything out. In truth, they are all a little frustrated to be here. Miles is so angry inside he wonders if anyone will notice if he gives Josh's embalmed body the middle finger. Buddy tries to think of why Ollie wants them here. He tries to put himself in his friend's shoes, thinking *what would Jesus do?*

Brandi just wants it to be over with. She wants to leave here and never think of Josh Acosta again. If she begins to she feels sick. She wonders why he was obsessed with her. She worries she did something wrong, something to provoke him. She doesn't wish she would have noticed him more, or ever have talked to him. She just wishes he never existed.

Every one of them is in a daze, thinking of other things, until Josh's parents stand at the podium. Josh looks just like his father. They both have jet black hair, greasy at the scalp but too dry at the ends, like the ends of it would poke through your skin if you touched it. They both have a long pointy nose with a bump on the bridge of it. But Josh has his mother's mouth and chin. Her lips are large and full and almost a purple shade, like she's been punched there. Her chin is small and round and today it quivers.

"We want to say thank you," Mr. Acosta begins. He's tall so he bends down to the small mike on the podium. "We know this is all difficult circumstances, confusing and hard to say the least." Mrs. Acosta blows her nose behind him. "We realize many of you probably didn't want to even be here." Brandi lowers her head to hide her face of the shame. Miles openly nods his head at the man. Mr. Acosta clears his throat again. "Despite what Josh did, he was still my son. He was a neighbor, a grandson, a nephew, cousin, classmate." He looks around the room at certain people when he says this. Mr. Acosta starts to cry. "He had his problems, but I loved my son." He wipes his face. Brandi wipes at the tears on hers too. "So thank you for being here," he finishes. He puts his arm around Mrs. Acosta who steps forward. She holds a tissue under her nose. She makes loud sucking noises as she tries to breathe through her mouth. It takes her a long minute before she is able to speak. By then nearly everyone in the room is crying too. She leans against the podium, her lips touching the mike. She whispers, "I love my son. I love him so much. I'm going to miss him so much," the words spill out of her like it is her soul speaking. "I remember when he was just a little baby in my arms. Then as he grew up he got bigger and farther away and harder to hold." She sucks in snot. "But he was always drawing. He always had a pencil in his pocket. He was magical with that pencil, just magical. He brought me so much joy with his pictures. He could have brought this world so much joy with those pictures." Mr. Acosta snorts back some tears. Mrs. Acosta shakes her head at the mike. "He wasn't a bad kid. He just did a bad thing. He lost his way. We lost him. His parents lost him.

He was in the dark for so long all by himself. He didn't mean to do this. He didn't deserve this life. I'm so sorry," she finally breaks. "I'm so sorry he," she tries to raise her arms like she's holding a large gun but her arms shake too much. Her husband takes her in his arms and leads her to their seats.

The room is quiet but for the sound of weeping. The line starts circling from the back of the room to the front. Brandi doesn't think she'll look in the casket but as she walks by she can't stop from glancing in. Josh doesn't look the same to her, almost unrecognizable. His long black hair is brushed over away from his face. He wears black, but it is a suit with a white shirt and black tie. He actually looks handsome but for the clay-like texture of his face. Brandi can't help but agree with Mrs. Acosta. Josh could have offered something to the world. She wishes things hadn't ended up this way. The rest of the team feels the same way, even Miles.

Ollie braces against his bed and also against the nurse who leads him down into a wheelchair. "You did really well with your muscle movements today," she tells him. She's almost as opposite as one can get from Sandra. She is a fat woman with short brown hair. She has a mole on the side of her nose that has little black hairs growing from it like trees on a hill. She's nice however. She slowly drops Ollie into his seat and moves behind him. "Brandi, do you want to push him?"

Brandi nods her head. She's been there since early this morning. She didn't even leave for lunch. Her mother bought her something from the cafeteria downstairs. She spent the morning telling Ollie about the funeral and how she felt through the whole thing. She asked him to explain to her why they needed to go. He said he didn't know how to explain it. He just knew it was the right thing to do. She's held his hand the whole day. She even snuck some kisses on his cheek while he dozed off. Now she carts him down the hallway in a position she never imagined she'd be. When she envisioned them growing old together she still saw Ollie tall, muscular and full of life. He'd have a head full of silver hair but his eyes would still sparkle with their brilliant blue. She couldn't imagine him in a wheelchair at the ripe age of eighty. Now she assists him in one at age seventeen.

They chat of little things as they stroll along. As they round a corner Brandi comes to a quick stop. Ollie grabs his chair so he doesn't fall forward. "What? What is it?"

Brandi leans down to whisper in his ear. "It's Josh's parents." Her eyes look straight ahead.

Mr. and Mrs. Acosta approach. Brandi straightens up, ready to push away if she needs to. Mr. Acosta speaks first. "Phil Oliver, I'm Josh's father."

Ollie reaches out his hand, "Mr. Acosta."

The man shakes it then side steps to reveal the Mrs. "This is my wife," he says.

Ollie shakes her hand too. "This is Brandi Bollinger," Ollie puts his hand above his head. Brandi doesn't look at them but nods her head.

Mr. Acosta squeezes his hands. "Phil, we just wanted to come and offer our apologies."

Mrs. Acosta tabs her eyes with a tissue. "We're really sorry for what's happened to you."

Mr. Acosta looks back to his wife then back to Ollie. "We didn't know. We had no idea."

"Josh was such a sweet boy," Mrs. Acosta says. "I still can't believe he did something like this." She hides her eyes in her tissue.

"Coach Jackson was at the funeral yesterday," Mr. Acosta says. "He told me you wanted him to give us your condolences." Ollie looks at the two of them. He feels so sorry for them he isn't sure how to talk. Mr. Acosta takes an audible gulp. "We were just in shock that you would think of that."

"We want to know if you could ever forgive us," Mrs. Acosta looks into Ollie's eyes with desperation.

"And forgive our son," Mr. Acosta finishes.

Brandi holds her breath. She's on the verge of bursting into one of two things: tears or shouts of anger. She isn't sure which.

Ollie tries to swallow through the lump in his throat. He coughs then speaks. "Of course," he shakes his head. "I forgive."

Mrs. Acosta buries her face in her tissue again and cries aloud. Mr. Acosta tries to stay in control. He swallows as hard as he can and looks to the ceiling to draw the tears back. Brandi looks down at her Ollie. He's sitting in a wheel chair. She'll never see him play basketball again; the sport that made her fall in love with him; the sport he loves so much. She doesn't know how he's doing it. If it were her she would be mourning in bed saying her life was over and everything is unfair. She'd cry and say she wishes she was dead. If she really was like Ollie with no future but basketball, no hope or chance but with an orange ball, she would give up. She wouldn't forgive. She'd hate for the rest of her days. She'd wish ill on Josh's family. She'd curse them and God. She feels Ollie's hand on hers. Mr. And Mrs. Acosta disappear into the elevator at the end of the hall. "Brandi," Ollie looks up at her. "Let's go."

Chapter Thirteen

Roses and Endings

Doctor Jameson informs Miss Stephen the children's home won't be an adequate place for Ollie to do his physical therapy. With all the children running around, wanting to climb on him, toys everywhere, a bunk bed . . . Miss Stephen agrees he shouldn't be there. The Bollinger's happily take Ollie home with them. Every day a physical therapist comes to work Ollie's legs. Every three days a nurse comes to check vitals and change his bandages. Carol takes charge of Ollie's medications. She sets timers through the house so pills are taken at the exact time every day.

They have Ollie set up in the living room. William pushed his recliner against the wall—a sacrifice he said he would only make for Phil Oliver. William is in charge of changing Ollie and taking him to the rest room. He lifts him from his wheelchair onto the toilet or into the bathtub. At first it was hard for them to look each other in the eye. Now they have inside jokes about poop. They tell the ladies *"What happens in the bathroom, stays in the bathroom."*

Carol says she's not used to having another man in the house so she makes double the amount of food she's used to. Ollie doesn't eat much but he still can't convince her to portion control. Left-over food piles in the fridge until Ollie finally has an idea. "Why don't you take the extras to Mr. Gibbs?" They all think it is a great idea. Before long, Mr. Bollinger has convinced Raymond to have dinner with them on occasion. He's worked his way out of his wheelchair. He uses his cane again. He tells Ollie he'll be in the same position soon.

A month into Ollie's new living arrangement the Bollinger's house phone rings off the hook. Ollie, unable to get out of the bed on his own, wonders where Carol is. William and Brandi are outside feeding the animals. After a couple minutes of ringing Ollie hears Carol running down the stairs. She slides into the kitchen in her bathrobe. Ollie figures she must have been showering. "Hello," he hears her say. A couple minutes later she's squealing into the phone, "Oh thank you so much! That is such good news! I can't wait to tell him! Thank you, thank you!" She puts the phone back on the receiver in such a rush it sounds like she's beat it into the wall. Ollie nervously sits up in his bed.

Carol appears in the living room with her hair up in a towel. "Ollie," she claps her hands together. She has the biggest smile on her face Ollie has ever seen. "That was Trinity College on the phone." Ollie's heart starts to race. He tries to sit up more in his bed. Carol comes to his side and fluffs his pillow behind his head. "They heard about the shooting on the news. That was Mr. Wackalliton," she grabs Ollie's hands in hers. Ollie feels slightly uncomfortable that she's in her bathrobe, but he also finds it funny that she's this comfortable with him. "He said to tell you that you have a full *academic* scholarship to their school. Ollie they want you to go there for free! Basketball or not," she squeezes his hands till he's sure his fingers are going to fall off but they laugh together.

"I can't believe that," Ollie beams.

Carol throws his hands in the air with her own. "We have to celebrate!" She twirls around to the stairs. "I have to get dressed. We're going to call everyone and have them over for dinner!" She disappears up the stairs in a hurry. Ollie laughs as he watches her go. He leans back in bed, exhausted from the good news. He closes his eyes and tries to understand why God is so good to him. He breathes in the goodness of the Bollinger house—the gingerbread and fresh linen smell. He is home. He has a family.

His life feels full that weekend when Mrs. Bollinger has everyone Ollie has ever loved into her home. Mr. Gibbs and Carl, Coach Jackson and the team, the Porters and Hammons, Roxanne and Angela, Miss Stephen and all the kids, and everyone from the First Baptist Church comes. The house is so crammed people fill the upstairs too. Luckily, the weather is perfect. Most people stay outside sitting on the porch swings or rocking chairs. Mrs. Bollinger fixes a large cake for Ollie saying "Congratulations!" Everyone applauds for Ollie when she presents it to him. Brandi kisses him on the cheek before she hands him the first piece of the cut cake. Up to this point, Ollie considers it to be the best day of his life.

Ollie's first outing is Easter Sunday. Brandi and her mom took off the weekend before to the nearest mall an hour away. They bought new Easter dresses, William a new button-up and tie, and Ollie a complete outfit. William helps dress him Sunday morning. "I've never wore a tie before," Ollie tells him.

William laughs, "You lucky duck." He smoothes out the shoulders of Ollie's suit jacket. "You look good kid,"

William says as he stands back. "You know, except for the face," he winks.

Brandi comes down the stairs in a flower peppermint green dress. She has little pink kitten heels on and a pink broach in her hair. She's curled it again in long little rings. She's powered her cheeks with blush and covered her eyelashes in mascara. Ollie's eyes light up when he sees her. "Brandi, you are so beautiful."

She is used to his complements now. She doesn't blush or stop. She walks to him and hugs him. She kisses him on the cheek as she pulls away. "You," she looks him up and down. "You look marvelous." Brandi has never seen him in such nice clothes. Her mom bought him new black church shoes, black slacks and a black suit jacket. He wears a button up light pink shirt that matches her shoes. They did that on purpose. His tie is light green with gold crosses on it. Ollie even wet his comb and brushed his hair over to the side. William gave him a bottle of cologne that Ollie splashed on his neck.

Carol comes down the steps in her new Easter dress, her husband matching her as well. "Ollie, dear, you look so handsome!" she says as soon as she sees him. "Oh, we have to get pictures!" Carol slaps her hands together and jumps on her toes. William pushes her toward the front door. "We'll get them after church Caroline. We're going to be late." The family squishes in the car and drives to Masonville First Baptist Church across town.

The people inside go bizarre when they spot Ollie rolling down the sidewalk. Many of them rush out to him and help him inside. A bright flash catches attention. A cameraman is there. He takes multiple pictures of Ollie and the parade of people that has gathered around him. Brandi tries her best to stay at his side but eventually the old ladies nudge her out of the way. When Ollie is pushed through the front door the photography stops.

Pastor Brown makes a special announcement to welcome back their Phil Oliver. All of the kids from the orphanage are there. Miss Stephen convinces them to sit in the pew behind Ollie, not on top of his broken hip.

Ollie can't think of a better day to have made his outing than the day of his Savior rising from the grave.

After church service there is a pitch-in dinner. It takes everything in Brandi not to lose her temper when the old ladies try to sit by Ollie. He asks the women to make room for her just in time. They are one of the last families to leave. When they get home Carol is pushing them all in front of the fireplace. "Brandi and Ollie, you first."

Mrs. Bollinger holds her camera to her eye. "Don't hold it against your face," Brandi laughs.

Mr. Bollinger helps Ollie onto his feet. He holds the fireplace mantle with one arm and the other he wraps around Brandi's waist. She leans her head against his chest. Carol readjusts and takes the picture. Ollie slides back into his wheelchair while Brandi takes pictures of her parents. Afterward, Carol sets up the camera to wait ten seconds before snapping another photo. The four of them cram together before the flash fires. Mrs. Bollinger looks at it and starts to tear up. "Oh look at my precious family," she says. William pushes her toward the stairs. "No crying Caroline. Come on."

Ollie returns to school the following Monday. In each class he turns in a large stack of homework Buddy and Corky had been bringing to the Bollinger house. All of his teachers are thrilled to see him back. They all have a special table set up for him that he can pull his wheelchair to in the back of the room. Mrs. Young hands him the *Masonville Tribute* when he enters. The front page is another article by Michael Deaton: *A Masonville Miracle*. A picture of Ollie in his wheelchair with First Baptist Church members all around him is under it. He chooses not to read it and hands it back to her. He makes his way to the back of her where his new desk is. It is placed behind where Josh used to sit. The dragon with flames coming out its mouth stares back at him.

The boys basketball team ended up losing the following two tournament games. They don't mention it to Ollie and Ollie doesn't say anything to them. What is talked about is the fact that the school year is nearly over.

"Just a month away from graduation," Corky says through a mouthful of sandwich. The boys sit at their usual lunch table in the middle of the cafeteria. Their girlfriends, or at least three quarters of the cheerleaders, join them. Ollie has pulled up to the end of it in his wheelchair.

"Let's not talk about sad stuff," Roxanne says.

"That's not sad," Buddy jokes.

"Let's talk about prom," Angela squeals. She flips her hair off her shoulder and flutters her eyelashes at her boyfriend.

"Not prom again," Percy sighs.

"Why? Don't you want you to go?" Patricia leans against the table so her boobs rest on top of it. Percy then nods his head.

"Ollie, have you asked Brandi yet?" Angela winks at him.

Ollie laughs a little and shrugs his shoulders. "No I haven't asked yet. Do you think she'll want to go when I can't even . . ." He looks down at this legs, "dance?"

Angela straightens up quickly. "Of course she'll want to go! Don't be silly. Prom is like the best thing ever. She'll be devastated if you don't ask her."

"Devastated," Patricia and Mandy echo.

"You've got to go Ollie," Buddy says.

"Yeah man, prom is your last hoorah with me," Corky pokes him with his sandwich.

"Alright," Ollie nods his head. "I'll ask her."

Ollie wheels his chair into the kitchen where Mrs. Bollinger flips pancakes in her skillet. "Breakfast for supper," she smiles at him.

Ollie figures he'll take advantage of this time while the house is empty but for the two of them. Mr. Bollinger is still at work and Brandi has class. "Caroline," Ollie says. "I've been thinking about going to prom."

She butters her skillet. "Oh, Ollie, you should!"

"Yeah, I probably will," Ollie lifts himself from his chair into the stool at the island.

"Is this about the money?" Carol asks. Ollie is taken aback by her question. "Money for the tickets," she clarifies. "I think it is silly juniors have to buy them." Ollie hadn't realized prom wasn't free. He begins to wonder how much the tickets will cost. "Well don't worry about the money," Carol continues to talk. "They aren't that much and William and I will happily pay for you and Brandi to have a night out." She quickly turns to Ollie. "That is, if you plan on asking Brandi." Ollie laughs. Carol presses her spatula against her heart. "Oh I knew you would," she smiles at him like she's a young teenager herself.

"Well," Ollie shakes his head still partly laughing. "That's what I wanted to talk to you about." Carol turns off the stove top and comes to the island. Ollie realizes how much he loves this family when she does that. He clears his throat. "You probably know I've asked Brandi to be my girlfriend before and . . ."

"She keeps saying no," Carol rolls her eyes.

"Yeah," Ollie nods.

"You're afraid she'll say no to prom?"

"No, not really."

"What then?"

"I want to ask her again."

"To be your girlfriend?"

"Yes."

"Because you want to take your *girlfriend* to prom," Carol nods like she's getting the full picture.

"Exactly," Ollie says.

Carol leans off the island. "Well I think if she says no again she's a lost cause."

Ollie and Carol smile at each other for a moment until she realizes Ollie's eyes looks sad. She smiles down at him. "I know she'll say yes Ollie." Ollie's heart lightens. His eyes fill with hope again. "That's all she talks about," she flings her rag over her shoulder. "Now, if you want to ask her in a special way I have the perfect suggestion." Ollie leans in closer. "My father has owned this farm for many years you know? He asked my mother to be his wife on this farm. She was a stubborn woman too. That's where Brandi gets it from, I know it—her grandmother. My dad asked my mother to marry him a good fifteen times before she finally said yes."

Ollie shakes his head, "How did he finally get her to agree?"

Carol leans away from the island in a smile, "With a rose."

Ollie crosses his eyebrows, "A rose?"

Carol nods her head. "My father planted that rose garden out back." Ollie sees the garden in his mind. A creek rock path winds from a gazebo in Brandi's backyard to the pond deck. When he and Brandi had gone the roses were trimmed back for winter. They were only short stubs with bare, thorny branches. Now, in the wake of spring, Ollie bets they are turning green and budding.

"He planted it because he knew roses were my mother's favorite flowers. He surprised her with it one day. It took him weeks to lay that creek path and then plant all those flowers. My mother nearly fainted when she saw it." She laughs a little like she's watching it all in her head. "He took her to the garden, picked a rose and held it up to her." Carol holds her spatula like it is the flower. "He told her he loved her so much he'd cover the whole farm in roses if that's what it took to get her to marry him. She said yes." Carol tucks the spatula in her apron pocket.

"So what are you suggesting?" Ollie asks.

"I've told that story to Brandi a hundred times. It's her favorite. She thinks it's romantic. So I'm sure you've learned the rose garden is her favorite place on this whole farm."

"In the whole world," Ollie says.

Carol nods her head, "Exactly. So," she smiles mischievously. "I suggest you ask her there, and maybe keep my father's story in mind." They smile at each other until the front door opens. Brandi hollers that she's home and Carol returns to cooking.

The later part of April is a constant drizzle of rain. It isn't until May that Ollie finds an opportune day to venture outside. While Brandi studies for a test in her bedroom Ollie pushes his wheelchair out the front door and down the short ramp William put on the side of the porch for him. It is difficult to roll the wheels through the grass but Ollie does so until he reaches the rock path by the gazebo. The roses are just starting to bloom. The garden area is beautiful. It reminds Ollie of a hymn.

I come to the garden alone

While the dew is still on the roses

And the melody that He sings to me

Within my heart is calling

And He walks with me

And He talks with me

Ollie pulls the scissors from his shirt pocket he snatched out of Mrs. Bollinger's basket by the door. He rolls his cart down the path until he finds the perfect rose. Mrs. Bollinger watches from the window. "William!" she yells. "William, get in here!"

Mr. Bollinger comes down the hall from the restroom. "What is it Caroline?"

"Come here! Look," she pulls his shirt until his face is pressed against hers looking out the window.

"What?" he asks.

"It's Ollie," she says.

"Yes, I can see it is Ollie." William thinks his wife has lost her mind.

"Don't you see what he's doing? He's picking out a rose."

"So?" William tries to move away from his wife but she tugs his collar until he's cheek to cheek with her.

"So he's going to ask Brandi to be his girl today," Carol looks starry-eyed.

William looks more closely at Ollie trying to understand how his wife knows this. Finally it clicks with him. "Did you tell him about how your parents . . ."

Carol jumps up and down on her toes like a child. "Yes, yes," she claps her hands together. She spins throwing her hands out. Her dish rag smacks William's face as she goes.

 The rose is just starting to unravel its red pedals. Ollie clips the stem then puts both the scissors and the flower in his pocket.

After he phones Mr. Gibbs he rolls his chair to the bottom of the stairs. "Brandi," he calls up.

Brandi appears out her bedroom door at the top of the stairs. She moves a pencil around her fingers. "Ollie," she says.

"Could you use a study break?" Without looking she throws her pencil through her bedroom door then hops down the stairs.

They drive to Mr. Gibbs house singing songs on the radio. When they arrive Brandi helps Ollie out of the car into his seat. "So what are we doing?" she finally asks.

"I have a surprise for you," Ollie smiles up at her. "Follow me," he rolls his chair around the house to the back yard. Mr. Gibbs stands with his back to them by the fence. He brings a hammer down over his head onto a stake in front of him. "What is he doing?" Brandi asks.

Mr. Gibbs turns from his work and walks toward them. His figure blocks the stake behind him. He nods his head at Ollie as he walks by them. He smiles at Brandi who stops to look at the old man. She turns to Ollie. "He didn't even say hi to us," she says aghast. Ollie chuckles. Brandi puts one hand on her hip as Ollie continues to roll by her. "What? Is something going on here?"

Ollie chuckles again. "Come on Brandi," he calls for her.

Brandi and Ollie reach the stake Raymond had hammered into the ground. A piece of wood is nailed horizontally at the top of it. In old man Gibb's shaky handwriting, it is painted: *Brandi's Flower Garden.* She looks down at the ground around the sign. A small rose bush is planted at the foot of it. Her mouth drops open and her heart warms her chest. Her eyes move to Ollie who is facing her. He puts two fingers in the little pocket on the front of his shirt. He pulls out a small red rose. Immediately Brandi thinks of her grandfather. The story of his proposal to her grandmother runs through her mind. "How did you . . ." she starts. "Did you know about my . . ." Ollie nods his head so she doesn't finish.

"Brandi," he says. "I know I've asked you a hundred times before but . . ." Brandi starts to smile as tears fill her eyes. She feels helplessly romantic. Ollie takes a deep breath. "I want you to know this farm will be ours one day and if I have to turn the whole thing into a rose garden, like your granddad said . . ." Brandi laughs and a tear runs down her cheek. Ollie laughs a little too. "I will do that for you," he finishes.

Brandi smiles so big her cheek bones push up at her eyes. She folds her hands over her heart as if it might really flutter away. "Ollie," she says breathlessly.

He holds the rose up closer to her. She looks down at it and laughs. "Will you be my girl?" Ollie says the familiar words.

She takes the flower from him nodding her head. "Yes Ollie," she says. "Yes."

Next Ollie breaks the news to her about prom. They sit on the front porch swing of what will be Ollie's farm house. "It's in three weeks if you want to go with me," Ollie says.

Brandi laughs one good time. She leans her head back on Ollie's shoulder and lays her hand on his thigh. "*If* I want to go with you," she laughs again.

Ollie chuckles. "Well, I won't exactly be the funnest date," he motions to his leg.

Brandi lifts her head. "You're gonna be great Ollie," she smiles at him. Ollie takes a deep breath and nods his head hoping she's right. Brandi kisses him on the lips. Ollie puts his hand around her ear and pulls her face to his again. They kiss slowly. Mr. Gibbs clears his throat as he steps out the front door. The banging sound of the screen door shutting draws Ollie and Brandi apart. Mr. Gibbs smiles at the two of them with his missing teeth. "Looks like she liked the roses," Raymond says to Ollie. The old man winks again at Brandi before he clumps his way down the porch steps with his cane.

The two of them laugh until Brandi suddenly sits up straight. She jumps off the swing then turns to grab Ollie's hands. She squeals like her mother, "I've got to buy a dress!"

Every evening when the Bollinger's slip away to sleep, Ollie maneuvers out of his bed. His nurse left him some crutches to practice walking with. She told him she didn't expect him to be rid of his wheelchair until mid-summer. But Ollie was persistent with her so she left some. He takes them out from under his bed and slips them under his armpits. At first he isn't able to put any pressure on his leg without grunting in pain. Tonight he crutches through the living room into the kitchen. He circles the island and stops by the stove. He leans one crutch against it. He balances with the other. He twists his waist like he's dancing. He raises one arm in the air and waves it over his head. He bobs his head and hums a song.

"Nice moves," he hears behind him. Ollie stumbles with his one crutch, startled by the voice. He grabs his other crutch and turns to find Mr. Bollinger smiling at him. Ollie puts his face down embarrassed he was just caught dancing in the middle of the kitchen in the middle of the night.

"You been practicing long?" William makes his way around the island toward Ollie but he goes to the refrigerator.

Ollie finds his balance on his crutches. "Yeah, I wanted to surprise Brandi."

"Oh you'll surprise her alright," William laughs, "with those dance moves." He chuckles as he pours himself a glass of milk.

Ollie laughs and shakes his head. "I'm not that bad," he says.

"Not bad for a guy with crutches, I'll give you that," William nods.

"I think I'm getting pretty good with them. I think I'm going to try to use them all day tomorrow."

William looks up at him in surprise over the tip of the glass he's pouring into his mouth. He swallows as he puts it down. "I think Brandi will really like that. She'll definitely be surprised." William takes his glass and walks around the island toward the stairs. He looks at Ollie before he goes up. "You'll do real good tomorrow," he says.

Corky and Buddy arrive at Brandi's hours before prom starts. They wear Roxanne and Angela on their sleeves like prized commodities. They crowd around Ollie who sits in his wheelchair by the fireplace. "You still haven't seen Brandi?" Roxanne can't believe Ollie. He shakes his head.

"I have to see what's taking so long!" Angela jumps up from the couch. Roxanne follows her up the stairs to Brandi's bedroom. The boys listen for any sounds. They can only make out faint squealing noises.

It's another twenty minutes before Roxanne and Angela comes thundering down the steps. "She's coming!" they yell as they go. The three boys get to their feet. Ollie holds onto the mantle for balance. William and Carol stand in the corner of the living room. Roxanne appears around the corner first. She claps her little hands together quickly in front of her chest. Corky's tie matches her crystal blue dress. Her dress is tight around her top making her waste look tiny. The bottom puffs out like a ball gown. Ollie thinks Roxanne would look just like Cinderella if she had blonde hair. But Roxanne has her dark brown hair in long curls down her neck. "Just wait till you see her," she says.

Angela bounces around the corner next. She throws one hand in the air like she's still cheering. Her dress catches the light like a disco ball. It is silver with large fake diamonds all over the bust. It hangs off her shoulders by two spaghetti straps in one long piece of material to the floor. Her little tiara matches and sparkles on her hair. "You're going to freak out," she tells Ollie.

Ollie runs his sweaty palms down the front of his rented black tux to straighten it out. Mrs. Bollinger picked everything out for him. He wasn't allowed to know what dress Brandi had picked out. Carol said he'd have a hint when she'd give him his tie and corsage. She dressed him this afternoon. She pulled a red tie out of a plastic bag and put it around his neck. Then she tucked a white handkerchief and small red rose in the chest pocket of his jacket.

It is no surprise then when Ollie spots the toe of a red shoe first. Brandi appears around the corner of the stairs into the living room in a vibrant red dress. Unlike Roxanne and Angela, Brandi's dress hugs her figure all the way down her thighs. Ollie is sure his face flushes to the color of red she's wearing. Brandi's hour glass figure shows she's not a high school girl. Ollie can't believe he's got a college beauty to take to the high school prom. She's going to blow everyone out of the water. Just standing in this room with the cheerleading captain—Angela, and the lead of all the high school theater productions—Roxanne, Brandi is already putting to shame. Her blonde hair is tied in a knot on the back of her head. Ollie has never seen her face so beautiful and bright. She's applied just enough make-up to make her cheeks glow and her eyes shine. Her neck looks long and slender. Her dress is strapless. The top is cut like a heart over her chest. The dress is tight to her knees then flares out at the bottom like she's a mermaid swimming in flaming lava.

"Isn't she beautiful?" Angela lays her hands to the side of her face and leans against Buddy.

Ollie blinks to make sure he's really seeing this. Brandi smiles at him sheepishly. William nudges Ollie from behind. He slips a clear plastic box into his hand. It is Brandi's corsage. She comes to him and puts her hand out. Ollie fidgets wondering how he'll hold the mantle and open the box at the same time. Again, William nudges him from behind. Ollie turns to see he's holding a crutch out to him. Ollie sets the corsage on the mantle then puts both crutches under his armpits.

"Would you look at that," Corky slaps him on the back.

Brandi holds her hand to her mouth in surprise. Ollie unsnaps the box and takes Brandi's hand from her lips. He slides the white band around her wrist. A little red flower is in the center with two green leaves on each side. Brandi's grandmother made it for her from a rose in their garden. "Thank you my prince," Brandi says.

Ollie looks up in surprise. She notices his large white eyes. "What?" Brandi asks. "Did I say something wrong?"

Ollie slowly shakes his head. A smile creeps across his face as he closes his eyes. Jane Oliver looks back at him from the front seat of the car. She smiles at him like the two of them have their own secret. Ollie opens his eyes. Before him stands his princess. He takes her in his arms.

Buddy and Corky's parents meet the Bollinger's at Masonville's Brewery down town. The vineyard is in bloom. They insisted this is where they have their prom pictures taken. The Brewery itself is a historically beautiful building. It is a handcrafted cedar structure. The wood is well maintained. The bright green grape vines stand out sharply against it. The couples stand in front of the long rows of purple and white grapes. Cameras snap away until the parents are fully satisfied.

Ollie goes everywhere on his crutches. "I can't believe you left your wheelchair at home," Brandi says to him. "Are you sure your leg won't hurt?"

Ollie wraps her in a hug. Carol takes advantage of the opportunity and takes a picture of them. "I'll be fine," Ollie says. "I've been practicing for weeks."

———————————

They wouldn't have known they were in the high school if they hadn't walked right in it just before. The gymnasium is unrecognizable. The senior student body, in which Roxanne is President, has decorated every inch of the place. The theme is *A Starry Night.* Thousands of white twinkling lights hang from the ceiling. *Speaker City's* light and sound system has come in handy once more. Music blares from the speakers and colorful lights dance in balls on the court from the ceiling. Around each wall white sheets are hung with more white lights behind them to make the place seem like one glowing candle. Tables are set up with bowls of punch, peanuts and mints. Staff spreads out through the gym.

Ollie realizes then that this is the first time he's been back in this part of the school since the shooting. His eyes wander to the hall leading to the locker room. A chill runs up his back as he remembers what took place there. Brandi is realizing the same thing too. All the decorations in the world couldn't make them forget what really happened here. Ollie suddenly feels sorry Josh won't be here tonight. He takes Brandi's hand and looks down her long red body. Ollie couldn't blame the guy for wanting this. Brandi is breath-taking. She looks at him now, sympathetically, as if she knows exactly what he's been thinking of. Her eyes talk to him; they calm him. She puts her hands on his cheeks and places her lips against his. Ollie kisses her until Corky smacks his butt. He glares at his friend who moonwalks away from him. Brandi laughs which makes Ollie laugh in return.

They watch their best friend's in the middle of the court. Corky grinds his buttocks against Roxanne who giggles so much she isn't really dancing. Buddy twirls Angela in and out of his arms. Miles pretends to fish for Bekkah Brown. He tries to lure her in but she stands shaking her head at him. Percy holds a cup of punch and nods at each and every girl that goes by.

Brandi and Ollie laugh at the sight of them. They look to each other, stars in their eyes. They move to the center of the court with their friends. Ollie lifts one crutch into the air high above his head. He moves in rhythm with the beat of the music. Brandi twirls in front of him. They are all young and alive. The music speaks to them like scripture; their hearts race and their blood pumps.

For Corky, it is the last hoorah of his senior year. He is a big fish in a little pond called Masonville. This fall he'll go

345

back to being lost in the big city. He'll be separated from Roxanne by time and distance as they travel to different states for college. He wants this night to last forever. He never dreamed all of this before him would happen when he left the Windy City for a dot on the map of Indiana. Now, as he watches Ollie thump his crutch toward the sky he recalls the first time he ever seen the kid. He was the threat. He was the big shot, pretty boy. The captain of the basketball team and he is only a junior. He looks down at Ollie's stiff leg, unmoving but holding him up. Ollie was almost killed. This tiny unknown town became a headlining news story around the nation because of him. Corky's world was flipped upside down that night he held Brandi to his chest. He realized then that love is all that matters in this world. He turns around and pulls Roxanne against his body because he is going to miss this.

Buddy puts his arm around Ollie's neck and roughs up his hair before he pushes away. The boys laugh. Buddy spins to try to toss his mind blank. He can't stop thinking about all that has happened on this court. He remembers the first time he and Ollie played here their freshman year. He sees all the times he lifted Ollie onto his shoulder; all the times Ollie led him in a play; the times they slapped each other in 'good job.' He replays the confetti falling, the buzzers sounding and the prayers said kneeling in the locker room. *"Thank you God for all that you give and all that you take away."* Buddy tries to pray that now as he spins. He'll never play with Ollie on this court again, not as a teammate, not in the same way at all. He isn't sure if he can play next year without him. *It's funny,* Buddy thinks to himself. *I've always leaned on him. But Ollie has the crutches now.* He stops spinning because spinning isn't working. He takes Angela in his arms and squeezes her tight against him. He'll have to be strong now. He'll have to lead the prayers in the locker room before each game. He'll have to say his own prayers in his car before the games begin. He will have to make his faith his own. Ollie has taught him all of this. Buddy will never know how to thank him so he simply smiles at his best friend over his girlfriend's shoulder. Ollie isn't looking at him. He has his eyes closed, his neck back so his face is toward the roof. The lights on the ceiling dance across his face. Buddy puts this picture in his mind to keep forever.

Miles picks up the crutch Ollie has dropped. He winks at Ollie who nods back. "That was nice of you," a voice says behind him. Miles turns around. Bekkah Brown, in her deep V-neck black dress, smiles at him. Miles shakes his head as he looks the pastor's daughter up and down. *Thank you Ollie,* he thinks to himself.

Brandi and Ollie dance the whole night. The gang stays as close together as possible there in the middle of the dance floor. Ollie has to think really hard about it but he finally makes up his mind: *today* is the best day of his life. "Thank you God," he says out loud. "Thank you."

Also read *Becoming Peace*, a historical Christian Fiction novel set in the time of Jesus.

Join Salome of Jerusalem on her path of self-discovery.